"*Pantomime* is a touching, amazing story of someone who simply wants to find their place in the world."
So So Gay Magazine

"A completely eye-opening, enthralling debut."
Once Upon A Bookcase

"*Pantomime* is a wonderfully written book, with a fantastic main character and I truly enjoyed reading it."
The Book Smugglers

"Well-written and intelligent fantasy with characters I loved and a wonderful protagonist, in a fascinating world."
Fantasy Faction

"A wonderful YA fantasy that address issues of sexuality in ways that I haven't seen before. It's a magical tale of accepting who you are, overcoming bullies and finding a place where you fit in."
Book Chick City

"This is a well-crafted tale of secrets and dreams, written with a satisfyingly rhythmic prose that lends itself perfectly to the slow beauty and tragedy of the story, and is certainly the most in-depth character based fantasy to have been seen in a long while."
British Fantasy Society

"*Pantomime* is one of the strangest, most fascinating, and daring YA debuts that I've read in a while and I mean that in the best possible way."
Jess Hearts Books

BY THE SAME AUTHOR

Pantomime

LAURA LAM

Shadowplay

STRANGE CHEMISTRY
An Angry Robot imprint
and a member of the Osprey Group

Lace Market House,	Angry Robot/Osprey Publishing,
54-56 High Pavement,	PO Box 3985,
Nottingham	New York,
NG1 1HW	NY 10185-3985,
UK	USA

www.strangechemistrybooks.com
Strange Chemistry #23

A Strange Chemistry paperback original 2014

Cover art by Tom Bagshaw

Distributed in the United States by Random House, Inc., New York.

ISBN: 978 1 90884 440 8
Ebook ISBN: 978 1 90884 441 5

Set in Meridien and Dirty Headline by Argh! Oxford

Printed in the United States of America

9 8 7 6 5 4 3 2 1

To my mother, Sally Baxter, for all she has done for me, but especially for showing me the magic of stories.

1
THE MAGICIAN

"I know I have created magic to rival the greatest anyone has ever known. What I do not know is whether the price of the gamble was worth it."

The unpublished memoirs of Jasper Maske:
THE MASKE OF MAGIC

We didn't run.

We kept to the shadows as we sneaked through the streets of Imachara. Any noise made us jump – any stranger could later be a witness to turn us into the policiers or the Shadow that pursued us. The Penglass domes threaded throughout the city reflected the full moon, and the cold blue light reminded me all too clearly of what had happened tonight. What I had done.

Don't think about it. Not now.

Every step hurt my broken arm, wrapped in a makeshift sling. Drystan, the white clown of R.H. Ragona's Circus of Magic and my fellow fugitive, reached out and clasped my shoulder, careful not to jostle me. We had reached our destination.

"This is where we'll find the magician?" I asked.

Drystan nodded. The flickering light of the gas lamps tinged the falling mist golden and cast shadows across the old Kymri Theatre. The boarded windows stared like blinded eyes from between the soot-streaked limestone. The columns carved with hundreds of glyphs and stylized demi-gods had once been painted, but only a few chips of teal and orange paint remained.

It was late, but there were still some hardy souls out, hunched against the rain: two men sharing an umbrella, a woman with her hood tight around her face, heels clicking along the cobblestones. I turned my face away.

The wide, impenetrable door before us was re-enforced with swirling tendrils of brass. Drystan hesitated before stepping forward and thumping the heavy lion's head-knocker.

We waited in silence, our breathing quick, my heartbeat still thundering in my ears. My pack with all my worldly possessions lay heavy on my shoulder. The drizzling rain turned into drops that snaked their way down my spine. Through the door, I heard footsteps. My pulse spiked.

"Someone's coming," I whispered to Drystan, who did not have ears as keen as mine.

The key clunked in the lock and one of the brass and oaken doors swung inward. Whoever was behind it remained in shadow.

"Who is it?" a voice asked. "We are closed."

"Someone you owe a favor, Jasper Maske." Drystan held up a coin, glinting silver in the light of the streetlamp. "And a séance."

The door opened further. A tall man emerged from the gloom. He had a pale, somber face flanked by dark hair and silvered temples. An immaculate beard framed his mouth. He held an orange glass globe in one hand, the light dancing against the dips and crevices of his face. He was the very image of a magician, from his shining boots to his neatly arranged cravat.

The magician regarded us for a long moment. "Drystan Hornbeam. It has been a long time."

He knew Drystan's full name, which meant he knew who he was – the estranged scion of one of the noblest families behind the throne of Ellada.

Drystan and I made a strange pair. Drystan's bleached white hair lay plastered to his skull. His pink and white clown's motley was translucent against his skin, thrown on in haste after his other clothes had been splattered with blood. Remnants of greasepaint smeared his cheeks. I made an even odder sight, in a patched coat over a torn wedding dress from my role in the pantomime of R.H. Ragona's Circus of Magic, half of its pearls missing. My broken left arm was wrapped in a hasty sling from a strip of the dress and my face bloomed with fresh bruises and cuts.

"And who is your companion?" he asked, turning his attention to me.

"Micah," I said, holding out my unbroken arm, which he did not take.

He peered at me. He did not ask why a beaten teenager with a boy's name and voice stood on his threshold in a torn wedding dress.

Drystan rolled the coin along his knuckles.

"Very well, Drystan. Keep your coin," Maske said. "And come inside."

2
THE SÉANCE

"Countless times, I have drawn closed the black curtains against the daylight, clasped hands with believers and cynics alike, and claimed to raise the dead. Some believe I actually bring forth ghosts, and others hold tight to their disbelief. But no matter how cynical, there is always the glimmer of fear in their eyes when the possible supernatural crowds the room with them. When the whispers fill their ears and they feel the brush of an unseen hand. Fear of the darkness, and of what they do not understand. Or perhaps it is not fear, but guilt.

"Is it ghosts that truly haunt us, or the memory of our own mistakes that we wish we could undo?"

The unpublished memoirs of Jasper Maske:
THE MASKE OF MAGIC

The magician stood aside.

Maske turned and walked down the entryway. Loose mosaic tiles slipped beneath my feet as I followed. Dust coated everything like a half-remembered dream. I shivered, the motion triggering a stab of pain in my broken left arm. Was Drystan right to trust this man, with the secrets that followed us?

Drystan's face revealed nothing. I slid my uninjured hand into his with the lightest of touches. I could not squeeze his hand – my recently dislocated thumbs were back in their rightful place, but every movement still hurt. He gave me a small smile that did not reach his eyes.

The magician pushed open a stained glass door that depicted a scene of one of the Kymri kings drifting to the afterlife on the River Styx, the boat laden with his possessions.

We entered the cavernous room of the theatre, though the magician's glass globe did little to illuminate the gloom. Dust dulled the once-burgundy seats, and peeling gilt glinted off the columns to either side of the empty stage.

"Do you need medical assistance?" the magician asked, nodding at my sling.

I said no. It didn't feel broken enough to need setting, and I did not wish to risk doctors. We'd splinted it hastily and if I didn't move too much, it didn't hurt.

"Very well. Wait here," the magician said, handing Drystan the glass globe. "I won't be long. I'll let you stay depending on what the spirits say." He gave Drystan a look I couldn't read before he navigated his way backstage in darkness.

Drystan and I waited, the glass globe flickering orange. The theatre was freezing, and I shivered beneath my damp coat. My voice caught before I could speak.

"Why are we asking him for a séance?" I asked. "We need him to harbor us, not spook us."

"Maske has been retired from magic for fifteen years, but he still performs séances. Trust me on this. It's nothing to do with what the spirits say. It's a test. It's about him evaluating us rather than some conversation with the dead."

I bit the inside of my cheek. I did not like trusting the somber-faced man, but I knew no one else in Imachara who would harbor us.

Any other words I wanted to say shriveled in my mouth. Drystan stared into the darkness like a haunted man. I knew what vision he must be remembering.

I tried not to think about what had happened, though it hovered at the edge of my mind. I could not think about the blood and the scattered pearls of my dress for the circus's pantomime, the way Aenea looked like a crumpled, broken doll after the ringmaster had thrown her across the room, her eyes unseeing, and the impossible, terrible thing I did to drive away those who chased us through the city... If I started thinking about it, I would never be able to stop.

The glass globe illuminated the mosaics on the wall above the darkened lamp sconces. They depicted scenes from the myth of the island of Kymri. The humans that appeared part-animal were Chimaera, creatures who may or may not have ever existed. The Holy Couple of the Sun Lord and the Moon Lady shone overhead, watching over their creations.

"It is ready," Maske said, coming back onto the stage.

We entered a smaller room, lit by several candles, the flames sputtering from their wicks. A table covered in thick, black lace topped with a crystal ball was the only furniture aside from a large spirit cabinet in the corner, a sort of portable closet for mediums to use in séances. A threadbare Arrasian rug lay on the floor, and oil portraits of long-dead monarchs hung on the walls, their faces disapproving.

"Sit," the magician commanded.

I perched on the hard seat. The Vestige metal base of the crystal ball shone like oil mixed in water.

"Now, hold hands," Maske said. I kept my arm in the sling, resting my elbow on the table. Drystan put his hand, damp from the rain, gingerly into mine, and I clasped the magician's cold, dry one.

"We call upon you, O spirits," the magician said. "We call upon you through the veil to answer our questions of the past and the future." His deep voice echoed in the room.

I heard nothing. I peeked at Drystan, but his eyes were closed. Then I heard it.

Tap.

I held my breath.

Tap, tap.

Tap, tap, tap.

"Good evening, spirits," Maske said. "I thank you for joining us this evening and honoring us with your presence and wisdom."

Tap. Tap, tap.

This was how the magician was going to prove that spirits existed from beyond the grave? I frowned, and the magician caught me.

"We have an unbeliever among us tonight, oh, spirits," he said.

I fought down a surge of fear. I did not know if I was an unbeliever, with the things I had seen, but I did not believe *he* was actually communing with the dead. But if there were spirits in the room tonight, I did not wish to anger them, either.

The table beneath us shook. I nearly snatched my hands away, breaking the circle, injured arm and thumbs or no. It wobbled and then rose several inches from the ground, but the Vestige crystal ball did not shift. My heartbeat thundered in my throat.

The table lowered. More taps sounded, as if from dozens of hands. Whispers rose, the words unintelligible. A woman sobbed in heartbreak before a wind, which ruffled my hair, drowned her cries. It reminded me far too much of the haunted tent of the circus, where I had first seen a ghost that was not a ghost.

"Oh spirits, please tell me about my guests. Where have they come from, and where shall they go? Are they friends or are they enemies?" Maske's face transformed. His wide eyes gazed into the crystal ball, and in the candlelight they looked like pools of darkness. Shapes flitted in the depths of the crystal. Drystan squeezed my hand gently, mindful of my thumbs, and I was grateful for the small comfort.

"Tragedy has struck you tonight," Maske said. "You must turn over a new leaf, and hope the old leaves you shed do not follow in the wind."

It would not take a psychic to deduce that tragedy had befallen us. I had fresh rope burns around my wrists.

"Your lives have intertwined together, but shall they strengthen into roots that run deep? It is too soon to say."

Drystan looked to me, and I glanced away.

"Your future is murky," the magician continued. He frowned into the crystal ball, as if surprised by what he saw there, his voice shifting into a deep, resonating timber. "But the spirits show me visions. I see a girl, no, a woman, in a wine-red dress. Her child is ill, eaten from the inside. I see figures on a stage, playing their parts, the audience applauding as magic surrounds them. I see great feathered wings flapping against the night sky. A demon with green skin drips blood onto a white floor. A man checks his pocket watch, and I hear a clock ticking, counting the time."

The crystal ball on the table brightened to a piercing light in the purest shade of blue – the blue of Penglass. I squeezed my eyes shut, terrified that the light would harm me. When the light cleared and I dared to open my eyes, Jasper Maske's face was lingering close to my own. He stood over the crystal ball, the blue light casting his face in unearthly shadow. When he spoke, it was in a voice entirely unlike his own, and echoed as though three people spoke at once.

"Take heed, Child of Man and Woman yet Neither. You must look through the trees to see the play of shadow and light. Do not let the Foresters fell you. The truth of who you are and who others once were shall find you in your dreams and your nightmares."

The metal Vestige disc I had stolen from the ringmaster's safe burned in my coat pocket.

Unseen hands tugged my torn dress and snarled hair. A cold fingertip danced across my cheekbone. Spots flashed across my vision. My breath caught. I could not have moved for the world. Maske fell back into his chair, his head falling to his chest as if a puppeteer had cut the strings.

My body tilted. The Vestige disc fell from my pocket onto the floor. Swirling smoke rose and I stared in fear at the face of the Phantom Damselfly. I had seen her countless times by now. On the first night in the haunted tent of R.H. Ragona's Circus of Magic, when she frightened me half to death. I had seen her every night for weeks in the pantomime of *Leander & Iona*, where she had played one of the monsters the Prince fought to win his fair lady's hand – me, for I had played the Princess Iona – and each night, the damselfly had looked over her shoulder at me before she disappeared. She leaned over me now, spreading her transparent dragonfly wings wide. *She's not a ghost*, I tried to comfort myself. *She's an ancient Vestige apparition. An illusion. Nothing more.*

"The spirits are wise, little Kedi," she whispered before she disappeared.

I blinked and the blue light faded. The room was lit only by candles. The raps and wailing faded. The disc was still in my coat pocket.

"Thank you for your time and your wisdom, spirits from beyond the veil," Maske said, as if nothing had happened. "As ever, we are humbled by your wisdom." He took his hands away, and it felt as though a current of energy had broken.

I rubbed my nose with my good hand, shaking. My eyes fell on the clock on the wall. I thought the séance had only been ten minutes. But unless the clock was wrong, half an hour had passed.

I wanted to leave this place, and as soon as possible.

"Thank you, Maske," Drystan said. "Enlightening, as ever."

"Drystan, a moment please," I said, terse.

Drystan raised an eyebrow, unfazed. How could he be so calm, after all that had happened to us? How was either of us able to function at all? Shock, perhaps. "Of course," Drystan murmured.

I nearly dragged him back to the empty theatre. I did not like the darkness surrounding us. Anything could be lurking in the corners.

"You were quiet in the séance," he said. "I almost thought you had fallen asleep. It was all up to me to tell Maske what he wanted to know."

I shook my head at that. I didn't remember him uttering a word. What had he said? My head hurt.

"I think it was a mistake to come," I said.

"Why? Did he scare you with the tapping and that balderdash about tendrils and roots? The woman's sobs were a nice touch."

"It was spirits," I whispered, hating how my voice quavered.

He chuckled. My unbroken arm's hand tightened into a fist as well as it could with my injured thumb.

"It was all trickery, Micah. None of it was real."

I shook my head.

Drystan smiled wearily. "He scared the Styx out of me when I saw my first séance as well, Micah. He's good. But none of it is real. The taps are nothing more than him crackling his toe knuckles, and there's an apparatus that lifts and shakes the table."

"What about the blue light of the crystal ball? And the three-toned voice? And the wind?"

Drystan pulled back from me, peering into my face. "Blue light? Wind? What are you talking about?"

He had not seen it, nor had he heard what Maske said. I crossed my good arm over my stomach, feeling sick. It was like the Clockwork Woman. And the Phantom Damselfly.

"Micah? What is it? Are you alright?"

"Nothing," I said, and just like that, I was lying again, though lies had brought me so much grief. "It's nothing. But I don't think we should stay here. Are you sure there's nobody else we could stay with? Anywhere else we could go? Anywhere at all?"

Drystan did not believe me, but he let it pass. "We don't even know if *he'll* let us stay," Drystan said, his voice low. "But I still mean to ask him. Like I said, we can trust him, and there are not many in Imachara I would. Especially now. This is the safest place."

I knew no one in Imachara I could trust.

Drystan looked so tired. I rested my head on his shoulder. His world had collapsed around him just as thoroughly as mine. All of my muscles shook, and I clenched my teeth hard so they would not rattle.

"Alright," I whispered. "I'll stay if the magician lets us. At least for a few days."

"Thank you, Micah." And he pulled away.

"Thank you for the séance, Maske, and for seeing us," Drystan said when we re-entered the room. Maske gave me a small smile, and though it did not put me at ease, he was not so frightening in the bright gaslight, when he did not speak with the voice of spirits.

I tried to pretend that it had all been from a lack of sleep and from the stress and terror of the night. But I knew, deep down, the séance had not been normal. My fingernails dug half-moons into the skin of my palm.

"Apologies, young... man," he said, the hint of an inflection on the last word. I did not acknowledge whether he was correct or incorrect. "I do realize my séances can be unsettling."

"I wasn't unsettled," I denied, rather unconvincingly.

"Of course not," he said. He steepled his fingers together. His face was calm. I wondered what he had decided about us from the séance.

"Now, why have an old friend and his companion appeared on my doorstep in the middle of the night, in quite the state of disarray, demanding a séance? I know you were fond of them, Drystan, but it is rather an imposition." A faint smile curled about his lips.

He had not been to bed when we had knocked, despite the late hour. His eyes held the puffy look of a man who did not sleep, contrasting against his crisp suit and neat hair.

"We need a place to stay for a time. A place with someone who does not ask questions," Drystan replied.

Maske's lips tightened. "Fallen into a speck of trouble, have you, Drystan?"

"You could say that."

Maske folded his arms, formless thoughts flitting behind his eyes.

Drystan's half-dried hair stuck up around his head in a blonde corona. "You once offered anything you could provide to me, Jasper. A life debt. I am collecting on the favor."

He held up his hand. "I did, yes. But I do believe that I am entitled to know why. It does not take a mind reader to see how much you need my help." His eyes flicked over to my battered face and my broken arm. I studied the lace of the tablecloth, noting a small burn in the fabric.

"It is a long tale for another time," Drystan said.

Maske stared at Drystan for a long moment. "Very well," he said, brisk. "I'll ready the loft for you. You can move to other bedrooms later on if you like, though most of them have mildew."

Drystan smiled, relieved. "The loft will be fine. My old room."

Old room?

Maske poured three glasses of whisky, not asking us what we wanted. I put my hand over my mouth, fighting the urge to retch. The ringmaster had stunk of whisky. I would never be able to drink it again.

"Is something the matter, Micah of-no-last-name?" he asked me, his voice cool.

I shook my head, the smell of the whisky and fear still in my nostrils. Maske cocked his head and turned away. Drystan understood and took my glass, downing first his, and then mine.

I wished that Maske had refused to keep us, so that I did not have to stay here. I knew I did not have to, and that Drystan might even come with me if I stood and walked out. But this was the only safe place in the city that Drystan knew.

We had nowhere else to go but this old theatre, with the somber man who raised ghosts.

3
A SCREAM IN THE DARK

"Never are we as honest as at night, alone with thoughts and nightmares."

Elladan Proverb

The rain drummed on the skylight of Drystan's and my new room. Maske asked us if we needed to see a doctor, but when we shook our heads – quicker than we should have – he passed us the bedrolls and a medic bag, complete with bandages and painkillers, and left us. The loft above the theatre was musty with dust and disuse, but the roof was sound. The long, narrow room was cluttered with several old apparatuses of wires and springs. There was a round porthole of stained glass, but it was too dark to discern its pattern.

Twin beds were on either side of the room.

"Why are there beds up here?" I asked.

"Maske had twin sons. They slept here when they were small."

"In the loft? But this place is huge."

"Probably farther away from the noise of the performances."

Behind the grime and the clutter were the remains of bright blue paint, and paler squares where pictures had hung. It must have been a cheery room, once.

"Where are they now?"

He shrugged. "Far away."

Drystan unrolled his blankets, moving mechanically. As soon as the bed was made, he crawled in and faced the wall. I wanted to say something to him, but the words would not come. His flaxen hair fell across the pillow, the muscles of his shoulders straining against the seams of his clown's motley. We needed new clothes, and desperately, but not yet and not with so many policiers after us for what we had done and what they thought we had done. Not to mention the Shadow, the man my parents had hired to find me.

I could not undo the buttons of the ruined dress with my broken arm, and so I ripped it from me, throwing it in a heap into the corner. After a long hesitation, I decided to sleep without the Lindean corset that bound my breasts.

A glance at my body showed my injuries and I fought down a pained gasp. I was mottled with bruising. My chest had been protected from the worst of the blows due to the corset, but most everywhere else was already turning purple. A long, shallow cut slashed across my lower ribs from the carved ram's head on the ringmaster's cane. I ran my hand along the ridged muscles of my torso. For all my body's strength from being an aerialist, I had not been able to free myself from Bil's grasp.

I adjusted the arm sling. In the darkness, the events of the night flooded back: the cheery bells of the circus music, the laughter of the crowd that warred with the feel of the strong hand on my shoulder, and the sickly sweet smell of chemicals. Waking up tied and gagged, the drunken ringmaster looming over me, his fingers working their way down my top to prove to himself that I was the missing noble girl he planned to turn in. But what the ringmaster did not realize until later was that he was not quite correct.

I did not want to think what might have happened, if Drystan and Aenea – my brave Aenea – had not saved me. I had escaped my bonds, but Bil was too strong. The blows of his cane had rained harder and faster, and I knew it was only a matter of time before he killed me. But then Aenea and Drystan had come. Aenea had thrown herself upon the ringmaster. And in half a moment, he had killed her. Drystan had taken up the ringmaster's discarded cane and brought it down for the killing blow.

I closed my eyes against the memories, but they lingered. The fading rage in the ringmaster's eyes, the way the blood flowed from his neck. Drystan splattered in blood. The feel of Aenea's slack neck beneath my frantic fingers and the absence of a pulse. My breath hitched in my throat, my eyes burning.

I couldn't cry. If I did, I wouldn't stop.

To distract myself, I disinfected the worst of the cuts with the unguent in the medic bag, but it did nothing to dampen the pain. I dug about in my pack and found a sleeveless undershirt. Working my way into it, I stifled more hisses of pain.

"Here," a voice said, and I jumped. Drystan's eyes were open and he stared at me from the bed, holding something out in his hand. I was only wearing my drawers and undershirt, which left little enough to the imagination. I turned away from him in embarrassment.

"Apologies," Drystan said, his voice closer, though he did not sound apologetic, only tired. He placed a small tin in my hand and made his way back to bed. When I looked over my shoulder, he was again facing the wall. How long had he been watching me? The blush stayed in my cheeks, though he had already seen everything under my clothes when I showed him and Aenea what I was.

It was a tin of pungent salve for wounds. It took a few fumbling tries to open it, but I nearly moaned in relief when I spread the unguent on my cuts and bruises. I set the near-empty tin on the small table by Drystan's bed, worried that he would turn around again. But he stayed facing the wall.

When the salve had dried, I put on bandages and crawled onto the pallet. Guilt pulsed through me in waves, tears choking my throat. I balled my hands into the thin coverlet. If only, if only, if only…

If only I had told Aenea the truth sooner, before the last night of the circus. We were going to go away to Linde over the winter holiday and I did not want there to be any lies. But I had told too many – too many for her to forgive. Still, she had come to find Bil when I went missing. She tried to save me. I failed her.

I lay in the dark for what felt like hours, my mind spinning over the same thoughts. If I had only done one thing differently, what would my life look like now? I had no answers – only fear both for the future and my past. Closer to dawn than not, my eyelids finally grew heavy.

A shout tore through the air.

I sat straight up in bed.

Drystan.

His face contorted as he thrashed against the covers.

"Drystan?" I said, coming closer.

He moaned, shaking his head from side to side.

"Drystan? Are you alright?"

I crouched next to the bed. He bolted upright and swung his fist, catching me on my injured arm. The pain seared through my arm, my vision tunneling. In reflex, I cried out and jabbed him in the jaw with my good arm, and then I crumpled.

The punch woke him. He stared straight ahead, shivering, not quite awake. He drew in several ragged breaths before coming back to himself. "Micah?" he whispered, a hand on his jaw. He wiped his ashen face and looked down.

"Yes?" I managed, pain coloring my world red and black.

"Why are you on the floor?"

"You punched me." I hissed the breath through my teeth.

"Did I?" He came down to help me up. "I'm sorry. I must have been dreaming."

"A nightmare, more like." He had swiped at Bil with his own cane at just that angle.

"I'm so sorry," he said again, his voice still unsteady.

The pain overwhelmed me. "You hit me in the arm," I grated.

"Styx, the broken one?"

I nodded, a gasp of pain escaping from me.

"We should really find a surgeon."

"No," I gasped. "No doctors."

Drystan helped me from the floor and to the bed. A knock sounded at the door.

Drystan opened it. Maske stood there, holding the glass globe, his face again half in shadow. He wore a striped nightgown and cap, incongruous with his neat beard.

"I heard a scream," he said.

"I had a nightmare," Drystan said, his voice flat to hide his embarrassment. "Micah came to check on me, and I'm afraid I have injured his arm further."

"Let me see," Maske said.

At least he was not a doctor. The magician came closer, setting down the globe and sitting next to me on the bed.

My torso was hunched, but I took a deep breath and straightened. His eyes lingered on the bumps under my shirt, and then the bump between my legs.

"It's complicated," I whispered.

"You should probably see a doctor for your arm," he said, as if I had not spoken. "Should I call for one?"

I shook my head. "A doctor cannot see me. They cannot know."

He nodded, placing his hands gently on my arm. I closed my eyes. One less secret to hide.

Maske's magician's fingers felt their way along my arm. I moaned, squeezing my eyes shut even tighter.

"I have had my share of accidents throughout the years, and I have set a bone or two. This is a simple fracture. I can re-splint it, and it should heal cleanly. But there are no guarantees."

I hesitated, and then I nodded.

Drystan brought Maske the medic bag. Maske continued his investigation of my arm.

He said nothing, but waited for me to speak.

There was no point pretending. I felt obligated to try and explain. "I was born different from most," I muttered, the mumbled explanation distracting me from my pain. "I was raised as a girl, but now live as a boy. But I am both."

"I see," he said, his eyes only on the bruises of my broken arm.

But he still didn't know anywhere near the full story. Truth be told, after the response of the Penglass to my touch, I still wasn't entirely sure what I was. I had been Iphigenia Laurus, the daughter of a noble family in Sicion, a society debutante. I transformed into Micah Grey, runaway on the streets turned aerialist and pantomime actor. I didn't know who I would be now.

This stranger now held more leverage against me, should he choose to use it. I had no such leverage in return.

Perhaps Drystan did.

Jasper took out a roll of plaster bandages from the medic bag and a new arm sling. He told Drystan to fetch the washbasin from the chest of drawers.

He held my arm firmly. Maske wrapped the damp bandages around my injury. I struggled not to move, stars of pain dancing in my eyes. The bandages dried, and the pain lessened to where I felt coherent again.

"This will take about six weeks to heal, and will be weak for a time," Maske said. "But you should regain full use of your arm."

Should.

A shiver ran through me. I could not imagine having a weak arm. Not being able to climb or tumble, always having to be mindful of how I moved. Such a possibility at sixteen was frightening.

"Here," Maske said, measuring a spoon of laudanum and passing it to me. "This should dull the pain and help you to sleep."

I gulped, grimacing at the overwhelming bitterness that all the honey and herbs could not hide. Maske patted me on the shoulder.

"I have a feeling you two are going to make my life decidedly more interesting," he said.

"I imagine you'll like that, Maske," Drystan said with a small smile. "Considering how interesting your life was when I knew you last."

"Perhaps, Drystan," he said. "Though I wouldn't want my life to be quite so… animated as it was when we last parted. I'm no longer that foolhardy man. Things have been far too quiet for far too long, but life is safer that way." He stared at us, and in the dimmer light his eyes were wide and dark again, and my skin pricked into gooseflesh.

"I shall see you two in the morning. I hope neither of you have any more nightmares."

"Me, too," Drystan said softly as Maske closed the door behind him.

"How long are we staying here, Drystan?" I asked into the darkness after we climbed back into bed.

"I hadn't thought much beyond this point, truth be told. At least until the trail runs cold."

"We need to leave Ellada, don't we?"

"It's probably our best chance. I know people in Byssia. But it'll cost more than we kept from... from the safe."

We lapsed back into silence.

"Do you trust Maske, Drystan?" I asked. "With no reservations?"

"I trust him. But I trust no one without reservation."

That did not comfort me.

And a small corner of my mind wanted to ask: *not even me?*

4
PENGLASS PERIL

"Most Elladans have not travelled beyond the island. Some may have gone to Girit to visit family, but very few have been to the Temnes, Linde, Kymri, or Byssia. Thus, the Archipelago must come to them in the form of entertainment – circuses or magic shows, theatre or vaudeville. Of course, by nature of this entertainment, many Elladans still know very little about the native culture of each island, no matter how much they think otherwise."

MODERN ELLADA, Professor Caed Cedar,
Royal Snakewood University

The next morning, Drystan's bed was empty when I awoke to a rainbow falling across my face. The stained-glass window showed a dragonfly, which startled me. I'd dreamt of dragonflies the previous night, weighing the darkness of my soul. I couldn't remember if the dragonflies decided whether my soul would stay in gentle waters or sink into the dark current of the River Styx.

After my first hot, proper bath in six months, I felt like a new person in my clean, if patched, clothing, even if I limped down the stairs. The Kymri Theatre was full of strange alcoves. The skirting boards and moldings were all carved with animals or glyphs, and walls painted shades of blue and terracotta; the floors dotted with colored mosaics.

Eventually, I found the kitchen, a cozy room at the back of the building, full of tiles of blue and green, warm varnished wood cabinets inset with blue and yellow glass, and shining copper appliances. The air smelled of coal smoke and coffee. At the worn kitchen table, Maske read the newspaper and Drystan stared at his hands, his drink growing cold. He wore a spare pair of Maske's trousers and a patched shirt. Dark circles ringed his eyes.

"Coffee," Maske said, his face still behind the newspaper.

"Thank you," I said, though I was not too excited by the prospect. The last time I tasted coffee was when I spent some brief time with a spice merchant, Mister Illari, before I joined the circus. It had been strong and just as bitter as the laudanum.

I sat at the table with them and took a sip, and found to my surprise that it was far milder than the stuff Mister Illari had made. With four lumps of sugar and a huge dollop of cream, it was actually quite nice.

A scrawny little calico with a torn ear sauntered into the kitchen and mewled, demanding food.

"Hey, hey, Ricket," Maske said, getting up and taking a plate of meat scraps from the chiller. He patted the top of the cat's head.

The cat contented himself with gulping the food, purring all the while.

It was so strange to be back among civilization. To not find granules of sand in each seam of my clothing, to have stone walls between me and the outside, not thin wood or the canvas of a tent. I was no longer surrounded by dozens of people. At the same time, the quiet was unnerving; the only sound the rustle of the newspaper and the ticking of the old clock on the wall. It was a domestic scene, except that the magician was a stranger and we were fugitives wanted for murder.

After a moment, Maske looked up from his newspaper. "As you're both here, I believe I may as well tell you that we have a problem."

I set down my coffee with a clatter. "Pardon?"

Wordlessly, Maske slid the newspaper across the table between Drystan and me.

The *City Searcher* was an Imacharan rag, and they would print even the most outlandish rumor. Unfortunately for us, those were the ones most likely to be true. Above a story about the rising ire of the Forester political party was an article about us:

Tears of Blood: Penglass Peril
Correspondence by Elena Gillen

The manhunt begins for the two fugitives from the terrible tragedy of R.H. Ragona's Circus of Magic. The circus is now dead and gone, never to camp on the beach again.

Yesterday evening, Ringmaster R.H. Ragona and one of his aerialists, Aenea Harper, were murdered in the ringmaster's cart by two members of their circus. A significant amount of money was stolen from the safe, and the two thieves escaped along the beach. The fugitives were cornered when something impossible happened.

The City Searcher *has an exclusive eyewitness account of a resident who claimed to see the event from her window.*

I fought down a choking noise. Seeing Aenea's name in print brought all the grief perilously close to bursting. And now all of Imachara would be after us. Drystan read next to me, his shoulder pressing against mine.

The woman, who prefers to remain anonymous, confirmed that noise drove her to the window. She witnessed the two fugitives cornered by their pursuers, the clowns from R.H. Ragona's Circus of Magic, and it seemed they would soon be brought to justice.

One of the fugitives screamed at the other to close his eyes and then pressed both hands to the glass. It was only after the fugitive, who was described as wearing a torn wedding dress, touched it that the Penglass began to glow. As the light brightened, the witness turned aside, saving her eyesight.

"When I turned back," she said, "the clowns were crying tears of blood. It was the worst thing I've ever seen." The fugitives had fled. The Imacharan citizen contacted the police and tended to the victims until assistance arrived.

Authorities are searching for the murderers and are confident that they will be apprehended soon. Fresh graffiti on a nearby municipal building stated: "TREES FOR ALL" and so policiers are not discounting that it could be a political Forester attack of some nature.

Experts were not available for comment on the claims of glowing blue Penglass. Doctors have urged anyone who observes Penglass behaving strangely not to look at it directly and to contact authorities immediately.

The two fugitives were the White Clown of the circus, known only as Drystan, and the other was the male aerialist of the final act, called Micah Grey. Former members of R.H. Ragona's Circus of Magic were unavailable for comment.

The clown is tall and slender, with white hair and blue eyes. The aerialist is the same height, with auburn hair and hazel eyes, seen wearing the torn wedding costume from the last performance of R.H. Ragona's Circus of Magic, which they both starred in before the killing began. They are considered dangerous.

Significant reward offered.

I took a deep breath and looked at Maske's expectant face.

"This article makes it sound much worse than it was," I said, and Drystan kicked me under the table. I rubbed my shin.

An eyebrow rose, but Maske said nothing.

"I once trusted you enough that I would stake my life on it," Drystan said. "Have you changed in the past few years?"

"I have taken you in," Maske said. "But being discovered harboring fugitives would prove quite tricky for someone with a past like mine. I want to know what I am getting myself into, should you both stay. I'm not demanding you divulge all of your secrets – just the most pertinent."

Secrets. Always so many secrets. Sometimes I felt as though I would drown in them.

"I'll tell you what happened," I said, on impulse. "But if I do, will you tell me your tale?"

Both of Maske's eyebrows rose. "My tale?"

"The theatre has been shut for years, and Drystan only told me you no longer performed. I would like to know what happened."

"It is not a happy story."

"Neither is ours."

He gave me a long look, but I narrowed my eyes, not letting him win so easily. I gestured at the newspaper article. "Please." I took a deep breath, holding it while I waited for his response.

"Alright, I shall tell you." He sipped his coffee. "But not yet."

I pressed my lips together.

He smiled wanly. "I'm a magician. You can't expect me to give up my secrets easily and so soon. All I'll say for now is that someone I thought was a friend, my partner Pen Taliesin, turned out to be no such thing, and I have paid the price for it these past fifteen years. I can never again perform magic in front of an audience. When the time is right, I shall tell you everything."

I'd have to content myself with that.

I licked my lips. Where to begin, and how much to divulge? Drystan still stared at his cooling coffee. It was up to me to speak.

And so, hesitantly at first, I told him the bare bones. That I had run away and joined the circus in early summer the previous year and trained as an aerialist's assistant and, eventually, the co-star of the pantomime. There was no need to mention that I had once been Iphigenia Laurus, the sixteen year-old daughter of Lord and Lady Laurus, and that the threat of surgery drove me from my home. I told him only that my life had once been comfortable.

I told him I had struggled to fit in at the circus at first, and then found my place. But the past would not leave me behind. The ringmaster decided to extort me for money. He was a man prone to anger and drink, and I provoked him enough that he would have killed me, if not for Drystan and Aenea.

At this last, Drystan looked up at me, eyes unreadable as I told Maske what Drystan did to save me. Bil had been a man to pity, but he was not innocent. In his anger, he killed his wife, poor Frit, and in his purchase of Vestige artifacts, he had all but brought the circus to its ruin. My throat tightened when I spoke of how he had killed Aenea, and Drystan had killed the ringmaster. We had no choice but to flee, leaving the circus a ruin in our wake. And I told him that what the newspaper wrote about the Penglass was true, but said that I did not think we were responsible.

Maske nodded to himself when I was finished. "You speak the truth," he said, no doubt coloring his voice. "Except for that last bit. You do think you were responsible."

I gaped at him. "How...?"

He gave an illusionist's smile. "A magician knows."

Drystan laughed without humor. "I wondered if you still owned your Augur. Let's see it, then."

Maske lifted his chin at Drystan, and in the tilt of the head, the curl of the lips, I saw something of Drystan's mannerisms as the White Clown. Drystan must have based his clown persona on Maske.

Maske tapped his pocket three times. Out crawled what looked like a small, iridescent beetle, which hummed softer than the far-off buzz of a bumblebee. It lifted its wings, and below them, Vestige metal cogs whirred.

Maske rested the mechanical beetle in his palm. "It is one of my most prized possessions."

I stared at the beetle, pressing my lips together. I had heard of Augurs before, of course, but never seen one. They were rare, and the few that remained were with the constabulary and the courts, for use in high-stake trials. They were not failsafe, though – some murderers had been so convinced that they told their own truth that they walked free. And, as with all Vestige, once the power ran out, it could not be rekindled. I swallowed. He had not used an Augur lightly on us.

"What happens when you lie?" I asked.

"Usually only the wearer hears the alarm, but there is a way that all hear it." He fiddled with a clasp on the Augur's underbelly.

"There. Tell a lie."

"My mother was a giraffe," Drystan said, straight-faced.

The room filled with a rhythmic, high-pitched clicking and whirring. Maske set the Augur on the table, and its wings opened and closed in time. It was not loud enough to drown out conversation, but it was definitely annoying. I grimaced. Maske switched it off, and the clicking returned to a buzzing, and then faded.

I did not like that he had used Vestige on us without our knowledge. But at the same time, I could not blame him. He knew Drystan long ago, and he might have changed in that time. And he knew little of me, though more than I'd have liked him to.

A coal popped in the fire, startling me from my thoughts.

"Where is Taliesin now?" I asked, deciding to risk the question.

"You know him."

"I... I do?"

"Taliesin's stage name is the Specter."

"He runs the Specter Shows?"

Every child knew of the Specter Shows, and I had even seen it when I was younger. Cyril and I had spent weeks afterwards trying to master card tricks after we saw them, but we never understood how they worked. The memory saddened me. I missed my brother.

But I couldn't focus on the past. I needed to know what we would do long term. Maske had agreed to take us in last night, but, judging by the state of the theatre, he did not have the means to support us out of charity. We needed somewhere to hide, and then a way to earn enough money for new papers, new identities, and new lives elsewhere in the Archipelago.

But would Maske let us stay that long, and then how would we raise the funds?

The idea occurred to me, brilliant in its simplicity. In the séance, Maske, or a spirit that spoke through him, had mentioned a stage, an audience, and magic. Something within me shivered. I knew how we could stay hidden for a time, and then make the money we needed to escape. Though it would be a risk, the gamble could work.

"Are you never meant to work in magic again?" I asked.

"That was the terms of our arrangement."

"But are you allowed to teach anyone else?"

Drystan perked up, and I felt his eyes on me as I studied Maske's face.

"That was not mentioned in the arrangement," Maske said, his gaze level with mine. "I've even taken on a student or two in the past, but none proved suitable."

The words came easily, like I did not even need to formulate them in my mind. "Then you could teach us," I said, my eyes on his.

Thoughts flitted across his face. "And why should I do a thing like that?"

His words momentarily stumped me. We were fugitives. Drystan had murdered the ringmaster. The policiers were after us. The Shadow was after us. Even if we let the trail die down, performing in public was not in our current best interests.

But it was better than working in the docks for a pittance to pay for our passage out of Ellada, where the authorities were sure to check. The policiers and the Shadow wouldn't expect us to perform in public. I could not stop the feeling that this would work.

I needed to convince Maske that we were worth training, and not tell him that it might be in vain, if we still felt we needed to leave Ellada. I didn't like to mislead him, but I couldn't see another choice.

"It could work," Drystan cut in, almost as if he read my thoughts. "You have hinted that you have money troubles, and I know you, Maske. I can tell that even all these years later, you miss magic and performance. We can, in turn, pay our way."

"I do not know if you could be taught–" he started.

Drystan laughed – a short, sharp sound. "You taught me plenty. I still remember it all. And I'm sure you'd find Micah a quick study. He learned the trapeze in a matter of months, rather than years."

Maske peered at me, and I could almost hear the cogs in his head turning as he considered our proposal.

"I have not performed in such a long time. All of my tricks and acts are years out of date. I do not know if I have that in me anymore." He stared at his coffee cup again. "And it would be risky."

Drystan smiled. "We could disguise ourselves. We're actors as well, remember. Who would expect it? Sometimes, it is better to hide in plain sight." His eyes were wide, and he was the most alert I had seen him since the night the circus fell apart. For a performer, the stage was a rush; a drug.

Magic illusion was a performance, like the circus, and abandoning the stage pained me already. The thought of never seeing the shocked delight on someone's face as I did something they thought impossible was unbearable. The circus had its own magic. I wanted to find more of my own. At least for a little while longer.

Maske stood and took our coffee cups to the sink, washing them as he faced the overcast sky through the window. Several orange and red leaves danced on the whistling wind outside. I wished I could know his thoughts.

Drystan met my gaze, and he nodded. He understood. We had both lost so much. We needed to gain something else in turn.

And maybe I wanted to find out how Maske had done the trick in the séance, or what it meant if there was no trickery involved.

The magician turned back to us.

"Alright," he said. "But I am not committing to anything long-term. You both need to hide while the authorities search for you, and to pass the time I will teach you, and you will create disguises and learn the basics. But if in three months, I don't think it'll work, that it's too dangerous, then you will leave. And Drystan, you will consider the life debt paid."

Maske and Drystan stared at each other. After a long pause, Drystan nodded.

"What kind of disguises?" I asked.

"Pretend to be foreigners, newly arrived from the Temnes, or Kymri. You will learn some of the language, and speak Elladan with an accent. With that and your magicians' uniforms and the wonders you create, no one will see you. They will see only the illusion."

I looked at Drystan's pale blue eyes and blonde hair. Drystan guessed my thoughts. "How will people truly believe we are Temnian?"

"I have a way, but it'll take some tinkering before I can show you. But, even with that, people will probably not really believe you. But you would not be the first magicians to pretend to be from a former colony, nor will you be the last. There is an air of mystique to the foreign, mostly born from rumor and ignorance, but nonetheless there. We may as well begin sooner rather than later. I will go into town and gather supplies." His enthusiasm faded from his features. "But I would appreciate it if, while I am away, you do not snoop behind closed doors. There are dangerous things moldering in the darkness, and other possessions that are for my eyes alone."

He held his gaze with ours, unblinking, and I was reminded of the man from the séance who spoke in three tones at once. What had been a growing sense of comfort around him dissipated, leaving a thick lump of misgiving in my stomach.

Of course, that only made me wonder all the more what he was hiding.

We broke our fast on toast and butter and marmalade – more luxuries. My breakfast for the past several months had been porridge and a fried or boiled egg. The second cup of coffee was a mistake, though, for I could not sit still.

Maske left. The kitchen seemed oddly silent once he left.

"Well, we should leave some things alone, but we can at least do a little exploring. Come, I'll show you the roof. It has some of the best views of the city," Drystan said with a ghost of his old smile, and we made our way up the dusty wooden steps. I paused at a landing, staring down its murky depths at the closed doors. Full of secrets – Maske's to tell, not mine to find.

Drystan laid a hand on my shoulder. I followed him up the stairs. On the landing opposite the door to our loft, we clambered onto the wrought-iron balcony, climbing the twining steps to the roof.

I gasped at the view, reminded of childhood memories of climbing buildings in Sicion. The theatre was taller than the surrounding tenements, so we didn't have to fear neighbors noticing two fugitives when they looked out of their window as they washed dishes. So many memories of life as Iphigenia Laurus flitted at the edge of my consciousness. My brother Cyril's face as he climbed with me. Tucking my hair under a cap before I stole through the streets to climb, and returning to change back into a dress and pretend I had been practicing the piano the entire time.

The gray-tinged clouds cast shadows over Imachara's swirling streets. Its tall buildings jutted toward the clouds, dark granite spotted with the colors of laundry hung between the wynds, and the flowers in the window boxes, still clinging to life before winter took them.

Twin spires of the churches of the Lord and Lady reached toward the sky, one made of white marble and topped with gold to represent the Lord of the Sun, and the other of dark marble and topped with silver alloy to represent the Lady of the Moon. And twining through the backbone of the city were the blue Penglass domes, their surfaces unmarked, taunting the world with whatever secrets they held within. I pushed away the memory of what happened when I touched them.

In the parks, the leaves were turning to fire, the grass dulling. The day was warm, but with a chill on the wind that promised true autumn and rain, tinged with the sharp scent of chimney smoke. The wind whipped our hair as we stared over the vast expanse of Imachara, Ellada's capital and former seat of the Empire of the Archipelago.

Drystan sighed and turned from the view, lying down on the sun-warmed roof slates, holding a hand to shade his eyes, gazing at the clouds.

Up here, I could not help but think of our troubles. Our tragedies. Tears pricked at my eyes, my breath hitching in my throat.

I stared up at the sky, trying to stop the tears from falling. Drystan did not notice my tears. Or chose not to.

I turned from him, lying down under the faint warmth of the sun, and, as if I could not stop it, a hole opened in me, and I bit down on a keening wail of grief. I let the tears come, dropping onto my shirt.

Glancing over my shoulder, Drystan's shoulders hitched. He, too, remembered our horrors. Eventually, the autumn sun dried my tears, though the pain felt no less. I turned over on my stomach, avoiding Drystan's gaze, the sun warming my back.

"So we'll stay," I said when I trusted my voice enough to speak.

His eyes flicked over to me, his skin blotchy from his tears. I looked away.

"Yes, Maske can harbor us for three months. If things are alright, then we'll perform with him for a time and then leave Ellada like we planned."

"Will that upset him – his taking the time to teach us and then us just leaving?"

Drystan stared into the distance. "He'll understand."

I hoped he was right.

"What else can you tell me about Maske?" I asked.

"It's his story to tell," Drystan said.

"Come on. You can tell me something. You might trust him, but I don't think I do."

"That's probably wise."

"You're not helping."

He half smiled, wiping at his face with the back of his hand. "Alright. Neither side is blameless in this story. Maske and Taliesin used to be best friends and partners – the best magicians in Ellada. And then it all went to Styx. Taliesin turned against Maske and became his enemy, but Maske drove him to do it. There're two sides to every story."

"What does that mean?"

"Maske slept with Taliesin's fiancée."

"Ah."

"Course, it's more complicated than that. Maske regrets it. And he's very different to how he was back then. They say your personality changes several times over as you age. You at sixteen will not be like you when you're thirty."

"I suppose," I sighed, looking up at the clouds. I wondered what I would be like when I was thirty. It seemed so far away. Almost half my life again.

We lazed on the roof, gazing at Imachara, each lost in our thoughts. The images of the previous night would not leave me alone. Playing over and over. When the clouds covered the sun, I shivered with cold. With guilt. With fear of what would happen.

5
TWISTING THE ACES

"Twisting the Aces is the oldest magic shop in Imachara, and possibly Ellada. It began as a small stall in the marketplace, with the old fortuneteller, Fay Larch, selling amulets against the evil eye. She later diversified, selling all manner of magical apparatus.

When attitudes toward magic shifted, her shop and wares likewise morphed. She bought the current premises and sold tricks to the early magicians of her day, from the simple cup and balls trick to the props for grand illusion. After her death, her son took over, and his child after him, and Twisting the Aces has continued for all these many years later."

Brochure for Twisting the Aces

We didn't leave the theatre for two weeks.

Even during the day, we kept the curtains drawn; hesitating to walk in front of them at night, for fear people would somehow recognize our silhouettes. An artist's impression of both of us appeared in another newspaper article, but luckily both sketches weren't quite right. There were door-to-door searches.

In the previous week they knocked on the door of the Kymri Theatre. Drystan and I waited with bated breath in the hallway, out of sight, as Maske opened the door. When the two policiers asked if he had seen two boys matching our description, he'd said: "Afraid not. I thought those two would have been found by now." A frown. A hint of disapproval.

The policiers bristled. The one with the higher voice said: "They will be, sure enough." There was a long pause, in which I imagined them trying to peer into the gloom of the entryway. I clutched Drystan, certain they'd demand to search the place, but in the end, they left, and we breathed a tentative sigh of relief, short-lived. All the neighbors knew Maske lived alone. What would they think when they saw us? I could only hope enough time had passed so they didn't make the connection.

The day before, Maske showed us how we could pass as Temnian. He passed us both Vestige pendants on thin chains, called Glamours, to wear beneath our clothing. The pendants were like little mirrors, shimmering with rainbows like soap bubbles. A flick of a hidden switch and, to the eye, our skin appeared to be burnished gold, our eyes and hair black, our features subtly transformed. We'd pass as Temnian. My eyebrows rose as I'd noted the changes in Drystan and seen myself in the mirror. I didn't know how I felt about wearing a face that was not my own, from a country that wasn't mine either.

And it was yet another illegal Vestige in Maske's possession.

I pulled a strand of my hair away. In the mirror, it looked dark, but when I saw it, it was its customary auburn.

"How...?"

"The illusion doesn't work on yourself," Drystan said as I'd switched it off, relieved to see my own face in the mirror again.

It was true we were not the only people to take on such disguises. Maske showed us several other magicians in one of his history books, and the ringmaster Ragona gave himself a foreign lilt, along with many members of the circus and carnival. I never learned where Bil had pretended to be from.

Now I'd never know.

We turned on the Glamours again, dressing in the costumes Maske purchased for us. I widened my eyes and stuck out my tongue at the stranger in the mirror.

We went down to the kitchen. "Hello, my Temnian visitors," Maske said, sweeping a bow, when we entered. "I am honored that you have come calling from your faraway land."

I gave him a small, stiff bow as the Temnians did, feeling uncomfortable, holding a palm resting on the tip of my nose to bisect my face, symbolizing the sun and the moon, the Lord and the Lady, and the light and the dark within us all.

Drystan spoiled the illusion by sticking his tongue out, and I laughed. We turned off the Glamours. This was the Drystan I knew and missed. Over the past two weeks, he had grown quieter than I remembered him being in the circus. When he thought I wasn't looking, he stared at nothing. I knew that thoughts of what he and I had done were never far from his mind.

I felt guilty for laughing. I had no right, with Aenea dead

and the circus in ruins.

"I'm planning on going into town today," Maske said that morning as we prepared a breakfast of toast and eggs. "To the Aces."

We both looked up. Twisting the Aces was the best magic supply store in Ellada.

He smiled. "That got your attention. Time to test your disguises."

"Is it safe to leave?" I asked, my voice quavering.

"You've been in here for weeks," Maske said. "I won't say it's riskless, but you can't hide in here forever. The disguises will fool the casual eye."

It was the other eyes that I feared. But in the end, Drystan and I shrugged into our patched coats. Maske had not started teaching us magic, and doing nothing all day in a dusty theatre where most of the doors were locked had grown rather dull. And dangerous. My mind often strayed to the locked door of Maske's workshop, wondering what lay within. The days were long and we both craved structure.

I missed so many people from the circus – Aenea, of course, with constant pain within my heart. But also those who, at the time, I did not think I had grown so close to. Bethany, the Bearded Woman and Madame Limond, the Four-Legged Woman. Juliet, the Leopard Lady of Linde. The strongman, Karg, and the small man, Tin. Sal and Tila, the dancers, with their ribald jokes that made me blush. Even Tauro, the Bull-Man, who could not speak but liked to ruffle my hair. I hoped they all found other work. Even if all of them must hate us for what we did.

We set off into town, though I was still terrified that

someone might recognize us. I turned up the collar of my shirt, hoping I looked like a convincing Temnian boy. I drank in the sight of unfamiliar faces. Men on a break from factory work in their dirty coveralls, their faces smeared with coal, soot, or grease. Children running underfoot, selling flowers or newspapers in the street, crying their wares. Harried women with bags of clothes for washing or mending. Here and there, well-dressed men and women in furs, picking their way carefully over the muck in the gutter.

It was a long walk to Twisting the Aces. Despite the oversized coat, I shivered in the chill wind. Granite buildings loomed to either side of us. Rubbish overflowed from bins. So many people crammed together, living and working but most never speaking to each other.

Twisting the Aces looked like the oldest shop in Imachara. Its cracked wooden sign hung over the teal door and needed a fresh coat of paint. The dusty front window display showcased playing cards dangling from strings, crystal balls, and magic wands lying on paisley Byssian shawls.

A bell chimed as we entered. A bored-looking boy, with a mop of messy brown hair and a mole near his mouth, glanced up at us from the book he was reading. The shop smelled of wood, beeswax polish, dust, animals, and the sharp tang of metal. Shelves were filled to bursting with all manner of magical tricks.

I gravitated to large canisters of coins filled with double-headed and double-tailed marks of bronze, false silver, and false gold. Haphazard stacks of card decks, both traditional and tarot, filled another shelf. I itched to run my hands along the rows upon rows of magic books made from crumbling and new leather. Nesting boxes and dolls of wood, rubber bands and balls, false gems, stuffed doves and rabbits as well as cages of live doves and rabbits, chalices, silk scarves, handcuffs and keys, coiled chain links, and all manner of wares whose purposes I did not know lined the rest. Small handwritten price tags peeked from the bottom of the shelves, ranging from the modest to the incredible.

A glass display case behind the bored teenager showed valuable antique wares. Crystal balls with Vestige metal, some possibly made out of Penglass, which would make them unimaginably expensive. A large tree made of gold, with the leaves from the Twelve Trees of Nobility carved of jade. A necklace on a mannequin that the sign proclaimed belonged to the first Byssian queen and was haunted by her spirit. On these there were no price tags.

To the left of the shop were large props – a carved Kymri sarcophagus, mysterious trunks and large crates stacked on top of each other, full-length mirrors, cabinets, and cages.

The teenager kept reading his book.

Maske rapped the boy on the head. He yelped and rubbed his head, glaring.

"I knew you was there, Mister Maske," he grumbled.

"Then you should have been more attentive, young Tam."

"Yeah, yeah, so you say. What'll it be this time?"

"Insolent ragamuffin," Maske said, but there was affection beneath his words. Maske must still come here regularly, despite his lack of performances. This boy was probably the son of the current owners and Maske had watched him grow up.

Maske rattled off a list of what he required, and it sounded like gibberish to me. The boy nodded, scurrying about the shop and picking objects from shelves, muttering under his breath. "Hey, miss?" Tam called to the back room. "Leave the stock checking and mind the till."

A woman of about forty years came to the front. Wisps of dark blonde hair fell about her face, and the rest strained against the pins confining it. She wore too much kohl about her eyes and had painted her lips a dark pink. Her dress was a matching hue of muslin trimmed with black ribbon.

"Hello," she said brightly.

"I haven't seen you before, my lady," Maske said. She giggled. "I've just been hired. Are you magicians?" she asked.

"Enthusiasts," Maske demurred.

She clapped her hands together. "Me as well! It's why I decided to try my hand working here."

"Have you worked in magic stores before?" Maske asked.

"No, sir. I don't need to work, you see. I'm a widow, the Couple bless my husband's soul. He left me with a tidy income, and we never had no children, so I grow so terrible bored sometimes. I saw the "help wanted" sign and fancied trying my hand at shop keeping! I've only been here a week, but I've met ever such interesting people." She chattered as she wrapped the goods Tam brought to her, speaking so quickly I could barely keep up. She had a girlish way about her, a faint bloom of excitement in her cheeks. "I'm Lily Verre," she said, holding out her hand.

"Jasper Maske. Charmed, I'm sure," he said, taking her

hand and bowing over it. "These are my associates: Amon and Sam." We gave her cautious nods and she gave us a sidelong glance. My heartbeat quickened – did she recognize us, or did Temnians rarely enter her shop? Maske kept up a repartee with the shopkeeper, flirting with remarkable skill.

"This place is just as I remember," Drystan said, sighing. He spoke with his Temri accent, placing the emphasis on the wrong syllables, the vowels sharp.

Lily rang up the purchases on the cash register, a gigantic mechanical beast.

As she did, I drifted back to the cabinet with the Vestige and other luxuries for sale. At eye level, next to the necklace that had supposedly belonged to the first Byssian queen, was a crystal ball with a Vestige metal base, much like Maske's at the séance. Something drew me closer. Maybe it was the overlay of dragonfly wings etched into the rainbow sheen of the Vestige metal. Through the glass of the display case, I gazed into its depths.

Images emerged in the crystal. A woman in a red dress, her back turned to me, pushing a carriage down the road, the wind whipping the scarf around her neck. A distorted voice cried out "Doctor!" as if yelling from underwater.

The vision shifted to a crowd of people with signs, shouting and shaking their fists at the Royal Snakewood Palace. By their signs, I recognized them as Foresters, the growing anti-royalist party. Overlaid on the angry crowd was the face of a man with a beard and piercing eyes.

An audience replaced the crowd, with Drystan on stage next to a girl I'd never seen before, both in Temnian dress. Drystan beamed at the audience, his face radiant with a happiness I had not seen since before the tragedy of the circus. He draped a handkerchief over his hand, and when he took it away a white dove flew over the stage.

The doves obscured the view in the crystal ball, and I heard the flapping of wings and the ticking of a clock. I reached my hand into the pocket of my coat. The disc of the Phantom Damselfly was there, though I thought I left it back at the Kymri Theatre. I blinked, and the Phantom Damselfly looked out at me from the glass, the silver tattoos on her forehead glittering.

"Soon, Child of Man and Woman yet Neither," she said. "Soon it will begin."

I was too frozen to do anything but look into her Penglass-blue eyes, full of ancient secrets and sad memories.

"Twenty-two silver marks and six bronze," Lily declared, drowning out the sound of time and feathers and the voice of the long-dead Chimaera.

I let go of the disc. The damselfly disappeared from the crystal ball. When I took my hand off of the glass of the display case, my handprint remained.

My head throbbed, and my throat hurt from biting back screams.

Maske took out several coins, but also looked at us expectantly. I leaned against the counter. Drystan side-eyed me and reached for our dwindling supply of money. Maske paid Lily and she thanked him cheerily.

Maske tucked the parcels under his arm, lingering near the counter and Lily Verre. "It was my pleasure, Mrs Verre." To us, he said: "Are you coming back with me or staying in town?"

Drystan and I exchanged a look and nodded, even though

I longed to go back to the safety of the theatre. Drystan's eyes were full of questions I would have to answer.

Maske smiled, as if he hadn't noticed that I was about to faint. He passed us a spare key and we left him.

The light outside was so bright I closed my eyes. My ragged breathing echoed in my ears.

"Old dog," Drystan muttered. "Never could resist a pretty face."

I stumbled.

"Micah? What's wrong?" Drystan asked, half-carrying me to a secluded alleyway.

"I felt faint all of a sudden," I said. I didn't want to tell him about the vision. I didn't want to admit to him or myself that I was seeing things that didn't make sense.

"I didn't eat much at breakfast," I added, hoping that would explain it. It wasn't a lie, but it wasn't the whole truth. When would I learn?

"Come on," he said, and he put his arm around my shoulders. I smelled the spicy scent of his skin. I used my weakness as an excuse to lean into him further, comforted by his warmth and nearness.

The streets were quieter than when Aenea and I had come into the city in midsummer. The clouds promised rain. We came upon one of the smaller market squares. The clock tower in the center was carved into an upright dragon, the clock face resting between its half-furled wings. At its base was a puppet show. Near the stage was a food stall, and Drystan bought me some almonds roasted in honey. The sugar melted on my tongue. Drystan stole a couple, the almonds disappearing into his mouth faster than sleight of hand.

We drifted closer to the puppet show. A gaggle of children too young for school sat cross-legged, staring up in delight at the display. It was a shadow play – the puppets were wood carvings, their clothes cut out from colored paper, their paper faces well-painted. The show had already begun, but I recognized the political fairy tale that I loved during my childhood: "*The Prince and the Owlish Man*". I watched the puppets act out the story against the late summer sun shining through the backdrop, losing myself in the tale to forget what I had just seen and couldn't explain.

A prophecy foretold that the young Prince Mael of Ellada would one day break into six pieces. To protect him, his mother and father locked him in a tower. He was not allowed to play. All of his possessions were soft and rounded. If he so much as pricked a finger, the greatest surgeon attended him. Prince Mael was watched and guarded by all, and the little boy was miserable.

One day, he was staring out of the window of his tower, watching the sun set. He clasped his hands and made a wish. He promised the Lord and Lady that if he could have his freedom, he would become the greatest king Ellada had ever known and he would go to the fate of his prophecy willingly.

He heard a flutter of wings. When Prince Mael opened his eyes, a young Chimaera perched on his window ledge. He was a youth with the large yellow eyes of an owl, and small feathers tufted his eyebrows. Great wings of banded brown and gray feathers sprouted from his back.

"The Lord of the Sun and the Lady of the Moon have

heard your prayer," the Chimaera said. "I have come to show you your kingdom and your colonies. You shall make friends and foes, you will love and you will hate, and during these ten years, no harm shall befall you. In return, you must promise to listen and learn from all those you come across. After the ten years have passed, you must return to the castle, your reign, and the fate of your prophecy."

"I swear it."

The owlish man held out his hand. "Then come."

And the prince climbed onto his back and they travelled the world for ten years. He saw all of Ellada's cities. He fell in love with a girl who did not love him back. He saw how the poor suffered, and how the rich profited from them. And then he went to see the rest of the world.

Danger had a way of finding him. A shark nearly devoured him off the coast of Northern Linde. He was kidnapped by bandits in Kymri. He was trapped in a landfall in Byssia. But he always managed to escape lasting harm.

Ten years passed. He had grown from a sheltered boy to a wise man. The day arrived when he must return to the castle and accept his fate.

Upon Prince Mael's return, his younger sibling abdicated and Mael ruled as king, marrying a beautiful princess.

Many years passed, and no harm befell him. King Mael became one of the most famous kings of Elladan history. He did not break. But he did bend. And when the colonies threatened war, he allowed them to secede. For that was how the prophecy was fulfilled – the Empire of the Archipelago broke into Ellada, Linde, Byssia,

Northern Temne, Southern Temne, and Kymri. He lived happily ever after.

Much of the political subtleties were lost on the children, but they delighted in the display of monsters and fighting and the happy ending. They clapped loudly and a man in a dark hood came around the crowd holding a puppet who asked the children for coins.

"That was one of my favorite tales, growing up," I said.

"Really?" Drystan asked. "It always seemed like so much propaganda to me."

"I always liked the message of it. King Mael chose to see the world and learn from it. And Mael Snakewood stopped wars."

Drystan shrugged. "More like he delayed it." That was so: Ellada had used the threat of Vestige to put the colonies under their rule again after King Mael died.

"That's true," I conceded. It had been a game of back and forth for centuries. I didn't think the former colonies would ever stand for being subjugated again. Ellada no longer had as much Vestige to use and it became an empty threat, and they knew it.

At the corner of the square, a small man wearing a billboard proclaiming "LEAVES FOR ALL" shouted at passers-by as he shoved leaflets in their faces.

"Are you tired of being cold and being hungry? Are you tired of the Twelve Trees of Nobility taking all the water and sunlight from us? Join the Foresters! Make a difference to Ellada!"

The boy caught sight of us and stomped over, pushing a flyer into our hands. "Make a difference," he whispered, impassioned. He trotted back to his stand and took up his place again.

On the flyer, the stylized image of the man from my

vision stared back at me. The man overlaid on the angry, shouting crowd. My breath hitched in my throat.

"What's wrong?" Drystan asked.

"Who's this?"

"That's Timur. The leader of the Foresters. No one ever sees him in person."

I shook my head and threw the flyer into a nearby bin.

When we turned around, two policiers stood before us. For a moment, I gaped at them, with their dark, pressed uniforms, their shining brass buttons, the guns holstered nonchalantly at their sides.

And then I remembered who I was supposed to be. The Glamour pressed against my sternum, buzzing softly.

"Sun's blessing," I managed with a smile and a passable Temri accent.

The policiers stared at me with a slight curl to their lips. It made me feel uncomfortable and small. I could barely breathe. They didn't seem to recognize me or Drystan. I schooled my face into blank, polite interest.

"Can we help you, gentlemen?" Drystan asked in that same, bland politeness.

"No, I don't believe so," one said, genially enough, but still they lingered. My forehead dampened with sweat.

"Well, good day to you, sirs," I said, nodding and smiling at them, though I avoided eye contact with them. They nodded back and bid us good morning, but they trailed us as we made our way across the square. We pretended to peruse the window of a second-hand bookstore.

"They know. They know!" I hissed under my breath.

"No," Drystan said, his voice sad. He still kept the

Temnian accent, just in case, and I made sure to do the same. When we left the square, they tailed off.

"They thought we were Temnian," Drystan said. "The disguise worked too well."

Relief flared for the briefest of moments before it clicked into place. We looked Temnian. We looked foreign. And many distrusted those who were not born on Elladan soil. "Those bastards. We weren't doing a thing." "They'd probably do the same to anyone they thought was Byssian or Kymri, too."

"That doesn't make me feel any better." Even as a runaway policiers hadn't looked at me with such scorn. And as Iphigenia Laurus, I could have very well passed those two as I took a stroll in the park with my mother, and they would have tipped a hat to me.

We picked our way back home, and I was silent, lost in thoughts.

He paused, considering me. "You've never noticed this? There's a reason the tumblers didn't go into town much. Wasn't worth the hassle."

My stomach flipped. "No," I whispered. "I never noticed."

Drystan rested a hand on my shoulder. The sky opened, drenching us with rain. We half-ran the rest of the way back to the Kymri Theatre. When we stood, dripping in the corridor, I snapped the lock shut with a clunk.

6
MOONS, CLOUDS, SUNS, STARS

"I could list every magic trick in the book, and in intricate, infinite detail describe the reveal behind each one. And you could understand it. But that does not mean you are a magician. It means you know a few tricks. For a trick without context is only a fold of the fingers or a tuck of a prop up a sleeve.

"I could teach you how to switch objects. A clown may pass a cloth over a false bird and bring it away to show a live, cooing dove to delight a sideshow. But a charlatan soothsayer may perform the same trick using misdirection to change the sacrifice of a live crow for a dead one covered in maggots. The same trick for different purposes, with very different results in the audience.

"There is no one way to be a magician any more than there is only one way to be human."

THE SECRETS OF MAGIC, The Great Grimwood

"Are you ready to begin?"

Maske held up a deck of cards.

We nodded.

The cards clacked together as he bridged them effortlessly. Maske brought his arms wide, a trail of cards following his hands. Flashes of red and black, the numbers jumbling together. He did it again, and I searched for hidden threads. He shuffled the cards in different ways, tumbling sections over each other; interlacing them and snapping them smartly back into a pack. The cards danced over his fingertips into circles and "S" shapes, each move flowing to the next without hesitation.

He fanned the cards, face down. "Pick a card," he said, flashing us a magician's smile. "Any card."

My fingertips hovered over the deck. The edges of the cards were well-thumbed, the silhouettes of the rampant dragons on the back faded. I touched the back of one card.

He held it up for Drystan and me to see, turning its face away from him.

I had chosen the ace of stars. I nodded and Maske shuffled the card back into the deck. He placed the pack upon his outstretched hand. The other hand hovered above the deck, and the top card levitated between his hands. He held it for us to see.

"Is this your card?" he asked.

The ace of stars. Amazed, I nodded.

He returned the card to its siblings and fanned the cards again. "Drystan. Pick a card. Any card."

Drystan selected one, tilting it to me. The six of clouds. Back into the pack it went. After more showy shuffles, Maske showed us the deck again, face up.

"Where is your card?"

We searched for the six of clouds, but could not see it. When we shook our heads, Maske opened his mouth and drew out a card. He passed it to us. Drystan took it with no small amount of trepidation, but the six of clouds was quite dry.

We clapped. He gave a little bow.

"What I showed you will not be easy to learn. For it is not just the manipulation of cards," he said, shuffling with various flourishes, "but having the instinct. And that cannot be entirely taught. Knowing how long to pause, what you say and how you say it, your body language, the confidence... all of this is what completes the illusion. Take an aspect away, and the magic is lost."

His demeanor changed. He stood stiff as an automaton, shuffling mechanically. He held up a card – the two of suns – and put it back. He fumbled. And in that hesitation, I saw how the trick was done. I met Maske's gaze, and he saw my understanding and was pleased.

"We start with cards, coins and other small objects: sleight of hand, or prestidigitation. This is where magic begins. You come from rich families – surely you have had a magician at a birthday party or something of the sort?"

I shook my head, but Drystan nodded.

"And what sorts of things did these magicians do at these parties?" he asked.

"Card tricks, coin tricks, cups and balls, things with billiard balls, eggs, flowers..." Drystan trailed off, trying to remember others.

"Exactly. Close up magic uses everyday objects and does something extraordinary with them. With grand illusion and séances, you can distract with great bursts of light, or darkness, but you cannot do that so easily with something so innocuous. It's all in your fingers."

He walked us through the very basics – how to hold the cards just so, and how to shuffle in different ways. We did these easy steps for over an hour, until we could do them without hesitation. Drystan far surpassed me with his fancier shuffles and flourishes. Half of the time I seemed to drop the cards. I decided it was the awkward angle I shuffled due to my sling. In fact, I was surprised Drystan did not comment on the fact I could shuffle at all. The bruising around my thumbs was almost gone, and they no longer hurt and only felt stiff.

We broke for lunch, and then the afternoon was spent amongst books. Maske brought us to the library, a dusty room filled to the brim with books and furnished with overstuffed armchairs. He chose some books and left us to it, saying he was going to his workshop.

"What is he doing in there?" I asked.

"No idea. Magic."

I rolled my eyes.

Ricket wandered in to join us, curling up on a small bed made of old rags in the corner.

Drystan chose a book – *Magick*, by a Professor Cynbel Acacia. He settled down into a chair, opening the tome and reading. His long fingers curled around the pages, the shadows of his eyelashes on his cheeks.

Not wanting to be caught staring, I picked a book entitled *The Secrets of Magic* by a name I recognized – the Great Grimwood, one of the most famous magicians from a century ago. The book looked to be about the same age, and I turned the crumbling pages gingerly. The type was small and difficult to read, but the voice engaging. The Great Grimwood, whose real name had been Adem Risto, had been born in the village of Niral. An incredible inventor, he transformed magic from sideshow entertainment into a show fit for nobility and royalty.

Ricket moved from his bed to my lap. I stroked his head idly as I read, his purring a calming sound. It occurred to me in that moment how very lucky we were to be here. Maske hadn't turned us in, we were warm and fed and learning a trade. I could only hope that this relative peace would last, even if it did mean hiding behind drawn curtains and locked doors.

The book had a brief overview of magic from its beginning: as basic illusions that priests would wield to cement their followers' beliefs and sway the cynical. Vestige artifacts were considered holy and proof of the divine. Yet when scientists deduced that Vestige might be technology and not magic, believers grew more cynical of the priests' effects. Magic for a long time was street entertainment, often married to vaudeville or circuses.

Grimwood also listed many of his tricks, from sleight of hand to grand illusion. Diagrams explaining the placement of mirrors and the position of fingers were difficult at first, yet when I understood, I felt a glow of triumph. I took a coin from my pocket and tried one of the tricks in the diagrams, frowning as the coin kept dropping from my fingers.

Drystan looked up from his book. "What are you trying to do?" I showed him the page. He studied the drawing before setting it aside.

He clasped my hands and walked my fingers through the trick, showing me how to hide the coin between my fingers. His hands were warm, and I watched his fingers on mine, trying to quell the feelings his touch stirred. A blush crept up my neck. Drystan met my eyes. We were inches apart. Everything in me seemed to stop – my breath, my heartbeat, my ability to blink.

Drystan made the smallest sound in the back of his throat. My breath left in a rush and we looked away from each other, confused and guilty.

Drystan's face was impassive as he focused on the trick. He performed it for me with no hesitation. His hands were steady.

"There," he said. "You try." It was if nothing had happened.

I took the coin from him, the metal warmed by our skin. I took a deep breath, and performed the trick, trying to copy Drystan's movements. I made the coin disappear. Drystan clapped and I smiled sadly.

"That's not too sore for your hands?" he asked.

Now he noticed.

"They're alright," I said, swallowing. "I heal… quickly."

"I'll say," Drystan shook his head. "I dislocated a shoulder once. I couldn't move it for weeks."

"How's your book?" I asked, to change the subject and distract me from thoughts that had nothing to do with magic tricks.

Drystan let the subject drop. "Good, though academic. All the salacious bits have been made as uninteresting as possible. Yours seems better. I'll read it when you're done." He set the book aside and stretched, the joints in his neck cracking, before standing and scrutinizing the bookshelves. He reached up for a book on the top shelf, and his shirt was short enough to reveal a flash of pale skin. *Pricks in Styx!* I stood and ran my hands down the thighs of my trousers.

"Fancy a pot of tea?" I asked, striving for nonchalance but sure I sounded slightly panicked.

"Please," Drystan said, taking his book back to his seat. For a moment I glared at the top of his head. He was so infuriatingly calm.

Or maybe he didn't feel what I felt. And what right did I have to feel anything, with our lives still in ruins, and Aenea gone?

I made my way to the kitchen. Far away, I could hear the whine of a drill against metal coming from the direction of Maske's workshop.

I tapped my fingers against the table, antsy. I still had not settled into this new life. Sometimes, I didn't know if I'd even settled into life as Micah Grey. Every now and again, it almost felt as though it was not my life I was living. I was not dressing as a boy, standing in a kitchen to run away from a blonde boy in the library with blue eyes and long fingers. As if inside, I was still Iphigenia Laurus and none of the events that had happened after she ran away had touched her.

But at the same time, I knew that wasn't true. If I woke up tomorrow in my old bedroom, with Lia singing her song to wake me up, if I dressed in skirts and found myself back in that life as a girl, I'd chafe even more than before.

I thumbed through a pile of old newspapers on the table while I waited for the hiss of the kettle. It was all the usual doom and gloom – prices would rise on glass due to a temporary shortage of shipments from Kymri. The Foresters lobbied Parliament for more seats on the council again and were angry that they lost, threatening more protests. Infected meat had caused sickness in one of the southern coastal towns. The Royal Physician was set to return from a brief sabbatical in Byssia and there'd be a banquet in his honor.

A scandal caught my eye. Lord Chokecherry had been caught having an affair with several young women from the docks. I closed the newspaper, my gaze lingering on the headline of the article about Drystan and me. Questions haunted my mind. Did Maske truly trust us? Could we trust Maske? What would become of us? No answers came.

Without a thought, I threw the newspaper on the fire, watching the edges of the paper curl like the dying leaves of autumn.

That night after dinner, my injuries ached, so I made my way to the loft, away from the quiet magician and his former apprentice.

I thought that as soon as I reached my bed I would fall into a dead sleep, but my mind would not rest. The shadows in the room were long and dark, and so I lit a candle and dragged my pack onto the bed. I took out my small treasures, laying them side by side. The soapstone figurine of the Kedi, given to me by Mister Illari, the spice merchant who took me in briefly after I ran away. I ran a fingertip over its rough face, remembering the two visions of the Phantom Damselfly where she had called me by that name.

A Kedi was worshipped as a minor deity in Byssia, a possible Chimaera born both fully male and female. Looking at the figurine again though, I wondered if a Kedi was actually a Chimaera. It looked human. It was not furred or scaled. Though its face was reminiscent of Alder features with its high cheekbones and long neck, like the Phantom Damselfly.

I held up the disc that contained her to the candlelight, rainbows flickering across the surface of the strange metal. I turned the disc over. A small clasp or button was on the bottom center. I did not press it.

I settled back onto the pillow, staring up at the rough ceiling beams. What did I hold in my hand? She was more than an apparition, more than an ancient recording. She spoke to me in the circus and met my gaze. I remembered the tilt of her head as she regarded me, the thoughtful pulsing of her wings. She told me that it had been so long since anyone had seen her or spoken to her. How long? Since the Alder Age?

I sighed. I tormented myself with questions I did not know the answers to. Maybe the Phantom Damselfly had those answers, but I was too afraid to ask.

I rummaged in my pack until I found my crumpled sheets of paper, an old stub of a graphite marker and a thin, ratty paintbrush. I took the lemon I'd claimed from the kitchen the other day out of the bedside table drawer. I squeezed the juice into a bowl, dipping the paintbrush into the juice in order to write a real, hidden letter to my brother:

Dear Cyril,

I hope you received the cipher I sent a few weeks ago, so that you know to iron the letter to show the ink. Might be the first time you've ever ironed anything, if so!

I know you'll have seen the newspapers. Please do not worry. What happened was beyond terrible, but the articles make it all sound much worse. But the policiers are looking for me. I don't know how to make it right. I wish I did.

I can't tell you where I'm staying. Perhaps in a few letters, when we know this method works.

Things are difficult. Aenea, the girl you saw me with in the park, is dead, and it's all my fault – but I didn't kill her. I know you'll believe that. Another friend had to kill because of my actions. I feel like my touch is poison.

I miss you more than words can say.

Love,
Your sibling

Once the juice was dry, very carefully, I wrote an extremely boring letter in pencil to Cyril on the other side of the paper, pretending to be his friend Rojer, who never wrote letters. I sealed the envelope with drops of candlewax. I would ask Drystan to write the address tomorrow for me, to lessen the chance of my parents recognizing the hand.

I had not spoken with my brother since the night he came to see me perform at the circus and tried to convince me to come home. Perhaps I should have gone with him. If I had, Aenea would still be alive, Bil would still be alive, and Drystan would not be a murderer. My eyes burned with tears, and a sharp pain bloomed in my chest. I pressed the backs of my hands to my face.

I stifled my sobs in the pillow. Aenea's face kept coming to me. The way she looked after we kissed. Her pink lips. The feel of her fitted against my side as we lay side by side, speaking softly as I rested my chin on her shoulder, her hair tickling my face. The sight of her flying off the trapeze, flipping and catching the bar at just the right moment. All the little facets that made her Aenea. Gone in an instant.

A long time later, my tears finally ran dry. I picked up the Phantom Damselfly again, turning it over, my fingertips following the snaking designs etched into the metal. I fell asleep with the secret held in my hand.

I walked through a blue fog so thick it suffocated me. I could not see, I could not hear, I could neither touch nor taste. I stumbled, my arms out in front of me, desperate to know I was not the only one in this strange and silent world.

Slowly, the vapor lifted. The Domes of Ven rose from the gloom. I flicked my wings in relief, running until I had enough momentum for them to carry me into the air.

The world was the purple and blue of dusk. The Venglass glowed as it did every night. I hummed the song of welcoming as I flew over the trees and the stream that led to Ven, a thanksgiving to the coming night.

But though I flew straight to the Ven, it grew no closer. The bright light faded, until the domes were as dark as death. I hovered in the air. Strange new buildings of dark stone grew around the Ven. I saw none of my kin among its bases – only humans, their faces serious and drawn.

Where had they gone?

I landed on a dark dome, looking out over this new world I did not recognize. The land was dead, no longer verdant. People passed below me and looked up, but they did not see me. I was nothing but a ghost among them.

"This is a dream," I said on top of the dome, coming back to myself. "I am dreaming. This is not me. I am Micah. I am Micah Grey."

I felt the person I dreamed I was smile sadly as she looked out at the ruin of the world she had once known.

"This is not your nightmare, little Kedi. It is mine."

I awoke, the Phantom Damselfly's disc thumping to the floor. Outside, it was the full Penmoon, the blue light filtering through the stained dragonfly window of the loft. I felt a longing to go outside and touch the glass, to see the soft glow. To find out its secrets. I didn't know why I felt this sudden urge – the last time I touched Penglass, it had caused pain and suffering. But the feeling lingered still, as I sat there bathed in the soft cobalt glow.

I did not sleep the rest of that night.

7
THE PHILOSOPHER AND THE FOOL

"Your whole life, you are told what is right and what is wrong. What you should do and what you should not do. What makes a good citizen and what makes a traitorous one. What happens, then, when you do everything you are not meant to do? Break down each and every barrier? Find out how good you are by how evil you can be?

"Some say this is how the Alder became great."

THE TYNDALL PHILOSOPHY, Alvis Tyndall

Over the next few days, Drystan and I spent so much time palming cards at the top or bottom of a deck as we shuffled, or hiding them behind our fingers, that new blisters formed on our fingertips. Eventually, we moved onto coins, billiard balls, eggs and flowers from paper cones. Soon, I felt as though my fingers had a mind of their own. My thumbs no longer caused me pain.

Drystan grew impatient, as many of the tricks were those he had learned from Maske before, or were a regular part of his clown's repertoire.

"When will we move onto illusion?" he would ask.

"When you are ready," was all Maske would reply.

At the end of the three months, Maske did not ask us to leave.

Neither did we ask to go.

The next day, he said that we were ready, and we'd meet the magician's assistant he planned to hire.

"I don't like that Maske is bringing in someone new," I told Drystan as we hung our paltry washing on the line attached to the roof.

"Maske has known her since she was a child, and says we can trust her."

"That's all very well and good that he knows her, but we don't. And he's being very cagey about this girl's background."

"He doesn't like to divulge secrets. His or anyone else's."

"I've noticed," I said, dourly, as we made our way back to the loft. "So maybe I should be the pretty female assistant. You're better at magic than me anyway."

"I've only had more practice." He cocked his head, studying me. "That could work."

I stifled a girlish blush, wondering if he had just called me pretty. Did I want him to consider me pretty, or handsome?

He continued without hesitation. "I think most of the illusions Maske is planning require two people, though."

"What about stagehands?" I asked.

"Maske doesn't like stagehands," he said. "Many of them have stolen or sold his tricks to his rivals. Besides, you're probably better off hiding as a man."

"Why?" I asked. "People are hunting for me as both a man and a woman. I'm not safe as either." Bitterness colored my voice. "They're looking for two escaped boys from the circus."

"Yes, but not two boys, a girl, and an old magician."

"And not an old magician, a boy, and a girl," I countered.

He paused at the heat in my voice. "So, are you saying you want to go back to dressing as a woman? Is that it?" he asked.

That brought me up short.

"I don't know," I said. "I suppose not. I've worn skirts for quite a long time. I've only worn trousers for less than a year."

Drystan looked as though he wanted to ask me something, but he wasn't sure if he should.

"What is it?" I asked, my stomach twisting.

His hair fell over his forehead. I fought down the urge to push it back from his face. Freckles dotted his nose and cheeks as though they were dusted with cinnamon. "We haven't really broached the subject, have we?"

We hadn't. Not since I'd shown him what I was. Before that, he'd thought I was a girl disguised as a boy.

"We have successfully avoided many things for months, yes." We never did move from the loft to separate bedrooms downstairs, but I always dressed in the bathroom. Drystan was less self-conscious, often lounging on his bed without his shirt after a bath, leaving me studiously avoiding staring at the flat planes of his stomach and chest.

He pressed his lips together. "It's hard to phrase it like I want to. But – how do you feel? About what you are?"

I turned the question over in my mind, trying to find the words that would articulate how I did feel. In the end, it was simple.

"I'm fine with what I am." It felt freeing to say that aloud. I would not change what I was. I ran away from the chance. "What I don't like is that many are not, and that I never know how people will react if they find out."

He nodded. "Was that why you hid it from Aenea?"

Aenea. Her easy laugh, the sound of her voice. Her dark eyes, the soft curl of the brown hair about her temples, the shape of her smile. I squeezed my eyes shut.

"I had sixteen years of being told that if anyone found out, it'd be shameful. The first boy to discover what I was…" I would not tell Drystan that it had been his younger brother, Damien. That would just be too bizarre. "He… He didn't react well. I was afraid that Aenea would be the same. But I took the choice away from her to decide for herself. I paid the price. But not as much as she did." I balled the fabric of the quilt in my hands.

I didn't want to talk about Aenea. I kept my grief tightly controlled so I could make it through the days, and I didn't want it to break free. But it would, in little ways. Going to bed alone, when often she'd come to visit me in my cart on the beach and we'd fall asleep together. Remembering something she'd find funny and being unable to tell her. Those stabs of guilt and grief I could not protect myself from.

"How did you feel? When you… discovered what I was?" As soon as the question left my lips I wished I hadn't asked it. I held the tip of my tongue between my teeth.

"Surprised."

I said nothing.

"How many others are there like you?" He said the words carefully, as if worried they would cause offense.

I shrugged, striving for a nonchalance I did not feel. "A doctor gave me to my adopted parents, so I don't know where I came from. I was trotted to plenty of others during my youth. There are other disorders, but they haven't come across anyone quite like me." How strange yet liberating to discuss this so frankly. I never had, except with Cyril, who had known almost his whole life what I was. Drystan seemed only curious and interested.

"What do you think that means?"

I frowned at him.

Drystan shrugged a shoulder. "What I mean is, do you think that's significant? That you might be the only one?"

I swallowed. "I don't think I am. I merely think it's rarer than the other forms they've come across."

Drystan had that look on his face when he wanted to say something else but was not sure if he should.

"You can say it."

"Do you... think you might be a Chimaera?"

I did not like this turn of conversation.

He sensed he had offended me. "You called yourself a Kedi that night," he said, defensive.

"It's as good a name as any – I'm not sure what else to call it. The doctors never shared their official diagnoses with me." I had taken to calling myself Kedi after Mister Illari gave me the figurine, but I did not know if I fully embraced it.

"They've been gone for millennia, if they ever really existed at all," I said.

Drystan made a noncommittal sound.

"What?" I asked him.

"Nothing. It just reminded me of something I read at university."

I looked at him expectantly. He shook the hair out of his eyes.

"It was a banned scientific paper looking at birth anomalies in the past century. They seem to be on the rise. Babies born with scaled legs, a tail, webbed toes, that sort of thing. The report said the findings were skewed."

"There you go."

"Some say it's a conspiracy to keep it quiet because they don't want to upset the public."

"And what happens to these babies?"

"They're operated upon to fix them," he said blithely and then winced at the look on my face.

"Sorry," he said, "I forgot."

"It's nothing." I hunched my shoulders.

"I didn't mean it, Micah. And a tail is different from–"

"A dick," I said, shortly.

He didn't bat an eyelid. "Well, exactly. If I'd had a tail removed, I don't think I'd miss it. The other, however…"

He shocked me into a laugh, dispelling some of the tension. We were so close to each other on the bed. I leaned back, but decided to take advantage of his talkative mood. "You haven't told me your story yet, you know."

He raised an eyebrow. "My story?"

"Well," I began, hesitant. "I only know you were born Drystan Hornbeam. I don't know why you left university, or how you know Maske."

He did not answer for so long that I did not think he would. "Do you realize, Micah, that despite all you've seen, even recently, you're still remarkably sheltered?"

"You don't know all that I've seen," I said, churlish, though I knew that in many ways he was right.

He laughed. "I would not assume to. But I have a feeling you have not truly seen the dregs of Imacharan society." He sighed and turned to me, the candlelight playing on the angular planes of his face, the circles under his eyes. Though he hid it well, he still suffered. As did I, but I had not killed a man. Though I had blinded men.

As Gene, I would have hugged my friend Anna without a second thought when she was upset. I'd not touched Drystan often, except during the pantomime and that night everything fell apart. How often did boys hug each other? My arms stayed heavy at my sides.

I did not tell him to forget it, that I did not need to know. Because I did.

We stared at each other, his blue eyes boring in to mine.

"Do you want the long version or the short version?" he asked.

"The long one," I whispered.

He sighed, composing his thoughts.

"I was raised with the best of everything," he began. "And I was a rotten child."

It was at odds with the Drystan I knew.

"It took an embarrassingly long time before I realized that the world did not, in fact, revolve around me. This happened when I was sixteen and about to start at Snakewood."

My age. The six years between us seemed impossibly far. And sixteen was a young age to start at the Royal University, which was notoriously selective in its exams.

"What happened?"

He shrugged. "I liked a girl, or thought I did. Linda Aspen. She was a pretty thing – long dark hair and blue eyes. I decided I'd court her, and my parents approved of the match. Thought it would be easy. Nothing challenged me, you see. My marks from the tutors were nothing but praise, and I did well at hunting and court dances. I had friends from the best families."

"Sounds like you were a plonker."

He laughed. "Oh, I was. You would have hated me."

"Maybe."

"Definitely. I gave Linda the best gifts – the finest chocolates from Byssia, bouquets of sugared flowers from Linde. I thought she'd be mine by month's end."

I wrinkled my nose. "Yech." Not that I'd been courted much as Gene, but I knew enough that it would not have turned my head. Though if it had been Drystan… I quelled that thought. "Didn't work, did it?"

"She was unmoved by my affections." He winked. "This, of course, made me think that the answer was simple: more gifts."

I groaned. "You cad."

"You're fond of insulting me tonight."

I pushed his shoulder. "I'm not insulting you *now*, I'm insulting you *then*."

"Of course. But yes, I gave her more gifts. Asked her to dance at all the balls. Came to her house unannounced and asked her to walk with me in the park."

"Good grief – you stalked her?"

"I didn't stalk her! Alright, maybe slightly. I thought it was romantic."

"Stalking is never romantic."

"True enough. Once, just the once, she accepted my invitation to walk in the park. And I thought I had her."

"Uh oh," I said.

"Indeed. She only walked with me to tell me to leave her alone. She turned and walked away, leaving me stupefied in the middle of the park."

"Poor little Drystan."

"You won't feel too sorry for him. Poor little Drystan made a spectacle of himself."

"You didn't." I leaned toward him.

"Oh, but I did. I yelled and stomped after her. Everyone turned to stare, and it was a fair summer's day. A lot of my peers were there with their friends or intendeds.

"She laughed at me." Drystan put on a falsetto. "'I can do as I please. And maybe if you bothered to try and speak with me you would have realized this. Do you know my favorite wine, or chocolate? My best friend's name? Do you even know what color my eyes are?' she asked.

"Naturally, I couldn't answer any of her questions. I remember her eyes were a bright green. 'Just because you want something does not mean it is yours to take,' she said. 'Especially when it is something as complex as a woman's heart.'"

I giggled.

"Yes, she was rather melodramatic, wasn't she?" He smiled wryly.

"Those were the last words she said to me, and I have not seen her since. She's Lady Linda Windbeam now. I wish I could thank her. Her words found something within me that I had dampened with fine horses and expensive cologne."

I smiled at him. "So what did little Drystan do next?"

"My, my, so curious, Micah."

I made a face at him, but I hung onto his next words.

"I continued with university. I wanted to understand people, so I started watching them. I sketched them, trying to see what they felt and who they were. I studied history, religion, and philosophy. I failed classes like law and business. My parents weren't too pleased."

"I'll bet," I said, thinking of the austere Lord Hornbeam.

"I considered studying antiquities, as I was interested in the Chimaera and the Alder, but in the end I settled on philosophy. I stumbled across the teaching of Alvis Tyndall – do you know him?"

I shook my head.

"He's quite obscure, and the monarchy don't quite... approve of his philosophy. He stressed that nobody could ever truly know humanity without first trying to be the best, and then trying to be the worst. You will find out where you belong on that scale of light and dark, but you will never, truly know until you do."

I swallowed.

"At university, I had been kind and courteous to all around me. I was on my way to being a saint. And so I decided to become a demon."

He leaned back on his elbows, the candlelight gilding his eyelashes.

"I had saved a small fortune from my allowance over the last year. But I stole money from my family as well. I took my mother's jewels." His mouth twisted. A blue eye peeked at me. "Some of them had been in our families for generations. I should have stolen their Vestige, or something that was valuable but not sentimental. My father was furious. My mother tried to be understanding – find me help. I kissed another boy at an afternoon tea, in full sight of everyone. I stole sensitive documents from my father's study and made sure they made their way to the press. I was kicked out of university. I left a young girl with child."

"You're a father?" I gasped.

He shook his head, his eyes shadowed. "She didn't carry to term."

"Did she miscarry?"

"No. It would have been too scandalous for her to have a child. But it went wrong and she... died."

My breath caught in my throat.

"I never heard about this."

"If I could go back in time to myself at that age, I'd... I don't know. But I can't. And it's why I left. They blamed me for leading her astray. Everyone knows it was an abortion and that I was the father. I was the monster."

"No one speaks about it, except in whispers. But they all know."

I rested my face on my hands, taking in his words.

"I hadn't even loved her. She'd died, shamed and hurting, because I was trying to anger my parents and prove some stupid philosophy."

I could go back. It'd be a scandal, but the life of Gene Laurus was not completely gone. But Drystan's was, or he considered it so.

"You were young. You didn't know that would happen. They'd take you back, surely?"

Drystan shook his head. "Not after what I did when I ran away."

My stomach twisted. Worse than this? "What did you do?"

He ran a hand along the stubble of his jawline. This was not an easy story for him to tell. And that, in itself, was a test of trust.

"I ran away taking most of my mother's jewels and heirlooms with me. I found the underbelly of Imachara," he said. "And it's dimmer and darker than you could imagine. There were many times when I could have died, and did not realize how close a line I walked…" He trailed off.

"That was where I found Maske," Drystan continued, eyes downcast. "Maske was infamous in the card circles. It was how he survived after he lost the duel. He went by a pseudonym and wore a disguise, for as soon as anyone knew a magician was in their midst, he'd be accused of cheating."

"And did he? Cheat?"

"Of course he did."

Drystan himself taught me the rudiments of card cheating with Aenea when we took the train from Sicion to Cowl, but that was only for sport. Using the tricks to steal from others was another matter entirely.

Drystan, as usual, guessed my thoughts. "Do not pity those he stole from. They were Lerium merchants or Vestige arms dealers, pimps or gang lords. But they were a very dangerous group to steal from."

My eyes widened. "And what were you doing with such a group?"

A side of his mouth tweaked. "I was one of them."

Wrapping my arms around myself, I looked at the boy I thought I knew. He was not that much older than me, but in that moment I felt so much younger.

"What did you do?"

"Lerium. I started using it at university, while I pondered the meanings of the universe." The words were sardonic. "After I left, I used more. Most of my mother's jewels went into the maw of addiction. When I ran out, I gambled to try and gain the money back. Lost far too much, and had to deal drugs to survive. I broke the habit and have not touched the stuff since." But a strange hunger came over his face at those words, and I knew that, whether he partook of Lerium or not, the cravings remained.

"After being roundly beaten by Maske at the poker table, I knew he cheated. I can tell when someone's lying. I could tell you were lying when I caught you in the circus tent."

"I was a terrible liar then."

"You've had more practice, now."

That bit deep.

"Sorry, Micah," he said, resting his hand on my arm. I nodded, not meeting his eyes. Drystan ran a hand through his hair, and continued. "I cornered him after the game. He probably thought I was going to throttle him. Instead, I asked him to teach me."

"And he did," I said, a statement rather than a question.

"He did. We rarely played at the same table, but we each did very well for ourselves. Too well, in fact. I never found out exactly who guessed our ploy, though I have my suspicions… I suppose it doesn't much matter now. Maske was in a bad state when I found him. If I'd left him there, he would have died.

"I brought him back to this theatre and helped him back to health. We both left the dark parts of Imachara behind. When he was better, he promised me I could have whatever I needed of him. A life debt. I grew restless and joined the circus. And there I remained, until you found me." He sighed deeply. "And that is the bare-bones tale of Drystan Hornbeam."

He had left much of it out, I was sure, but he'd told me enough that I was touched by his trust. Drystan stared at me, but I was unsure what to say. He was still the one who had helped me.

He's still the one who killed for you, a sneaking thought danced across my mind. *And his actions unintentionally resulted in the death of a girl.*

I put my hand in his. He turned over his palm, and squeezed my hand. I felt a thread of connection thrumming between us.

I sighed. "It's late. Good night, Drystan." I gave his hand, still in mine, a last squeeze before I padded to the bed on my side of the loft.

"Good night, Micah," he said softly. "Sweet dreams."

8
SHADOW OF A SHADOW

"A magician creates magic and mesmerizes the audience. But it is a pantomime, and the audience knows that it's a ruse. It's in the name: a "magic trick". They play along when the magician tugs his sleeves to show there is nothing hidden within them, or that the top hat is empty of a rabbit, or eggs, or flowers. Beneath the façade there is only sleight of hand, wires and contraptions, misdirection at a key moment.

"But what the audience does not realize is that it's not always trickery. Or at least, not quite."

The unpublished memoirs of Jasper Maske:
THE MASKE OF MAGIC

"Sir, please, do you have a cigarette I could borrow?" I asked.

Drystan and I stood on a street corner, in full Temnian regalia, the Glamours humming beneath our clothes, so softly that only we could hear them. We unfurled a small Arrassian rug, arranged our props, and stuck up a sign saying: "The Magicians of Temne – Wonders and Delight from the Southern Archipelago".

The man gave us a mistrustful look, but he patted the pocket of his winter coat and drew out a cigarette. His wife looked on.

"Thank you, sir."

I rolled up my sleeves. Taking a pack of cards from the pocket of my cheap silk robe, I let the man pick it up to see it was a normal deck. When he passed it back, I tapped the cigarette gently against the top of the cards. Then, I made it seem as though the cigarette passed through the cards before passing it back to him, the cigarette completely unharmed.

"Fantastic!" the woman exclaimed.

I gave her a small Temnian bow. "Thank you, my lady."

After that, Drystan and I amused them with more standard fare, such as presenting a bouquet of paper flowers for the lady. A small crowd gathered around us. Though we hid it well, we were both nervous that someone would stand at the wrong angle and see how the tricks were done, that they'd catcall derisively, or that we'd come across more rude policiers. But the group was appreciative, even if a few were wary and muttered about foreigners, and soon we heard the clink of coins thrown into our offering box.

Drystan called forth a man wearing a bowler hat who stood at the back, holding an open bottle of dandelion and burdock cordial. He asked the man for the bottle, which Drystan set on the ground. I licked my lips. This trick was complicated.

"Pick a card, any card," Drystan said. The man pointed at one, and it was only then I had a good look at his face.

It took everything within me not to swear out loud, grab Drystan, and run.

It was the Shadow from the circus.

It was a face that would blend in anywhere and that stood out in its very sameness. The even features, slightly puffed with age, and bland smile. It was the man who wanted nothing more than to take me back to my parents for his hefty finder's fee.

I held my breath as Drystan performed the trick. He shuffled the deck several times, the man cut it, and then Drystan leaned the deck against the bottle on the ground. People strained to see. Drystan waved his hands over the deck, murmuring a "spell" in Temri, which was really a list of random objects: "apple, butter knife, shoe, toothbrush". The chosen card levitated out of the pack. We bowed to scattered applause.

Drystan performed the trick perfectly. I did not think he recognized the man when he originally picked the Shadow as our mark. But surely Drystan recognized him now? I'd been hit on the head, in extraordinary pain, half-mad with grief, and I still knew that face with a certainty.

Did he recognize us? He gave us a nod and threw a few coins into the box with the rest of the crowd, retrieved his drink, and ambled away.

Though we planned to perform for longer, we said our farewells and packed up our kit.

"We can't go home first," I whispered to Drystan.

"No," he said.

We smiled genially at those who spoke to us after the show. A few tried to bribe us into explaining the trick, or performing them again, but we demurred, stating that a Temnian sorcerer would surely curse us if we did so.

When the last of them had scattered, we started toward the markets. We stopped at shop stalls every so often, feigning at browsing but watching our surroundings. I could not be sure if anyone pursued us.

"Lady's nightgown, this is not good," Drystan said, hefting the knapsack of supplies on his shoulder, as we wove our way through the throng of people.

"I know," I said. "What are we going to do?"

"Hope he doesn't follow us and that we can shake him."

I glanced behind me. I couldn't see a man in a bowler hat, but that didn't mean anything. From far away, his face would blend into the crowd.

My heart in my throat, we turned corner after corner, winding a circuitous and aimless route.

We stopped short.

In front of us was the Shadow.

He clapped, slowly. "I wanted to congratulate you on a wonderful performance."

"Thank you, sir," I said, trying to keep my voice even and my Temri accent flawless. "But I'm afraid the performance is over. If you please, we will be on our way."

"Ah, but you're still performing, Iphigenia."

Moving with a tumbler's speed, Drystan slid the knapsack off his back and hit the Shadow in the head, the coins clinking within. The Shadow cried out and clutched his face. But he managed to grab the back of my robe as I made to escape. I struggled, kicking backwards.

"Come on, girl, you're only delaying the inevitable," he

hissed in my ear. His breath smelled of chewing tobacco. "I'm the best Shadow in this city – you can't hide from me forever."

"Fuck off, you prick," I snarled, and then I kicked *up* and got him right between the legs. He crumpled. The few people on the street gazed at us in shock.

We ran like the River Styx flowed behind us, but we didn't run far. Around the corner was scaffolding on one of the many crumbling buildings of Imachara. We climbed to the rooftops. I had to climb almost one-handed, for my healing arm was still weak.

As quickly as we could, we shimmied out of our Temnian robes, stuffing them in our pack. Underneath we wore Elladan clothes. We kept the Glamours on, because any disguise was better than no disguise. I cursed myself for not asking Maske to enter another disguise for us in the event something like this happened.

I peered over the rooftop, scanning the crowds below.

"What are you doing?" Drystan asked as he recovered his breath.

"Trying to find him so we can follow him."

"Follow him? Shouldn't we stay as far away as possible?"

"He's not going to give up, Drystan. We have to beat him at his own game, it's the only way. There he is!" I hissed.

The Shadow stopped and glanced around. I ducked back. I gestured at Drystan, who crept closer.

The Shadow limped away, slightly bent over. I hoped it hurt. I steadied myself and scampered over the slanted rooftops and Drystan followed me.

The Shadow headed toward the Glass Quarter. We jumped across another narrow roof. I landed on a loose shingle. I wobbled.

I fell.

Drystan cried out. The shingle fell into the alley below, clattering and breaking on the pavement. I grabbed the rain gutter, my legs swinging dozens of feet off the ground. The gutter groaned ominously. I forced myself to stay calm. This was just like a trapeze. A trapeze that could break at any moment and send me falling to my death.

I tried to pull myself up, but my grasp slipped, and I held on with my good hand.

I took a deep breath. I had a good grip. I would not fall.

Muscles straining, I clambered back onto the roof. I collapsed face down, hugging the slate to me. With a clatter, Drystan jumped across and landed on a sounder tile.

"Are you alright?" he asked me.

"Fine," I said, still winded. "I hope we didn't lose him."

We crawled to the edge of the rooftop. The Shadow was far off in the distance, and turning right. We made our way along the rooftop until we climbed down a drainpipe, praying that nobody would look in the narrow alleyway.

I jumped onto the ground, knocking over a bin in my haste. Drystan and I trotted after the Shadow, ignoring the strange looks we received. No one would recognize us as the circus fugitives beneath our Glamour. So I hoped.

We saw the Shadow's bowler hat far ahead, and we ducked and wove our way between the pedestrians.

The Shadow turned right again. As we rounded the corner, we slowed. He paused and peered over his shoulder. We darted behind a stall.

The Shadow entered a large granite tenement. The

door swung shut behind him. We made for the tearoom across the road. Drystan and I hid under the shadow of the veranda and parted with enough of our remaining funds for two teas, our eyes never leaving the door.

"If he looks out, he'll see us."

"He might not expect us here. And now we know where he lives. Or might live."

We sipped our tea as we watched the building, but we did not see the Shadow leave. Plenty of other people left and entered the apartment block – a man in a dapper pinstripe suit and purple handkerchief, but he was too large to be the Shadow. A girl in the starched uniform of a maid hurried back with overflowing bags of food shopping. A woman in a red dress struggled to hold the door open. A man on the street paused to help her. She pushed the wicker chair around, speaking to the child within. He was a small boy, long-limbed but with the unnatural thinness of illness. The boy clutched a blanket about his face, looking up at his mother.

I see a girl, no, a woman, in a wine-red dress. Her child is ill, eaten from the inside…

The words Maske spoke at the séance came back to me. The woman's hair fell from her bonnet, obscuring her face. She thanked the man and continued up the road, her dark red dress swirling behind her like a waterfall of blood. I wanted to follow her, but what if it were only a coincidence and we missed the Shadow as a result? And how would I explain it to Drystan? *We need to follow this woman I saw in hallucinations…*

I shook my head.

We had lost the Shadow. He might have left through a back door, or slipped out when we were not looking. Or, most likely, he lived there and was having his dinner behind one of those windows. Watching us.

"We can't keep sitting here. And we can't perform publically until we've done something about the Shadow," I said.

"I know." He sighed. "I've been thinking. But I don't think you'll like my idea."

He leaned close and whispered his plan.

He was right. I didn't like it at all.

But it was the only way to catch the Shadow.

9
MIRROR MAZE

"I had to sell another of my automata today. Each time, I sell my least favorite, but that means that each time I part with the next, it grows harder. I sold the golden tamarind monkey, and it was a shame. I hope its new owner cherishes it.

"At least soon it will be the Night of the Dead, and I should have more bookings for séances. It will delay the date I must sell the next.

"I still have all of Taliesin's automata. Those I shall never part with, no matter my finances. Someday I'll figure out how he makes them tick. Then I'll be one step closer to revenge."

Jasper Maske's personal diary

I grew no closer to learning more about Maske.

My arm healed, until it no longer hurt to perform card tricks. Maske taught us magic daily, and he spent a lot of time in his workshop, the distant buzzing of saws and drills drifting down to us as we studied. I tried asking Maske questions, but he found a way to dance around them.

Drystan and Maske went out one day to play cards with some of Maske's friends. I raised an eyebrow at that.

"They're only Maske's friends, and innocent ones," Drystan told me. "They bet with buttons, not coins."

I declined joining them. I had no desire to play cards with strangers while keeping up a false accent and disguise all evening. In any case, it was my "woman's time", which still made me feel… conflicted. Mostly, I felt more or less masculine, but during these times I felt more female.

I tidied the loft. Ricket the cat rubbed my legs, demanding that I pick him up. I did, and he tucked his head under my chin, purring. I wandered through the hallways with him.

My feet took me to Maske's workshop. I stopped and stared at the black door, the doorknob in the shape of a brass fist. I set Ricket down, and he trotted away. I tried the doorknob. Locked.

I remembered the key ring in a drawer in the kitchen and made my way there. One of the keys was made of brass; the key head an open hand with an eye on its palm. I took the key ring back upstairs, staring at the brass fist of the doorknob.

I should not pry. I should not pry….

I twisted the key in the lock. The door swung inwards. Darkness greeted me. I hesitated, almost closing the door and locking it again. But then I stepped into the blackness.

A small light switched on automatically and I jumped.

It was not a workshop.

Mirrors surrounded me. Some were normal and some

warped, making me look short and fat or long and gaunt. Everywhere I turned, a version of a guilty Micah Grey looked back at me. I tried to walk forward but I kept bumping into mirrors. I knew there had to be an opening, if I could only find it.

Eventually, I found one and stumbled forward. The air felt cool. I could smell sawdust, oil, and metal. The workshop was just behind this maze, but I couldn't find it unless I found my way through it.

I do not know how long I spent in those glass hallways. I admitted defeat and tried to leave, but I couldn't find my way back. I held my hands out in front of me, leaving smudged fingerprints on the glass.

After a time, I gave up. The mirrors must have moved and I was trapped. All I could do was wait and hope that when Maske returned from his cards, he checked his workshop. I did not relish being found out, but it was my own damn fault.

Time dripped past. After an hour, hunger gnawed at my stomach, and I had to use the washroom. I took a coin from my pocket and it flashed, reflected in many mirrors, as I walked it over my fingers. I tossed it and it tumbled toward me. I reached up to grab it, but it bounced off my knuckle and rolled.

"Styx," I muttered. I crawled on hands and knees, groping after the coin, which had rolled under a gap beneath a mirror. I pressed my face to the floor, careless of the dust. The coin was too far for me to wriggle my finger under to grab, but that didn't matter. I had a very small view into Maske's workshop.

I couldn't see much, but I saw the legs of tables, wood shavings littering the floor. Saws, dowels, clamps and nails. Giant frames of wood and metal. I squinted. In the far corner, something gleamed bronze in the low light.

Footsteps from the hallway cut the silence. I held my breath, scrabbling back, trying to make my way back through the mirror maze, but glass met me from every direction. Maske.

The footsteps drew closer. A mirror tilted inward.

Maske stared at me, a sardonic smile on his lips, but his eyes flashed in anger.

I brushed my hands over my dusty clothes, trying to look nonchalant. Maske crossed his arms over his chest.

"I thought I told you that things behind closed doors were best left that way," he said, and I knew without a doubt I had infuriated him.

"I– I'm sorry."

"Why'd you do it?"

I swallowed. "I don't know anything about you."

"You could have asked."

"I did ask, on the first night."

"And I told you I'd tell you later. You never asked again."

"I hinted."

"Hints can be ignored. Bit of advice, Micah. If you want something badly enough, it's best to say you do."

"Alright. I want to know more about you. If I haven't angered you too much for being an idiot."

He paused, looking me up and down.

"I'll tell you, then. But you'll stay out of this room unless I expressly invite you inside. Do we have an agreement?"

"Yes. I swear it."

He nodded. "Good. Come on, Micah."

I followed him out of the maze and down the stairs, feeling very sheepish and grateful he hadn't been so angry as to throw me out. I had been childish and rude, and I knew it. Maske made a pot of coffee. Drystan was up in the loft. I wondered how the card game had gone, and if they had won.

The tense silence seemed to stretch for ages as the coffee steeped. He brought it through to the parlor and we made our cups. I clutched mine close to my chest.

"So, what exactly are you most curious about, that you break and enter my workshop?"

"Or tried to," I said. "I wanted to know what you were working on, though I know I shouldn't have. But I couldn't find my way past the maze."

He nodded. "Glad I am so mistrustful. You can never be sure. I wouldn't put it past Taliesin to send spies to try and steal my secrets, even after all these years. Mirrors are a relatively easy trick to keep them out."

"I see."

"I am working on an illusion, but I want no one to see it before it is completed. I am superstitious in that way, I suppose."

"I breached your trust," I said. "I'm sorry."

Maske sighed. "No lasting harm done." It wasn't quite forgiveness. "But I'll tell you what you wish to know, at least in part." He inhaled the steam from the coffee, settling back into his seat as he gathered his words.

"Fifteen years ago, I was the best magician in Ellada. I performed for the King and Queen and the other monarchs of the Archipelago. This theatre shone like a jewel. I made more money per month than your little circus made in a year. The papers all proclaimed my tricks the best illusions anyone could find."

He rested his fingers against his mouth. "I took on a partner. Pen Taliesin." His voice curled around the words. "He could perform any trick seamlessly... but at the beginning, his stage performance was atrocious. Though the trick was faultless, it would fall flat. The patter was not quite right, the movements too stilted or too energetic for the last, delicate flourish. He gained his renown as an escapologist, for his energy and persona suited that raw, heightened flush with danger. But he did not want to be known as the man who could escape.

"We went into business together. For many years, all worked perfectly. We would invent tricks and illusions, and Taliesin was a genius. His automata alone... some of them were almost enough to rival the Vestige ones. I still have a few of them, despite all that's happened, purely because I cannot bear to part with them.

"Together, we were unstoppable. I performed, and we collaborated on the new illusions, stretching the limit of magic. It was the most wondrous period of my life. I had my wife and my sons to whom I would leave all my secrets."

Maske sighed. He recited the tale as though it were a story he had written. "But, as you may guess, that is not what happened.

"I didn't know that Taliesin burned with jealousy and rage that I was the one in front of the audience. He felt cheated. You know what I speak of."

I did indeed. A memory of flying through the air, the perfect tautness as I controlled every muscle to propel my body about the trapeze. Knowing the exact moment to hold out my hands to catch Aenea. Training with both Aenea and Arik, laughing together, trusting each other. I longed to be back on the trapeze.

"Unbeknownst to me, he had been perfecting his own stage persona. I thought he was content to be behind the scenes except for his escape acts.

"He decided that I craved the limelight for myself. And I did. I was young and foolish, confident in my own power and blind to the jealousy that turned my business partner against me."

Maske paused. "I'm not proud of what happened next. There was a show held in the Crescent Hippodrome. The King and Queen chose the Maske of Magic and the Specter to mark the opening of the season.

"Taliesin asked me if he could perform at least one of the grand illusions in addition to his escape act. His betrothed was in the crowd, and he wanted to impress her. I was hesitant. But he showed me the act he intended to perform and it was… extraordinary." He trailed off, studying his coffee cup.

"And so I agreed.

"The night of the grand performance, Taliesin and I used all of the best illusions that we had created throughout the years. I brought forth ghosts and transported my assistant from a spirit cabinet into the audience. I levitated a tea set and the teapot poured a cup of tea for a member of the audience. Silken handkerchiefs transformed into white doves, one of which landed on the Queen's outstretched hand. It was perfect." His voice vibrated with emotion.

"During the intermission, Taliesin readied himself for the grand performance. I was jealous: Taliesin had an illusion that was perfection itself, the star of the night's performance on the most important moment of our career to date. And so I made a throwaway comment, telling him that everyone was watching, even his intended, Margaretha, so he should not mess up if he wanted to keep her." He cleared his throat. "I meant it as a jest… or, at least I think I did. Events are hazy, as it was so long ago… I often wonder what my life would have been like now, if I'd only been kinder, more encouraging… such a little thing to lose so much over…"

I knew he had slept with Taliesin's fiancée. I suspected it happened right around this time.

He sighed. "On stage, Taliesin saw the blank, expectant faces. Perhaps he caught sight of his beloved's face, or the King and Queen. He started the trick, but he moved stiffer than his automata. And I realized: he couldn't produce that wonderful illusion. His hands were so stiff the reveal would fail and all would see the deception.

"So I went onto the stage and saved him. I worked it into my patter, made it seem like his hesitation was all part of the act. We performed together, and he recovered. I thought he would be grateful, but he stormed off the stage as soon as the curtains closed.

"The next day, it was my name in the papers, and he was relegated to the "escapologist". He left, demanding his share in the company and loading as many of his props and devices into a cart as he could and driving it away. He said I was poison. I was dismayed, but thought the split was the end of it.

"It was far from the end.

"With his share of Specter and Maske, he purchased a crumbling mansion in the Gilt Quarter and transformed it into a theatre to rival my own. Soon, his name was as infamous as mine. At first, I wished him every success. Our acts were different enough that neither of us suffered, though we were not as profitable as when we worked together."

The words tumbled from him, as if he could not stop the tale. "Taliesin still loathed me, and he was determined to bring me down. Small things, at first. He'd schedule his shows to coincide with mine, with cheaper prices to drag away my customers. He'd take a trick he knew I was fond of, and find a way to make it more exciting.

"A newspaper article would appear the night after a performance revealing how I did my illusion, meaning I could not do it again. During my show, an apparatus would not work properly, meaning he had bribed a stagehand. Once it resulted in an injured volunteer who nearly sued me.

"I fed the flames in turn, finding my own ways to foil his shows and poison his reviews. And so we went, back and forth, each trying to outdo the other. I stayed up long into the night in my workshop, inventing and dreaming up new illusions.

"I did not even notice when my wife began to grow ill. My sons were about your age then. Old enough to hate me."

He bowed his head. There was the smallest bald spot at

the crown. "She died. I went to the funeral in a daze, and each time someone comforted me over the pain of my loss, I looked at them as though they were only phantasms of the living.

"My sons left for the former colonies. I think they're in Kymri, now. They only wrote when they needed more funds, and several years ago, I could no longer accommodate their requests, and so I have not heard from them since then.

"I lost everything to Taliesin. Everything. So I challenged him to a proper duel. I called upon the Collective of Magic and they witnessed our terms of agreement. One performance, with each of us showcasing the best of our acts. The audience and the Collective judged the winner.

"I thought for sure I would win. I barely ate. I barely slept. My whole life was magic."

He looked up from the table, to the ceiling. He looked old. His magician's façade had cracked.

"But I lost."

I wanted to know about Taliesin's great illusion at the Crescent Hippodrome. I wanted to know the tricks he and Taliesin performed, and what trick had beaten him, but I knew now was not the time to ask.

"He cheated – sabotaged a bit of my equipment – and I lost. I shut down the Kymri Theatre. I foreswore grand illusion. And here I have remained for the past fifteen years, surrounded by the memories of who and what I used to be."

We sat in silence.

"Taliesin has fallen on hard times," Maske said, a

shadow of pleasure and satisfaction coloring his voice. "He was caught possessing a large amount of Lerium and has been fined so much the Specter Shows are barely keeping him afloat. Then the two magicians who worked for him, Mandrake and Crowley, quit due to the shame. The Collective of Magic was all set to ban him from continuing to perform. Ever."

"That's wonderful," I said.

Maske nodded, but I sensed that even this satisfaction came nowhere near to making up for the fifteen years of success and comfort his rival had experienced. "But he talked them out of it. He's good at that. He's training his twin grandsons, who are about your age, and has started the shows with them again."

He half smiled. "And that, Micah, is the tale of the once-great Maske of Magic. I trust that satisfies your curiosity enough to leave my workshop alone." He left. In the kitchen, I heard him pour liquid into a glass. I guessed it was whisky.

The thing was, it did satisfy my curiosity. I had seen behind the mask of Maske, to the sad man within. He was in good company with me and Drystan.

The next morning, I woke far too early to the sound of another of Drystan's nightmares.

I crept from my bed, shivering in the early-morning chill. Drystan's entire body tensed, his brow furrowed as he tossed his head from side to side. His breath rasped in and out, ragged with fear.

Mindful of startling him from sleep, I sat next to him. When his questing hands brushed against my arm, he stiffened. I held my breath, hoping he would not hit me again.

Drystan's hand rested on mine. I lay down carefully on the bed, half propped-up against the headboard. His hand squeezed mine, and then relaxed. He turned toward me with a sigh, settling into a deeper sleep. I held my breath. When awake, Drystan kept his distance. Now, his face was vulnerable and open as he breathed – the deep, dreamless sleep of the exhausted.

Fighting the urge to stroke his hair, I sat there until I could just make out the design of the dragonfly of the stained glass window.

Time for the sunrise. And the magician's assistant.

10
THE TRUE TEMNIAN

"If the Kymri are more predisposed to worship the sun, then the Temnians have more respect for the lunar cycle. During the full moon, or the night the Penglass glows under the stars, there is a huge celebration and feast. Elders dress as the moon and stars and bestow blessings upon those who need them. Special food is created that may only be eaten that night – sweet mooncakes and small sips of a drink called Dancing Water made from almonds, fermented honey, and small gold flakes, which is meant to be an elixir for long life. Small amounts of the drug Lerium are also sampled. On this night, men and women are meant to become closer to the Lord and Lady and their prayers will more likely be heard and wishes granted."

THE FORMER ELLADAN COLONIES, Professor Caed
Cedar, Royal Snakewood University

The girl Maske wanted for the role of the magician's assistant arrived the next morning. She walked onto the stage as if it were an audition.

My skin prickled into goosebumps at the sight of her. I knew her face. She was the girl on stage with Drystan in my vision at Twisting the Aces.

She was Temnian, with dark eyes, golden skin, and hair that fell in a dark river to her waist, small sections braided with ceramic beads. She wore a simple dress of Temnian linen, secured about the waist with a silken scarf.

She gave us the Temnian bow, her hand across her face.

"Good afternoon, Cyan," Maske greeted her. "Thank you for considering my proposal."

She smiled. "Pleased to help you, Mister Maske, after all you've done for our family." She spoke with an Elladan accent. Her eyes darted to the side, a shadow crossing her face. I leaned forward, sensing a secret just out of reach.

"Well, my dear, let's see what you can do." Maske gave her some simple instructions: could she touch her toes? Fit into the cabinet? Had she learned any magic tricks? She performed them all gracefully. She drew the eye, but did not command it to the exclusion of all else. She would be perfect and help with misdirection without stealing the show.

For our benefit, she told us she had been raised among sideshows and circuses where she'd picked up various skills, from fortunetelling to contortionism. Her parents currently performed in Bil's old rival circus, Riley & Batheo's Circus of Curiosities. This put me on edge – we'd almost certainly have acquaintances in common.

We thanked her for her time and asked her to return the next day, but I could tell Maske's mind was made up. He wanted her to be the new assistant.

I was still worried. "She could be a spy," I said to Maske and Drystan over lunch.

Maske speared a potato. "I've known her since she was six."

I'd known my parents my whole life, and they still turned out to be duplicitous when it came to a surgeon's knife.

"She worked in a circus," I said.

"Yes. We'll be mindful of what we say around her, naturally, but we need an assistant. I will vouch for her. She also needs our help."

"What do you mean?" I asked.

"She's run away from the circus and her parents. She came to me after leaving but wouldn't take me up on my offer to stay. She's been staying with someone, but he'll be leaving soon. I don't want her on the streets, so I approached her again. She agreed when I told her she could work for her board."

"She seemed truthful to me, for what that's worth," Drystan said, mouth full. I think he delighted in having rough table manners, after the rigorous etiquette training he must have had as a youth. I, however, could not shake my upbringing, holding the cutlery just so.

"She could be a very good liar," I grumbled under my breath.

"She's a truthful girl," Maske said, the edge of his voice sharpening. "I used the Augur and she didn't lie. Now, please leave it."

I stabbed a piece of overcooked beef.

There would be so many opportunities where we might make mistakes. Even three months later, newspaper articles about us still appeared, reminding citizens of the potential reward. There was no longer anything about

Lady Iphigenia Laurus, but I knew people were still searching for her, too.

Drystan and I had gone to watch the apartment tenement where we had last seen the Shadow, but saw no sign of him. We began to doubt he even lived there.

We had to find him to find a way to be rid of him.

I tossed and turned that night, jumbled dreams jolting me awake more than once. Drystan was restless, but not crying out in his sleep. I sighed, giving up on rest long before the sun rose, hoping that we were not making a terrible mistake by hiring this girl named Cyan.

She arrived at noon. Yesterday she had been cool, calm, and collected as she performed. Now, she looked nervous, younger, standing on the threshold of the theatre with a large carpetbag, the hood of her coat up against the cold.

We invited her in and introduced ourselves.

"I'm Sam," I said, holding out my hand to hers.

"Amon," Drystan said, nodding.

"Well met." She inclined her head.

She was perhaps around my age or a little older. We had hidden all personal possessions and we wore Glamours beneath our Temnian silks. Of course, she knew full well that we were not Temnian.

"Are you going to turn off your Glamour?" she asked. "You're not Temnian."

"No, they're not. Don't rush them, Cyan. You'll see them when they wish to show you their true faces. Though I hope, for the Glamours' sake, that it's sooner rather than later." Maske gave us a pointed look as he passed her a mug of coffee.

She gave him a smile, her nose crinkling. "Thank you," she said as we clustered about the kitchen table. She held the cup in both hands, warming her fingers. Her hair lay in a shining plait over her shoulder.

"I've made up your room," Maske said. "May I take your things?"

"If it is not too much trouble, yes."

Maske took her bag. "I'll bring this up and let you three become acquainted."

"My thanks," she said.

Maske left us. The lull in the conversation stretched to an awkward silence.

Her expression was polite and impassive, but even beneath the nerves her eyes were lively, as if laughter could erupt at any moment. Through my suspicion, I found myself growing curious about her.

"Have you been in Ellada long?" I asked. Yesterday we'd kept up the Temri accents, but that day, we left them behind.

She broke into a smile, and it was so open, I found myself warming to her, despite myself. "I was born here," she said. "My family is from Southern Temne, near Muyin and Chinsh."

"Do you ever go back to visit?"

She nodded. "Every few years or so. My mother is very close to her side of the family." Her smile faltered. Something had happened with her parents, especially the mother. She fingered a ceramic bead at the end of her plait.

I knew with certainty that she was running away from something. She looked at me sharply, as if she guessed my thoughts.

"How long have you known Maske?" Drystan asked.

"Since I was a child. He knows my parents. My mother was a great admirer of his when he was a magician." A twist of the mouth, tinged with bitterness. I kept the frown from my face.

"You must find it a little silly, that we pretend to be Temnian," I said. I felt protected by the illusion cast by the Glamour. She saw a stranger.

She smiled, holding a hand in front of her mouth. "It is, a bit. So many Elladans dislike us, yet find us fascinating. It grows tiring. The fact that you'd court that is… odd, but I know others who did that, even in my circus. And your accent is terrible. Though I can at least teach you the curse words."

We smiled weakly.

There was an indignant meow. Ricket, the little calico, investigated Cyan's skirts. "Hello, small cat," she said, holding down her fingers for him to investigate. He sniffed her suspiciously. She passed the inspection, and he rubbed his face against her hand before pouncing into her lap. She stroked his back. His purr rattled into the silence as he kneaded her legs.

Determined not to let the small silence relapse into awkwardness, I spoke.

"We're both new to Imachara. I'm from Sicion," I said. "But Amon here is from a town so small you'd never have heard of it."

We planned our whole make-believe lives to the smallest detail – what our parents did, our fictitious siblings, old addresses, friends, and the like. My fictional father was a luminary, selling Vestige glass globes and gas lamps, and my mother was a seamstress. Drystan, as Amon, was an orphan whose parents had drowned on a fishing boat, and had been raised in the tiny fishing village of Neite by his aunt. Drystan softened his accent to sound as though he were from there.

She nodded. "I've been to Sicion for the circus, but never as far as Niete. How do you like working in magic so far?"

"I imagine it's much the same as the circus, except you don't move around as much," I said.

"Have you been to see Riley and Batheo?" she asked us. We shook our heads, too quickly.

"You should see it sometime. It's something to behold." I made a noncommittal sound, unable to speak.

"New people just joined, I heard," she said. "They came from Ragona's Circus after the ringmaster died."

My breath caught in my throat, almost choking me. "We heard about that," Drystan said. "Terrible." How could he sound so calm?

"It seemed so. The people who joined were still broken up about it. Couldn't believe it."

Did she know? Was she threatening us? She didn't seem to be, but I couldn't be sure.

"Sometimes you think you know someone and realize you know nothing at all," Drystan said. I bit the inside of my cheek until my eyes watered.

Cyan took a sip of her drink, petting Ricket with her free hand.

"What is your favorite sound?" she asked us.

I was taken aback, but relieved, by the abrupt change in conversation.

"I was just thinking," she said, stroking Ricket, "how the purr of a contented cat is one of my favorite sounds in the world. There's something so comforting about it, isn't there?"

"I suppose there is," Drystan said, bemused.

"So what are your favorite sounds? I'll give you some others of mine. The first birdcall of morning. The whistle of the kettle. The sound of far-off singing not quite heard." She lapsed into silence, as if embarrassed by the sudden outpouring of words.

I considered. "The sound of waves washing along the beach. The rustling of wind through the trees. The steady sound of someone breathing peacefully." I looked at the floor when I said this. It had become one of my favorite sounds only lately, when Drystan slept without nightmares.

Cyan nodded. "All excellent sounds. And you, Amon?" she then asked Drystan, polite but her face alight with curiosity.

"The crackle of the fire," he said, and I knew he was thinking of the bonfires at the circus. "The ethereal sound of the chorus in the Celestial Cathedral on Lady's Long Night. It fills you up until there's no other thought left. The crunch of walking on fallen autumn leaves." I smiled at him, and promised myself that we would go to the cathedral on Lady's Long Night in a month's time.

"All very good sounds. And intriguing."

"Intriguing?" I asked.

"Yes." She smiled at us widely. From our answers, she suddenly seemed much more at ease around us. I wondered what we had unintentionally given away.

The magician returned. "I've turned out your room, Cyan, if you wish to go and investigate. I'll lead you to it."

"Of course, that would be wonderful," she said. As they walked out of the kitchen, I heard her ask: "It's been a while since I've asked you, Mister Maske: what are your favorite sounds?"

As they walked away, I could not hear his answer.

"I finally saw the Shadow this morning," Drystan said that evening, as soon as we were alone in the loft.

I sat up straight in the bed. "Why didn't you tell me?"

"I didn't have the opportunity. I returned just as Cyan arrived. And I'm not entirely sure it was him. It was a man wearing that broad-brimmed hat he'd been wearing when he was sneaking around the circus. It's not like he's the only man in the city to wear that type of hat, but I was pretty sure it was him."

"And?" I prompted.

"I followed him, but he shook me."

My stomach dropped. "So he knows we're following him?"

"I was discreet. But I think he sensed someone following him. I've narrowed it down to the Brass Quarter. I lost him near the marketplace."

"Let's go there tomorrow. All we need to know is where he lives..." He'd never entered that other apartment building we saw, so he must live somewhere else.

"We're close." Drystan picked up the book of magic history by his bed but set it aside again. "I couldn't find any signs of deception in Cyan today."

"She's hiding something, though."

"Without a doubt. But I don't think it affects us, at least not directly."

"I'm not trusting her."

"Me neither."

"Why was she asking us about our favorite sounds?" I asked.

"It's a Temnian thing. They ask about favorite sounds, favorite tastes, favorite textures and the like quite often in conversations. They say that it gives away things about a person, so they can make up their mind about them. Sort of like how Maske makes up his mind about someone in a séance."

"I wonder what we gave away."

"I don't know. If she turns out not to be a spy, we can ask her."

We murmured our goodnights but, as usual, sleep evaded me. I was so tired of never feeling safe, always wondering who I could trust. I did not know this Cyan girl and whether she would grow too curious about us. It seemed inevitable that the Shadow would find us. I turned the Phantom Damselfly over and over in my hand. The metal thrummed under my fingers. I watched Drystan's back rise and fall in sleep and listened to the rain drumming on the rooftop.

I debated falling asleep with the disc in my hand again, but at the last moment, I set the disc aside, fearful of what I might learn.

I need not have bothered.

This is a memory that I do not wish to remember.

Only fragments remain – like a jigsaw puzzle scattered on the ground, some pieces the blank brown of the backs, and others bright specks of color. But they are without context. I do not remember how long ago this was. A long time. If only I could choose to forget the rest.

My charge was in the next room. I was in stasis. My real body had perished, and my new one of flesh and bone still gestated. For now I was all cogs and metal and crystal. Something triggered my warning mechanisms, and I found myself awake. In the next room, my charge was screaming.

I ran through the door, trailing my false fingers against the smooth Venglass walls, and my charge – my boy – was dead. I do not remember the sight of his body. That is a puzzle piece with a blank front. Nobody was in the room, but the window portal had been left ajar. I rushed to the window, the glass glowing with the coming dawn, but saw no one. I went to the bed, cradled my hand against his face. I could not feel him through my false skin. To me, he had no more substance than a wraith.

I believe I was there for a long while. It is impossible to know. I sent out my sensors over the ground, but all was quiet. The night flowers closed, and morning blossoms opened. The Venglass around us glowed brighter. The hanging gardens swung in the warm, summer breeze. I could not smell the flowers, though the old me, the me who had been real, almost remembered what they would have smelled like.

Normally, I would be awakening my charge. But there was no way to do so. Blood had stopped dripping onto the floor.

The Alder burst into the room. I failed them.

"Did you do this?" they asked me.

"No."

"Who did? Who did this?"

"I do not know."

They accessed my memory banks. They did not believe me, and so they relived what I saw. But there were gaps in the data. They decided someone had corrupted me. Or I had corrupted myself. That I had been compromised.

I was put to sleep.

And I remained asleep for ever so long, my little Kedi.

I awoke, bolt upright in bed. The Vestige was on the bedside table where I had left it. It was only a dream. Wasn't it?

In this dream, I saw inside Penglass. No one has ever been able to penetrate it. No one. It had been calming. As calming as that yearning I felt to touch Penglass on the Penmoon – as though it held the power to take away my troubles.

I remembered the sound of dripping blood from the dream, and I shuddered, wrapping my arms around myself. In the dream, I had *been* the damselfly. All senses were muted. I could not smell and I could not feel. Sight and sound were strange – the colors lacking subtle shades, and sounds almost mechanical. My fingers had rested on a still cheek, unable to even kiss the boy goodbye.

A sob caught in my throat. My eyes burned. My vision blurred. Grief for a young boy who may not even have been human tore through me, for a boy dead for centuries, possibly millennia.

My gaze fell upon the small, innocuous disc. I did not even know if it was my grief, or hers. I picked it up, and the sorrow grew stronger. Another sob threatened to choke me. I walked to the stained glass window and opened it with a creak, preparing to throw the disc out onto the pavement below, where it would shatter and never bother me again.

"Micah?"

I flinched. Drystan was sitting up in bed. The open concern on his face undid me again. The disc thumped to the floor from my numb fingers. I sobbed, and not just for the long-dead boy. I cried for Iphigenia Laurus, for Micah Grey, for the boy Drystan Hornbeam had been and the young man he had become. I cried for Aenea, for Frit, even for Bil, the clowns, and everyone in the circus I had hurt. I cried for Maske. Everywhere I turned, there was nothing but fear and heartache.

Warm arms wrapped around me. A tear that was not mine dropped on the back of my hand. I rested my face against his neck, his heartbeat against my lips. This simple touch was what we both needed without realizing we did. That it was alright for us to grieve for what we had lost. For what we had taken.

When the tears dried, we each went to our cold, lonely beds. The next morning, neither of us mentioned it and we avoided each other's gaze. By the afternoon, I almost wondered if it, too, had been a dream.

11
THE FORESTERS

"We are the roots of society – we give them the soil and the water to help them thrive, but receive naught in return but promises and worms. It is time, my brethren, to step into the light and take charge of our own destinies."
Pamphlet of the Forester Party

While I was no less suspicious and still feared the knock of the Shadow or the policiers at our door, time passed, easing the worst of the rough edges from when I had torn myself in the circus.

I still knew little about Cyan and what to make of her, even though Drystan and I had spent hours with her during magic lessons. She took to the lessons with glee, and her fingers were soon just as nimble as our own.

"My merry magicians. I'll be going for supplies from Twisting the Aces. Fancy coming along after lessons?" Maske asked one morning.

We needed an excuse to go into town, and this seemed almost fortuitous.

"Of course," I said.

"Wonderful," Maske said, finishing his coffee. "To the lessons."

We were learning to place needles in our mouths and draw them out, linked, on a piece of string. It was a fairly safe trick, but my tongue was still sore from dozens of minor pinpricks. I kept fearing I'd accidentally swallow a needle.

I fought down nerves during the lessons, which only resulted in another few jabs of my tongue. Drystan mastered the trick easily, his arms crossed as Cyan and I struggled.

Afterwards, the four of us set off into town, well-wrapped against the cold.

The distant strike of a blacksmith's anvil echoed as we walked toward Twisting the Aces, the wind whipping our hair into a frenzy. The bell tinkled as we entered.

The store was much the same, with Lily behind the counter.

"Hello, my dears, it's been a time. So wonderful to see you again," she greeted us, her eyes on Maske.

He consulted the list of supplies, rattling off replacement machinery parts and their measurements, taking care to linger close to Lily. I picked out the smaller items – candles, invisible wire, magnets to conceal within clothing.

Lily flitted about the shop. "I think the spare cogs are up here," she muttered. Stretching up, she knocked something off the shelf. Out of reflex I caught it and passed it to her – a square of deep purple glass, set in a frame of lacquered wood of red and blue. The frame reminded me a little of the clown's motley at the circus, and my gut twisted.

"Thank you, my sweet! I was wondering where that was," she said, hanging the glass in the window so that the playing cards dangling from strings shone purple in the light. She resumed her post behind the counter, wrapping the purchases as we brought them to her.

My eye fell upon the cabinet with the Vestige artifacts for sale, but I stayed far away from the crystal ball. I wanted no more visions.

"When we have our first show, we'll be sure to invite you," Maske said, smiling at her. "We may be performing séances shortly as well."

She clapped her hands together. "Oh, please do let me know when you perform! I consider myself quite the spiritualist. I went to a séance at Lady Archer's not long ago – she was a frequent customer o' my late husband's – and it was so frightening my heart just about burst from my chest. Lady Archer communed with her long-lost brother, and she had no doubts that it was him. Not a doubt in the world. I haven't been to one since, but I'd dearly love to!"

"Of course, my lady," Maske said, making a show of bowing to her. "Could we arrange for the larger purchases to be delivered?"

"No problem at all, sir, no problem at all! Tomorrow?"

"Tomorrow will be fine," he assured her. "Just to the Kymri Theatre, please."

She bobbed her head. "That's an awfully nice building. Is it just as pretty inside?"

"It's a beautiful building, though sadly in a state of disrepair."

"Oh, but if you hold performances there I've no doubt you'll spruce the place up. I know a nice florist, if you need, closer to opening night. Bouquets of roses do ever so brighten a place."

Maske nodded to us. "You three run into town if you like. Mrs Verre and I have made arrangements to meet for a cup of tea."

"Oh, have you now?" Drystan drawled, amused.

"Indeed. Off you go."

"Thank you, my lady," Drystan said gallantly to Lily, giving her a bow before we stepped out onto the cobbled street.

"She's a good-looking woman but I can't say I see what attracts him. That woman is exhausting," Drystan said once free of the shop.

"She's nice!" I protested.

"She's very… enthusiastic," Cyan said, diplomatically.

"She's nice," I insisted. It was refreshing to be around someone who had such a sunny disposition. So often people were full of doom and gloom. Maybe that's what Maske liked about her.

Drystan frowned. "What's that?"

Up ahead, we heard shouting. A group of people holding signs marched down the street, and we were swept up with them and herded toward Golden Square in front of the Snakewood Palace.

"What is this?" I cried over the din. The yelling coalesced into chanting.

Men and women crowded the square, holding signs and chanting "Equality! For the Tree!" over and over, their voices rising to a fevered pitch. The horde blocked traffic. Men and women driving carriages and carts yelled obscenities, adding to the fray. The gates of the palace were locked, grim guards posted behind the wrought iron.

The palace lay in the center of the city, the three large Penglass domes peeking over the roof. It was costly to integrate Penglass into architecture, as it was so smooth that buildings erected around it tended to leak. I wondered if the young Princess Royal peeked out from behind one of the closed shutters.

We were caught within the press of people, Cyan and Drystan pushing against me, Cyan's elbow digging into my side.

"What should we do?" I yelled over the melee. We stumbled toward the middle of the square. I could not believe how many people there were. I knew a bit about the Forester party. They wanted to abolish the monarchy and establish a democracy like Southern Temne. But I always imagined they were a small faction. This protest made me realize that, as first a noble's daughter and then as a circus performer, I was, in many ways, out of touch with how Ellada actually felt.

Drystan pointed toward a staircase at the corner of the square. While it was filled with people, it wasn't the same crush, and we'd be able to take the pedestrian bridge to escape. We pushed our way through the throng, people stepping on our feet. I smelled unwashed bodies, coal dust from workers, and cheap perfume. Some were trying to profit from the protest, selling food and blank sign boards, a bucket of paint at the ready. People were chanting so many slogans that I could no longer tell what anyone was saying.

A commotion at the podium in front of the palace made us pause. A man appeared, and in the push and pull of the throng, he was the picture of calm, holding his arms out. He was tall and blocky, wearing simple clothes, though they fit him well, with mutton chops on his cheeks. I recognized the face instantly, from both my vision during the first visit to Twisting the Aces and from the flyer foisted into my hands afterwards.

Some people chanted his name: "Timur, Timur, Timur."

The leader of the Foresters. Rumor had it that he once worked for the bureaucracy before he became disgusted with politics and took matters into his own hands. Nobody knew his full name. He rarely appeared in public.

"People of Imachara," he said. "It is time to reclaim our rights. For too long have we been the servants of those who claim themselves higher than us. It is time to bring equality to the entire tree, from the roots to the highest of branches."

People cheered and he smiled at them magnanimously. Something about his manner reminded me of the ringmaster of the circus. He had an air of the showman about him. The air of a liar.

"I do not wish for violence. I wish this to be a peaceful change. A government where the people have the right to make the decisions of our country, and not just the monarchy and the nobility. Ellada is wearing down. As more Vestige breaks, we are left weaker and more vulnerable than ever before. But what will the current power do about this? I do not know. Do you?"

People cried out that they didn't, stamping their feet.

"We are not autonomous. We need far more from the former colonies than they want to give. They are bleeding us dry, my brothers and sisters. But through negotiations and diplomacy, perhaps a new government, free from the taint of the empire, will make a true and lasting peace with our neighbors."

I could not trust him, despite his pretty words. There was something he was leaving out, some plan beyond the promises he was offering.

"Bollocks," Drystan whispered next to me.

Below us, the carpet of people screamed in agreement with Timur, from the gates of the palace onto the spiral of streets. It was madness. Despite promises of peace, a fight broke out on a corner, two men tussling. People backed away to give them room. One of the brawlers picked up his discarded sign, which read: "LEAVES FOR ALL". He smashed it over the other man's head. I sucked in my breath and grabbed Drystan's clammy hand. I did not need to glance at him to know that the gesture reminded us of Drystan's fatal swipe at the ringmaster with his own cane.

But the man below was not dead. He staggered to his feet, wooden splinters in his hair. More men joined the fray, swinging fists. I heard the distant wail of sirens and a group of policiers pushed through the crowd, and more sentries emerged from the palace gates.

"Something tells me this won't end well," Drystan said.

Down below, I saw a distinctive hat. "Look," I pointed. "It can't be–"

"It might be."

All three of us stared at the hat as it moved and bobbed its way through the people. The man paused and looked up toward the palace. I could just see his profile, but my eyes were keen enough to know that it was the Shadow.

"It's him," I said. We'd planned to leave Cyan and find the Shadow on our own, and here he was, right in front of us. Was he here looking for us?

"Someone's looking for you?" Cyan asked.

I said nothing.

"Come on," she said. "Let's get out of here before the mystery man finds you."

The three of us dodged the crowd and made our way down the flight of steps back to the other side of the cobbled street. We ducked into an alleyway and waited for him to pass. When he did, none of us dared to breathe, terrified that he would see us. The Shadow continued without a sideways glance. We made our way toward the Nickel Quarter.

The people were thick enough to give us cover but not impede us. My breath caught in my throat as we followed. Perhaps he would take us back to the same building. Or perhaps he would take us somewhere else.

Cyan's gaze fixed on the hat. For a moment, I was worried that this was a ploy – that she knew exactly who he was. Why else would he have been here at the same time as us, in the entire sprawl of Imachara? When she saw me looking, her features smoothed. Did she know him?

The Shadow walked with purpose, head up, back straight, hands deep in his pockets. A balloon vendor obscured our vision, and we impatiently pushed around her. When we emerged from behind the multi-colored balloons, we barely saw him turn a corner. Our feet thumped along the cobblestones.

He stopped in front of a tenement. We jumbled to a halt. The back of Cyan's hand brushed mine, her skin warm.

With bated breath, we watched as the Shadow slid a key from his pocket into the lock and made his way inside.

"It's no use," I moaned. "It'll be just like the other building, where we'll never see him again, and it's not as if we know which room is his, even if he does live here."

"You need to know where he lives?" Cyan asked.

We said nothing.

"I have an idea." Cyan walked toward the door of the building. Drystan and I followed at a safe distance, poised to run if it turned out she was in league with the Shadow.

Cyan shook her hair from its plait, letting it flow free down her back. She let her shawl hang closer to her elbows. The collar of her dress was high, but the posture was still alluring. She glanced back at us and gave us a dazzling smile. We both gawped back.

Confidently, she rapped on the door and spoke to the porter, with much flicking of her hair.

"Why do I have the feeling she's done this before?" I wondered aloud.

"Oh, she most definitely has," Drystan said, admiringly.

My merriment faded. Drystan's eyes locked on her as she charmed the doorman. I had never learned such feminine wiles. My childhood friend Anna Yew had mastered the art of flirting – gazing coquettishly over a fan at a ball, knowing just what to say to have men hanging onto her every word. I'd always been the one to make them laugh. But now, I had not mastered masculine wiles, either, come to think of it.

Looking at Cyan so comfortable in her skin struck me to the core. I could never imagine flirting with such assurance. The porter blushed beet red, and when he answered her questions, she giggled and kissed him on the cheek before sauntering back toward us, her hair swaying from side to side.

I fought the urge to *harrumph*. The curl of Drystan's lips made me wonder if he knew exactly what I was thinking.

"Well, you're in a pretty pickle, and that's the truth," she said. "What with a Shadow after you and all."

"Um," I said. But there was a tension in her neck and shoulders, and she glanced over her shoulder at the building.

As if she sensed my gaze, she relaxed into a smile.

"Shadow Kam Elwood lives on the third floor in suite G," she said.

"Wow," Drystan said. "Well done, Miss Cyan."

"He's evidently a nice enough fellow. Tips now and again and always has a smile."

"How did you get him to tell you that?" I asked. *And did you know his name already?* I wanted to ask.

"I said I was one of his clients' maids, and that she was so impressed with his service that she wanted to surprise him with a present. She knew the building but not the number to send it to, and struggled with the spelling of his name."

"Wow, he's a gullible fellow," Drystan said.

"I suppose he is. Rather handsome, though, don't you think?"

"His face is a bit too blocky for my tastes," Drystan said, deadpan.

She laughed. "Aha! I knew it!"

"Knew what?" Drystan said, innocent as a lamb.

She chuckled. "Pity, you're just my type. What about you, Sam?"

"Oh, so I'm second choice? Way to make a boy feel special," I drawled.

She glanced between us. "Aha. I see."

Drystan did not miss a beat and smirked, snaking his hand around my shoulders. I sputtered as the implication sunk in. I shot a glance at Drystan. His expression only said "come on, play along."

I rested my healed broken arm around his slender waist, leaning against him. It did not feel like playing along. The memory of putting my hand around Aenea's waist cut me, and I almost took my hand away.

Cyan sashayed ahead of us, her hair swaying like a pendulum.

When she was out of earshot, he leaned close: "She knows more than she's letting on."

"Undoubtedly."

Drystan kept his arm about my shoulders the entire walk home.

12
THE VANISHING GIRL

"Oftentimes the answers that you seek are not the ones you were expecting to receive."

Elladan proverb

There was a knock on the door.

We all started. I spilled a bit of my tea on the worn table. The knock sounded again. Cyan, Drystan and I all froze like rabbits spotted by a fox.

"I'll get it," Maske said, amused at our apprehension.

We waited as his heavy footsteps made their way down the hall. Who was it? Shadow Elwood? The constabulary? Should we run?

"Good morning, Madame! Ah, I see all the parcels are here. Always a pleasure for such a lovely woman to stand on my threshold." Maske called, loud enough for us to hear. I heard a giggle. "Oh my, what a rogue you are, Jasper!"

Jasper? I mouthed at Cyan and Drystan, raising an eyebrow.

"Come in, come in," Maske said. "Leave the parcels here in the hallway and then you must have a cup of tea. No, no, I insist, just leave them there in the hallway. I'll put young Amon and Sam's backs to work later."

Drystan and I exchanged an alarmed glance. Why did Maske invite her inside? Luckily our Glamours were on, as we didn't yet trust Cyan.

Lily entered the kitchen, well turned out in a dress of cobalt blue trimmed in black lace. A ridiculous hat festooned with feathers and veils sat perched upon her head. She looked about in wide-eyed wonder.

"This place is a marvel. An utter marvel," she said. "I can't wait to see it when it's bright and cheery."

"Is it as gloomy as that, my dear Mrs Verre?" Maske asked.

"Just a little," she said, crinkling her eyes at him. "It needs a good dusting, that's for sure! When it gets closer to the time for you to open, I'd be happy to come lend a hand on an afternoon."

I frowned, not sure if we should be letting strangers into the theatre.

"You are too kind, my lady," Maske demurred, but two spots of color appeared on his cheekbones.

My eyebrows rose.

"Oh, Jasper, I'm no lady, so call me Lily." She waved her hand carelessly and then sipped her tea, crinkling her eyes at Maske. She only had eyes for him and barely glanced at the rest of us. I considered Maske. He was a fine-looking man, with those doleful eyes and mysterious smile.

The cat, Ricket, stretched and padded his way over to investigate the new intruder. Lily crouched under the table to say hello. We perched around the table. Lily and Maske flirted with each other. Cyan hid a smile behind her hand.

Lily chatted away, her mind jumping from topic to topic with a speed I could not follow. Soon, I gave up and just watched in amazement as she kept on.

After drinking three cups of tea, Lily begged to use "the facilities" before making her way back home. I escorted her to the washroom, not wanting her curiosity to lead her down darkened hallways. As I waited for her, I rubbed my temples. Maybe Drystan was right, and small doses of Lily Verre were more than enough.

"This place is a treasure trove!" she exclaimed as we walked back to the kitchen. "Well and truly. My offer to help make it presentable still stands. I mean it," she said, taking my hand in hers.

"We'll definitely keep you in mind." I disengaged my hand. The thought of an entire afternoon with her made my temples throb anew.

She bid her farewells, giving each of us kisses on both cheeks. Her lips lingered on Maske's, and his face split into an inane grin. Before Lily, I had a feeling it had been many years since a woman kissed him.

"What a marvelous woman," Maske said, more to himself than us. "Extraordinary. Such vivacity!" He shook his head in amazement.

Drystan, Cyan, and I all exchanged smiles.

"Well, that's quite enough of that," Maske said, briskly. "Let's to our lessons."

• • •

It was dark inside the spirit cabinet.

The bonds chafed my wrists and brought back memories of Bil leaning over me, the sharp smell of whisky on his breath, the pain as I dislocated my thumbs to break free. My breath came faster.

"Are you ready?" Maske called.

"Almost!" Drystan said. "Are you alright?" he whispered close to my ear.

"I've remembered I don't like being tied up overmuch."

"Ah."

Inhale. Exhale. I forced my breath to slow.

"It's fine," he whispered. "Remember. You can escape these bonds at any time." His lips rested against my forehead, light as a sparrow's wing. He leaned away from me, though our shoulders still touched. The dim light fell on the eyelashes resting against the curve of his cheek, the slope of his nose and the curl of his lips.

Inhale. Exhale.

"Ready!" Drystan called.

"On my count," Maske said. "One, two, three!"

In a thrice, we were free from our bonds. Drystan dropped through the trapdoor at the bottom and I slipped behind the hidden mirrors.

I heard the door open.

"As you can see," Maske said to our audience of one, Cyan, "the magicians have disappeared into the ether in the blink of an eye, the magic too much for their veins."

The door slammed shut. I counted in my head as Maske continued his patter, describing how magic was all around us and all we had to do was know how to tap into its hidden power.

When I counted to twenty, I slipped back into the darkened spirit cabinet, looping my bonds loosely about my neck.

The door opened.

I stepped calmly onto the stage, the ropes slithering from my neck and onto the stage like snakes. Cyan clapped.

"Two have freed themselves and one has gone. Or has he?" Maske gestured to the empty audience. Drystan emerged onto the balcony, unruffled, the bonds about his neck.

Cyan jumped from her seat and laughed in delight, clapping even louder. We had kept this trick from her as a surprise.

"Marvelous! Is it the finale?" she asked.

"Oh, no, no, my dear." He took her hand and led her onto the stage. "This is practice. You, Cyan, are the finale."

She cocked her head. "Me?"

"I have designed a trick that shall be magnificent," he said. "It will take a lot of work to get it right, but if we succeed, we will be the talk of Imachara."

Drystan and I had already been the talk of Imachara. Again, I wondered why I was so intent on learning magic, despite how dangerous it could be. But even still, I wanted to learn, to perform. And it'd only take one sell-out performance to give us enough money to leave Ellada behind. Though the more time passed, the less I wanted to leave.

Maske continued. "It'll take perfect timing. There can be no room for error, for if there is, it could be dangerous."

"Dangerous?" Cyan echoed.

"Have you seen the old pantomimes performed?"

I starred in one as a girl, I thought. *With Drystan as my true love*. I could still recite all of the lines without hesitation.

"They are fond of characters coming up through trap doors," Maske continued. "They call it a star trap.

"A star trap is dangerous, however. It's very quick. If you're not aligned just so, then you could injure yourself terribly," he said. "So we will have to be careful. And we will have to trust ourselves and each other to perform."

I bit the inside of my cheek, my eyes darting to Cyan. Nice a girl as she was, I had dozens of doubts about her. Nearly a month with her and we had learned almost nothing, although we hadn't asked many questions, fearing questions in return. She also hadn't turned us in.

"Are you sure it's not too dangerous?" I ventured. "We are still amateurs, after all."

Maske waved away my fears. "I'll only be showing you the basics for now. But you will master it, and it will be a show to remember." He radiated a quiet joy at this. When he was teaching us about magic and illusion, he stood straighter and his voice boomed. On stage was when he came alive.

Maske disappeared backstage and bought out a cylinder of fabric held apart by metal hoops, the sleeves fashioned as crude, feathered wings.

"What… is that?" I asked. The strange contraption was made out of old, threadbare sheets.

"It's a prototype," he said, defensive. "Now, Sam and Amon, shift the cabinet, will you?"

We obliged, the wheeled cabinet sliding away from the hidden trapdoor.

"Cyan, you stand over the trapdoor, please?"

She shuffled over, her brow crinkled. Maske slid the frame over her body, forming a decidedly odd dress.

Maske looked her over. "I'll make adjustments to the shape, never fear."

Cyan slid her arms into the winged sleeves. She held them out to her sides, stiffly.

Maske circled her. "I'm not sure what type of wings to make them in the end. Feathers? Bat wings? Gossamer won't do – too transparent. No matter, no matter. Plenty of time for that later." He moved the fabric from side to side, making notes in a small book. He licked his finger, flipping through pages of intricate diagrams and cramped writing.

Drystan and I watched, transfixed, as Maske continued his lone diatribe. Cyan gave us a helpless look as Maske muttered about necklines and angles. I found myself stifling a grin.

"Alright. Put your wings in front of your face like so," he instructed, helping her move her arms. "Now, there're two small hooks at the end of the cuffs. Fasten them together and then take your arms out of the sleeves and stand with them close to your sides."

She must have done so, for he said, "Good". But it looked as though her arms were still in front of her face.

"Sam or Amon will be under the stage and will catch you, and you will the vanishing girl."

"What about the dress?" I asked.

"I won't ruin the final reveal just yet," he said. "But it will vanish in a way you'd never expect." He muttered to himself again.

"Can I come out now?" Cyan asked from inside the wire and cloth.

"Certainly, my dear, certainly. Thank you for your help."

Cyan wriggled from under the dress, dusting off her robe. She had several Elladan dresses, but far preferred Temnian tunics. They did not require corsets, and well did I know how uncomfortable those could be.

Cyan fiddled with the end of her silken sash. "Mister Maske? Would it be possible to have the rest of the day as leave? I left my parents in a rush, and there are some loose ends I must tie up." Her eyes darted to the floor. But Maske told us she'd run away from her parents. Would she go back so easily?

"No bother at all. I've much to do in the workshop. Sam and Amon, you can either choose to study history or you can take the afternoon off as well. You've done well today." He amended the diagram of the vanishing lady before leaving us to return to his workshop.

"He's certainly driven, isn't he?" Cyan asked once Maske left. She shook her head. "He's been like that as far back as I can remember."

"He is at that," I agreed.

"Such a shame he was banned from magic. My mother said he was the best magician that ever lived." She chewed her lip. "The duel with Taliesin seems silly to me. What is it with men holding such grudges?"

Drystan snorted. "I don't think such stupidity is only limited to men."

Cyan waved her hand. "In this case, I do not think women would carry such hatred for so long. Honestly, Maske and Taliesin should have just whipped them out and discovered once and for all whose was the longest."

Drystan laughed outright at this, and my eyes bulged.

"They were fighting over a woman who sampled the both of them. That would have solved it, with much less bother," she said, her eyes merry.

I glanced around. "Don't you ever let Maske hear you say something like that."

"I'm not stupid."

"No, I don't believe you are."

Her merriment faded. "Besides, evidently Maske was quite the ladies' man back at the height of his power. Taliesin couldn't have been all that surprised."

I remembered his blushes with Lily. "He still appears to have the touch with the ladies, but he doesn't seem a womanizer."

"Fifteen years is a long time," she said, staring into the distance. "In any case, I must be getting on." She rubbed a hand on the back of her neck.

"Are you going back to visit the circus?" I asked lightly.

"Just for a little while. Will be good to see them." She smiled, but the expression didn't quite reach her eyes.

"We'll see you for tea then?" I asked.

"Of course. See you soon," she said before hurrying away.

"It's your turn to keep watch for the Shadow," I whispered once she left.

"Yes."

"I'll follow Cyan," I said.

Drystan nodded.

• • •

Cyan did not, in fact, go to Riley & Batheo's Circus of Curiosities.

Cyan went to her room before leaving. I changed as quickly as I could into the spare dress in my pack, wrapping my head in an old rag. I filled a basket with laundry, which I rested against my hip as I followed Cyan at a discreet distance.

She headed to the Penny Rookeries, the worst part of town. I was worried to even follow her there. Dressed as a woman, I felt vulnerable. Men leered at me with smiles with more gaps than teeth. A man clutched at my skirt and asked how much for a "quick wash", but left me alone when I kicked at him and growled in my best Rookeries accent: "more n'ye can afford, awa' wi ye." He cackled as I wandered down the street.

The skirts were strange and heavy against my legs. I feared my jawline was now too strong for a dainty woman's, and I had down on my cheeks, which I shaved. My lips were still feminine. I ran a hand over them.

Cyan's plait thumped against her back as she walked. My hair had been that long once, before my brother chopped it off with scissors in the middle of the night when I ran away. The night I learned my parents were going to have me cut.

Even if Cyan dressed like a boy, with her heart-shaped face, small nose and rosebud of a mouth, she could only be a woman.

She swept down a side street. I liked her, with her quick wit and open laugh, but now I was certain that she was going to meet the Shadow. What would I do if she was? I had no weapon with me, and in any case I did not think I could harm anyone. Not after that night with Bil. Not after what I did to our pursuers the night of the Penglass.

All I could do was to follow, wait, and listen. And then I would have to race home, and Drystan and I would most likely have to run again and hope that Maske did not get into trouble for harboring known fugitives.

I thought of how crushed Maske would be if we left, if he never got to see us perform his magic in front of a crowd again. How once we did perform, we might leave Ellada as soon as we had enough money to escape. It would break his heart. I could kick myself for being such a fool.

Cyan stopped in front of a crumbling tenement. Many years ago, it had been a fine townhouse, like all of the houses in the Penny Rookeries. But bit by bit the neighborhood had been overtaken by the poorest dregs of Imacharan society. I paused as Cyan knocked on the door.

Had Drystan stayed in a place like this? Perhaps he had once knocked on a peeling door, entered a murky doorway, gone down the rickety steps into a smoke-filled room, with a circle of hard men holding well-thumbed cards, a pile of money on the table.

A man emerged from the crumbling house, distracting me from my thoughts. He nodded to her and they made their way down the road. He walked with the loping gait of a sailor, looking behind him several times, as if worried that someone followed them. Each time I pretended to search my washing basket. I did not want this man, whoever he was, to know my face.

They meandered through the streets until they reached the beach. My heart flipped in my chest as they made their way along the promenade. My traitorous feet stopped just short of the wooden planking of the pier. I did not wish to follow them farther; round the next bend, and see where I had spent several months camped out on the beach, living my old life in the circus. Down there was where I had kissed Aenea. Where I had flown on the trapeze, eaten candy floss and swigged beer at the bonfires, brought water for Saitha the elephant and scrubbed her rough skin. Down on that beach was where I had found myself and lost myself all over again.

Cyan and the unknown man sat down on a bench. I took a deep breath and hurried down the wooden stairs. My illusion as a washerwoman was not as strong here – washerwomen did not wash their clothes in the ocean. I hugged the basket close to my chest and kept under the pier. I stopped below Cyan and the unknown man, the shadows of their feet above me, their toes turned toward each other. I dropped the basket and climbed the log support of the pier until I was close enough to hear what they were saying. I could only hope someone would not see me and shout an alarm.

"...and I'm not sure what I should do," Cyan was saying. I strained closer.

"Why do you have to do anything? They have made their choice." From his accent, I guessed he was from the northern town of Niral.

"I feel like I should do more," she said. I craned my neck. There was a wider gap in the planking. I could see their faces, though it was at a rather unflattering angle. The muscles in my neck ached as I studied them. Cyan looked upset, her fingers dancing across her knees.

"It's my fault," she said. "All of it. I've ruined their lives and mine."

"You couldn't control it, Cyan. And it's a blessing."

"It's no blessing." Her voice was bitter. "It's a curse."

They were definitely not talking about me and Drystan. So what were they talking about?

Cyan looked to her left and her right, lowering her voice. "I'm sure it'll happen again, where I am now. There's lots of it in the theatre – I can sense it. I can hear the whispers at night, when I try to fall asleep. One is particularly strong. I feel as though it's calling to me." She sounded weary.

"You've not been sleeping well, have you?"

She sighed. "No."

"I can always tell," he said, and his words were tender. Cyan turned her face to his and they kissed gently. He held her face with his hand, the other on the back of her neck. She rested her arms around his back.

I blushed, abruptly ashamed. I had been so quick to think the worst of her, and she had only snuck off to see her beau. I knew I should shimmy down the post and return home, but I stayed despite the splinters digging into my palms. I wasn't proud of that, but I was curious. What was in the theatre that called to her? What choice had who made?

Cyan leaned her head against the man's shoulder.

"I still feel like I should go and speak to them. Before things get any worse."

The man shook his head. "They said if they ever saw you again that they would put you on the first boat back to Temne. You don't want that, do you?"

She shuddered. "No."

"But there ain't no demon. Styx below, they're not seeing sense."

"They fear what they don't understand," she said, heavily.

"Well, what you did scares me too, a little, but I know there was a reason it happened."

Curiosity burned brighter within me.

"I don't know. I hope it never happens again. I like where I am now. I don't want to leave just yet. And I'm close to you." She reached out and touched his face.

"So it's good with Maske?"

"It is, so far. Although I can tell the two trainees are so stuffed full of secrets that they're practically spilling out of their ears. They're so scared I'm going to discover them! There's a Shadow after them for something. And it worries me – makes me think about my parents' threat to hire one to find me and drag me back."

I blinked.

"You know that was just a threat. Are you sure it's safe with then?"

"I don't know. I have one of my feelings..." She glanced down, and I held my breath and wished for the power of invisibility. If she saw me through the slight gap in the floorboards, she gave no sign of it.

"Maybe you should leave then. I don't much like the thought of you bunking with criminals, I must admit."

Cyan chuckled. "Oh, Oli, don't fret. I don't think they're

criminals. Just people with secrets. I'm used to that. I did grow up in the circus, after all. Everyone there had a tale or ten to hide. I'll be careful. And if they are dangerous, I'll take care of it." She sighed and leaned further against his side. "When do you sail out?" she asked, sadly.

"Three weeks tomorrow."

"I wish you didn't have to go."

"I know, sweet. But it won't be long. We're just going to Kymri and back. Quick cargo trip. You won't even miss me."

"I always miss you." They kissed again. I reckoned I had eavesdropped enough. I made my way down the pole, glancing up a last time at the shadows of their feet turned toward each other before I headed back to the Kymri Theatre.

My head was heavy with storming thoughts. She wasn't a spy, but that did not mean she was not dangerous.

A few days later, I was up in the gridiron – the section above the stage where we attached the near-invisible wires for tricks such as levitation, or for people to manipulate objects above the stage or throw confetti. The wires had grown tangled in practice that morning and I'd agreed to fix them. Drystan was in the library, Cyan in her room, and Maske in his workshop.

Cyan had not left the theatre since she visited her sailor. As far as we could tell, she sent no missives or messages. But I could not shake my unease.

"Drystan," I said one evening before we went to sleep. "Should we just leave and make a run for it? Make the money for passage elsewhere? We don't know what Cyan's up to."

"That's probably the wisest thing to do. But do you really want to run? And we have no concrete proof that she's up to anything." He paused. "And I like it here. Seeing Maske again. We were so close, and that connection is still there."

I liked him too, though at times he grew far too quiet, and he kept his own counsel.

"Alright," I had said, turning to the wall. "We stay. For now."

I drifted from the memories and back to the present, balancing on a gridiron twenty feet above the stage of the theatre. I held my tongue between my teeth and I plucked apart the wires, drawing them up from the stage and winding them into loose spools. It was cramped up there, and dusty. After I finished, I worked my way to the ladder down to the stage. But I had missed a wire, invisible in the dim light. I tripped, though I managed to grab the railing and dangle above the stage.

I sighed, annoyed. I made to pull myself up, but before I knew it, my damp hands slipped and I fell twenty feet through midair. I had enough time to be surprised and angry at myself and try to twist for a better landing before I hit the wooden stage.

I landed with a sickening thump. For a second, I felt fine. And then: pain. I had landed on my side, my hip on fire. At least I hadn't landed on the arm I had broken. My head rang. I was winded and couldn't cry for help. I lay sprawled on the stage, hoping someone would come and find me.

Pain warped time. At some point, I heard footsteps. A cool hand rested on my forehead.

"Sam?" Cyan asked. "Are you alright?"

I couldn't remember who Sam was. I mumbled something.

"What happened? Did you fall?"

I blinked. It was so bright.

"Are you hurt?"

Was I? I couldn't tell. "Dunno," I managed to mutter.

"I'm going to help you up. If something hurts, tell me."

"Everything hurts."

She pressed her hands along my spine. "Have you hurt your back?"

I considered. "No. It's more my side."

"Good." She made comforting noises, and slowly, she helped me into a sitting position. The ringing in my ears faded, but nausea roiled in my stomach.

"I'm alright," I said. And I was. Just very, very sore. I rolled over onto my uninjured side and lifted my shirt, pulling away the waistband to my trousers. I would have quite the bruise.

More than the ache in my side, my head throbbed anew as I realized she had no reason to come to the theatre at this time of day.

"How d'you know I was hurt?"

"I thought I'd walk around. My legs had stiffened from reading for so long."

I moved a little and grimaced. Maybe I hit my head as well, for I seemed to lose my good sense as I said, "Oh, that's bollocks, Cyan, and you know it."

She coughed. "Alright, it is. I was reading in my room and I had the strangest feeling that you were hurt." She fiddled with a bead in her hair. "So... So I came down to see."

I blinked at her. "Maybe you're a psychic."

She laughed, but it sounded nervous. "What happened?

Did you fall?"

"I did."

She looked up. "From... from the gridiron?"

"Yes."

"That's a good twenty feet or more. Nothing's broken?"

She helped me stand. I took a few cautious steps around the stage. "I seem to be alright."

"You were lucky."

"Looks like."

"Sam."

I glanced up at her serious tone. "Yes?"

"I know you followed me yesterday."

I froze. How did she know?

"It's alright. I don't blame you. I'd have followed me, too." She grinned, a little wickedly. "You look quite pretty in a dress."

I coughed again. Pain still thrummed through my body. "Thank you. I suppose."

"I wouldn't have mentioned it, but I want you to know..." She trailed off, her fingers worrying a bead in her hair. "I want you to know that I'm not out to get you. I'm just trying to find my own way. And you have a Shadow after you. And I have a feeling one might be after me. Maybe even the same one."

I blinked.

"I know, it seems unlikely."

"How do you know a Shadow is after you?"

"I don't, not really. Oli went to the circus, after we spoke. He spoke to my parents to try and make amends. I didn't ask him to, but it's the sort of fellow he is." She smiled sadly. "My parents did want me back, but wouldn't tell him anything. He asked some other circus folk, and they told him my parents hired a Shadow. I don't know why, but I think it might be Elwood. I want to find out for sure."

I felt as though my head was stuffed full of spider webs. "Cyan, why are your parents after you?"

She opened her mouth, but no sound came out.

I waited.

"I let them down. I scared them. But I'm no threat to you. And I want to get rid of him. You and Amon must be planning something. I wanted you to know that I'm in. We need to get rid of him."

I hurt too much to think straight. I still didn't know if I could trust her, and I didn't like that she wouldn't tell me what she had done. Then again, I hadn't exactly been forthcoming with her either.

"Sam." Her dark eyes bored into mine. "Please. You can trust me."

I looked at her, as if I could see straight into her. "How do I know that?"

"Because your Glamour doesn't work on me. I've seen yours and Amon's true faces from the first day. You have reddish brown hair. Greenish eyes. Amon's blonde, with blue eyes. I know who you really are."

With a shaking hand, I reached to my chest and turned off the Glamour. Cyan smiled at me.

"That's better. Before, I'd sometimes see both – it'd look really strange." She exhaled in relief.

I had to trust her. After all, she was in that vision I had in Twisting the Aces – she performed magic with Drystan, both of them smiling from ear to ear. I wanted to believe in that vision.

Convincing Drystan proved to be another matter. I convinced him that while we were in the theatre, we could turn off the Glamours. There was no point wasting the power when Cyan knew our secret.

And eventually, Drystan too realized we needed all the help we could get.

13
Night Errands

"There is always the chance that darkness can conquer the light. The sun and the moon may light the sky with their love, but the darkness of the universe is wide and deep. Styx may find a way to snuff the stars one by one and to wrap the sun and the moon in its sable embrace."

The Aphelion

We shadows of the Shadow dressed all in black.

I shrugged into the dark shirt, wondering if I should have left the Linde corset off. In the darkness, Cyan might not see the small proof that I was not entirely male. But there was a chance, and so the corset remained, my skin itching beneath the linen.

Drystan and I tied dark rags around our faces.

Cyan waited for us on the roof. She wore a dark Elladan dress and an old coat of Maske's as opposed to her customary tunic. A plaited crown framed her face.

"I still don't see why I have to stand guard. It's because I'm a girl, isn't it?"

"Of course not. Are you an acrobat?" I asked.

"Are you?" she countered, derisive.

My pride smarted. "Yes," I said. Her eyebrows shot up.

I bent down and then lifted my legs into a handstand. The arm I had broken was slightly weaker than the other, but my balance was perfect. I hadn't lost much of my strength from the circus. Drystan I still exercised almost every day up in the loft.

"Nice trick. Where'd you learn it?"

Even upside-down, I noted Drystan's suspicious glance. "I taught myself. Mostly." I came back to standing.

Cyan half-smiled. "Not bad." She flipped head over feet. Her skirts slid up, giving us a glimpse of petticoats and pantaloons and her shiny, low-heeled city boots. Her form was perfect, even wearing a corset.

We gaped at her.

"Honestly, you two. I grew up in the circus. But I'll keep watch. I'd probably come up with better stories than you two to keep us all out of prison."

"Probably," Drystan agreed affably, though he was a wicked liar when he chose to be. "Let's be about our business." His breath fogged in the cold air.

We shimmied down the drainpipe rather than risking the creaky front door. The metal of the drainpipe was so cold I worried my skin would stick to it. The air was crisp enough to snow.

Once on the ground, I rubbed my hands together. Clouds all but obscured the half moon. Cyan landed beside me with a swift puff of breath. Drystan landed without a sound.

We kept to the darkest parts of the streets.

Drystan and I had taken turns watching Shadow Elwood's apartments. Cyan came with me a few times and continued her flirtation with the young porter, who had overheard Elwood mentioning he was going to the opera this evening. We decided that this was the night to seek the answers to our questions.

Just in time, we slid into our hiding places. Shadow Kam Elwood appeared in a tuxedo and top hat. Under the street lamp, he tapped a cane against the pavement impatiently as he checked his pocket watch.

The words Maske said at the first séance came to me: *A man checks his pocket watch, counting down the time...*

I swallowed. The tapping of the cane reminded me of the ringmaster. The Shadow's head swiveled from side to side as usual, but he did not see the three of us.

A cab arrived, its engine sputtering in the darkness.

Cyan leaned against a street lamp. She had a whistle in her pocket that sounded like a train, which she would blow three times as a warning. If anyone asked why she was lurking, she was waiting for a sweetheart to meet her and take her dancing after he got off work at any moment.

Drystan hadn't wanted to involve her at all, but I told him to believe me when I said I thought she was worthy. And Maske trusted her as well. Having her on the lookout would be better than having no one at all.

I could not help worrying for her. I had been raised to believe that a girl alone at night was never safe. That men would automatically assume her a Moonshade and try to purchase her services. Or find her easy prey.

But Cyan was not as easy prey as Iphigenia, daughter of the Laurus family, would have been, especially with the little knife in her pocket.

I took a steadying breath. "Are you sure this is a good idea?" I asked Drystan.

"Not entirely, no, but at least this way we'll have more of an idea of who we're up against. He knows where we are, but I don't think he's reported us to the authorities."

"Doesn't mean he's not reported us to someone else."

"Course not."

"This is a terrible idea," I whispered. "We're a couple of amateurs. He'll have all manner of ways to know if someone's been rifling through his possessions, surely."

"I know a lot of them. I've investigated a few people's personal possessions over the years." I remembered he had searched through my pack not long after I joined the circus, when the other clowns had stolen it as a joke. He hadn't told them what he'd found – a dress and a strange figurine of a Kedi, a letter to my brother signed "your sister." He had kept my secret.

"He could hide them cleverly, or have a cipher, or booby traps, or..." I continued.

Drystan smiled in the dark, and I fought the urge to back away. With his soot-stained face and feral grin, I wondered if I knew him at all. He pressed his palms against his thighs and the smile faded. He was not as fearless as he pretended to be.

"There's no need to worry because I lifted this from Maske." He held out a wand-like device made of Alder metal, the end pointed like an insect's antennae.

"What is that?" I asked.

"It's an Eclipse. When it's switched on, it'll turn off all other Vestige within a certain radius. Even if he has a Banshee."

"Lord and Lady," I breathed. A Banshee was the most advanced Vestige alarm that civilians could buy. I squinted at the Eclipse. "I've never even heard of such a thing." I took it from him delicately. It weighed little more than a feather.

"That's because it's highly illegal."

"Why does Maske have so much illegal Vestige?"

Drystan gave me a look.

I sighed. "Yes, I know. Former card sharp and criminal. But why does he still have it?"

"They're dead useful. If you had one, would you let it go?" He tucked the Vestige back into his coat pocket. "Come on. Let's go."

"I sure hope we don't regret this," I muttered. I peeked over the edge of the building. Cyan's small face tilted toward us for the briefest of moments before she resumed her watch.

Up here, the plan seemed, if possible, even more ill-considered. Once we entered the apartment, Cyan could dart off to the authorities and we would be none the wiser. Half of me wanted to tell Drystan that we weren't doing this. But we were so close.

Drystan switched on the Eclipse. Its end glowed green, pulsating like a heartbeat. Energy prickled along my skin. Nausea whirred in my stomach. I swallowed, and the feeling passed.

Drystan took out a lock pick roll and jimmied the window open with a screwdriver. It wasn't the strongest of locks, but then this was not an easy ledge to climb to. The window opened and Drystan peered in.

"I think he does have a Banshee," he whispered. "But we're alright with the Eclipse."

Drystan took off his muddy boots, wedging them into the corner of the windowsill, and I did the same. Drystan crept inside, every muscle poised for flight. But the flat was silent. He made a slow circuit of the room, prowling like a hunting cat, the Eclipse doubling as a quivering torchlight. With a nod, he gestured at me to enter.

I slunk into the room, leaving the window open only a crack. I rubbed my hands against my arms as I glanced about.

Shadow Elwood was messy. This was worrying. He could have done this on purpose, so that if anyone came snooping he would know from one single askew fold of cloth.

Despite the disarray, the trappings of his wealth were obvious. Crystal decanters for brandy on the kitchen island. A rich Arrasian rug beneath our feet. If I were not an escaped noble myself, I'd be tempted to set up a business sniffing out adultery among the Saps, as it seemed to be a lucrative line of work.

I gravitated toward the desk in the corner of the room. There were several framed prints of young children, and a woman half-smiling at the camera, her face tilted upward. A wife? Children?

"His family is dead," Drystan whispered in my ear, causing me to jump. "Once we figured out his name, I found out a little about him."

Why hadn't he told me? "What happened?"

"Wasting sickness. They went abroad to Linde. Elwood

stayed here, to work. They caught the illness and never came home."

Maybe that was why Drystan had kept quiet about it. It was harder to fear and hate someone when you pitied them.

Drystan looked through the other rooms of the house. I rifled through the desk, meticulously keeping every paper where it had been before.

Elwood's filing system was neat, at least – labeled by last name and date. Sure enough, there was a file marked "Laurus, Iphigenia." I drew it out with shaking hands.

In it was a page of information on me. Birthplace: unknown. Birthdate: unknown. The stark, black words stared at me accusingly. My parents must have filled this out. The birthdate they had given me was a lie. It was another blow when I thought that they could not hurt me any more.

I read on, rubbing the back of my hand against my nose. It stated the schools had I attended, the lists of tutors. My last recorded height and weight was listed, along with my hair, eye color, and blood type. The notes and observations section was completely blank. I recalled his notebook from when I saw him on the beach by the circus, scribbling and squinting at the canvas tents. I searched the other drawers for it, but Shadow Elwood probably kept it with him at all times. I kept my file out on the desk.

My gaze lingered on a file titled "Chokecherry, Malinda". Lady Chokecherry. I took it out. Shadow Elwood had been hired by Lord Chokecherry to spy on his wife to see if she was cheating on him. The file was cursory; the sum marked "unpaid". I held my tongue between my teeth and put the file back. Obviously someone found something for him to land in the papers.

There were so many folders. I searched for the people I knew. There were no other Laurus names but mine. Neither of my parents suspected the other of adultery. Or, they hadn't hired Elwood. Hornbeam was another absent name. Hawthorne was there, though. Lady Hawthorne had hired Elwood to see if her husband was seeing other ladies while she stayed at the Emerald Bowl to grow her flowers. He had been, at least as of three years ago. I put that folder away with a sigh. Their son, Oswin, was Cyril's best friend and, for a brief time, a possible future husband of mine. I wondered if he knew about his parents. I peeked in other files of familiar names. It was incredibly nosy of me, but I could not help myself.

The very last folder in the filing cabinet held another surprise. Zhu, Cyan.

"Drystan," I called, softly, but he did not answer from the other room. I opened the file. Someone had hired Elwood to find her, but there was no name. Her parents? The details of her background were scarce. She was two years older than me, born in Southern Temne, as she'd said. Her mother was a contortionist and tarot reader, and her father was a juggler and fire eater.

The observations section only contained the following: (IL). KT (JM), GD.

I frowned at the letters for a time, and then the blood drained from my face. IL for Iphigenia Laurus. KT could mean Kymri Theatre, JM Jasper Maske, and GD the Glass District. If I read that correctly, then he knew where we were; why had he not told my parents? Or Cyan's?

I picked up my file and Cyan's and walked through to the bedroom. Drystan sat on the floor, staring at an open box as if mesmerized.

I padded toward him. He was looking at a box filled with vials of a black substance, a little syringe, and a long tie for the arm. My heart constricted. Lerium.

Before I could say anything, Drystan looked at me.

"This isn't Lerium," he said.

"It's not?" I said, creeping closer. "What is it?"

He took out a vial, holding it to the light, and I could see that it wasn't black, but dark green. Its viscous liquid clung to the inside of the glass vial.

He unstopped the vial and took a sniff.

"Drystan!" I hissed.

He gave me a look. "You have to inject it or smoke it to feel anything."

His condescending tone grated on me. "For Lerium. Maybe not for whatever that is."

"It doesn't smell of anything. I have no idea what it is."

"Look." Under the dip in the velvet where the vial had been, something glimmered.

Drystan picked up the top layer with the drug vials. Underneath was a blue oval of Penglass set in a Vestige metal frame.

I reached out for it but Drystan snapped my hands away. "Don't touch it. It's a Mirror of Moirai."

No one knew what the Alder had used it for, but it could find people's locations. Only the constabulary had these, or so I had thought.

Drystan put on his glove and switched on the Vestige mirror. Alder script emerged on the screen, as well as the outline of a hand.

"If someone touches it, it tracks them," Drystan whispered. "Even a piece of hair will do."

"Do you think I'm in it?"

"Probably. If Elwood has this, he must know what it is. Explains why he's the best Shadow in the city, as he claims. Wonder where he got it."

"Can we… erase my record somehow, if I am in it?"

"I don't know how it works."

Neither did I. "We could steal it," I said.

He looked at me. "He'll know we took it."

"We can't leave it."

He nodded, wrapping the Mirror of Moirai in a cloth and putting it in his pack.

"What did you find before you came through?" he asked.

I looked at the forgotten files in my lap. I passed the papers to him and he scanned them. "Not a lot here to surprise us, except Miss Cyan here." He narrowed his eyes.

I crept back to the window. She stood just out of the light of the streetlamp, her hands deep in her pockets, her breath misting in the air. I came back to Drystan. "She hasn't moved."

He tapped his teeth together. "I found the drugs here," he said, tilting his head. I followed his gaze to a large, antique tapestry that would not have been out of place in the public wing of the palace. It depicted a kelpie – a smooth horse the color of green-glass, rising from the ocean, water weeds in its black mane. Dark storm clouds lurked on the horizon. The kelpie's eyes showed the whites in fear, as though something in the water pursued it. I did not like it.

"A lot of these flats have the same floor plan. I lived in one much like this at university. There was a door here in my bedroom," he said, pulling the tapestry aside. Sure enough, there was a small alcove and a safe, which Drystan had broken into.

In the safe was where he had found the box of Lerium-like drugs. Inside was another filing cabinet. I rifled through it, taking out other files with the name Chokecherry, Laurus, and Zhu. I scanned Chokecherry's file first.

"He's blackmailing his clients," I said, passing the papers to him.

He whistled low. "Looks like we're being pursued by a crooked Shadow."

Ignoring the two other files for the time being, we searched through other folders at random. More than once, it was obvious Elwood fabricated evidence, or withheld vital information. My stomach twisted. Some people had gone to prison or died because of him. People who shouldn't have. Any guilt about our plan evaporated.

I looked in Cyan's file, still avoiding my own.

I read aloud: "'?C's parents mentioned a Shai – when they spoke to each other in Temnian, they did not realize I spoke the tongue. If she is a Shai, would make case v. interesting.'" So her parents hired the Shadow. How had they afforded it? Shadows were not cheap.

"What's a Shai?" I asked Drystan.

"Sounds familiar. Something to do with Temnian mythology."

"She isn't... like me, is she?"

Drystan shook his head. "No idea."

I grunted, still reading.

"Anything else?"

"A lot of it is abbreviated. I don't know... Something about an event that happened at the circus. Caused her to leave. She ran away two weeks before we left our circus. Can you make anything else of it?" I passed the papers to him and then, with trepidation, picked up the folder with my name on it.

It had nearly everything. A detailed summary of Bil's death, Drystan's first name – though not his surname – and the Kymri Theatre. But what really worried me was that Elwood had written: "Location determined. Parents not informed. Waiting confirmation for the next course of action. Suspicions of being watched. Second Shadow? Linked to RP?"

A shiver ran through me. Another Shadow? As if one wasn't enough. And who was RP? I looked in the folders, but there were no names with those initials. My breathing seemed to come from both very far away and close in my ears. I swayed on my feet, my vision darkening.

Drystan's hands closed about my shoulders as I slumped against him.

"I'll never be safe," I muttered. "It'll never stop."

Drystan led me to the bed and sat me down, guiding my torso until my head was between my knees. I focused on my breathing.

Drystan rubbed my back as I sucked in deep breaths.

"Your brain bathed in blood again?"

"Think so. That's never happened to me before." Sitting up, I touched my hand to my head.

"First time for everything." He sighed. "We've got enough to hang him. We'll trickle the information to the right people and Shadow Elwood will disappear."

"It's too late anyway. Someone else is looking for me and we don't know how current that file is. Who is he waiting for?"

"I don't know."

We were surrounded by meretricious displays of wealth. Alabaster naiads and sylphs held up the marble mantelpiece. How much of it was bought through blackmail and double-crossing?

"He will have enemies. Anyone who came looking might have found this," I said, gathering up the papers.

"Very true."

"Let's go. We've snooped enough."

A train whistle blew once, twice, and then a third time. Drystan and I froze. Cyan's alarm. I dashed to the lounge, ensuring all of the desk drawers were shut. I returned to the bedroom where Drystan was putting the safe to rights and stuffing the last of the papers into his pack. We took a deep breath and I clasped his hand.

But just as we reached the door to the bedroom, the front door opened.

A man coughed as he stumbled into the lounge. Quickly, Drystan and I slid under the bed. It was dusty, with spare socks and a few books. Drystan and I lay pressed against each other, the bedsprings scant inches above our heads. We heard Elwood stomp into the apartment. He must never have made it to the opera, to be back so soon.

He was not alone.

The woman laughed low in her throat. She tottered about the lounge, as drunk as he was. I could hear them kissing – sloppy, sucking sounds. Drystan's gaze met mine, wide in the darkness beneath the bed.

"I hope they don't decide to fuck in here," he whispered, his voice little more than a breath in my ear. I clamped my hand over my mouth, fighting down a hysterical giggle. All the nerves and fear of breaking and entering a stranger's house threatened to burst from me. I buried my face in Drystan's shirt, silent laughs racking my body. He shook with laughter as well. I thought of how perplexed the Shadow would be if he stumbled into his bedroom and discovered two hysterical boys beneath his bed and that started me all over again. Tears gathered in my eyes and my face must have been tomato-red from the effort of keeping quiet.

When the silent laughter finally ebbed, the fear returned, stronger than before. The only solace was that, if he found us, the Shadow needed us alive to collect his reward. I also realized that I was very close indeed to Drystan. I could smell the lemon soap he used to wash, the spicy scent of his skin. His heart beat quickly, his stubble scratched against my forehead. As the Shadow and his lady embraced in the next room, I wondered how we were ever going to get out of this.

"Oh, Leda," Elwood said. They came into the bedroom. Leda tripped and left her shoe by the bed, a little satin dance slipper, decorated with crystal beading. *Please, please don't let her bend down to pick it up.* My nose tickled with dust. I pinched my nose shut to stop the sneeze. The other satin shoe joined the first as Elwood threw Leda onto the bed.

"My sweet summer rose…" he murmured, and I made a face at Drystan. He bit his lip to keep from laughing, but he was pale beneath his freckles. They were making all manner of noises on the bed, and the springs sagged alarmingly in the middle. Would we be trapped here all night?

Articles of clothing littered the floor of the bedroom. Leda's dress, a pale, watered green silk decorated with pink roses. Her corset. Elwood's coat and waistcoat. His notebook peeked out from the pocket of his coat. What I would not give to take it, but it was clear on the other side of the room.

"It's cold, my love," Leda said, her voice low and sultry.

"I'll soon warm you," he said.

"The cold from outside is deep in my bones." I heard the rasp of her hands rubbing her skin.

"I have an idea. Come, my dove."

Elwood and Leda's naked feet came into view. A ropey scar twined about Elwood's hairy ankle. He led her into the washroom, turning on the tap for the bath, but he paused before joining her.

"A moment, my sweet."

His feet grew closer. He paused by his trousers, which were right by the bed. He reached down and I saw his hand, a scant few inches from my face. He rummaged in the pockets of his trousers and found a lambskin prophylactic. We were as quiet as could be, but his hands and feet stilled. He went about the room, opening the wardrobe door and rifling behind his clothing. The Shadow came back toward the bed. He began to crouch. I tensed, ready to fight him, my body thrumming with nerves.

"Sweetling," Leda called from the washroom. "The water is warm. What's taking so long?"

Shadow Elwood paused. He laughed ruefully. "Coming, my darling." He padded to the washroom. As soon as the door closed, Drystan and I were out from under the bed, covered in dust. At the door from the bedroom to the living room, I paused to crouch and grab the notebook, but Drystan's hand stopped me. He shook his head.

"He'll know someone was here," he mouthed.

He'll know anyway, I wanted to say, but I left it.

We darted through the lounge and opened the window, hoping the running bath would cover the sound. Within moments, we were back on the frigid windowsill, stuffing our feet into our boots, and then shimmying down the frozen drainpipe. Drystan took the Eclipse and turned it off. This time, I felt a surge of energy. The street was empty and deserted but for Cyan. She started walking toward home, and we followed her, shadows with secrets.

14
THE DAMSELFLY

"Dreams hold the answers, even if the questions are not yet known."

Elladan proverb

I was in a garden.

Chimaera strolled along the paths. Most were dragonfly, like me, but several fauns and naiads lounged beneath the trees. The air was thick with a sweet perfume of hundreds of blossoms. Early afternoon lengthened to evening. The small Venglass domes that lined the path glowed in the soft dusk.

I stretched my arms over my head, content in the moment. All was well. I ran my hands over the warm, iridescent flesh of my arms. Blood flowed through my veins, not metal wires. My wings buzzed behind me, swirling my hair about my face. I turned to the Chimaera beside me. My love.

"I like this life," he murmured. "Everything seems to have worked out well this time, has it not?" His voice was

as familiar to me as the birds' calls at dawn. The peacock blue and green sheen of his markings glittered in the glowing light of the Venglass.

"It has. It is a welcome respite." Unbidden, the memories of the murdered boy, my dear Nian, came to me. I wished I could forget it, but there are some memories that even dozens of lives will not erase, no matter how much we would wish otherwise. "That death is still a black mark in my ledger."

"We have all the time in the world to make it right," he said, his hand just grazing my jawline. "All the time we need."

I stared at two fauns on the grass, one playing music that drifted through the air like the scent of the flowers. "I hope you are right. Sometimes, I cannot lose the feeling that we do not have as much time as we would like. That there are only so many lives we can live."

"I am always right, when it comes to these things." He held me close for a kiss. He tasted of honeysuckle, his fingertips as light on my face as rose petals. I drew him in for a deeper kiss, pressing against the man as familiar to myself as my own skin. In every life, we found each other, no matter the distance. My Relean.

Above us, the sky blazed. We broke apart, shielding our eyes from the light with our hands. It was as though the sunset returned, lighting the sky with the colors of a forest fire.

It was a ship with furled wings curling over the prow. It landed on the grass, glowing blue. I clasped my love's hand in mine.

The door opened, and two Alder emerged from the ship. It had been years since I had seen an Alder. They were scarcer in the Ven now, preferring to stay farther up the mountains with their own kind. And many had grown tired of this world and left in search of other moons and stars.

They came straight for us, as I knew they would. Relean and I waited. They were so tall. I always forgot how tall they were, the unnatural thinness of their limbs, the blue sheen to their skin. Their large eyes glowed the same cobalt as Venglass.

They inclined their heads at me, and I bowed my head in turn. All the Chimaera were gone, the music silent, leaving the garden private for me, my love, and the Alder. One of them – a female – held a small bundle in her arms. I fought the urge to sigh even as my heart constricted.

"Your newest charge," one said in Alder, the three-tonal voice echoing in my ears and mind. "We trust you will look after this one better than the last."

My cheeks burned at the rebuke, though the death had not been ruled my fault. I held out my hands for the bundle.

It looked like a human child. I saw no iridescence, no scales or feathers. They had never given me a humanoid Chimaera before, usually leaving humans to care for them. I looked up at the Alder in confusion.

"Unwrap this one," the taller Alder intoned.

I did, and nearly gasped with shock.

The Alder inclined their heads at me and turned, walking with their liquid grace back to the ship. Within moments, they were gone. But the spell of the garden had *broken. The air seemed colder, the scent of the flowers cloying and suffocating.*

The child gurgled in my arms. I looked at Relean. He touched my face with his hands.

"All will be well, my love. All will be well." I drew him into another kiss in the silent garden, the child a barrier between us.

"Little Kedi…"

I awoke, every nerve of my body on alert, memories of the strange dream echoing in my mind. It was only a remnant of the dream. Nothing to fear. I closed my eyes and willed my racing heart to stop.

"Little Kedi…"

No. I was not hearing voices. I was not.

"The time has come."

I found myself climbing out of bed. I clutched the warm damselfly disc. It hummed like an Augur. I shrugged into my coat and stepped into slippers, almost as if I were sleepwalking. I climbed to the roof. Small snowflakes danced along the wind. I stared at the small disc in my hand. As if in a dream, I flicked the switch and set it on the ground. Backing away, I hugged my arms around myself as the wavering image of the Phantom Damselfly appeared.

In the sideshow Pavilion of Phantoms in the circus, she had a loop of actions she performed, walking in a circuit, looking up overhead. She had frightened the visitors of the Pavilion so much that the tent closed down, the disc returning to the safe with the other Vestige pieces the ringmaster collected. She had returned to the stage of the pantomime of *Leander*

& Iona, becoming a monster that Leander must battle. She had not been a frightening monster. Not until she broke her normal movements and glanced over her shoulder, directly at me, before she disappeared.

There was no pretense of those motions, now. She shook her head as though awakening, and then she gazed at me with intelligence and sadness.

"Little Kedi," she said, and sighed soundlessly, snowflakes falling through her transparent dragonfly wings. Her features were almost Alder proportions – bigger eyes, cheekbones that could cut glass, and a wide, thin mouth. Strange tattoos traced her hairline, following the long line of her neck, and disappeared under her gossamer dress.

My tongue stuck to the roof of my mouth.

"I know what you want to know, little Kedi. Of the many things I have been, and the many names. You may call me Anisa."

"Anisa." I pulled free my tongue from the roof of my mouth and rolled her name on it.

She shook her head sadly. "You wonder why I speak to you and no one else."

I nodded, terror stiffening my muscles.

"I can speak to so few, and you are the first in such a very long time. There are others who would also hear me. I feel them, flickering like a candle flame, just here." She tapped her heart. Through her torso, I could see the glow of a gas lamp, as if her heart were aflame. "Some are closer than you know."

"Why...?"

She shook her head. "Because we are alike."

I took a step backwards. "We are not alike at all. You're a ghost. Or a mirage. Vestige trickery."

She moved closer to me, her feet trailing a light leading back to the disc. "I have lived thousands of years. I have seen marvels and horrors you cannot even fathom. You have lived but a few scant years. Sixteen years is but a blip of time in the span of the world." She held her hand to my face, but I could not feel a thing. "Tell me, then, little Kedi. Which of us is more real?"

"What do you want of me?" I whispered.

"I have waited so long. The time is not yet right for the other chips to fall, and I still see little of the pattern."

"You speak in riddles."

She smiled. "I speak more plainly than you know. One day, you will see."

I was tempted to tell her she was only proving my point, but I stayed quiet.

She turned out and looked over the dark skyline, the yellow windows of far-off buildings like stars. "The world is so different, now."

The dream came back to me – the verdant fields of green, the Penglass buildings glinting in the sun. "I remember."

Anisa swept a transparent hand toward the city. "You already know more than all of these people do about what happened long ago."

I did. In a few scattered dreams, I knew more about the Alder Age than those who have spent their lives studying Classics and Antiquities.

"What do you want from me?" I asked, the fear blooming again in my chest.

"Do not fear, little Kedi. Nothing you cannot give. You will help me when the time is right. You will know what to do."

I pressed my lips together to stop them from shaking. This was too much. "Can... you tell the future?"

"I can see possibilities, and which are more likely, no more. Sometimes, it feels as if I know less than anyone else."

"How?"

"They're written on the wind, in the stars and the sunlight. In dust motes swirling through the air. The world knows what has happened, and what may happen. You need only to look for it. You could learn, if you wanted to."

I pinched myself to make sure I was not still dreaming.

"You do not believe me. You will in time. Do you recall the night you first arrived in this place? The séance?"

"Yes." How could I ever forget?

"The magician said more than he knows and yet has no memory of the saying of it. The woman in the red dress. She is important to you, though I do not yet know how. The two of you are linked."

I held my hands to my temples. I remembered how strange I felt when I suggested Maske teach us magic. Had that been her? I should grab the disc and throw her from the roof to smash upon the pavement below. But I knew I would not. She looked at me as if she knew all I thought. Perhaps she did.

"Do you know who chases us? The second client of the Shadow?"

Her eyes unfocused. "I cannot. I can see the shape of the person, but not their face. It is blurred like the reflection of a puddle."

How conveniently unhelpful. I backed a little further away from her.

"Little Kedi, you need not fear me. You are my charge. As I am yours."

I shook my head. "I am no one's charge but my own." I picked up the disc. She stayed where she was, but her form grew more distinct, almost alive.

"I know you are afraid, little Kedi." She tapped her temple. "I can wait. But know that if you need me, I am here. And when I need you, you will help me."

Before I could lose my nerve, I flipped the switch on the disc. She stared at me as she faded from view. She was gone, but I could still feel her, thrumming with energy in my hand. I had been numb with fear, but now the full cold of winter gripped me, as though the very core of me was frozen. I gripped the disc and walked to the edge of the rooftop. I held my hand over the ledge. My fingers would not let go. The wind whipped my hair and snowflakes landed on my face.

When I could stand the cold no longer, I put her back in my pocket and returned to the loft. My teeth chattered from ice and fear. The edges of my vision blurred as I stumbled into the room, a pounding headache in my temples.

Drystan was restless, burrowing deeper under his duvet. I looked at my own empty bed and I could not face it. Only nightmares waited for me there. I wrapped my arms around myself, squeezing my eyes shut as hard as I could. I fell to the floor and curled into a ball, too scared to even cry.

"Micah?"

The sleepy voice broke through the paralyzing web of fear. I sat up, feeling as though I had run clean across Imachara.

Drystan was not awake. His eyes were closed, his forehead furrowed. He said my name again, more of a sigh. His eyes opened, his gaze blurry. I stepped toward him. Stopped. With a sleepy smile, he held up the blanket. Was that... an invitation?

I licked my lips, wondering what to do. In the end, it was simple. I set the damselfly down on the bedside table and slid into bed with Drystan, curling my body around his. He shivered once at my coldness, but then he relaxed. I rested my head against his shoulder.

I told myself that I'd only stay there against him until I had warmed up and the worst of the fear fled. Moments later, darkness claimed me, mercifully free of dreams.

15
THE SHAI AND THE SHADOW CAPTURE

"Could a mermaid love an angel?"

Translated fragment of ALDER SCRIPT

When I awoke, my mouth felt fuzzy and my eyes bleary. Then I realized where I was and felt wide awake.

I faced the center of the loft, daylight streaming through the dragonfly stained glass. Drystan lay curled against my back, his breath warm against my neck. His arm lay around my torso, his hand on my chest. My chest, which did not have the corset underneath my shirt. My entire body tingled, my face burning in a blush.

My mind whirled as I wondered what I should do. What had possessed me to crawl into bed with Drystan? I had been frightened and cold, and perhaps he had invited me, but maybe he hadn't been fully awake. For Cyan's sake we were pretending that we were a couple, but this skipped a few steps. Drystan even had a…well, morning condition, as did I. I scooted forward, feeling so many emotions I couldn't give name to.

But even as I prepared to sneak from the covers and back to my own empty bed, I did not want to. Drystan's warm arms cocooned me, and I felt safe. Sleep still lured me with its siren call.

Drystan yawned and stretched, pressing against me again. My muscles stiffened, even as I hoped he would not pull away. I should leave now, before he awakened. He would never need to know my momentary weakness.

"Micah?" Drystan asked, sleep thickening his voice.

Styx. "Yes?"

"Any particular reason you're in my bed?"

"You invited me. I… I had a nightmare," I lied, my voice small as a sheepish child's.

"I… didn't," he said, surprised. "First time I've slept the whole night through, since…"

Since the ringmaster.

I turned to face him. "I'm sorry, I shouldn't have presumed–"

He silenced me with a finger to my lips. The words died in my throat. I swallowed. He took his finger away, and my lips tingled. Without a thought, we moved closer to each other. He rested a hand on my cheek and his lips pressed to mine.

It was not the first time I had kissed Drystan. I had kissed him dozens of times. But this was the first kiss without hundreds of eyes on us. The first kiss without pretense.

A small sound escaped his throat and he pulled me closer to him. My hands twined about his neck and tangled in his hair. Our bodies fit against each other, a thin layer of clothing all that separated us. I could feel every muscle, and shivered as he ran his fingertips up and down my side, before his palm lay flat against the small of my back and pressed me even closer to him. I felt a tightening of my nipples, a clenching in my stomach and a stirring between my legs.

Embarrassed, I broke the kiss and shifted my hips back from him. Drystan's pale lips were pink, his pupils wide and dark. He was heart-wrenchingly beautiful. What would he want with me?

"What is it?" he asked, his voice husky. My stomach tightened with desire.

"But I'm–"

"Micah," he breathed, and I was not sure if he was answering or interrupting me. He pulled me back to him, and I pushed away my fear.

We only kissed, for he sensed my hesitance and my nerves at doing anything more. But in that kiss, Drystan held nothing back, and I responded in kind.

I concentrated entirely on Drystan – the sight, smell, touch and taste of him. I did not kiss him as a man or as a woman. I kissed him, and he kissed me.

Our farce for Cyan became a reality. If Maske or Cyan sensed the change between us that morning at breakfast, they did not comment upon it. I was amazed, and terrified. It seemed like it could disappear at any moment. I didn't tell anyone, and neither did he. Each night, there was a kiss, a caress, and a continued closeness. I was shy and he knew that, never pushing. But what was this between us? What were we to each other? I didn't know, and to be honest, I didn't think Drystan did, either.

Drystan disappeared the morning after we searched Elwood's apartments, with an unmarked envelope full of purloined documentation for the constabulary. We included a note made from letters cut from lithographic posters and newspapers, saying only, "Beware the crooked Shadow. More in the safe behind the kelpie tapestry."

Now all we could do was wait and hope that Elwood had told no one else of our whereabouts. The pessimist in me feared that we would always be running. The second client could still find us. The policiers could follow a clue. Life in the Kymri Theatre could be only another temporary respite.

But if Drystan came with me again, perhaps I would not mind so much.

We were practicing our first grander-scale illusion: "The Sleeping Kymri Princess". Drystan performed while I sat in the audience with Maske, holding two cymbals.

"I learned of this magic from the great wizards of the golden Kymri plains," he said, his Temri accent now flawless thanks to Cyan's tutelage. "There, in a ritual under the full Penmoon, they performed a spell that would help me harness the powers of the ether of the stars. Starlight lives within me still." He held his arms apart. His palms were coated in glitter. This he sprinkled over Cyan, resplendent in full green Kymri robes stitched in golden hieroglyphs, a circlet upon her head. She sparkled in the light of the glass globes and lanterns scattered about the dusty stage.

Drystan laid his hand against her forehead, bidding her to close her eyes. When he took his hand away, he left a smudge of silver. He held his hands wide, muttering an incantation.

Cyan collapsed backwards, her nickel and copper bangles clinking. As her head and torso fell, her legs raised until she levitated off of the floor, her body level with Drystan's waist. Her unbound hair brushed the stage. Drystan moved his arms, my cue to crash the cymbals. Cyan rose higher until she was level with Drystan's chest. Drystan grabbed a hoop hidden behind him on the stage. He passed the hoop around Cyan's "sleeping" body, to prove that wires were not holding her aloft.

"Through the ether the Princess of Kymri is now light as a feather," Drystan intoned gravely.

The moment was magnificent, and I set down the cymbals to clap. But perhaps I clapped too soon – the screech of metal echoed through the dusty theatre. The hidden metal ledge Cyan lay on tilted madly from the harness attached to Drystan's waist. Cyan yelled as she crashed to the floor.

Maske ran onto the stage. Cyan sat up, indignant, her circlet askew on her forehead. Maske disentangled Drystan from the entrapment. I came onto the stage, trying, and failing, to stifle my mirth.

"Are you alright?" I asked Cyan through my laughter, reaching down to help her up.

"I'm fine. And it's not funny." Cyan scowled.

"It's a little funny."

One side of her mouth quirked. "Only a little," she said, straightening her circlet.

"What happened?" Drystan asked.

Maske studied the metal framework. "My figures must have been slightly off. It should have supported her."

"Maybe I've gained weight," Cyan quipped.

He gave her a smile. "Unlikely, my dear. I'll fix it. It should not happen again. Are you unhurt?"

"Just a sore bum."

"Apologies again. I am entirely at fault."

"Starlight," she muttered.

"I think that's enough practice for today," Maske said, his arms full of metal. "I'm going out. Spend the afternoon in the library if you like."

"Where are you going?" I asked. His suit was especially immaculate today.

"I am meeting Lily again."

"Ooh, another date for Mister Maske," Cyan teased, singsong.

"It is merely a meeting between two new acquaintances."

"What is this, the third such meeting now? With an attractive widow," Drystan pointed out.

Maske waved a hand, but the spots of color returned to his cheeks. "I doubt anything will come of it, but it will be a delight to be in her presence once again."

"I'll bet," Drystan drawled. Maske straightened his suit jacket and walked off, as dignified as he could be with the three of us giggling behind him.

"I think it's sweet they're growing close," I said, and then realized the turn of phrase sounded more like something Gene would say, and not Micah. I peeked at Cyan, but she did not seem to notice.

"It is," she agreed. "I've never known him to have a lady friend."

Drystan brushed himself off, only covering himself in more glitter. "Ugh, remind me not to let Maske make me use this stuff for practice."

"You look as pretty as a pixie," I chided. He stuck his tongue out at me, but his eyes twinkled. A warmth flared in my torso and I looked away with a small smile.

"That fall was well-timed, in any case," he said.

"What are you talking about, Amon?" Cyan asked.

"Well, it distracted Maske, and he doesn't need to know…" his voice trailed off and he reached to the back of the waistband of his trousers. He held a newspaper.

"Oh, no. What now?" Dread snarled my stomach.

Cyan tilted her head at me, and I cursed myself for my slip.

Drystan unfurled the newspaper. Front page headline: "CROOKED SHADOW BEHIND BARS". He passed it to us. Cyan and I read it side by side.

I studied it. An anonymous tip off had informed policiers that the eminent Shadow Kameron Elwood fabricated evidence in many of his cases. When all the documentation seized from his apartments had been categorized, it became clear that nearly half of his cases had been tampered with in some way. An innocent man had been falsely imprisoned for the past ten years due to erroneous information presented in court by Elwood.

"Couple above, I hope we didn't miss any documentation about us," Drystan said.

"Me too." I looked back at the newspaper. "Ten years."

"I know. This man was a…" Cyan called him something so rude in Temri my eyes nearly popped out of my skull.

We kept reading. Shadow Elwood protested that the documentation had been falsely planted by two people in an active case. Naturally, there was no documentation of any such cases found at his premises. We breathed sighs of relief. Reporters contacted the alleged employers, who said they never hired the services of Shadow Elwood.

I smirked. If Cyan and I were the active cases mentioned, then Styx would sooner freeze over before my parents, the Lord and Lady Laurus, would ever admit to hiring a Shadow with such a taint upon his name.

The Shadow claimed this case was the root of his downfall. Authorities were listening to his claims but disinclined to comment further. Shadow Elwood was being held in the Snakewood Prison, awaiting further justice. I wondered if they had housed him with anyone he ever investigated.

I looked up when I finished reading. "So it worked?" I didn't feel any better.

"Looks that way, doesn't it?" Drystan's eyes, conversely, glowed with triumph.

"There's still the second client or a second Shadow to worry about, though," I said.

"What's this?" Cyan asked.

"We found it in his notes. Elwood sensed he was being watched."

Cyan gave a low whistle, resting her head on her hands. "More problems." She paused. "I've been hoping you two would tell me, but it seems I must ask. When you went to Elwood's," she said, choosing her words carefully, "did you find anything about me?"

I was tempted to lie, to say we had not found anything, that the Shadow had not been hunting her or us at all. That would probably have been the wiser thing to do.

"Follow me," I said instead and made my way from the main theatre.

I felt Drystan and Cyan's eyes on my back as we entered the gloomy hallway. My foot kicked a loose mosaic, sending it skittering into the darkness.

We went to the loft and I pulled her file from where I had hidden it under the mattress. Her sharp eyes saw the second file underneath. I ignored the questions in her eyes and slid my own story from sight.

"He *was* following me." Her voice was flat with surprise. She cradled the files and perched on my bed. "You could have pretended you never found anything," she said, head bowed, hands curled loosely around the brown paper of the folder.

"That's true enough."

Her head rose. "So why didn't you?"

I turned the words over in my mind before I uttered them. "You live here. You work with us. You knew who we were and you said nothing. You've trusted us, or I believe that you have. The least I can do is offer the same courtesy."

She ran a fingertip over the front of the folder. "Thank you."

I said nothing. She opened the folder and read. Drystan kept trying to catch my eye, but I would not meet it. Yes, it was perhaps foolhardy to trust her so readily. But I had lost Aenea through lies. And I did not think I trusted the wrong person. She was on the run, like me. Like us. I could find out what a Shai was from elsewhere, but the best way to hear it was from her own lips.

She closed the file.

"Well," she said. "You read it, didn't you?"

"Yes." Before I could lose my nerve, I asked, "What's a Shai?"

"Hogwash, that's what." She fed the papers to the banked coals of the fireplace, where they smoked, blackened, and then curled.

I almost threw Iphigenia Laurus' file onto the coals as well, but I was certain that some of his notes were written in code. I did not want to miss anything.

"How'd he find us?" Cyan asked. "It's a big city."

Drystan and I exchanged a look. Maybe she'd know how to work it. I retrieved the Mirror of Moirai from where it remained in Drystan's pack. We explained to her what it was and turned it on.

Drystan and I had spent hours trying to puzzle it out. We knew that we'd both touched it enough that it would probably be able to find us. Sometimes, I almost felt as if I could puzzle out the strange Alder characters, but then they eluded me. At one point, something that looked like a stylized map appeared on the screen, but we had no idea what to do from there. Even if the second client or Shadow was somehow stored in the mirror, we did not know how to locate him through the Vestige artifact. Again, Anisa would know, perhaps, but I wanted to see if we could somehow discover its secrets ourselves, first. I wouldn't put it past her to bring up results and then lie to me about what they were.

Cyan frowned at the mirror, touching it at random. She managed to pull up the map. "It's Ellada," she said. She made the area that was now Imachara bigger. Over the centuries, it had somehow mirrored the layout of the capital, and we could see its tangled streets as if we were birds flying overhead. But after a few more attempts, she gave up in defeat as well, and I put it back into the pack with a sigh. I'd hide it somewhere else later.

"Well, at least we have it, versus someone else. I wonder if we're safe now," she said.

"For a time, perhaps," Drystan said. "If we really don't want to be found, we should probably go take up in a tiny fishing village somewhere."

Or out of Ellada. Like we planned. Though was that still the plan? Drystan and I hadn't discussed it in ages. It seemed more a nebulous possibility than a decided future.

"Where we'd instantly be the "new strangers" in town?"

"There is that. Safety in numbers." He ran his hand through his blonde hair.

"You two know why I left." She gestured at the flames. "Why was Elwood looking for you?"

I shot a glance at Drystan. He raised an eyebrow. "Tell her your side if you like, but leave me out of it. You're a nice enough girl, Cyan, but my secrets are my own."

With that, he left. By the stiff way he held his shoulders, I could tell he was upset. There was a rightness to what I was doing. Like it had already happened and I was going through the motions like an automaton.

"My name is not Sam," I said.

She said nothing.

"For the last few months, I've gone by the name Micah. But that's not my name, either. Or at least not the one I was given." I slid the papers out from under the mattress. "If I show you this, will you tell me what a Shai is?"

She pressed her lips together, pulling her hair over her shoulders and twisting it into a thick dark rope. "I'll do better than that. I'll show you."

The silence hung between us.

Drystan had "borrowed" the Augur from Maske without his knowledge. Why, I wasn't sure. He could be a bit of a magpie for shiny things. He'd give it back – but he wanted to prove he could take it without his old mentor noticing. Using my newly acquired sleight of hand, I had taken it from the bedside table and turned it on while she wasn't looking. The mechanical beetle rested in my pocket, silent as could be. She told the truth. I turned it off.

I passed her the folder. She opened it and read, trailing her fingers down the vertical columns of script.

Her eyebrows rose, but she said nothing until she read the entire thing.

"You're a girl?" she said, and she looked at me like Drystan had the night I told him on the Sicion pier. She was trying to see the woman in me. I met her gaze steadily.

"Not quite. Or rather, not only."

Her brow furrowed.

I took a deep breath and decided to tell her.

"I'm both."

Her eyes widened. "Really?"

"Really."

"We had someone of both genders in the circus," she said.

My mouth fell open. "Are they still there?"

"No. They left not long after they joined, but I don't know why."

"Was that person in the freakshow?"

She hesitated, then nodded.

I bit my lips. "I never was. I didn't tell anyone in the circus what I was. Not until the very end."

"So Amon knows?"

"He does." I licked my lips. "Do you… care?"

"Why should I care?"

I smiled from ear to ear. I almost felt like crying.

Her fingers toyed with a corner of the paper. "That must have been difficult for you. Raised as a girl, then to leave everything that you've known, to have to change who you are… hide who you are again…"

"I haven't thought of it quite like that. I'm still who I was before. But freer, despite all that's happened."

She smiled. "Perhaps I should switch my skirts for trousers."

"And cut off all that hair? That'd be a tragedy." I pulled out a strand of my shorn locks. "I still miss my long hair, sometimes." And I did. Though I most definitely did not miss corsets and hated the one I still wore.

She clutched her hair protectively and laughed. "True." The smile faded. "Thank you for telling me. I promise you that it'll go no further." She passed the file back to me.

I inclined my head and waited.

"Alright. My end of the bargain. Close your eyes," she said. I obeyed.

"Think of your fondest memory and hold it close. Try and remember every detail."

My mind scrabbled in circles. What was my fondest memory?

It came to me. My brother Cyril and I by the fireside one winter's evening in the nursery. I was young, barely old enough to read. Five, six perhaps. Cyril, two years older, seemed so big and grown up. I was trying to read an old picture book of his, frowning and frustrated.

Cyril put down his own adventure book and came over and read me the story, pointing out each word on the page as he did so. It was the tale of *The Prince and the Owlish Man*. The artwork had been beautiful printed watercolor paintings swirled through with black ink lines. The owlish man looked like death himself and frightened me. But Cyril's presence comforted me. I leaned back against his torso, his voice reverberating against my ribs as he read. I remembered the crackle of the flames and the smell of smoke and furniture polish. I almost sighed with longing. The scene was so real in my mind's eye. I wished I could step back into it, when my greatest difficulty was not being able to puzzle out the words on the page.

"You're remembering a boy. He's close to you. A brother? Sandy hair. There's a room with a marble fireplace. A painting of trees in a gilt frame. He's reading to you. *Prince Mael and the Owlish Man*. You are warm and safe."

I opened my eyes and stared at her in horror. I felt dizzy, and the room wobbled.

"How did you...?"

"I don't know," she said, tears swimming in her eyes. "I don't know."

"You can read anyone's thoughts, all the time?" She could have learned so much from one careless thought...

She shook her head. "It takes a lot of concentration. Sometimes it doesn't work, but other times it comes out of nowhere. I try not to intrude. I have learned that people think such terrible things. Things they perhaps do not truly believe or would not do..."

She trailed off, playing with the edge of the bed quilt, and I wondered whose thoughts she remembered. I tried to concentrate on her and see if I could read her mind. Maybe I could sense a flicker of an image – a tear falling down a woman's cheek – but I could not be sure. I blinked, a headache throbbing at my temples, my stomach roiling with nausea.

"That's why the Glamour didn't work on you?" I said, quietly.

Cyan bent her head, silver dust from the Kymri Princess levitation falling to the floor. Her eyes were downcast, her fingers intertwined. She rubbed her thumb pads together. "You knew what you looked like. Both of you. That's why it didn't work."

"And that's why you were a fortuneteller in the circus."

"Nay." She shook her head. "I learned to read the tarot first, and nothing strange happened for years. But then a man came to have a reading and I had... a vision. My first one. What I saw didn't make sense. The man gripped my hands so hard it hurt. He kept ordering me to tell him what I saw, over and over again. When I did, he nodded, threw some coins on the table, and left."

"What did he look like?" I focused on her again, but saw and sensed nothing. I felt a surge of disappointment.

"I don't remember what he looked like. When I try, his face is blurred, like the reflection in a puddle." She shrugged. The wording of it mirrored how Anisa had described the second client of the Shadow. The same man?

"What did you see?"

"Flashes. Monsters. Chimaera. A woman with bat wings. A boy with a scaled face. Blue light. The sky on fire." She shook her head. "Nonsense."

"You have no idea who he was?"

She shook her head. "No. I asked around the circus, but no one else even saw him. After that, I started hearing or seeing things more often. I responded to others' thoughts, thinking they spoke aloud. I learned who in the circus did not like me one bit. Or liked me too much. Sometimes, my dreams come true. Or my nightmares," she whispered.

"Nightmares?"

She nodded. "The night before I left the circus I had a horrible dream. A circus accident. The animal trainer, Liam. Someone in the audience was going to frighten the lion. I told my mother I was going to go warn him. Plead for him to take the night off and not perform that day. My parents... they wouldn't let me. Said it was only a dream or a dark spirit possessed me. They feared I was a Shai.

"I let them convince me it had all been in my head. They took me away from the circus, saying that a day in the city would do me good."

Cyan was lost in the memory, her eyes unfocused. "They bought me chocolate limes. I remember the flavor. They took me to the Temnian Temple, and I prayed... I prayed so hard..."

She swallowed. I covered the back of her hand with mine.

"I fainted in the temple when it happened. And when I woke up, I ran back to the circus, leaving my parents behind.

"It happened just as I'd seen it. Liam was dead, mauled by his lion. He loved that lion. Called him Pip. Pip was dead as well. They'd shot him, I think. They lay side by side, their bodies still warm."

Another flash of an image. Cyan, crying, her hands entangled in the lion's tawny fur. A man and a woman pulling her away. My headache worsened.

"My parents realized what had happened." Her words thickened. "They said as soon as they could, they'd book passage back to Southern Temne and leave this godless land."

"So that was why you ran away."

She nodded.

"Why come to Maske? He said you came to him just after you left."

"Did he?" She stared into the distance. "Can you keep a secret?"

My mouth twisted. "I've had a fair amount of practice."

"After Liam, my mother and I fought. And I heard what she was thinking."

I said nothing, waiting for her to gather the courage to go on.

"She thought that it was all my father's fault, that it served her right for sleeping with a magician, to birth a cursed babe."

I blinked. Opened my mouth to ask the question, but she cut me off with a nod. "I don't look half-Elladan. Maske doesn't know."

My head spun. I thought back to Drystan's hints that Maske had been a different man at the height of his power. "Well."

"Well indeed." She chewed her lip.

I searched for something to say. "Are you... different?" I asked.

"Um. Were you not listening? I just told you I can read minds."

"Well, yes. But what about physically?"

"I've no idea what you're talking about."

"How often do you fall ill?"

"Hardly ever. My f–father used to say I was hearty as

an ox." She smiled, but it faded. "Why?" She shifted closer on the bed, her dark eyes peering into mine. "What aren't you telling me?"

"You might…" I swallowed. "You might be different from other…" I trailed off, not quite sure how to finish.

"From other what?"

"From other… humans."

She blinked. She started to laugh, and stopped when I didn't join in.

"Am I lying to you? You can check." The thought of her peering into my mind frightened me, but I knew it was the only way she'd believe me.

She closed her eyes, and I followed suit. I sent a small tendril of thought toward her that I knew she'd hear.

We are Chimaera.

I opened my eyes. She was staring at me, her lips parted. Her eyes rolled up in her skull and she fainted.

The threatened headache bloomed in my skull, and I followed her into the dark.

16
THE NEW WAGER

"Sometimes I cannot believe the anger and hatred I am capable of. These many years later, I still despise Taliesin with every thread of my being. I blame him for everything. For throwing my life away, for costing me my family and my livelihood. That anger was what drove me to the darkness where I lived for a long while. I stole and I cheated and I lied and I liked it. I learned just how evil I can be – all thanks to the evil of Taliesin. One day, I will get him back for how he hurt me. For now, I'll nurse the hatred."

Jasper Maske's personal diary

I awoke before Cyan did, clutching my head. I'd never fainted before coming to the theatre and now I'd fainted twice. After a few minutes, I felt better and splashed water on Cyan's face and tapped her cheek gently. When she did not awaken, I went to fetch Drystan, terror growing within me. He was reading the history of the Great Grimwood. He closed the book when I entered, his fingertip marking the place.

"Cyan's fainted and she's not waking up," I said, dread rising in my stomach at the words. What if she was trapped in a vision? Or the vision had affected her physically? I followed Drystan up the stairs, feeling strange. I stumbled over a step. My stomach was in knots of fear for Cyan and yet almost... excitement.

I might not be the only person who could do things that no one else could. And if Cyan and I were different, there were most likely others. I felt heady with the possibilities.

Drystan knocked at Maske's workshop. The sound of drilling ceased. Maske came to the door, pushing a pair of greenish goggles up on his forehead. His face was smeared with black oil. I searched his face for echoes of Cyan's features, and I found them in the line of his nose and the curl of his lip.

"Yes?" he asked, annoyed at the interruption.

"Your medic bag is still in the kitchen, right? Where is it again?"

"The cupboard to the right of the cooker. Why?" He peered at us.

"Nothing to worry about," Drystan lied smoothly. I wondered why he lied. Perhaps not to worry him? "Cyan's delicate derriere needs the bruising cream."

Maske chuckled. "Well, let me know if it grows worse. It's my fault she was hurt." His face creased. "I'll be down soon for tea. My turn to scrounge something up, more's the pity for you all."

"I'm sure we'll survive, at least," Drystan joked. While Drystan and Maske spoke, I craned my neck, trying to see past Maske into his workshop. He spied my blatant attempt and raised an eyebrow, leaning back to show me.

Mirrors. I should have known they would still be there. He smirked and closed the door. The drilling resumed.

"I still want to know what he's doing in there," I said as we trotted down the hall.

"And you'll find out when he's ready, Micah. How many times have I said this to you now?"

I snapped my mouth shut. He didn't usually snap at me – he was definitely cross with me for being so frank with Cyan.

Grabbing the medic bag, we dashed to the loft. Cyan lay on my bed, arms akimbo, hair tangled about her face.

Drystan peeled an eyelid back, showing the whites of her eyes. Plucking the smelling salts from the medic bag, he waved them under her nose. She groaned, turning her head away.

He tapped her lightly on the cheeks. "Come on, Cyan. Wake up now." To me he said, "What happened?"

"It's complicated."

"Isn't it always?" he asked, more to himself than to me.

Cyan's eyes fluttered. Drystan helped her sit up and passed her a glass of water, brushing the hair from her face.

Her forehead crinkled. "My head," she moaned, pressing her hands to her temples. "Are you meant to dream when you faint?"

"What did you dream?" I asked, alarmed. Drystan noticed the sharp tone of my voice.

"I dreamed of a woman with great dragonfly wings. Tattoos on her face and hands. She was crying. She missed someone. Wanted to find him. More than anything…" She shook her head. "It's fading, like water through a sieve. Just a dream. But it was so clear… it was almost as though I *was* her…"

My blood drained from my face. Drystan mouthed "damselfly" at me, and I shook my head, as though I were just as confused as he was. I glanced at where the damselfly disc lay hidden beneath the loose papers on the table by my bed.

Maybe Anisa wanted to sway Cyan to her cause as well, whatever that may be.

"I'm fine. How embarrassing, to faint!" She laughed, unconvincingly. She smoothed her crumpled skirt with her hands. "I think I'll go to my room. You've given me a lot of think about, Sam. Or should I call you Micah? Or Gene?"

"Either Sam or Micah," I said, ignoring the way Drystan's eyes narrowed. "I'm not really Gene. Not anymore." My throat closed. Was that girl who climbed trees and shirked piano lessons well and truly gone? Debutante turned runaway turned murderer.

Cyan moved like a drunken woman, stumbling and holding onto the wall for support. At the door, she paused, as though she would say something. But she carried on, leaving us in silence.

Drystan crossed his arms.

"There's no point in being mad. It's already done. And we can trust her. She knows some of my secrets, but I've learned some of hers as well."

"And?"

"And they're not mine to tell. Had you stayed and told her something of yourself, you'd know them too."

He waved a hand. "So you're saying we shouldn't worry about her?"

Only if she invades our thoughts. I tried sending the

thought to him, wondering if he would hear it.

Drystan frowned at me.

"Why are you squinting at me like that?"

I sighed. "Never mind. No, I don't think we need to worry about her. She's lost everything, as we have. She's merely trying to pick up the pieces."

"If you say so," he said, folding me into his arms. I rested my hands on the wings of his shoulder blades and he placed his chin on my shoulder. He did not say anything, and after a time, I met his lips with mine.

This thing between us was still so delicate, just blossoming and seeking the light. We still did not give it a name – no declarations of love, no promises. Though kisses always felt a little like a promise of what could be. A wordless reassurance of trust and longing.

We heard the distant ding of the doorbell.

"Cyan or Maske will get it." Drystan nuzzled my neck.

Any thought of leaving vanished. Small shivers ran down my spine.

Drystan's hands pressed against the small of my back. A tip of his finger rested on the bare skin where my shirt rucked up about my waist. The front of his thin white shirt was open, and I rested a palm against his chest, feeling the ropes of muscle just under the skin from years of tumbling and hard circus work.

Someone knocked on the door. We broke away.

"Yes?" I said, my voice strangled.

Cyan poked her head into the room. She was still pale but more alert. She did not seem to notice our flushes or the sly way we rearranged our clothing.

"What is it?" Drystan asked.

"That magician Taliesin is here."

There were three men in the parlor. Maske sat, every muscle tense, pointedly staring at the younger man and not his age-old rival, Pen Taliesin.

Maske, though in his late fifties, never struck me as middle-aged. Taliesin may have won the old feud between them, but he had lost against time. Deep lines engraved his face, and his back was humped underneath a rich mink coat. Golden rings bedecked his long, gnarled hands, which shook badly. The whites of his eyes had aged to the yellow of old parchment. He looked like a man twice his age, held together with string and matchsticks, as though a strong wind could blow him away.

The other man next to Taliesin, by contrast, was all straight lines and calm stillness in his smart suit and expertly folded green cravat with an emerald pin. His sideburns and waxed mustache were of the latest style, and he had the long fingers of a magician.

"Good evening," the coiffed man said. "I am Christopher Aspall, the representative of the Collective of Magic of Ellada. I am the solicitor of the organization, and a retired performer myself." A thin leather briefcase leaned against his shin. "I am here," Aspall continued, "to deduce if you are violating the terms of your legal agreement between one Jasper Maske and one Pen Taliesin, signed by both parties on the fifth of Lylal, 10846."

Maske's eyes snapped to Aspall's face. "I have not violated the agreement."

"Horse piss," Taliesin spoke. Most of his teeth were gone, the rest ruined gravestones in his mouth. "You think I don't know what you're doing here? Why did you hire these pups?" He gestured at Drystan, Cyan, and me, clustered at the séance table in the corner of the room. "You're recreating our show!"

"You know full well no performances have been held at the Kymri Theatre in these many years."

"But you're planning to." Taliesin pointed a shaking hand at Maske. The teeth, the shaking, the unnatural brightness in his yellowing eyes: Taliesin was truly one of the Delerious – a Lerium addict.

"Per our agreement, I'll never perform magic again. But, if you recall, the wording did not ban me from teaching magic and allowing others to perform, even in this building."

Taliesin sputtered. "It is your magic they'll perform, and your magic cannot go on the stage."

Aspall cleared his throat. He brought a legal folder from the leather briefcase, opening it to reveal the printed and signed contract between Maske and Taliesin. He made a great show of reading it over silently before he spoke. Showmen. They never lose their taste for the dramatic.

"While I have come here at Taliesin's behest, I am impartial." He gave the last word the slightest emphasis. "I am here to represent the Collective of Magic's best interests. And, after much careful study of the syntax of the agreement, the Collective's official announcement is that…" He paused again for dramatic effect. We leaned forward in our seats.

"Jasper Maske is not violating the terms of this contract. As long as the performers are not performing the exact same tricks that were well-known to be Jasper Maske's and Pen Taliesin's when they were in business as Specter and Maske."

Taliesin gave a wordless cry of rage. "This is not what I wished."

"What you wish does not matter in this case," Aspall said, his nose wrinkling in distaste. He was not as impartial as he pretended to be. Disgust and pity coursed through me as well. How could that old man have been a performer? Everything about him looked twisted – his features, his spine, his grin and his scowl. I would bet that if souls were visible, his was as twisted as they come. Every fiber of my being wanted to lean away from him. He could not have been like this when he performed. Had the drugs transformed him so completely? What would Taliesin be like now if Maske and he had never parted ways?

A small thought trickled through my mind, despite my best intentions. I wondered what Drystan would have looked like now, had he not given up Lerium, and what he would have looked like in another decade or more. It did not matter, I told myself. He'd never be like Taliesin.

"I thank you, Solicitor Aspall, for your ruling on the agreement," Maske said.

Taliesin grinned, a fearsome sight in his ruined face. "Ah, but Jasper, my old friend, what would you say for a chance to absolve our old contract, eh?"

Maske stared at Taliesin's face for the first time since he entered the parlor. "You would abolish it?" he said, his voice carefully neutral.

"Not for nothing, no."

"What are you proposing, then?"

The silence in the room was almost another presence. Taliesin rummaged about in his coat pocket, bringing out a crumpled, wax-sealed envelope.

"From my own solicitor," he wheezed. "Just in case." He passed it to Aspall.

The solicitor held the envelope delicately, investigating the seal. "Are you sure you would not wish to have your own solicitor present? Should we arrange another meeting at a later date?"

Taliesin motioned for him to open it. "Let him see what it says. We can sign it all official-like later if he agrees to it now."

Aspall broke the seal and read the letter. His eyebrows rose, just once. I nudged Cyan with my elbow, but she was already staring at him with a distant gaze I recognized.

Aspall passed the crumpled paper to Maske. As our mentor read, his face flushed, and then blanched.

"Alright," he said. "I will consider it." Maske's eyes flashed to us, and the look in them made me shiver – there was rage, but also the fierce excitement of a gamble.

Taliesin leaned back, a shaking hand resting against the patchy stubble of his cheek. "I thought you might, Jasper. I thought you just might." Taliesin, too, relished the gamble, but what was to be gained or lost? We were ignored – children to be seen and not heard.

Cyan knew. Her face grew thoughtful, but she couldn't tell us.

"Well," Aspall said, somewhat taken aback by the turn of events. "If you are both in agreement, then we shall meet at the Collective of Magic's headquarters on Thistle Street in a week's time at 10 o'clock. I will discuss this with the Collective and ensure that this meets with their approval. Though the thought of two magicians emerging from the shadows to the limelight again will no doubt please them immensely. I know that many, like myself, were great admirers of the Specter and Maske shows as children." He coughed, and the brief glimpse of the man beneath the solicitor's façade disappeared. "You have until next week to change your mind. Once you put the ink to paper, it is done."

"I expect much the same result as last time, young Aspall. Merely proving another point." Taliesin heaved himself to his feet. The shaking grew visibly worse.

Taliesin took a cool look in our direction. I forced myself to meet his stare. "Hope these little ones don't embarrass you as much as I think they will, old boy."

Maske's knuckles tightened about his knees.

"We shall settle this again," Maske said. "And you may find that the last fifteen years have treated us differently."

Taliesin looked about at the faded glory of the Kymri Theatre. He arranged his fur coat, the gold rings on his fingers glinting. "That they have. Until next time, Jasper."

"Pen."

Maske stayed poised for flight until we heard the front door close, and then he collapsed onto the sofa.

"What happened? What's going on?" I asked.

"A rematch," he said, his voice faint. "In three months' time. Between you two and Taliesin's boys. The Specter Shows only started up again in the autumn. Perhaps when the Collective of Magic was going to ban him permanently from performing, he cooked up this scheme. With the expenses on his theatre and the lavish way he lives, money must be precarious. He wants the notoriety – the Specter Shows on everyone's lips." Maske seemed to be speaking to himself more than us.

"You are going to accept it, aren't you?" I asked. "And we'll put Taliesin and his boys to shame."

Drystan perched next to Maske, taking his hand in the first sign of affection I had seen between them. "He has no choice. The Collective already know of it."

The Collective. It sounded so sinister. "Why?"

"The Collective would have salivated at a chance for this much publicity. Magic shows have fallen a bit out of favor lately. They get amalgamated into circus or theatre acts rather than having the starring headline. They'll never keep it quiet."

"So if Maske turns it down, everyone will know anyway," Cyan said, and I wondered if she were voicing her own thoughts, or echoing Maske's. Or Drystan's. The thought of her reading Drystan's mind made me uneasy.

Maske nodded miserably.

"But why wouldn't you say yes, Maske? It's a way to get Taliesin back and show him who the best magician is." I frowned at them.

"Well, we still don't know the entire rules of the game," Cyan pointed out. "Mister Maske, what happens if we lose?"

Maske wilted even further. "My ban on magic remains in place, but is also passed onto you. And… I'd have to give Taliesin the Kymri Theatre."

"Lord and Lady," I breathed. "This time you'd really lose everything. What would he lose if we win?"

"His ban is put into effect for a certainty, and extends to his grandsons. We gain his premises."

High stakes indeed. "No matter," I said. "We'll win, right?"

"Sam," Maske said.

I sighed. "You can call me Micah if you wish. Cyan knows."

He blinked in surprise. "Micah. Taliesin's grandsons might be new to magic, but they'll still have been around it their whole lives. And Taliesin has been designing tricks for the last fifteen years, studying the psyche of the audience, which always shifts with the times. I'm a decade and a half out of date. Washed up."

"Rubbish!" I said. Maske blinked at me as I continued. "You're the Maske of Magic! You taught him everything he knows. And he's a ruin of a man, now. We'll beat him and his kin, no problem." Though I was not as confident as I pretended to be. We were outcasts from the circus, novice magicians and would be up against performers trained enough to star in the Specter Shows. We could not even pull off the levitation illusion yet.

Drystan and Cyan echoed my reassurances, knowing it was what Maske needed to hear. From the stiff way he held his shoulders, it was clear that seeing his old rival had unnerved him. And no wonder – he had been living in his workshop, dreaming and creating. Occasionally, in the evenings, he went off for séances or card games with his friends. It was a rude awakening from his dream world, with performing only a distant fancy. Not three months from now. Not as a duel. All of his old hate, betrayal, and jealousy were naked on his face, warring with a forlorn fear. Taliesin had tricked him again.

As we told him we could do it, that we knew that we could beat him, he straightened and his eyes grew beetle-bright with the challenge.

"You're right. I was only being foolish. We'll win. And then I'll perform again..." He faltered. His next words were whispered in awe: "I'll perform again."

"You will," I said, clasping him on the shoulder.

He looked up at me, a slow smile on his face.

"We'll beat him," I reassured him.

Inside, I hoped so. And I could not shake the feeling that while the Shadow was off our trail, other problems still darkened our path.

17
Dust Motes

"With each life, they learn more, they become the truer essence of themselves. With each passing generation, our children are growing into what we hoped they would be. Of course, there is always the threat that they will learn too much."

Translated fragment of ALDER SCRIPT

The next day, we threw open every window of the Kymri Theatre, despite the thin layer of snow on the ground and the bite in the wind.

The work warmed us. We swept dust from the stage, and then sanded, stained, and varnished it until it shone. We scrubbed the aged velvet of the seats, mending the tears. We mopped the mosaics and glued the loose tiles back into place. We washed the stained glass windows. I climbed to the roof and made it possible for light to shine through the grimy skylights again.

Lily Verre, true to her earlier promise, helped us during two afternoons. Maske said nothing of their date, but I knew that they planned to meet again. Lily kept meeting his eyes and smiling as she chattered and dusted vaguely. She brought bouquets of roses "to freshen the air," even though it was rather pointless. No members of the public would enter the Kymri Theatre during the remaining life of the dying roses.

At the end of the week, the theatre was in a semblance of order. Decades of grease and grime no longer coated everything. We discovered the original pinkish beige of the walls before we coated them with warm yellow paint.

When the paint had dried, we surveyed our handiwork. My back ached from the dull, repetitive motion of scrubbing. I was weary to the bone, and my palms were wrinkled and chapped from filthy soap suds.

In that moment it did not matter. The Kymri Theatre sparkled. It looked like a place for magic shows and wonder. I could imagine audience members in the seats. The rustle of skirts, the waving of fans and the crinkle of paper as men and women consulted their programs. Before, the dusty seats only seemed like they could be filled with ghosts.

"Tomorrow is the meeting with Aspall and Taliesin," Maske said, breaking the silence of the theatre. "You three still want to participate?"

We did.

"Then we'll see this through to the end."

With that, he twisted the controls, and the chandelier of gas lights above us shimmered to life, bathing the empty theatre in a warm yellow glow to match the walls. I breathed in the smell of the varnish, lemon-soaped water, and roses.

It was not a circus ring, but it was our new stage.

• • •

To celebrate the scrubbing of our home, we invited Lily for tea. She hadn't reported us to the policiers, after all, and Maske wanted every opportunity to see Lily Verre. Around her, Drystan and I always wore our Glamours, just in case.

We cooked the most lavish meal within our capabilities, with Cyan making traditional Temnian dishes, the recipes passed on from mother to daughter for generations. Cyan wore a bittersweet smile as she kneaded the dough for mooncakes, the smell of yeast and spices in the air. She marinated chicken and vegetables in a thick, spicy sauce before cooking them on a skillet and made rice, a fluffy grain I had only tried a time or two before.

To showcase my cooking lessons over the past few months, I made little savory tarts filled with leeks, cheese, and bacon. Drystan made an old circus favorite for a second dessert – peanut brittle. It was an extremely disparate meal, but it was ours.

Lily brought a bottle of wine and a bottle of whisky, which I still could not stand to drink. She wore a russet dress, her hair tumbling from its chiffon in its usual disarray.

We gave her a tour of the finished Kymri Theatre.

"You worked your magic on this place, right enough," Lily said.

"Thank you, my dear Mrs Verre," Maske said.

We sat in the kitchen rather than the formal parlor. For a time, the only sounds were the clink of cutlery and the splash of wine into glasses, then Maske and Lily carried the conversation through the meal. I was too hungry from a solid week of cleaning to do much but put one spoonful of food after another into my mouth.

"It's a shame about those Forester protests, isn't it?" Lily said, fluttering her hand. "Frightful, really. Not that I'm completely unsympathetic to their cause, mind, but the protests are truly getting out of hand, aren't they?"

"Out of hand?" I asked.

"Well, there were those fights outside the palace the other week, and now there's the vandalism of the estates in the Emerald Bowl. They cut down all the trees around it and painted: "LEAVES TO ROOTS" across the windows. That's a bit much. They're even threatening a civil war if their needs aren't met."

Civil war? Surely it wouldn't come to that. "Which family was vandalized?" I asked, nervously.

"The Ash-Oaks, I believe."

They were staunch royalists. I knew them. Lord Ash-Oak was an adviser to the Steward and very active against the Foresters. Their son was only eight. He must have been so frightened.

"I bet the Steward wasn't too happy about that," Drystan said.

"I'm betting that's a gross understatement," Maske said. "That man will be calling out for their blood, and that leader Timur's especially."

"He won't be able to do anything to them. And no one knows where Timur is hiding, do they?" Cyan asked, biting her lip.

I felt a... knocking on my mind, like someone was asking to enter. Cyan's brows furrowed.

I know a few Foresters, she said in my mind. *Some of those in the circus left to be Timur's followers.*

I nearly reeled in shock at the sound of her voice in my head, setting down the wine glass with a clatter. Cyan's voice in my head. What had she discovered? What had I unwittingly disclosed?

Sorry. I didn't know if this would work. I won't do it without warning again.

Don't! I thought. I tried to push her from my mind, and "felt" her drift away.

I stared into the coffee cup. I did not like her invading my head at all. It felt like a violation. Maske and Lily continued speaking, but my mind did not follow the words. I clutched the coffee cup until my heartbeat returned to normal.

But then I wanted to know something. After the initial shock, it seemed silly not to take advantage of something so extraordinary. I did not relish the thought of her in my mind again, but at the same time, I was curious. I sent a wisp of thought toward her, which she met, almost like taking my hand.

Are you one? I asked. *A Forester?*

No, but I agree with some of what they want. Don't you?

I don't know. I guess they're protesting against pretty much everyone I knew in my previous life. I had overheard many heated discussions of politics, at dinners. The circus folk, after drinks at the bonfire, had also complained at length about the monarchy. Tin and Karg, the strongman and the dwarf, often had arguments. But perhaps now was the time to study all the sides of the issues and find out where I stood and what I believed.

Maske had been speaking: "...they may wish to overturn the monarchy and plenty of people are sympathetic, but these antics make them look like little more than petulant children full of theatrics. What happened to petitions and due process?"

"Petitions were ignored." Drystan swirled the wine in his glass.

The conversation meandered in that vein for some time, and eventually I grew a little bored. I didn't know enough to be able to add anything meaningful to the conversation. Ashamed, I focused on the food.

"Oh, did you read the paper this morning?" Lily asked. I took a large bite.

Maske shook his head. "Didn't have a chance to yet. We were busy finishing up the theatre. Why? More disaster and dismay?"

"A Shadow was murdered in prison last night."

I started choking on my food.

"Are you alright, my dear boy?" Lily asked. I nodded, my eyes watering as I forced myself to swallow. My throat felt raw.

"What Shadow?" I rasped.

"That one who was done in for fabricating evidence a few weeks back. Shadow Kameron Elwood? Shocking, isn't it? To think! My dear late husband hired him once to see if our supervisor was skimming from the top and sneaking off his shifts early. He was and was fired. But now I do wonder if perhaps he made the whole thing up!" She waved her hands.

"How did he die?" I whispered.

"Oh, it's terribly tragic," she said, sounding more delighted than saddened. "He was housed with one of the men whose evidence he'd fabricated. The man had been innocent of the crime he was imprisoned for, but he wasn't released quite yet as Elwood had notes that pointed to even worse crimes, so the constabulary decided to investigate. But the man had been in prison for over ten years – lost his business and everything. He'll be in that prison for a long time more now, though, on account of strangling Elwood in his bed."

I pushed my plate away, my appetite gone. I'd had no love for Shadow Elwood. He had tried to send me back home and was not the most honest of men, but that did not mean I wanted him murdered. Dead. If we hadn't turned him in, he wouldn't be, and there was no denying that fact. I felt sick.

I met Drystan's gaze and I couldn't read what I found there. Another death to our ledger.

Cyan whispered in my mind again: *No, Micah. Elwood chose to fabricate the evidence and put men and women behind bars. The man chose to take Elwood's life. The fault is not with you.*

Stay out of my head unless I invite you. It's crowded enough in here with my own thoughts.

She drifted away.

I said little for the rest of the evening. Lily seemed to notice she had upset me and grew even livelier to try and cover the silence. Drystan came to my rescue, bantering with Maske and charming Lily. Underneath the façade, though, I knew he felt as empty as I did.

• • •

It was such a simple thing, in the end, to sign a piece of paper.

We stood in the headquarters of the Collective of Magic itself, a large house in the Gilt Quarter. I felt grubby in my patched shirt and worn trousers. Somehow, in the last two months I had grown so much that my ankles peeked out from above my shoes. Showing my ankles in public. How my mother would have been scandalized.

I felt especially ragged next to Cyan's composed grace. She tucked her hands into the sleeves of her tunic, staring down her nose at Aspall and Taliesin. She could have worn an Elladan dress, but she wanted to look Temnian. Taliesin was unsettled by her, me and Drystan. We looked foreign to him.

Many older Elladans were still uncomfortable around foreigners, for they'd grown up during a cold war. The other islands didn't have as much Vestige – it had decayed in the warmer climates. Ellada held its power through its stockpile of Vestige weapons. Sometimes, the colonies would rise up but the skirmishes never lasted long. Older Elladans still remembered when the other islands were colonies, and few travelled between the islands of the Archipelago unless they needed to.

Our rivals, Sind and Jac Taliesin, stood across from us. They were short, with solemn faces and hair pomaded into perfection, their new, crisp clothing contrasting with ours. I could not tell them apart. They met our eyes with haughty gazes of their own. Maybe they didn't understand all they stood to lose.

Aspall read the new agreement aloud. A duel in three

months' time – the winner could perform magic and would gain the other's profit.

The agreement was long and peppered with legal jargon. Briefly, I wished my father was here. He would have noticed any sneaky turn of phrase in a second and made sure the agreement was as fair to our side as possible. Homesickness echoed through me. Once, I lived in a place such as this: rich woods and fabrics, and a warm fire in every room. Now I lived in a draughty theatre that was never fully warm.

I lost the thread of Aspall's droning words, but his next words snapped me to attention.

"Now, for the specifics. How many performers?" Aspall asked.

"Two magicians and an assistant each," Maske said.

Taliesin waved his hand, his gaze lingering on Cyan. "No. No assistants."

Taliesin and Maske went back and forth, their voices rising in anger.

"Why shouldn't there be assistants? They were always a part of our shows!"

"Magic against magic, Jasper! No... distractions."

"You jealous old fool."

"You insufferable git. What, afraid if the audience looks away from your pretty Temnian girl that they'll see how poorly your amateurs perform?"

"It's nothing to do with that!"

"Please," Aspall said. "Let us discuss this rationally."

In my mind, I asked Cyan a question. She answered with a grim smile and a nod.

"I can step out, and Cyan can take my place, not as an assistant but as a full magician," I said.

The room grew quiet.

One of the twins spoke. "A... female magician?"

Cyan put her hands on her hips, narrowing her eyes. "What's wrong with a female magician?"

"Nothing," the other said. But he muttered something to his brother, who fought down a snigger. I narrowed my eyes at them.

"Has... the young woman been trained?" Aspall asked.

"Yes, she has," Cyan answered, testily.

"Is that what you wish, Sam?" Maske asked.

"Yes," I said. "I'll be your stagehand."

"Does this meet your agreement, then, Mr Taliesin?" Aspall asked.

Taliesin looked shocked by the turn of events. "That'll do," he managed.

"Then we have come to an arrangement." Aspall noted the amendments. Maske managed to make one more concession: an assistant could appear as a prop in one illusion on each side, which tied into his mysterious finale.

Everyone signed the agreement, from Taliesin's blotty scrawl to Maske's impeccably tidy signature. Technically the contract was not legally binding for me, Drystan, and Cyan. We all signed false names in Temri script.

After the contract was signed and the seal pressed into hot wax, the head of the Collective of Magic himself, Professor David Delvin, came to congratulate us. He was a wizened old man, but the wrinkles on his face showed he spent most of his life smiling. He thanked us, shaking our hands. He discussed business and publicity, saying that he had some excellent plans for the final venue. The Collective, in return for its support and management, would take a fifty per cent commission of ticket prices. Steep.

Professor Delvin gave us all a pointed onceover and an advance on our profits to buy new clothing. I did not think it was possible for any of us to blush any more than we did at that.

After what felt like ages, we were let free. Maske went back to the theatre, instructing us to go to the tailor's. Cyan forewent new clothing, and I asked for a set with the same measurements as Drystan, as we were close enough in size. In my mind, I told Cyan where I planned to go. I nodded to them both in farewell.

The tailor scowled at me, but I left without further ado, breathing in the frozen winter air. I hated being touched by strangers. Growing up, I saw doctor after doctor. Nurses, medical students – so many peered at me undressed, poking and prodding. I did not realize that I still had such a phobia of being measured and examined. Just before I ran away, I learned that a Doctor Pozzi gave me to my parents and another doctor planned to operate on me to make me marriageable.

I ran a hand over my cheeks. I still had no stubble to speak of – only the soft down of peach fuzz. I would turn seventeen soon. My parents celebrated my birthday on the first day of spring. A new beginning. I ran away from them in late spring of last year. It was almost spring again. Eleven months away from ballrooms and tutors and tea parties.

I had not sent Cyril a letter in some time, and I decided

to correct that. Parting with more coins, I bought the cheapest supplies at the stationer's. I made my way back to the tea room where I had first followed Shadow Elwood when I had seen him spying on the Kymri Theatre.

For though he was gone – dead – something did not quite add up for me. Why had he gone to that building just after spying on ours? Had it just been another case, completely unrelated? But I remembered the woman in the wine-colored dress. That could only be the woman in a red dress with a child "eaten up from the inside" that Anisa, through Maske, had spoken of. Who was she and how were we linked?

I ordered a pot of tea, though I knew I would have to skip out on the bill. In between writing a draft letter to my brother, which I would transcribe later in lemon juice, I watched the building. I sat near the front, the heat from the tea room steaming the windows. I wiped at them occasionally, making a show of glancing at the clock as though I waited for a tardy someone.

Dear Cyril,

I am well. The Shadow that darkened our path is gone. A different sort of shadow looms before us. We're being put to a test. I'm staying vague, but when you hear of it, you'll know. It has to do with an old feud and settling old scores. Perhaps you could find a way to come.

All seems quiet enough for now, but I can't let myself become complacent. I've learned that life can change quicker than the blink of an eye. But I am happy, I think, or near enough. I may have found someone who has helped with that. I feel guilty, though – as though

I'm betraying the old love through finding a new one.
Though it's not love, not yet. It's too new for such a word
as that.

How are you? It's been so long since I've had a letter.
You must be nearly finished with schooling now. Will you
come to the capital for university in summer?

So much to say, but so difficult to put into a letter. I
miss you each and every day.

All my love,
Your sibling of many names

It was such a paltry letter. When my brother and I were together, we could talk for hours. He would know I was upset before I would. We would fight, as all siblings did, but he was a constant for me. I ripped off the bottom of the paper and wrote a shorter note to my old friend Anna Yew, hoping she was well. I'd taken the risk to write to her, and she'd passed on my messages, keeping my secrets. Anna had always loved fairy tales and wanted her one true love and a magical wedding. I hoped she found them.

I folded the paper into the envelope. I sniffed, hoping the tears would not fall. Looking up, I caught sight of the woman pushing her child in the wheelchair. She wore a brown dress this time underneath a thick woolen coat, her hood up against the cold breeze, again obscuring her face. The boy was bundled up like a babe in blankets.

I thought back to the séance, and to Cyan. Perhaps the boy was special, like us. But while Cyan and I were healthy, his skin was a pallid yellow, with no flesh to his features. He was a boy with an old man's face and sad eyes.

They passed right by me. I watched her hooded form retreat, knowing that this was another mystery I would have to solve.

With a sigh, I waited until the serving girl was distracted and snuck from the tea room, guilty at having to steal. I had not been quick enough, however, and the woman and her child had gone with no way for me to follow.

Snowflakes fell from the sky, dancing to and fro on the wind. I opened my mouth and caught one on my tongue. It tasted of nothing.

18
THE SPECTER SHOW

"The sun comes up, the sun comes down.
At night the moon goes round and round.
Chimaera creep and sneak and peek.
They'll gobble you up then pick their teeth!"
                              Elladan children's nursery rhyme

When I stumbled down the stairs for my customary cup of
coffee at dawn, Lily and Maske were at the table.

They looked up, guilty as children with stolen biscuits.
Lily wore a robe and her hair was in disarray, while even
Maske's perfect hair was mussed.

We stared at each other in an impasse. I had the feeling
that Lily planned to leave early, so that no one would ever
know she had spent the night. The widow and the magician.

"I… I…" I sputtered, and then, though I wasn't proud
of it, I ran away.

As I scurried back to the loft, Cyan poked her head out
of the door.

I opened my mouth, but she said, "I know."

"Does Lily care for him?" I asked. "I don't want him hurt."

"I don't either. But if you think she's talkative, then you haven't heard her mind. So much noise I can't pick out a thread, but sometimes I pick up emotions. And she glows when she's around him."

"Good. I'm going to tell Amon." I grinned at her and dashed up the stairs.

Maske refused to mention the incident, pointedly ignoring our titters over breakfast. Soon, we had other things on our mind. That night, we went to see the competition: Taliesin's grandchildren at the Specter Show.

Maske came with us. The large Specter Show theatre was half filled. It was not the week's end, and most laborers would not be paid for another few days.

The light dimmed and music from a gramophone played with a pop and a hiss. My stomach dipped with the same excitement as before I watched the circus on that last day of spring. The curtains pulled back and the first twin entered the stage. I could not tell if it was Sind or Jac. He was soon followed by the other. They gave a short bow and launched into the tricks, aided by their assistant, a girl with curly brown hair and long legs.

As the show progressed, excitement twisted to dread in my stomach. The Taliesin brothers were talented. Their patter was witty, weaving in topical commentary, from the political upheaval of the Forester protests to the Princess Royal's birthday to the upcoming festivities of the Night of the Dead and Lady's Long Night. They started with small tricks – scarves appearing from sleeves, opening a closed palm to reveal a live butterfly fluttering away – before rolling out a spirit cabinet and having their assistant disappear. I breathed a small sigh of relief that she did not appear as she did in our tricks, but having her drop down to the stage from a rope from the gridiron above was dramatic all the same.

They continued to abuse their poor assistant, sawing her in half and then quarters, levitating her and then having her disappear in a shower of sparks. Though I thought I could figure out many of the tricks, some of them eluded me.

The Taliesin brothers chose volunteers from the audience and performed mentalist tricks. They guessed how many siblings they had, what objects would be in their pockets, the name of an uncle that had died.

"They're planted," Cyan whispered into my ear. "Talented actors."

After the intermission, the brothers raised a phantasmagoria, telling a story through images projected from a magic lantern onto a shifting canvas of smoke. Skeletons and hooded figures trailed along the smoke. The Night of the Dead had come early.

"Once, old man Styx came to the world himself to collect the dead," one said.

A large hooded figure with a scythe emerged onto the vapor.

"He would take the dead one by one in his robe to the River Styx, where the good would cross to the twilight lands by gentle waters and the wicked would sink to the dark currents below before returning to the land of the living. As they passed through him, they forgot all they were and all they had ever been. Each life was a blank slate, as it is for us now."

Men and women swam in a great, swirling river that undulated on the shifting canvas.

The brother changed the slide. "A woman decided to trick Death. She sought the help of a Chimaera wizard, who gave her a spell so that she would remember who she was when she passed through the river."

A Naga, a snake man, gathered a great ball of energy, which moved toward an older woman bent with age. Death came and held his cloak open, and she moved into his embrace.

"When she crossed through, she remembered all those many lives. And she knew if she returned to another life, she would forget it all again. So she stayed in the river.

"This upset the balance. Because of Death's error, the Lord of the Sun and the Lady of the Moon forbid him from coming to earth to collect souls. Now, we find our own way to the river, but we all find it in the end."

The smoke swirled into darkness and the gaslights rose. The magician's assistant stood on the stage, wearing a white wig. The other brother stood in a dark robe. The "old" woman shimmered with the light of her "spell". She ran at the hooded Death. Death held its robe open to her and when they met, they both disappeared.

Applause deafened my ears as the curtains closed. They opened again to show the two Taliesin twins, their assistant between them. They lifted their joined hands and bowed before the curtains fell.

● ● ●

As people rose to leave the theatre, Maske scowled, and I didn't need to look at Cyan to know that the last trick was related to the dress he had shown us. Maske's fingers twitched, as though he were already drawing new diagrams to make his illusion better.

"Are you alright?" I asked him as we threaded our way through the seats.

"I will be when we beat Taliesin," he said, and I reeled from the heat in his voice. "He knew that trick was one of my favorites."

I rested a hand on his shoulder. "We'll beat him, Maske. I promise."

"I hope you're right." He twirled his hat in his hand. "I'm going to see Lily."

We nodded, and he gave us a curt farewell before heading off, his shoulders slumped.

Cyan, Drystan and I waited near the backstage. We spoke to the stagehand and told him who we were. After a wait that was long enough to border on rude, we were led backstage. We wanted to speak to our competition. Cyan would try to see if they planned to cheat.

The Taliesin brothers lounged in their dressing room, their bowties loosened and their shirtsleeves rolled to their elbows. They regarded us coolly.

Cyan took a step back from them, as if their thoughts repelled her.

Which is which? I thought at Cyan.

Pencil Dick is on the left and Styxhead is on the right, she shot back at me.

I sent a wordless burst of surprise and affront.

I "heard" rueful laughter. *Sind's on the left and Jac's on the right. They think I'm beautiful. But in a skin-crawling way. They're both imagining me undressed.*

I sent her the mental equivalent of "eugh!"

"So," Sind drawled. "You're the magicians we're to thrash in a few months' time?"

"We're your opponents, sure enough," Drystan said, and Sind's attempt at dryness was *nothing* compared to his. He was the White Clown, even if he spoke with the Temri accent of Amon.

"I think I've seen enough," Jac said. Neither of them bothered to rise.

Drystan leaned forward until he was uncomfortably close to them. "I think you two need your arrogance brought down a peg or two. I'll be happy to oblige in a few months."

I let Drystan handle this. I became flustered in a fight and never knew what to say. This hadn't served me well in the circus, nor as a noble's daughter.

The brothers rose, and Drystan faced them. Sind and Jac's hands were balled into fists. Drystan's were lax at his sides, but he stood in a tumbler's ready stance.

"You three will never beat us, and we'll see to that," Jac said, his face twisted into a snarl. "We've only just started performing, but we were born for the stage."

"And we were born to win," Drystan said. "Believe me, you have no idea who you two are tangling with." His face was perfectly calm, but his eyes scared even me. It was the face I had seen when he struck Bil with the cane. That stillness when we found out about Shadow Elwood. I forced my head high. *Show no fear.*

"Get out of here before we bloody that pretty face of yours," Sind growled.

Drystan batted his eyelashes. "Oh, you think I'm pretty, do you?"

Sind swung his fist. Drystan dodged it easily and jabbed Sind in the throat, just hard enough to make him sputter and drop back. Jac jumped in next, but they were magicians, not brawlers. They were no match for Drystan and his tumbler's reflexes. Within moments, they were both on the ground, gasping, with Cyan and I looking on in amazement.

"We'll see you in three months," Drystan said. "And I expect the result of the wager will be much the same as tonight." He left, and we followed.

After returning from visiting Lily, Maske didn't emerge from his workshop all night. He fought his own demons there, trying to solve them with diagrams and equations.

When Drystan and I were in the quiet of the loft, I didn't ask him about the altercation with the Taliesin twins. I knew his anger hadn't really been about them. He still felt powerless over the thoughts of the deaths against his name. He had a bit of power over the Taliesins, two boys as rotten as overripe plums. I gave him a long, wordless hug and went to my bed.

I licked my lips in the darkness. It would feel good to beat Taliesin and his twins.

19
THE BLUE LIGHT

"The strange, unearthly light,
On the full Penmoon night.
The blue glow on your skin,
You and I are here again."

THE BLUE LIGHT, by Micah Grey

The next morning, Maske was in the kitchen drafting a revision of the winged woman trick, drawing the delicate cogs of the machinery onto the checked paper.

Cyan and Drystan and I opened the books Maske had left out for us for that day's lessons.

"Séances?" I asked as Drystan passed me a cup of coffee. I smiled at him gratefully as I cupped the warm mug in my hands. Ricket trotted into the kitchen, demanding food, and Drystan obliged.

"We need capital. My séances alone aren't enough, especially after all the repairs on the theatre. It's been long enough that I think you two will be safe to perform them. I had to pawn a few things yesterday before we went to that Specter Show, and I'd like to avoid doing that as much as possible."

"What did you pawn?" I asked, curious.

"Old Vestige. I used to collect it. A lot of it's not functional or low on power, but I hate to part with it." I wondered if he ever pawned the illegal Vestige he owned, or if it hadn't come to that yet.

"Is there a lot of Vestige in the theatre?" Cyan asked, twisting the end of her braid around her fingers.

"A fair amount," Maske said evasively.

"Hmm," she said. I looked at her questioningly.

I think that the more Vestige I'm around, the stronger my abilities. It's so easy to speak to you like this, here. It was a little harder at the Specter Theatre, even though I could sense some Vestige there. Maybe that's why it didn't happen often at the circus.

Well, that is… interesting, I thought.

"The Night of the Dead approaches," Maske said. "I want us to begin séances at least two weeks beforehand, in pairs. One to perform at the table, and another to perform behind the scenes."

I shivered. The Night of the Dead was the night before the Long Night of the Lady, the longest night of winter. The Night of the Lady represented the hope of a turning point – that longer days and spring would return.

The Night of the Dead symbolized lost hope. Some say the currents of Styx that trapped the dead could flow back through the world and the dead could walk among us.

It was a night for séances.

Cyan met my gaze. She did not have to read my mind to know what I was thinking – with her in our midst, we were sitting on a goldmine. We had a Vestige crystal ball, and numerous other small artifacts we could spirit away in our pockets. If we went to the house of any rich merchants or nobles, they would be sure to have collections of their own. All Cyan needed to do was ask them to picture the dead person they wished to speak to in their mind.

I pretended to read from one of the books of séance as I pondered the implications.

Cyan?

She looked up. *What?*

Can I tell Drystan what you can do?

I thought you were still insisting on calling him Amon?

Styx.

She kept her composure, but only just.

Why?

He'll know the best way to approach this. How not to be too obvious.

There was a long silence as my heart thundered in my throat. I was speaking to a girl with my mind as Drystan and Maske sat at the table with us, none the wiser. She read my mind and spoke back to me. None of it was my own ability as far as I could tell. But even so, it was extraordinary.

Alright. As long as he keeps quiet.

He's much better at secrets than I am, I thought wryly.

Her laughter echoed inside my skull.

I hid a smile of my own, but I was relieved. I could tell Drystan. The secret was eating away at me. I had lost Aenea from the little threads of lies that spiraled into a web and caught us. I knew I did not want to lose Drystan.

That evening, after lessons, I pleaded taking a chill and announced I was going to study in bed until teatime.

"Of course," Maske said. "We'll start practicing in earnest tomorrow." He rubbed his face with his hands, tired. He was doing séances three nights a week, and spent hours and hours in his workshop or instructing us on magic tricks. He was patient, never snapping even when we kept making the same silly mistake over and over again, or dissolving into a fit of giggles. But he was tired.

I crept upstairs with my séance book. I tucked myself into bed, but could not concentrate. Setting my book aside, I held the disc that contained Anisa. Had it really been weeks since I had spoken to her? I sensed she was waiting for me to let her out again, to learn more. She possessed so many answers, if only I could ask for them...

My eyes grew heavy.

Drystan's tread on the stairs woke me up. I slid the disc under the pillow.

"Come in," I said, before he knocked.

He entered, closing the door behind him. "You slept through dinner. I tried to wake you."

I was usually a light sleeper. I wondered why I hadn't woken before. "Did I? I suppose I was tired."

"Strange day," he sighed.

I murmured my agreement. He made his way partly to his bed but then stopped, looking at the crumpled sheets as if they held no comfort. I scooted over on the bed, my heartbeat quickening. With a smile, he slid in next to me, settling his head on my shoulder.

I loved this simple affection. When I first met him, he was so aloof and removed. He still was, in many ways, but like me, he craved physical contact. And this closeness was so nice. Only Cyril had ever given me any physical affection growing up. My parents had never hugged me. Not once.

For a time, we said nothing. We listened to each other's breath as the flames in the fireplace made shadows dance on the wall.

"Is this uncomfortable?" Drystan asked, tapping the Lindean corset I wore under my clothes.

"There's no such thing as a comfortable corset." I strived for lightness.

"Then why do you wear it?"

"Because a boy with breasts is a bit of a curious sight, even if they're not very large," I said, a blush creeping up my cheeks.

"Well, everyone here knows the truth. So if it's a day where we're just around the theatre, I don't see why you couldn't leave it off. No one would mind." Drystan traced his fingertips lightly over the corset, and I swallowed hard.

"I suppose," I said. "Here, budge up."

He sat up, and I loosened the corset stays under my shirt, sliding it over my hips and throwing it onto the floor. I took a deep breath, my ribs free. In that moment, I felt so fully aware of all the parts that made me: the breasts beneath the rough cloth, the little extra between my legs, the shaved down on my cheeks and the wider spread of my hips. I felt… comfortable.

"That is better."

He chuckled.

We rearranged ourselves. This time, I rested my head on his chest. Drystan stroked a hand along my spine, up and down. I grew dozy with the feel of his feather-light touch.

"Before I fall asleep," I murmured. "I have to tell you something."

"Mm?" he said, and I felt the sound echo in his ribcage.

"Cyan said I could tell you. About her."

I felt his breath hitch.

"You don't have to. Or she could tell me herself."

"She knows that. I think she'd rather me tell you. Rather than her having to show you."

"Is she like you, then?"

"What? Oh." I coughed, remembering the horrible night I showed him and Aenea what I was rather than tell them because I did not know how to explain. Just before our lives fractured further. "No, it's not that."

"How do you know? Have you seen her naked?" he jested.

"No!" I sat up. His eyes dropped to my chest, lazily. I fought the urge to cross my arms over my chest. "You are not making this easy."

"Sorry, I'll behave. No more jokes. Cyan?"

Lord and Lady, how to say it? "Cyan can, um, well... She can read minds."

He stared at me, and then he began to laugh, just as I had responded to Cyan. He kept laughing though, even when my face remained still as stone.

"Did she do some mentalist trick on you? Cover her eyes and ask you to choose a number between one and twenty?"

"She asked me to think of my fondest memory. And she told me every little detail about it. Including what painting was on the wall, and what book lay open in my lap."

He sobered at that. "That's not possible."

I waved my hand vaguely. "Plenty would say the same about me."

"But isn't yours mainly physiological? It's not mindreading!"

"I've been seen by a lot of doctors. None of them have ever come across a case quite like mine. Besides, don't you remember what else I can do?"

"Remember what?"

"The night we ran away from the circus." We'd never spoken of it. In the beginning, we were both too broken. And then... it was easier not to discuss murder and death.

A shadow crossed Drystan's face, his pupils wide and dark. "I don't remember most of that night... after the cane."

"You blocked it out?"

He shrugged. "I suppose."

I didn't want to bring up that night, but I pushed on. "When the clowns were chasing us, and they trapped us. I told you to close your eyes. There was a flash. And we escaped."

His brow crinkled. "I think I remember a flash. It's all jumbled." Had he truly forgotten the memories to save himself from the pain? I wished I could do the same.

I puffed my breath out from between my cheeks. "Come on," I said, leaving the warm cocoon of the bed. "As ever, it's easier to show people than to tell them."

"You could show me what's under your clothes again. I remember that clearly enough."

I threw him a dirty look, even as my face burned. "You said no more joking."

"Maybe I wasn't joking," he said, sending another shiver along my spine.

Unable to articulate my thoughts, I turned from him. We shrugged into our jackets and shoved our feet into our boots. Up to the roof we went, and down the frozen drainpipe. Snow lay thick upon the ground. The world was dark, the sky brilliantly clear, each star shining down on us like a pinprick of light through black cloth. The air was fresh and cold.

It took a long time to find a Penglass dome that wouldn't be easily seen by people in the tall buildings to either side. Finally, I found one a little taller than us, hidden just inside an alley next to a shop with boarded windows.

Drystan looked at the dome in confusion, his teeth chattering with cold. "Why are we here?"

"Stand here, so anyone walking by won't see."

He complied. I took a deep breath, my bare palms hovering above the dome. Excitement coursed through me. And fear. Had it really been months since I had done this? Penglass called to me, especially every Penmoon, but I always resisted, not wanting to risk someone seeing... someone being hurt. But would the glass be like it was the night with Cyril, or like the night of the Penmoon?

"Keep your eyes shut until I tell you it's safe," I warned.

He did, and I closed my eyes to near slits.

I pressed my palms to the cold glass. Beneath my hands, the dark cobalt Penglass began to glow. The light reflected off the snow until it seemed as though we stood on diamonds. I took my hands away, widening my eyes. It was safe. The imprint of my hands remained.

"You can look," I said.

Drystan crept closer, the blue light illuminating the planes of his face. His eyes were wide with wonder, his lips parted.

"You created the flash?"

"If I touch it on the night of the Penmoon and focus, it becomes blinding." I swallowed, thinking of the clowns. I had tried to forget that, because of me, they would never see again.

"How is this possible?"

I tried to lock away the memory of that night in a corner of my mind, along with the other horrors. It was the only way not to be haunted. "I don't know. I discovered it by accident, when I was climbing with my brother." That memory had been one of the most amazing of my life, and then utterly terrible. Cyril had fallen off the smooth surface of the Penglass, breaking his arm. I had jumped down the Penglass after him, leaving two long trails of light as I did so. Nearby residents had seen them, and the next day photos graced the cover of the newspaper. No one had ever linked it to me. At least, I did not think they had.

Drystan reached out to touch the glass, but it remained dark under his fingers. I drew a few swirls like the winter wind, illuminating the snow a little more.

"So you see," I said. "There's much in this world we don't understand. I can do this. I never grow ill. My arm healed before I stopped wearing the sling. So if I can do all of this, then what Cyan can do does not seem beyond the realm of possibility."

His head jerked back at that. "How much quicker did your arm heal?"

"Two weeks or so."

"Why didn't you tell me?" He sounded hurt.

"I wanted to pretend it was not that odd. That I was not that odd." My voice caught, surprising me.

"You're not odd. This, what you can do… it's beautiful." He came close, and wrapped me in his arms. "You're beautiful."

My breath hitched in my throat.

Our lips met. I pushed him against the glowing glass, the stubble of his chin scratching mine. I rested a hand on the Penglass, the cool blue light bathing us as we kissed, careless of who might see.

20
HIDDEN MESSAGES

"Sometimes, I wish séances were real. That I could reach through the veil and speak to those I have wronged. I wish I could apologize to my wife. I'd apologize to Taliesin's lover, who I stole away because I could rather than out of any real affection. So many men and women I have wronged, reduced to ghosts and shades. They surround me, but I can never let them know I regret what I have cost them, both the living and the dead."

Jasper Maske's personal diary

We clasped hands about the round table, me with no small amount of trepidation.

With Cyan here, sharing skin-to-skin contact, who knew what could happen? Dread prickled the back of my mind. Cyan's gaze flicked to mine as she sensed my unease.

We had studied nearly nonstop the last few days. The mornings were for magic, and the afternoons and evenings for séances. Maske gave us many lectures on the history and the importance of séances.

"The atmosphere must be just so," he had said the previous night at the dinner table. "Dark enough so that if one of us needs to sneak about, we'll be able to, but not so dark that nothing can be seen. Props are useful, especially in superstitious households. I've kept a record of almost every house I've been to, writing down the names, appearances, and dispositions of each member. Many of my clients are repeat business, so I tailor my approach. I'll teach you several variants, but only practice, time, and intuition will help you discover which approach is the correct one for you and those you hold the séance for.

"A séance is very different from stage magic. In a magic show, most of the audience doesn't believe you're really doing magic. But with a séance it's entirely different. Some are complete cynics, others are not sure, and others believe or desperately *want* to believe." He squeezed his eyes shut and opened them again. "And you'll have enemies and allies both at the same table. They are also active participants. It's not one volunteer called up to the stage from the audience. Each person in turn may be asked to divulge something personal. Each will have loved and lost.

"I view séances differently from my magic performances, though in the last fifteen years, they have not exactly warred for my attention. Though I am aiming to deceive people at a séance, sometimes I feel as though I help them. Grown men have wept like broken-hearted babes at my table when they think they have made contact with a long-dead loved one. They've felt like they've been able to say goodbye, even if, deep down, perhaps they know they have not."

Tonight, Maske was the same somber-faced man I had seen on my first night at the Kymri Theatre.

"Show me what you've learned," he said. We had studied, and now was the test. If we performed well, we would start performing séances next week, beginning small with merchant and tradesmen families, and working up to nobles as our reputations grew. I was glad to learn the skill – if magic shows proved not to support us, between séances and street magic, we would never starve. That comforted me. I had spent several days on the street just after I ran away from my old life as Iphigenia Laurus. I had been hungry and scared, terrified that I would have to return home.

In my new home, the curtains of the parlor were drawn, and candlelight flickered, casting long shadows along the walls. The Vestige crystal ball rested on the table before us. Alder script had been drawn on the dark tablecloth in chalk.

Maske was our subject, and so Cyan led the séance. During our practice sessions this morning, I learned that for séances, I was also better suited to being an assistant, sneaking behind dust curtains and folding myself into small spaces. I could not speak the lies with the same assurance that Cyan or Drystan could. I did not know what that said about them or me.

"We welcome you to our sacred circle, Jasper Maske," Cyan intoned. Her face was covered with black gauze, a bride of darkness. She wore a dark Elladan dress, wasp-waisted in a corset. Only her hands were bare, decorated in swirling designs of silver paint, her nails black as night.

"Tonight we call the spirits to peek their heads up from the currents of the River Styx, to whisper the words they wish they could have told us in life. I have known a heartache that few others have possessed. Through this grief, I may pull back the veil and pass along the messages of the dead, Jasper Maske. Close your eyes and imagine who has passed that you wish to speak with. For we have all known, loved, and lost."

Maske concentrated. Cyan's brow crinkled as she spied on his mind. Drystan opened his eyes. I squeezed his hand and he squeezed back.

"Someone comes to me through the mists of the otherworld…" Cyan shuddered, her head falling forward on her chest. I felt a humming deep within my chest.

Whispers in Alder echoed in the room. "She hears us, too. She hears us, too. *She hears us, too.*"

Cyan's head rose, and my spine turned to ice. Though I could not see her face through the veil, I knew that it was not Cyan.

Before I could break the circle, her veiled head turned to mine. The gauze faded to mist, drifting from her face. Her eyes glowed the bright blue of Penglass, and the crystal ball on the table blazed the same hue.

Maske and Drystan had frozen, as though time had stopped. Cyan, or whoever she now was, began to mutter under her breath in Alder, far too quick for me to understand. Like Maske when he had spoken during the séance the first night I joined him, her voice seemed to echo with three tones at once. The last word ended in a scream and she tilted her head to the ceiling. Her hand gripped mine so tightly I feared she would break my fingers. I heard sobbing, and it took me a moment to realize it was me.

Cyan broke her handhold with Maske, her free hand moving toward me. I sat, paralyzed in fear. Her fingertips rested on my forehead and I jerked with the force of the vision.

Cyan and I were side by side. I knew it was her, though her body was different. A severe widow's peak topped her new, heart-shaped face. Her lips were small and thin, her hair a cap of feathers banded brown and gray. Her tawny, yellow eyes blinked at me once. She was far shorter than the Cyan I knew, thin and bird-boned, her skin a dark olive.

And then there were the wings.

They rose behind her, impossibly large, all faun and chestnut and charcoal. She flapped them, buffeting me with gusts of air.

I looked down at my own shimmering limbs, knowing that I was Anisa. My wings rose behind me as well, as insubstantial as a wish compared to Cyan's.

We stood on the edge of a cliff made of white stone. Venglass sprawled down to the crescent of a bay. Ships with purple and red sails drifted on the water. We were not in Ellada. The air was too warm and humid, close as a lover's touch. Between the Venglass, tall tropical trees twisted toward the cerulean sky. The wind carried the scent of hyacinth, dark, loamy soil, sea salt, and an unfamiliar spice. I guessed that we were in Linde – Linde as it was when Alder and Chimaera lived side by side with humans.

"Matla," my mouth said in a voice that was not my own. Cyan, *I tried to say.* Are you there? *But my mouth*

would not form the words. I was only a passenger in this body. As she spoke, my sense of self, as Micah Grey, faded. "Why are we here?" Anisa asked. "Why bring me half a world away?"

"Someone will die here, unless we stop it. And this is what we must do, at all costs. The alternative does not bear thinking about."

"Who will they kill? Who is killing?"

Matla, the owlish woman with Cyan hiding behind her eyes, shook her head. "Not all is clear to me. Not yet. But the steady dripping of blood on Venglass haunts me."

The memory of my murdered ward haunted me as well. The phantom memory filled my nose with the iron tang of blood. My newest ward was safe now, at home with Relean.

"Come," Matla said, spreading her wings. "We haven't much time." And she dived off the edge of the white cliffs. I brought my own wings to life and dived after her, cutting through the thick, warm air as though it were water.

As we flew toward the Venglass Domes of Sila, I wished Matla had told me more. I had nothing to protect myself but the small dagger in its sheath at my hip and an Acha in the pocket of my robe. I was weary from our long flight, for though we took the portal from Ellada to Linde, it had been on the other side of the tropical island.

A few inhabitants of Sila looked up as we passed. The Chimaera here were more aquatic than those from the mountains of the Ven, with fish scales that glistened in the light, the beaded skin of lizards, or the moist hides of salamanders. Paths lined with colored stones wound through the cobalt Venglass. An open market released the scent of sizzling meats and spices, and the sounds of goats bleating and the laughter and haggling of Chimaera, Alder, and humans alike rose to us.

The jovial atmosphere of the market warred with the absolute dread and fear Matla emanated as she darted through the air, bringing us over the town and into the dark jungle. We landed on the branch of a breadfruit tree, tucking our wings to our backs as we climbed down the trunk.

We pushed our way through the undergrowth, not speaking, spurred on by an undeniable sense of urgency. My hand never strayed far from the hilt at my hip.

We came to a small Venglass dome, incongruous in the middle of the jungle. There were no nearby growths. Matla glanced over her shoulder at me, blinking owlishly. She held a finger to her lips and set her hand on the glass and it lit. She drew the glyph for opening, and it did, the glass melting away to a hole large enough to admit us.

Underneath Anisa, the part of me that was still Micah Grey tried to memorize that glyph, but it drifted away.

Matla entered, drawing her long, thin Acha. The part of me that was Micah recognized it as an Eclipse. It cast a light that only the two of us could see, and broadcast a subtle illusion, so that someone glancing down the hallway might not see us at first. She held her curved scimitar in her other hand. I drew my own weapon. It was dark, but Matla could see in the gloom, so I followed the whisper of her footsteps.

We went deeper and deeper into the earth. It was hard for both of us, who preferred wide, open skies. I wondered again why I was here, why Matla had asked me and not a stronger fighter or someone higher in the ranks of the Chimaera.

Far off, we heard agonized cries, as if something or someone was being tortured. My wings shivered. I did not want to be here.

We entered a room. Two Alder loomed over a creature strapped to a table. Engrossed as they were in their grim task, they had not yet seen us.

Matla crouched into a fighting stance, a hand still holding the Acha. She brandished her curved sword, and the light glanced off the bright green poison at the tip. My blood ran cold, for I wondered how she possessed Vitriol, the only poison that could kill an Alder.

She launched herself into the room, at the last second giving an avian shriek.

The Alder turned from their charge on the table, raising the surgical instruments in their hands. Matla swiped one of the Alder through with her scimitar, and he dropped, the wounds smoking. The other whirled, skittering back from the table. They fought, the Alder just barely holding back Matla's furious attack. Matla shrieked like a banshee.

"Get the boy!" she cried at me. "The boy must be saved!"

I broke from my paralysis, moving to untie the bonds holding the creature on the table. For I was not sure if I could call the thing a boy.

He had the flat face of a snake and reptilian eyes. His body glistened dark green in the light. His eyes were the brilliant emerald of a cat or a snake. He was hairless and naked, and two jet black horns sprouted from his forehead. How could Matla have brought me here to save a demon?

He panted in pain. Red blood splattered his skin from where they had cut him. It looked as though they were planning to implant something into his torso. It rested on the table next to

*the surgical instruments, dark green, speckled with intricate blue
and black designs. Other cuts on his head were sewn shut. I put
the object in the pocket of my trousers.*

*I untied his bonds, keeping an eye on the fight between Matla
and the other Alder. I stepped over the corpse of the first one. I
knew what group these two belonged to. How could I not? They
were Kashura. And they wanted to kill us all.*

*The Alder made a mad swipe and grazed Matla's wing. She
screamed in pain and rage. Leaving the boy, I took my little
knife, darting in from behind. He twisted away, but I managed
to leave a long gash along his ribs. Matla recovered and stabbed
him in the arm, grimacing in triumph. He would die, now, from
the poison. No matter what.*

*But Alder, our makers, are a strong and strange folk. His eyes
blazed with disgust, his lips curling. With a move too swift to
follow, he grabbed the weapon from Matla's hand and plunged
it into her stomach.*

*I cried out as though I was wounded. I launched myself at
him, stabbing my little knife into his throat. I did not stab as
deeply as I would like, but I hit his jugular. Blood poured and
he dropped the scimitar. I grabbed it, letting my knife fall to the
floor. Wasting no time, I plunged it into his chest. He fell.*

*"You're too late," he whispered to us in his three-toned voice
before he died. "All has already been set in motion."*

*I ignored him, bending over Matla. She sucked in wet, sticky
gasps.*

*"You'll be alright," I said, though I knew I lied. Tears streamed
down my face as I ripped off a strip of my shirt and held it to
the gaping, smoking wound in her stomach. Vitriol could slay
Alder, and it could kill us just as easily. Underneath Anisa's*

consciousness, the me that was Micah railed against the walls of her mind like a moth in a lampshade, wondering if Cyan was alright.

"Save the boy," Matla whispered. "Raise him with your other charge. Raise him to be good, and kind, or all is lost."

I heard a great shuddering gasp from the table. The strange, horned creature jerked and went still. I did not know if he was unconscious or dead.

Matla groaned in pain. "He must be good, or all is lost. All is lost and we are all doomed." She coughed, a wet burbling in her throat. I clutched her hand.

"I'm sorry," I said, over and over. "I'm so sorry."

"Not your fault," she managed. "It's mine. I can only hope I did some good, and there's some chance to save the rest of us… or we're all dead… we're all dead and lost…"

As Matla's life slipped away, the strange medical room deep within the Venglass began to dissolve. I rested my hand on Matla's cheek.

And then I was gone, thrown from the Phantom Damselfly's ancient life and back into my own.

Cyan fell from her chair and lay jerking on the floor, clutching her stomach. She was choking out "or we're all dead, we're all dead and lost" in Alder, which she didn't speak as far as I knew. Maske went to her, peering at her expanded pupils. He turned her on her side so she would not choke on her own tongue.

I swayed in my seat, the edges of my vision darkening.

"Micah," Drystan said, snapping his fingers in front of my face. "What's wrong?" He shook my shoulders gently.

"The Alder wanted to kill us all. All the Chimaera. And I think they did. When they left, I don't think they took us with them…"

Dimly, I realized I was babbling and should guard my tongue.

Maske ran to get the medic bag. With Drystan's help, I stumbled to where Cyan still writhed on the floor as Maske returned.

"You're alright, Cyan," I said. "It wasn't real. Only a memory. A very old memory." I meant to send that to her as thoughts, but Drystan and Maske's gaping faces told me I spoke aloud. So much for guarding my tongue. My secrets scattered about the room.

Too late now. I steeled myself. "Matla?" I asked.

An eye rolled toward me.

"Are you Cyan or are you Matla?"

"I do not know," she moaned, not realizing she still spoke Alder. "I don't know," she repeated in Elladan.

Her words struck such a fear into me. What if we had lost Cyan and now Matla somehow possessed her?

"Cyan. You are Cyan," I said, more firmly than I felt. "You were born in Temne. Your mother is a contortionist and your father is a juggler. You were raised among circus folk and you told fortunes. You love a boy who is a sailor. You see more than most."

She inhaled. "Yes. Cyan. I am Cyan." She muttered to herself in Temri, and the fluent outpouring of her mother tongue reassured me. Matla was gone, dead thousands of years.

Maske returned. "What is going on? Cyan, was it some sort of fit?"

With a sigh, she said, "I had a vision."

His brow furrowed.

"I'm not lying." The truth spilled out of her. Let the chips fall where they may.

"A vision," he said, slowly, as if he was not sure he heard her correctly.

"You deserve to know," she said. "There's more. If I concentrate, I can sometimes tell what others are thinking."

He didn't believe her.

She shifted. "Think of your fondest memory. Hold it close. Imagine every detail."

Maske harrumphed in consternation, but he closed his eyes.

A long moment passed. Cyan grew paler.

"You're not imagining your fondest memory at all," Cyan admonished. "You're wondering if the screws you bought will fit the mechanism of the–"

"Enough!" he cried, shaken. "A lucky guess."

Cyan smiled weakly. Focusing on Maske, her father, even if he did not know it, seemed to bring her further to herself. "Then try again. Think of your favorite memory."

Maske took a deep breath. He closed his eyes.

"You're in your workshop. You're younger. Your hands are unlined, and you don't have the scar on your left thumb. You've created a little automaton. It swings from a little trapeze. Its motley is gold and silver."

Maske's eyes opened, rounded in surprise. Cyan met his eyes, exhaustion in every feature. Drystan and I gawped in amazement as well before exchanging a glance. He made a trapeze artist that wore motley?

"Will this… kind of vision happen to you if you attempt

another séance?" Maske asked, his voice wavering.

"I don't know."

I was coming back to myself more with each passing minute. Anisa was behind this. She had grown impatient and wanted to speak to me, and to prove her point she had dragged Cyan into it.

Cyan stared at Maske. She was still pale, her hair matted with sweat against her forehead. But she was desperate to ask him something else, I could tell. What had she seen in his mind?

Perhaps it was for the best that I could not read minds as she could. I doubted I would be able to show any such restraint.

"You should rest," Maske said. You've overstressed yourself and we all have... much to think about."

Maske helped Cyan stand and totter to bed. She looked back at me. I nodded. I had seen everything she had seen. I had watched her die in another's body. That tied us together in a way that could not be broken.

I started shivering and I couldn't stop.

"Micah?" Drystan asked.

I did not answer, my head bowing to my chest. Drystan carried me to the loft. All energy left me, and I still did not feel entirely like myself. I could still sense the phantom wings against my back, and catch the echo of iridescence on the skin of my arms.

"What's happening to me?" I moaned.

"What do you mean, Micah?"

I tried to answer him, but my tongue was a slug in my mouth and would not move. My eyelids fluttered. *Don't faint*, I pleaded with myself. *Not again. You're not a fainting maiden.*

I felt a sudden stirring of dread. I heard the plumbing of the upstairs bathroom rattling the walls.

"Cyan," I tried to mutter, and made my uneven way to the door. Drystan helped me, sensing my unease. The door to the washroom was locked. I looked at Drystan mutely. He ran to fetch his lock pick and within a moment the door opened.

The bath was running. Cyan lay slumped on the floor against the tub, still fully clothed, eyes closed. Drystan turned off the water and I checked her pulse and color.

"She is not well," I said, alarmed at how the whites of her eyes were yellow when I pulled back the lids. "She needs a doctor."

Drystan nodded and dashed from the room.

"Cyan," I said, slapping her cheek gently. "Come on, Cyan." She opened her eyes but they couldn't focus.

Maske came and carried her like a child downstairs. She wrapped her arm around him. "Daddy," she moaned, piteously, and my heart went out to her. She spoke the truth and he did not recognize it.

"Don't tell them what happened," I said to Maske.

Maske hesitated, but he nodded.

And then they were gone.

"So cold…" I muttered, still swaying. Drystan rubbed his hands against mine, but I only shivered all the more.

"OK," he said, and threw me over his shoulder, bringing me back to the bathroom. Dimly, a part of me was insulted by this treatment. He turned the water on again, the tub half full of steaming water. He stripped me down to my undergarments, chafing my arms, hands, legs, and feet. Another part of me was touched and embarrassed in equal measure.

Without ceremony, he placed me into the tub. I gasped with shock, sputtering. My limbs tingled like they were recovering from frostbite.

I sagged against the tub and rested my hands against my temples.

"Micah, what is going on?" Drystan asked, stroking my hair back from my face.

"I don't know."

He perched on the edge of the tub. "You do know."

He was right. I did. Well, almost everything. I left out the previous visions with Anisa. I intended to tell him. The words were in my head, but when I told the story, the tale slipped past those visions. I frowned and tried again, but the same thing happened. Drystan held the back of his hand against my cheek, checking to see if I was fevered.

So I told him only of the most recent vision, skimming over some of the details, and made it seem as though it was the first time it had happened. Drystan put together a few of the pieces on his own.

"The dragonfly woman… was she like the Phantom Damselfly from the circus?"

"It was her."

"And you and Cyan both had the vision?"

"Yes." I hoped she was alright.

"Lord and Lady," he breathed.

We stared at each other in silence. "Come on, help me out. I'm warm enough, now."

He did, and we both paused when I was out of the tub.

His eyes were on my face, but I knew he sensed my body so close to his. Still, I hesitated. My mother had made so many comments about how no one could see my body, no one could know...

His arms slid around me, even though I was slippery. He drew me close and I clutched him, comforted by his solid presence. Through his damp white shirt, I could see the outline of his muscles and the pink blush of his nipples. With a burst of bravery I did not know I had, I pulled his shirt off, gasping at the feel of his skin on mine, only the Lindean corset separating us.

My lips left his and worked their way to the soft skin of his neck and he gasped. We were frightened, me by what I had seen and Drystan by what he had watched me go through. We kissed and touched each other, exploring a little more than we had before, but both of us kept our trousers on. As I ran my fingertips over his skin, I felt the last tatters of Micah Grey come back to me. Drystan centered me. No matter how much we scrabbled for purchase, our world continued to crumble about us. So we held onto each other and let the world fade away.

21
Confronting the Chimaera

"In all these many years, we have found no archaeological evidence of either Alder or Chimaera bodies. No graveyards. No mummies found in ice. No bones. Only Vestige, as if one day they all left. It is a small wonder that many believe the Chimaera never existed at all. Sometimes, in a darker mood, I wonder that, myself."

Unpublished article by Professor Caed Cedar

Cyan returned from the doctor's a few hours later, pale as milk, and went straight to bed.

"How is she?" I asked Maske.

"Faint, but she should be fine within a day or two." Outside her door, he held up a hand. "Come. Time you told me what's going on under my roof."

Nerves sent a shiver down my spine. He led us to the library. I curled against the seat cushions gratefully, for I still felt as weak as a newborn kitten. Maske folded his fingers in front of his face, his eyes piercing and unreadable.

"Tell me," he said.

I took a breath. We hadn't told him initially, and I still didn't really want to tell him now. It made it feel too real.

"Cyan and I had a shared vision. We don't know how or why." Though I had my suspicions.

"What did you see?"

I told him the tale. As with Drystan, I made no mention of the earlier visions. I couldn't.

"As well as reading minds, Cyan has a sort of prescience, then? But of the past?" He was animated, but not as surprised as I would have thought. I peered at him. Here was a man who had seen much that could not be explained.

"We don't know. Have you ever known anything like this?"

"I met a woman once, who seemed as if she could read my mind. I volunteered for a mentalist show. You already know that, for mentalist shows, a magician phrases a question a certain way, giving hints. This mentalist guessed without the magician asking her a single question. Could be they had an advanced system or a hidden earpiece, but part of me wanted to believe that it was… magic. Funny, isn't it? I'm a magician, and I know the secrets to almost every trick ever performed. But I'm always hoping to stumble upon a little bit of real magic. And magic was right under my nose. In both of you."

"It's not Micah," Drystan said. "Just Cyan." He gave me a warning look. I looked away, guilty.

"Micah saw the vision, too."

"She let go of our hands, but not Micah's," Drystan said. I bit my lip, feeling like we were spilling Cyan's secrets without her permission.

"When you came back, you said something about Chimaera. You said 'we'." He missed nothing, the old card sharp.

"I was... confused. From the vision," I said, hoping I sounded convincing.

He let the subject drop. A gleam came into his eyes. "Is there a danger of such a thing happening again, or can we harness it? Think of it, for both our séances and the magic show. There is a way to use this to beat Taliesin." He rose and paced, his eyes alight with planning and cunning.

"Wouldn't that be cheating?"

"Pah!" he laughed. "If it takes a little cheating to beat him, then so be it. I doubt he'll be so scrupulous."

"Do you really want to beat him by cheating?" At the look on my face, his pacing slowed.

"No." He sighed. "Not at all."

"Right." My eyes narrowed. "Cyan nearly died tonight. Do keep that in mind."

His chest puffed in rage. And then, he deflated. "You're right, you're right." He rubbed his face with his hands.

Maske left, his footsteps heavy in the foyer. Drystan stared into the banked coals of the fire, looking almost as tired as I felt. His hair fell into his face.

It was late and I wanted to sleep. But I feared the dreams I might have.

Neither of us spoke, each with our own thoughts. When we went to bed, I stared at the ceiling until Drystan's breathing evened in sleep.

I crept down to Cyan's room, the Phantom Damselfly disc in the pocket of my coat.

She opened the door before I could knock, motioning me inside. Dark circles bruised under her eyes. I had not been in Cyan's room before. She had pinned Temnian wax-dyed cloth on all the walls and the ceiling, which made the room feel like a circus tent. From the light fixture in the center of the room she had hung prayer scrolls – ribbons printed with prayers in Temri script. The room smelled of orange oil and incense.

I sat on the rickety rocking chair by her bed.

"You saw everything that I did, didn't you?" Cyan asked me without preamble.

"You know I did."

"What does it mean? Was it real?"

"I think it was an echo, or an old recording played. I think it happened, but long, long ago."

"I remember dying." Her voice collapsed.

"I know," I said. "I don't think you'd ever forget something like that."

She took a shaky breath. "Why are you here?"

"To give you answers. I don't have them all, but I have a few."

She covered her mouth with her hand. "Will the answers frighten me?"

"Probably."

She put her head in her hands. "I don't want this. I just want to be normal."

I drew the Phantom Damselfly disc from my pocket.

"What's that?" she asked.

The disc warmed in my hands. "Anisa," I said.

Cyan's mouth dropped open as she recognized the name.

I pressed the button and set the disc down, and the tower of smoke swirled in the middle of Cyan's room.

The smoke cleared and Anisa materialized, her wings flickering to life. Cyan cried out in fear, looking between us. She recognized the damselfly – how could she not? Those hands had cupped her cheek as she died on the floor of Penglass in another land and another time.

I should have warned her, but I did not know how. I should have tried though – it was cruel to shock her so. I was unnerved to see Anisa again as well. I had *been* her three times now, in visions so clear they felt almost more real than my actual life.

"Anisa," I said again.

"Little Kedi," she greeted me. She never called me Micah Grey, or any of my other names. Her gaze fell upon Cyan. "The one who was Matla."

Cyan stood and backed away until she reached the wall.

"I am not Matla," she gasped.

"This I know. But you saw what she saw." Her eyes fell back to me. "Just as you have seen through my own eyes, little Kedi."

I took a shaking breath. "Why did you show us this?"

"There is no one else to show you. Almost all of us are gone now. Some return. Here and there, scattered among the Archipelago." Did she speak of people who could do the things that Cyan and I could, or did she mean more discs that contained ancient Chimaera?

"Why?" I repeated.

"So that you would learn what happened to your kind. And so you might learn what could happen again, if a certain man has his way. All is at stake. All might be lost."

"I do not see what this has to do with us," Cyan spoke, her voice high but steady.

"In all the many years I have waited, you two are the only ones I have sensed that could hear me that could also help me."

My breath caught. "But… there must be others. There has to be."

"None that I would trust." She held her arms out to us. "You two are children almost grown. Your hearts have not hardened to the realities of the world. Your dreams have not fallen through your fingers. You still know hope."

"We are not children," I said, my voice shaking with a sudden anger. "We have both left everything we've ever known. My parents lied to me and Cyan's fear her." Cyan flinched, and I felt a stab of guilt at my words. But anger spurred me on. "My first love is dead because of me. Cyan has seen horrible things in people's minds. Don't call us children."

She held her hands up in amused supplication, the ghost of a smile playing about her lips. "To me, you are children, and you would be if you were wrinkled as grandparents. I have lived a hundred lives. I have lost my love many, many times, and sometimes in ways far worse than either of you could ever imagine."

"Please." The word tore from my mouth, ragged as a shard of glass. "What do you want from us?"

"We have to stop the man who wants to take away what has begun to flourish again. To kill the Alder's dreams."

"Not the dreams of all the Alder," I muttered.

"No. Not all of them," she agreed. "Not the Kashura.

They considered the Chimaera an abomination. A man is forming his plan. And he will eradicate the new Chimaera. Like you," Anisa said.

"Who is this man?" I asked.

"I do not know. He hides from me."

"We're not Chimaera," Cyan said, gesturing to her body. "We're human. We have no horns like that creature in your vision."

"You know little of how the world was." She held out her hand and created an illusion. An image of an Alder appeared, hovering over her hand. Long limbs, large eyes, no hair. "The Alder made humans first." A little human appeared over her other hand.

"Why?" I asked.

"As slaves."

My breath hitched in my throat.

"But humans were weak. They lived a few scant years, succumbed to illness. Some Alder decided to make beings that were more like themselves. And so they created Chimaera. But what has been lost to history is that there were two strains of Chimaera." She balled her hands into fists and the little Alder and human disappeared. She held open her palms again. A creature who looked not quite human and not quite Alder appeared on one hand. The proportions were almost human, but the eyes too big, the cheekbones too high, the lips too small. On the other hand was a damselfly, a self-portrait in miniature.

"They made Chimaera who looked human, the Anthi, and who looked hybrid, the Theri. The Anthi came first, and in them the Alder instilled abilities like they had.

Now, when your historians study ancient statues and see one with no scales, no wings, no horns, they think, 'they must be human, and not Chimaera,' but there were Anthi with abilities and power, and the odd Theri with none."

"So I'm not human?" Cyan gasped.

"I do not know," she said gently. "You two are different. The Anthi looked similar to me." She gestured to the little illusion hovering over her palm and then at her longer neck, her high cheekbones. "But I was not privy to the Alder's secrets. None of the Chimaera or humans were.

"And so you will help me stop him, for there is not much I can do." She indicated at her insubstantial body.

"And why should we?" I asked.

"Why, I should think that would be obvious. For he will come for you, too."

I swallowed. Cyan turned gray.

"So what should we do?"

"For now, nothing. He has not started yet. But when the time is right, you will know. And I can only hope you fare better than Matla and I, all those years ago. I am glad I called to you." She nodded. "You will help me. And all will be well."

"Called to us?" I asked, dread like a stone in my stomach.

"Surely you guessed, little Kedi?"

The air left my lungs. "Guessed?"

"Do you know why you went down to the beach that night, the night you found the circus?"

"Because... I love the ocean," I said, faltering.

"I called to you and you heard me. It was soft as a whisper, but you felt it. I thought you would come to me, that first night in the circus, but you came to me the next night. You were so frightened."

I was sure I was more frightened now. I backed away from her, my breath gasping in and out.

"And me?" Cyan asked, faint.

"Oh, one who was Matla, I sensed you from afar as your powers grew. Who do you think sent you the dream of the lion tamer?"

She clapped her hands over her ears. "No! I don't want to hear you anymore. I don't know what to believe. I don't know what is real. Go away!"

I darted forward, clutching the disc in shaking hands. "Stop sending us dreams and visions without warning. Stop speaking in riddles. Or I won't call you out, and I won't help you."

"Oh, but you will, little Kedi." She smiled beatifically. "You will."

I pressed the button savagely. She disappeared, and I went to Cyan. She folded into my arms, and I held her as she cried. "I'm sorry," I said, over and over. "I'm so sorry."

22
THE NIGHT OF THE DEAD

"On the Night of the Dead, the dead come out to play.
On the cold, dark wind of winter, they come to stay,
They whisper to remind us before the light of day:
You will join us one day."
    Elladan children's rhyme about the Night of the Dead

Blissful routine followed over the next few weeks, and I sank into it gratefully.

Mornings were for magic lessons, early afternoons for constructing the apparatuses and costumes, and late afternoons were for séance work. I cemented my role as a stagehand. If both Cyan and I were at the same table during a séance, visions plagued us, though we broke physical contact before they could take hold. Anisa kept her visions away, or so we thought, but all Vestige seemed to contain echoes of their past. Whenever we went to Twisting the Aces, I avoided the whispers just out of earshot that came from the display cabinet. We returned the Augur to its rightful place as I began to feel uneasy around it. As far as we knew, Maske never knew we had temporarily borrowed it. Even the Glamour felt uncomfortable next to my skin, and I was glad I didn't have to wear it as often anymore.

Cyan and I agreed not to talk about what happened between us in her room. It reminded us too painfully of our differences, and the fact that we had no idea what Anisa planned. We focused on the stage magic to distract ourselves from the real kind.

But that did not mean that thoughts did not plague me. Scattered among the many magic books in Maske's study were a fair few about ancient magic and antiquities. I had never looked at them – too afraid of what I might discover, perhaps. But I couldn't keep running away. I took down a book by an author I recognized: Professor Mikael Primrose, the husband of the famous Lady Primrose, on etiquette.

After the long days of study and work, I studied more, pouring over the dense text. We knew so little. Already from Anisa's visions I had a clearer context of the relationships between the Alder and the Chimaera and what life for them was like. Already I knew that Vestige was far more powerful than we had ever dreamed.

Professor Primrose still taught me a thing or two. He held many postulations on Penglass – that it was created from the same substance as their ships, which I could confirm from my vision of Anisa in the garden. He thought that the Alder had left and taken the Chimaera with them, and that humans chose to stay. But soon after they left, a tragedy had struck the earth. Smoke scorched the sky and most of the world drowned beneath the waves. I had the feeling that the Alder had still been involved in that in some way.

For though I knew more than most about Chimaera, the Alder were still an enigma. Many times, I considered asking Anisa, but I still feared her and feared what she would ask of me in return for her answers. Everything seemed to have a price.

I dreamed of that ancient Lindean forest many nights, but I did not think Anisa sent the dreams to me. In them, I loved the forest, with its primordial feeling of age and power and life. I prowled through the jungle on all fours, content that I was the king of my domain. Nothing could hunt me.

Maske came in late one afternoon after going to the auctioneers to sell another of his precious Vestige automata. He showed it to us before he left – a mermaid, her skin a luminous brown, her hair cropped close to her skull, and eyes dark as coal. Her neck had little gills, and small fins sprouted on the backs of her forearms and along her spine. The mermaid's tail was an emerald green, and she wore a heavy necklace of shells and stone that did not quite cover her breasts. Maske said that if he switched the lever on her back she could swim underwater, but Maske did not wish to use any more power before selling her, not even to see her swim one last time.

"She's lovely," I said.

"So she is," Maske said, stroking her face with the back of a fingernail before wrapping her in cloth and sliding her into the case. "Another woman I've abandoned, eh?" He said it with a smile cracked with sadness.

"What do Taliesin's automata look like?" I asked, remembering him mentioning that he'd never sold those. Maske hesitated, but in the end he came down with a little tortoise. I could tell it was not Vestige – the limbs were articulated, and I could see the seams between the painted tin of the shell. When he switched it on, it moved well enough, though jerkily, and I could hear the mechanisms within. It was still a clever bit of machinery. With a sigh, Maske tucked Taliesin's tortoise away and left for the pawnshop.

When he returned, no sadness remained. He held a letter aloft as he entered the library where Cyan, Drystan and I were having biscuits and tea as we studied.

He placed the creamy sheet of paper on the table between us. His face was flushed, flakes of snow on his coat and hat.

"We have an invitation to our first séance and private magic show of note," he said, nearly bouncing on his heels like an excited child.

We had performed a few séances, small ones for Maske's more regular clients. Cyan had proved a great success. Evidently word travelled fast, or perhaps the Collective of Magic had a hand in it. They were doing everything they could to push publicity for our duel – printing lithographic posters and taking out ads in the newspapers for an event that was still two months away.

"Of note?" Cyan echoed.

"Look."

I read the invitation:

Mr Jasper Maske and his Marionettes:
You are cordially invited to entertain with a night of

*séance and magic at the residence of Lord and Lady
Elmbark on the 21st of Dalan, the Night of the Dead.
Kindly provide your response by week's end.*

   Cordially yours,
   Mr Edgar Nautica, Head Butler of the Elmbark Residence

"Wow," I breathed. "The Elmbarks are a prestigious family." Cyan looked at me blankly, but Drystan's jaw muscles tightened. I felt similar to Drystan. I had once dined at the Elmbark residence with my parents and Cyril after going to the opera in Imachara.

But I remembered the Hornbeams were much friendlier with the Elmbarks. Drystan had probably been to their estate in the Emerald Bowl. He would have played with their son, Harry, who was about the same age. Harry's younger brother, Tomas, was Cyril's age.

"Who else will be there?" Drystan asked, his voice terse.

"I asked the messenger about the guest list and, with but a small parting of coin, he was happy to gossip." A small smile of triumph curled on Maske's lips.

"Oh, was he now?" Cyan asked, delighted. Drystan and I, by contrast, clutched the edges of the table in dread.

"The Lord and Lady Elmbark will be inviting some very important guests: Lady Rowan, Lord Cinnabari, Lady Laurus, and the Royal Physician himself, who has just returned from abroad. A few others as well, but the man did not remember the names."

My eyes burned – I was so surprised I had not blinked.

"I can't go," I said.

Drystan stared at me in mutual horror.

"But you have to go!" Maske said. "The séance we have works only with all three of you. And this is essential for us – Taliesin has never performed for them as far as I am aware."

"There's a slight issue with the fact that one of the attending members of the séance is my mother," I said, teeth gritted.

Maske jerked his head back in surprise. "Oh."

Cyan sent me a wordless wave of concern and comfort, tinged with her own surprise.

Maske's shoulders slumped. "They're offering us two hundred gold marks. That's enough to last us months, plus buy the materials we need for the finale. We can't turn this down."

"Two *hundred* gold marks?" Cyan echoed. I felt the same. Our cut would be almost enough to buy false papers, though Drystan and I had not mentioned leaving Ellada for months, now. I think we both still hoped that it wouldn't come to that.

Maske sat up straighter. "Micah, you will be behind the scenes. Behind the walls."

"Behind the walls?" I asked.

"Lots of older houses have space behind the walls for servants to get around the rooms. Or for people who shouldn't be there to make a… discreet escape."

Cyan laughed. "Shocking."

"Not particularly. Nobles are as twisted and devious as you'd expect." Drystan drawled.

"Well, I've only you two to judge on, so obviously that's true." She wrinkled her nose.

"Who, little old me? Noble? How amusing," he said.

Cyan goaded him to try and learn more about him, but he never cracked, though he let the fake small town accent fade gradually. In turn, she stayed well out of his mind as far as I could tell.

I did not join in their levity. Panic fluttered in my stomach. "It's still very risky, for me to go. If Drystan or I are recognized, that's the end of your duel, Maske."

Maske rubbed his chin. "That is a point. Damnation. But think of it this way. The nobility are our prime clientele. I can charge a noble family ten times what I charge a working class family for the same séance. If you're to stay a magician you'll always be rubbing shoulders with the nobility. Who better to test your disguises with than those who have the most chance to recognize you? They asked us. Not Taliesin." He grinned, his teeth white and sharp. I knew it was the thrill of the gamble that excited him. The threat of discovery made the prospect all the sweeter.

"That they didn't," I said.

We asked for an advance on our wages, which Maske reluctantly gave us, and we bought false identity papers, hiding them in the loft. If we were discovered, we'd make a run for it. Maske was the one who put us in contact with the man for the papers. I know he hoped we'd never have to use them. So did I.

In the end, Maske won the gamble, or at least partly. Drystan and Cyan would wear their disguises and stay in the limelight. And in the séance, as with the magic duel, I would stay out of sight in the shadows.

Come what may.

• • •

It was the night before Lady's Long Night. The Night of the Dead.

We rode in the carriage, the curtains drawn tight against the cold. We huddled beneath the blankets, but our breath still misted in the air as the driver took us through the winding cobbled streets of Imachara.

Cyan wore her black Elladan dress with a Temnian silk sash. In her bag was the dark veil for the séance and silver paint for her face. In addition to the Glamour, Drystan's eyes were darkened with kohl and he wore a suit with a Temnian silk cravat.

I was dull in an all-black suit, black gloves, and I would wear a black knitted sock over my head, with two holes cut for the eyes. Invisible.

As we rode, I berated myself, trying to clamp down my unruly nerves. All I could think of was that somehow my mother would see me and would recognize me and drag me back to Sicion. She would find a way to explain away the scandal and try to have me engaged or married off by summer's end.

We pulled up to the apartments on a rich street of the Gilt Quarter of Imachara – Amber Dragon. I had spent much of my life on streets as sparkling clean as this one. Statues graced every corner, the streets lit by the sodium yellow of gaslight, and the turrets of the buildings topped with oxidized copper.

We exited the carriage. The cold wind nipped at our fingers and ears, its teeth finding its way beneath our coat collars. I pulled my coat up higher against the stinging snow. The doorman gazed at us disdainfully as he gestured us inside.

The lobby was a mirror image of my old apartment building in Sicion. Both of them had been built during the Astrid era, two hundred years ago. Our shoes clacked along the granite floor. When we knocked on the door to the Elmbarks' suites on the top floor, the butler welcomed Cyan, Drystan, and Maske to the foyer and, with a knowing wink, ushered me to the hidden entrance behind the wall. Maske and the butler shook hands, and I knew Maske would have slipped a coin into his palm. A token payment for continuing our ruse.

Part of me wanted to sneak back to the Kymri Theatre and not have to spend a long evening staring at the woman who used to be my mother. The woman who had convinced my father that surgery was my only hope for a normal future. She had raised me to be ashamed of what I was, banning me from telling my closest friends to avoid even the hint of scandal.

But I could not let the others down, and so I crept along the dusty corridors behind the walls. Magicians, spies, or jealous lovers had already been here, for there were little peepholes in the walls. The room was bedecked in Night of the Dead memorabilia, the walls draped in black velvet, white wax candles illuminating the carved fauns and fairies of the wooden columns to either side of the stage.

Guests trickled in over the course of the next half hour, ignoring Cyan and Drystan at their posts on the stage but greeting Maske. My breath caught when I saw my mother and Cyril. My mother smiled, a cat with the cream at being included at such a prominent evening. But her face was thinner, the lines about her mouth and eyes deeper. Her nose and cheeks were flushed with the rosacea of drinking, even through the powder. She always enjoyed her wine a bit too much, but I could tell her penchant had grown. Her hair was a different shade of brown; she dyed it to cover the gray. I could not believe how much she had changed in so few months.

My brother, in contrast, was the picture of good health. He was taller, his face somehow more mature, as if he had settled into his features. His fair hair curled over his ears. I smiled to see him. I had a note in my pocket I'd have to find a way to give to him, so that we could meet tomorrow.

The Lord and Lady Elmbark were both dressed in somber gray with matching necklaces of bird bones and feathers. Lady Elmbark wore preserved bats' wings in her hair. The Elmbarks loved anything to do with the macabre and always dressed and behaved as if one foot were already in the grave. A tall man with a trimmed mustache and beard and a finely tailored brown suit stood next to them, a bright feather boutonniere on his suit coat as if to deliberately clash with their solemn apparel. He wore a small, derisive smile that reminded me of Drystan's – as if he knew the punch line to some amusing jest that none of the rest of us could hear. He must be the Royal Physician, whose true name very few knew. It was safer that those trusted to be so close to the crown – the Royal Physician, the Royal Taste Tester – went by their title, to protect their identity and families. A few faces registered: Lord Wesley Cinnabari, Lady Rowan, Lady Ashvale, and several others.

I was not sure why my mother and brother were here. My father often came to Imachara in winter for the partners' meeting and seasonal party, but most years we stayed home. The Lauruses held a good standing among the nobility, but these were all families closest to the Snakewood throne.

Soon, the Elmbarks led their guests to the dining room. Drystan would entertain with close-up magic. Cyan remained in the parlor, preparing the séance. I wondered how many of the Elmbarks' guests were cynics or believers.

I snuck further down the walls, hoping to spy on the dinner. In my mind, Cyan asked me to send her anything that might be useful for her séance.

Through another peephole, I saw the guests sitting about the black draped table. A gramophone played eerie, appropriate music. Candles flickered, the only source of light. Unfortunately, I was right by the gramophone, so it was difficult to hear what anyone said to each other. As they ate their lavish meal, Drystan entertained them with prestidigitation. I found myself unable to concentrate on his patter as he amused the audience, distracted by his long fingers and the tilt of his smile as he performed the tricks.

I blinked, forcing myself to concentrate and deduce who was most impressed by his magic. Though I could barely hear it, Drystan told a story about a young jack who fell in love with a queen despite the jealous king, cutting the deck and drawing up the relevant card at just the right moment in the story. I found myself smiling as I watched him. The jack disguised himself as the queen's joker and they ran away together. Drystan had invented the trick.

He made coins appear from behind ears and produced endless falling blossoms for the Lady Rowan, who blushed like a maid. He had people choose cards and made them appear in different places about the room, or he levitated and threw them onto the ceiling, where they stayed for the rest of the meal. By the end of his entertainment, people had stopped eating and were watching him in awe. The man in the brown suit clapped just as hard as the rest of them, though his eyes narrowed as though he were trying to figure out the method behind the tricks. I noticed he still wore his white gloves. When Drystan gave a last flourish and left, talk resumed and people finally remembered the food in front of them.

Lord Wesley was especially impressed. I heard him exclaiming to Lady Rowan – who wore one of Drystan's paper blossoms in her hair – that he had never seen such a display. I tried to eavesdrop some more, but the music was too loud. I snuck back to the parlor, sticking my head out of the concealed door.

Cyan and Drystan were murmuring to each other. Cyan saw me first. "Stars and sky! You startled me."

I grinned. "You did an amazing job, Drystan."

He gave me a little bow. "Why thank you, thank you."

"Need any help setting up for the séance?" I asked.

"Nay," Cyan said. "Not yet. After the Vestige demonstration, though."

Her eyes grew unfocused. "Oi! They're coming!"

I closed the door behind me, setting my eye back to the peephole. All too soon, my lower back cramped and my stomach rumbled. As the guests went back into the room, I rummaged in my pack and ate some cheese, nuts, and dried fruit. I smiled – I was a little mouse behind the walls, eavesdropping on the big cats of Imachara.

Cyril conversed with Tomas Elmbark about starting their studies at the Royal Snakewood University next summer, their conversation the stilted words of childhood friends who realized they no longer have anything in common.

The Royal Physician spoke with Lady Ashvale about hunting in the Emerald Bowl. The physician said he was looking forward to going back to his estates, but that he did not think the hunting could compare to the great cats of the Lindean jungle. I remembered my dream and shivered.

My mother's earlier jovial mood vanished. She kept looking at the door as though she wished she could leave. She had no great love for magic tricks or the supernatural.

Her profile was turned toward the only window not covered by dark velvet. I remembered when we were young, during a summer at the Emerald Bowl, she told us to count the stars outside our window until we fell asleep, since we could not do it in Sicion with all its city lights. I closed my eyes against the sudden pang of homesickness. Had I taken a different fork in the road, I'd be a guest of this party, possibly, murmuring with my brother and Tomas, waiting for the séance to begin. My legs would be crossed demurely, with less between them, the scars from the surgery healed. The physical ones, anyway.

Lord and Lady Elmbark began with a brief Vestige demonstration. Almost all nobles had a collection to rival the Mechanical Museum of Antiquities, except for my family. My mother had tried to convince my father to let her collect, but he always felt the money would be better put to use elsewhere. Like saving for that surgery, perhaps. To me, it always seemed a bit foolhardy to blithely show guests one's most valuable possessions. But I was curious all the same.

The butler unfurled a tapestry, though perhaps tapestry was the wrong word, for it was not woven, but made of Vestige fabric that did not decay like wool or cotton. It had been painted or stained with Chimaera – centaurs, angels, and other beings. I even spied a damselfly woman. As the butler rolled the tapestry away, I thought I caught sight of another figure hiding behind her – a creature with green skin and horns. Before I could blink, the tapestry was back in its canister, and I was left with more questions that I could not answer.

Next, the butler pulled out a small hand harp. He ran his fingertips along the strings. They made the high, pure sounds of a finger dancing along a wine glass's edge. The haunting melody lingered in the air before fading.

After setting aside the harp to muted applause, he brought forth a cloth-wrapped globe. I thought it would be a glass globe of a rare color – deep purple, for instance – but when he pulled away the silk, I muffled a gasp with my hand. Inside the glass was a flower similar to a rose, though its blossom was more bell-shaped. Its petals were a brilliant turquoise that darkened to blue-black at the tips. The now-extinct flower was preserved at the height of its beauty for all eternity.

The next item was an oval mirror framed with shimmering Vestige metal. But when someone looked into it, they did not see their reflection, but the vision of a beach, waves lapping across white sand. It reminded me of the Mirror of Moirai we stole from Shadow Elwood.

Lastly, the butler showcased the automaton collection. All noble families had them. Even mother had convinced father to let her buy just one – a little sleeping baby poking out from the spiral shell on its back, like a hermit crab. My breath caught once again. The Elmbarks possessed an impressive collection, but I recognized the mermaid with the emerald green fin and close-cropped hair that Maske had sold. Maske's smile remained fixed upon his face, but his eyes did not leave the mermaid.

His show ended and our show for some of the noblest faces in Imachara would soon begin. The Collective of Magic had a hand in our invitation, but that did not mean I was not nervous at how the séance would be received.

The guests drank aperitifs and ate little desserts of cream-filled pastries. I nibbled more fruits and nuts, but my stomach rumbled and I thought longingly of the mooncakes we had back at the Kymri Theatre.

I was distracted from my hunger as the guests left the room so it could be prepared for the séance. I ducked out from my hiding place and helped fold the chairs and put them back in the storage cupboard behind a fold of black velvet. We set up the round table for the séance and draped it with more black velvet before topping it with the Vestige crystal ball. Cyan went to the washroom and returned with the black veil over her head. The guests came back to a transformed room. The winter wind shrieked against the windows, rattling the glass.

The guests took their places about the table, and then Cyan stepped forward, a sadness that could not be contained emanating from her. A servant turned on the gramophone in the corner and it filled the room with soft, mournful horns.

Cyan sat at the head of the table, gathering her skirts about her.

"Good evening, fair sirs and ladies," she said with a Temri accent. "I welcome you to our humble séance."

She lifted the dark veil from her face, revealing silver swirls painted across her forehead, a crescent moon and stars in the center. With a start, I realized that the glyphs echoed Anisa's facial tattoos. The Royal Physician narrowed his eyes at her, as though he recognized the symbols. I wish she had told me what she planned, as I would have dissuaded her. However, the result was undeniably haunting. She looked like a Chimaera ghost. She looked like Anisa.

"Please join hands so we may find you the answers you seek from beyond the grave. I have lost all of my family, all of my childhood friends, and my one true love. All were taken from me too soon by death. In return, death saw fit to let me peek beyond the veil and share what I know. To let others have the solace I cannot find." Her voice thickened, and tears slid down her face.

The Royal Physician joined hands, but he still wore his gloves.

"Please remove your gloves, esteemed sir," Cyan said. "The skin-to-skin contact of the living strengthens the bond to the other side."

"Alright," the doctor said, amused, taking off his gloves. His wore a small gold ring on his left pinkie finger that glinted in the candlelight.

But his right hand...

I had seen a clockwork woman's head at the Museum of Antiquities last year with Aenea. The hand looked as though it could have matched, though the hand was masculine and the head had been feminine. Clockwork gears and pistons shone a dull brass, the hand covered with a substance that could be mistaken for skin but for the fact it was transparent. He flexed the hand, a sardonic smile on his face as everyone about the table gaped, open-mouthed. It moved as smoothly as any human hand.

Who was he, to have such a priceless piece of Vestige for a hand, and where had he found it?

Cyan was at a loss for words.

What can you glean about him? I thought at her. The Royal Physician was not in the public eye much, so I knew next to nothing about him. Sometimes the Royal Physician gave lectures or went on research sabbatical, but most of his time was spent looking after the ailments of the royal family.

Not a thing, which is strange. This house is full of Vestige and I can hear the others as clear as a bell. She frowned.

The physician studied Cyan as if he found her fascinating.

You've been silent too long, I told her

"Lord Elmbark, please grasp the Royal Physician's wrist above his... hand, and we will proceed." Lord Elmbark gingerly touched the skin above the physician's clockwork hand.

The illusion of mystique had briefly shattered, but Cyan fell back into character.

"Please. Give me the name of a beloved you have lost to the dark currents of the River Styx."

Silence. And then: "Robbie," Lady Ashvale said. Her son

had drowned in the Jade River, the river that ran through the Emerald Bowl.

"Close your eyes, Lady Ashvale," Cyan said, and the table gasped that she commanded her so plainly. "Close your eyes and think of young Robbie. Remember what he looked like and sounded like. Everything about him. A mother's heart never forgets."

Lady Ashvale gave a small sob. Cyan kept her eyes closed. "Come, Robbie Ashvale. I call upon thee. Your mother is here. Come back and visit, just for a time." She waited for a moment as I grabbed my props from the bag. "Robbie, are you here? If so, please give us a sign."

I rang the bell, and everyone at the table jumped except for the Royal Physician, Maske, and Lady Rowan.

"Robbie?"

I rang the bell again and tapped my fists against the walls, like footprints.

"Robbie, will you share your story with me? Will you let me see?"

Another ringing bell.

Cyan tilted her head back. "I see Robbie. He is seven – the age he was when he was taken from you. He remembers drowning, that it was so cold. He remembers you trying to wake him. He was standing right next to you, but you could not hear him or see him.

"Age beyond the veil has no meaning. Now he is a young boy of ten, the age he would be now. He's sprouting like a weed. I see him as a youth of fifteen. He is so very handsome, the dark hair falling into his blue eyes. Now, he is a grown man.

"He is that age, the prime of his life, after death. He misses you. He loves you. But he is happy. And he says soon he will travel down the River and join the world of the living again."

She opened her eyes, and I thought I caught a flash of cobalt blue. I shuddered and shook my head. It felt like such a cheap ruse, to take the images of a grieving mother's son and weave a web of lies.

Yet Lady Ashvale was crying with relief and heartbreak. Normally, in noble gatherings, such a display of emotion would be unseemly. But not here in the circle of the séance. These were the words she wanted to hear. Now, she could imagine her son, grown and happy and waiting for new life.

"Who else has lost?"

"I... I am not sure if I have," Lady Laurus said. My breath caught in my throat. My mother's voice quavered, and in the dim light of the candles she looked even more worn and wan.

Cyan nodded. "I know of whom you speak."

She's thinking of you.

I know.

What do you want me to say?

I took a shuddering breath. And I thought the words at Cyan, who spoke them to my mother.

"The one who you miss is lost but not gone, this much I know. She has not passed into the currents of the River Styx. But she is dreaming at the moment, and so the spirits can sense her."

"Where is she?" my mother whispered.

"The spirits choose not to say. But they do say... that she is safe."

"Will I... ever see her again?" There was stark hope in her voice. I doubled over behind the walls, my eyes stinging with tears.

Will she?

I don't know. I don't know.

Cyan said her own words. "You might. She has her own journey to follow. It may lead her back to you, or it may lead her somewhere else. But I hope that you find her again, my lady."

My mother bowed her head, not speaking, and behind my wall I cried silently into the sleeve of my suit. I should hate her. She tried to change my life for me without giving me a say. At every turn she tried to make me someone I was not. But I could never hate the woman who raised me.

One by one, the members of the table asked for a message from the dead, all save Maske and the man with the clockwork hand.

"I've said all I wanted to say to those I have lost," were the physician's only remarks. I wondered if that were true. By that point, my tears had dried into stiff tracks on my cheeks.

Cyan performed beautifully, perhaps too beautifully. She plucked the details from their minds, molding them to the tale they wanted and creating the illusion of what life was like after death. A world much like ours, but softer around the edges, like a dream. The dead could shift their realities, and time and pain left no mark. Religious Elladans believed that the dead rested in the afterlife before coming back to the world for another life. But if the Lord and Lady felt they had lived their lives with sin and evil, then Styx kept them submerged in darker currents for longer.

I flitted behind the walls, adding the sound effects as needed.

She should have not been so detailed. If they knew what she was really doing, they would lock her in prison. Or put her into a hospital and examine her. Just as they would do with me.

At the end of the séance, she asked all of the spirits to congregate in the center of the table to prepare to return to the spirit world through the crystal ball. The servants blew out more of the candles. In the near darkness, I sneaked from the hidden wall and crouched between Cyan and Maske, reaching through their legs to wobble the table. If we'd been able to take our mechanized table from the Kymri Theatre, I wouldn't have needed to leave my hiding place, but it was too heavy to move. People gasped. The center of the table had a hole so I could reach up and switch the lever at the bottom of the crystal ball. It glowed blue, a cheap trick rather than true Vestige. Cyan chanted in Temri, and the glow faded.

Before I retreated, I crept around to Cyril and slipped a note into the pocket of his blazer. But as I left, the physician's elbow grazed me. He looked down and met my eyes.

I felt a visceral shock. We stared at each other in an impasse. He turned from me, letting me scurry back to the wall, with the rest of the séance none the wiser.

I darted behind the wall and glanced through the peephole, shivering at the near miss.

Tears still slid down Lady Ashvale's cheeks, and other eyes were wet.

Cyan, I thought. *In the future, I think you should tone it down. You've really upset them.*

I know! I know. Her thoughts were frantic. *I thought I was helping them.*

Maybe you are in the long run. In the short term, they are heartbroken. And remember, we're using them for our own gain, too.

As they left, they took a moment to thank Cyan, holding her hand, sliding extra coins into her palm. She thanked them with a grave incline of her head. The Royal Physician was effusive, saying it was a marvelous performance. She shook her head haughtily at him. "It was far more than a performance," she said, her voice sharp.

"Ah, but of course."

Lord and Lady Elmbark took Maske, Cyan, and Drystan into the other room to settle payment.

"I'll be just a moment," he said, pulling his gloves back on slowly. "And meet you in the hall. I wish to ruminate on the séance if it's not too much trouble."

"You're never trouble, Doctor," Lady Elmbark demurred. "Thank you for coming, and we'll see you at your lecture next week."

"It will be a pleasure."

When they left, he finished tugging on his gloves.

"Well," he said. "You can come out now, if you wish."

Bollocks.

"Just want to say a quick hello and congratulate you on a job well done. I almost did not see you."

If I stayed silent, would he leave me alone?

He waited, patiently staring at where I was hiding. He wasn't going to give up.

Resigned, I took a breath and opened the hidden door and peeked around it.

"Hello there," he said. He squinted at me. "I assume you're there under that mask."

I coughed, embarrassed, and feeling unsure why I had come out from behind the walls. Curiosity. Idiocy.

Quicker than I expected, he darted toward me and pulled off the mask. His eyes flashed with recognition, and I realized my error too late.

"I thought so. Nice to finally meet you, Iphigenia."

I froze.

He held out his hand and he said the words that, somehow, I almost expected. "I believe you know who I am. I am the Royal Physician of Imachara. My name is Doctor Samuel Pozzi."

23
THE DOCTOR

"The Royal Physician of Ellada is one of the most esteemed positions. The doctor, when in residence, attends to the royal family in all of their health needs. Sometimes, the physician is called abroad to oversee important medical developments to take back for the good of the citizens of Ellada. Often, Royal Physicians have known more about the royals than even their closest advisers, and have therefore become advisers in turn."

A HISTORY OF ELLADA AND ITS COLONIES, Professor
Caed Cedar, Royal Snakewood University

I stumbled backward. The physician held out his hand. "Wait."

"What do you want?" My eyes flashed to the door, hoping Drystan or the others would come through.

"I want to speak with you. We have much to discuss, do we not?" His voice was clipped and perfectly articulated.

"How do you feel about pretending you never saw me,

don't know who I am, and I just go on my merry way?" I hid behind the sarcasm, but the quiver in my words gave me away.

He laughed.

"I'm not out to capture you, Iphigenia."

"That's not my name."

"No, it isn't any longer, is it? Alright then. Micah."

Styx. "How do you know who I am?"

"A little birdie whispered in my ear."

The gears fell into place. "You. You're the second client of the Shadow."

"And which Shadow would that be?" He smiled and tilted his head, as if confused.

"Shadow Elwood."

"Ah, yes. He found you for me. I wasn't planning on meeting you, until I realized you'd be here tonight."

"What do you want?"

He shook his head. "You're not acting very ladylike."

"Never did. Caused my mother a lot of grief."

"The Lady Laurus. It must have been difficult, seeing her here tonight."

"You don't know how I feel." I sounded so surly, but I could not help it. The man who gave me to my parents had appeared out of nowhere like a ghost. Shock knocked all manners aside.

He rubbed the back of his neck with his false hand. "This is not going well."

"You're being enigmatic. I don't like enigmatic people. Why'd you hire a Shadow to spy on me?"

"No nefarious reason, I assure you. I was merely curious

to see how you have been doing. You were my charge, and I felt responsible. When I discovered you ran away, I wanted to find out why, and see how I could help."

I narrowed my eyes. Help? He had given me to strangers and never taken an interest in me. Why now?

"Did you find out why I ran away from the Lauruses?" I asked.

"No, I did not."

"They were going to operate on me." I gestured to the general vicinity. "Make me more... marriageable."

His mouth dropped open. "They would not dare."

"I overheard them and left the day before they scheduled it."

"I would never have allowed that."

"Who are you to allow anything? You gave me to strangers and you threw dice with my life." The words came out in a hiss.

"I'd say the dice rolled in your favor, young Micah. You were raised in comfort and safety, until your parents acted against my express wishes. Would you rather I had left you with paupers?"

The anger left me in a shaking rush. I sounded quite the spoiled brat. But I still wanted answers, and I still did not trust the man standing across from me.

I heard the murmur of voices through the walls, coming closer.

"We need to speak privately, and soon," Doctor Pozzi said. "We have much to discuss."

My mouth tightened. "What's so important?"

"It's about your health. I need to make sure you're developing normally."

My breath caught in my throat. Developing… normally? The voices grew loud enough that Doctor Pozzi could hear them.

"Come see me the night after Lady's Long Night. I am staying on Ruby Street. Number 12G. It's the top window to the left of the ivy trellis."

"Oh yes. I'm on the run from the policiers so I'll just wander onto the street where the constabulary headquarters are. If this is an attempt at a trap, it's pretty blatant."

"No trap. This I swear to you. Come now, you've shown you're quite adept at not being seen when you wish." He smiled.

"Not good enough," I muttered.

The doctor grabbed my arm and drew me close to him. I could feel the coldness of his clockwork hand through his glove and my sleeve. He had dark eyes, his skin tanned from countless days in the sun. "I'll leave the window by the trellis unlocked," he whispered. "You have to come."

"Why?" I whispered.

"It's one reason I had to find you. Because you might be ill. You might be dying."

And Maske, Cyan, and Drystan walked back into the parlor to see me fainting into a boneless heap on the floor.

I dipped in and out of consciousness as they took me back to the Kymri Theatre. Up in the loft, Drystan removed my coat and shoes. I was in his bed rather than my own. I stared at the ceiling, focusing on my body. Was I ill? I did not feel as though I was dying. Not so much as a cold had troubled me. I did not know what Doctor Pozzi meant, and I did not know if I could trust him. But I needed answers.

And I had now fainted or nearly fainted three times, when before that, I'd never fainted in my life. A tiny corner of my mind wondered if he was right.

Drystan came in, visibly relieved when he saw I was awake. "What happened?"

"The Royal Physician."

He frowned. "What about him? What did he do?"

"He's Doctor Pozzi, the man who gave me to my parents. And he was the second client of Shadow Elwood."

"Styx."

"Yeah."

"What does he want?"

I told him.

"Are you going to go?"

"Do I have any choice?" He didn't threaten me, but if I didn't go, he knew who I was, where I worked, where I lived.

I rubbed my temples. I decided not to tell him what Doctor Pozzi had said about my health. I had no proof. And, truth be told, I could not say "I might be dying" aloud.

"Do you want me to come with you?" he asked.

I nodded. "Not into his house, but if you were nearby, it would be a comfort."

"Of course." He settled into the bed, wrapping an arm around me.

"Considering how often we're sleeping in each other's beds, maybe we should push them together."

He made an affirmative noise against my hair. "Tomorrow. Can't be bothered tonight."

"Agreed."

The strong, steady beating of his heart lulled me to sleep.

24
LADY'S LONG NIGHT

"Once there was a prince who was very cruel. The king and queen lived in fear of him. Though nearly grown, he was prone to tantrums and violence. One day he went hunting in the woods and came upon a lovely nymph. He ordered her to be his lover, but she declined. He was enraged and took up his bow, meaning to shoot her.

She laughed instead, and the wooden bow grew leaves and branches and twined around his arms, pinning them to his sides. The nymph showed him his own cruelty in visions, until he wept and begged to be let go. But still she kept him pinned to the forest for a day and a night before making him promise that if he were ever cruel again, any scrap of wood around him would pin him and not let him go.

The prince came back to his land and ordered all wood to be burned and only stone and metal used. This proved to be difficult, but everyone did as he bade. He married a timid princess from a faraway land and was very cruel to her. One day she went into the woods to cry. The nymph found her, and gave her a wooden staff to bring back with her to the castle, asking her to leave it underneath the bed that night. She did, smuggling it into the city under her cloak, and the next morning, she awoke to find the prince pinned to the stone bed, no longer able to hurt anyone."

"The Cruel Prince and the Wooden Staff,"
HESTIA'S FABLES

The low gong of the doorbell tolled.

"I'll get it!" I cried, bounding down the stairs from the loft and dashing to the door. I dampened my enthusiasm long enough to check through the peephole that it was the guest I was expecting.

Earlier that afternoon, I had waited for Cyril at the spot I mentioned in my note, breaking into a smile when I saw him walking up the path of the park toward the fountain where I stood. We hadn't spoken properly since he'd come to the circus and tried to convince me to go home. He knew I was wanted by the law, but I hadn't been able to properly explain. So over a cup of coffee I'd told him about what really happened the night R.H. Ragona's Circus of Magic fell. Grief and guilt still hit me in the stomach. I would never forgive myself for the mistakes I had made. I would never forgive myself for Aenea, and for the clowns I hurt.

He'd understood, as I'd hoped he would, though I could tell he hurt for me, and realized that I was, in many ways, a completely different person from the sister he had climbed trees with. He in turn told me about what happened at home

– that mother drank more than ever and might be coming to Imachara for the "ladies' spa", the polite phrase for the Fir Tree Hospital for Women, which had two wings: an asylum and a treatment center.

"Is this my fault?" I gasped.

Cyril hesitated. "You may have been the catalyst, but it's not your fault. They knew what they planned to do to you, and they're the ones who chose to lie. Mother and Father haven't been getting along for some time now. It's her idea to go – to make sure she's better before she grows any worse."

He didn't try to convince me to come home with him again – he knew that home was broken. I decided to invite him around to the Kymri Theatre for Lady's Long Night, for levity and to put him at ease about my new life. Hopefully. I knew I could trust him with it – if there was anyone I trusted, it was Cyril, the brother who'd always been there for me.

Now, I threw open the door, dragged Cyril into the hallway and embraced him. He hugged me back. The others came into the foyer to greet us, and then gaped at me.

I wore a dress of cheap muslin. It felt strange to have skirts swishing around my ankles again. I bought it on the sly a few weeks ago, and decided that having my brother come to visit on Lady's Long Night was as good an excuse as any to dress up. I had even attempted a hair style with my shorn locks, though it ended up looking more like Lily Verre's, with bits escaping the pins and falling into my face.

"It's my sister!" Cyril exclaimed. "She's all grown up."

"I could still beat you in a fight and you know it."

"Oh yeah?"

"You know it. I've more muscles now." I strove for composure. "Cyril, these are the friends I live and work with. Well, you've already met them after a fashion. Jasper Maske is the head magician and our teacher. Cyan led the séance and is a magician, and Drystan is also a magician and, um, my good friend." I trailed off, blushing. Drystan's eyebrows rose, but he smiled. I fought the urge to shuffle my feet like a shy child.

"Pleased to make your acquaintance, Lord Laurus," Maske said, shaking hands.

"Please, call me Cyril."

Cyan gave my brother an approving look from the top of his head to his toes.

Hey! I thought at her. *You have your sailor.*

Sure I do. Doesn't mean I don't have eyes. I noticed him at the séance. You never told me you had such a handsome brother.

He's my brother!

She sent me a smirk, but kept her face pleasant as she held out her hand to Cyril. "Lovely to meet you. Again."

"You're not as frightening today."

She laughed. "I'm glad."

I shot a look at Drystan, who also gave me a smirk.

"Come in," I said, playing the host. "Are you going to spend Lady's Long Night with us?"

"If you'll have me. I told Mother and Father that I was going to the cathedral with Oswin."

"Wonderful! How is Oswin, by the way?" I asked as I led him to the kitchen while Maske made a pot of coffee.

"He's good. Engaged to Tara Cypress. They'll marry when he finishes university."

Engaged. So strange. Once, there had been talk of Oswin and I... but that would never happen now.

"Hah, he got into university?" I tried to make light of it. "Can't believe he passed his exams."

"It was a near thing."

We lapsed into silence as Maske poured the coffee into our cracked cups. I stirred my customary sugar and milk into it, but Cyril kept his black. My brother looked about with unabashed curiosity at my new surroundings.

Drystan kept sneaking glances at me.

"What?" I asked, resisting the urge to pat my hair.

"You look different."

"You've seen me in a dress before." I smoothed my hands down my skirts. "What, do I look silly?"

"Not at all," he said with a smile that warmed me straight through.

Normally, people exchanged presents right before they went to sleep on Lady's Long Night, but we opened ours before going to the cathedral, since Cyril would make his way home straight from there. We passed our wrapped parcels around. Cyril brought little presents of sweets for Maske, Cyan, and Drystan as well as me. He also gave me a stash of coins, which I protested but was secretly grateful for, and he brought some of the possessions I had left home without – some of my old Ephram Finnes novels and a new one to go with them, a blank leather-bound diary, my half-filled sketchpad, and my music sheets for the piano. I ran my fingers along my old possessions, half smiling. They were familiar, yet they did not feel as though they belonged to me at all.

Cyan gave me a preserved dragonfly cocoon from Temri, painted a bright blue and lined with gilt paint. I thanked her with a nod. I gave Cyan a pot of gold eye paint I had seen her linger over at a marketplace, and to Maske I gave – well, a mask. It reminded me of him, the Maske of Magic, made of black velvet embroidered with six-pointed stars, the thin crescent of a moon curling over an eye. He said that if we won the duel, he'd wear it for his first performance.

Drystan and I exchanged gifts last. He had been the most difficult person to find a present for. In the end, I gave him a small flute that sounded a bit like an owl's call, for he used to sometimes borrow Sayid's instruments and play at the fireside at the circus. I bought him the nicest I could afford, with little vines carved into the wood and colored with green enamel. His face lit up when he opened the case and I flushed with pleasure that he liked it.

When I opened his present, I felt as though I had offered him a lowly trinket. He gave me a necklace that was somehow neither masculine nor feminine, but just right for me. It was long enough that I could hide it underneath my clothing and was made of thin metal rectangles strung together. Each had an Alder word engraved on them, like "luck" and "faith" and "goodness" and… "love".

I blinked so that the others would not see the tears that marred my vision. Drystan seemed to understand. He put the necklace on me and it settled under my clothes. We finished our drinks and the cold metal of the necklace warmed against my skin.

We made our way down to the Celestial Cathedral as dusk fell. It was the night of the Penmoon, and so all of the Penglass glowed blue, tingeing the snow around us. I steeled myself against its wordless call. I tried to recall the glyph I had seen in the vision of Anisa and Matla, but though I could recall the general shape, the rest eluded me. Did Cyan remember? There were so many more secrets inside of them, I was sure of it, but perhaps it was for the best I didn't remember. I had enough mysteries.

On the long promenade that led down to the Snakewood Palace, floats draped with white fabric fluttered in the winter wind. Snowflakes danced from the clouds. We bustled through the crowds until we found a good view of the parade. Men and women dressed as Chimaera – angels, dragonkind, mermaids, and others – waved as the floats moved down the boulevard. They wore all white, as though frosted, the blue light of Penglass settling on them like a shawl.

Music drifted through the streets. Imachara was fragmented lately, with the rising Forester protests, but at that moment, any animosity faded away as the citizens listened to the flute music rising and falling with the whistle of the wind, mesmerized by the slow waving of the false Chimaera.

After the parade had made its way back to the Snakewood Palace, we went to the Celestial Cathedral, our feet sliding on the frosty pavement. It was the largest cathedral in the city; its spires of white and dark marble some of the tallest in the city.

I did not consider myself particularly religious, but there was something about sitting on a pew under such a high manmade ceiling, and seeing the monumental religious figures in the stained glass that made me feel so small. I liked the near silence, but for the low murmurs of a few prayers, or the shuffle of feet. Like holding one's breath.

The High Priest trundled onto the stage, awkward in his heavy white and gold vestments. He led the people in prayer, and I mumbled the verses along with the countless others around me. I lifted my eyes to the windows, wondering if the Lord and Lady heard our prayers.

The priest finished his sermon, and relinquished the stage to the choir. Two dozen men and women in dark blue robes embroidered with stars lifted their faces toward heaven and sang, their sweet voices reverberating throughout the cathedral. Drystan's hand found its way into mine. They sang of love of the night and the day, and how the darkness made the stars and moon shine that much brighter.

When the last note faded, the silence was absolute.

And then it shattered.

A keening wail echoed about the chambers, so loud that I clapped my hands to my ears. All the gas lights outside on the street and inside the cathedral extinguished, leaving only the glass globe chandelier bathing everyone in an unearthly glow. Outside, a loud voice asked all to gather around.

My hand still clasping Drystan's, I filed out with the others. Faces were tight with worry. Curiosity drove us forth.

Timur, the leader of the Foresters, stood on a makeshift podium in the square outside the Celestial Cathedral opposite the Royal Palace – the same square where Foresters had protested in the autumn. He waited, arms open, for us to gather below.

"Friends, welcome. I thank you for joining us on this most special occasion. The Long Night of the Lady." He gestured at the moon. "I apologize for interrupting your festivities. But the Long Night of the Lady marks a new beginning. The night grows shorter. The light wins against the battle of darkness, snow melting into the life of spring."

He gestured to his fellow Foresters fanned out behind him. Many of them had the look of bodyguards, their massive arms crossed over their chests.

"For years, I was one of you. Working in a job that poisoned my very soul. Paper after piece of paper crossed my desk. Eventually, I realized what the papers said. They said that the nobility and the royals had everything. The large holdings of land. The vast wealth. The hordes of Vestige. I'd leave my office and see people with soot or grease on their faces, their clothes shiny with use and their faces pinched with hunger. Where is the justice in that? That those who live in comfort are blind to the reality and the pain that many of their citizens live each and every day?

"I left and founded the Forester Party. And there was an enormous response. The people of Ellada yearn for justice, and I aim to bring it to them. First, I hoped to work with the system, and I brought forth petitions and worked within the confines of the law. The petitions had thousands of names but nobody within that building" – he waved behind him at the Snakewood Palace – "was listening. They hoped that if they ignored us we would go away. As you might have noticed, we haven't."

Snow swirled around us. People's faces were serious, their noses pink with cold. Some murmured amongst themselves, but most were quiet. It was not a mob like last time. People were listening.

The first few days after I ran away from the Laurus household, I had a taste of what many people went through every day. Being hungry, unable to find work, scrounging and trying to make the most of nothing. I'd found another bubble of safety within the circus, and now the Kymri Theatre. I had luck on my side. A lot of people did not.

"I'm here tonight to tell you that enough of Ellada wants a change. We do not want violence and bloodshed. But we want to be heard. And we will do whatever it takes. The Snakewoods and the Twelve Trees cannot ignore us forever, especially not now that we know their secret."

He paused again, letting the words sink in.

"The royals have lied to you, citizens of Ellada. They have lied to their very core. We do not wish to expose them, for it would turn both our worlds upside down. So we give them this chance to acquiesce to our demands. To let our voices be heard, and changes be made. If they do not, then we will let the secret of the Snakewoods be known. So spread this knowledge far and wide. Together, Ellada can be great once again. And we will do what it takes to make this happen. Whatever it takes."

Fog filled the stage. I smelled pine needles and dried roses. It was the same Vestige machine Bil had used at the start of every circus show. The smell filled me with such nostalgia and loss. When the fog cleared, the Foresters were gone.

I shivered in the cold. The snow still danced upon the wind. The gaslights rose, bathing us all in a yellow glow. I looked back at the Celestial Cathedral, light again blazing from its windows. Yet the sight of it gave me no comfort. A small trickle of people returned to the cathedral, but most of them stayed in the square with us, cold and confused.

"What secret is he talking about?" I wondered.

"No idea. Hence the secret," Drystan said. I glowered at him.

"Maybe they don't even have one, and they're hoping the threat will work," Cyan said. "What royal family wouldn't have secrets that would turn the world upside down if they were known? I must admit, I hope the royals don't comply and we can find out what it is."

Cyril's face was especially drawn. "Do so many of the people really feel that way?" he asked. He looked lost.

Cyan looked at him, and there was no pity in her features. Her long hair whipped about her face. "Many of us do, young Lordling. So many of us have so little, and you have so much you don't even realize it. I've slept in a cart most my life. Your world and mine are too different for us to ever understand each other."

Cyril stared at her, mouth agape.

"I've been in both worlds," I said, hesitantly.

"Not for long," Cyan said, and though her words cut me, they were true.

My brother hunched his shoulders. "Perhaps things will change."

She laughed, and it was not a friendly sound. "The nobility will never give up a copper of their wealth to help the like of us and you know it. This isn't going to end well."

A strong winter wind whipped around us, snow flurries so thick we could barely see.

"I should head back," my brother said, and we all knew he was heading back to a room of comfort and roaring fires, while we returned to the old theatre that was never warm.

"Luck be with you on the Lady's Long Night," I said the traditional words, but they sounded hollow.

"And Luck of the Lady to you, Gene," he said, bending down to kiss me on the cheek. We watched him walk back toward the Gilt Quarter.

25
THE DOCTOR'S APPOINTMENT

"The loss of Miss Iphigenia Laurus as a subject is great. The slow, steady heartbeat, the oxygenation of her blood, the immunity to illness – all combined is something I have never seen in the history of my medical practice. Selfishly, I hope that they find her, and bring her back to me for further study."

UNPUBLISHED NOTES of Dr Leonard Ambrose

The next day I couldn't focus at all on magic practice. My only thoughts were for the night and the looming visit with Doctor Pozzi. Maske told me off multiple times for dropping things or for missing my cues. He was wound tight. The Specter Show had unnerved him. He was redesigning the final act and would tell us nothing about it. He said only that he was close and we would know soon enough.

Maske grew thinner, his eyes wide in his skull. The only breaks he made were to visit Lily or when she came to visit him, and he was only briefly rejuvenated before disappearing back into the depths of his workshop.

I went up on the roof to watch the sun set. Cyan came up to visit me.

"I hope you've stayed out of my head," I said without turning around.

"I've tried, but you've been shouting your thoughts. I know where you're going tonight."

I turned toward her. "And?"

"And be careful. Pozzi is the first person I've come across I couldn't read at all. I don't like that."

I rolled my eyes. "Welcome to how the rest of humanity feels."

She glared at me. "No need to be sarcastic."

"Sorry. I didn't realize until recently just how much I want answers about where I came from."

She sighed. "I wouldn't mind some answers, either. But... you won't mention me to him, will you? I don't think he learned much from Shadow Elwood, and I'd like to stay beneath his notice. Just in case."

"No problem," I said. "I wish I hadn't poked my head out from behind the wall like an idiot. Now I have to see him. He knows everything about me. He could force me back with my family at any time. And what he said..."

"Yes. That you might be dying." She rested a hand on my shoulder but I shrugged it away. "It might be a lie. Just saying it so that you'll come. Do you feel like you're dying?"

"No." Even with the fainting, I felt perfectly fine the rest of the time.

"See? It could be a trick."

"Doesn't feel much better, going to the house of a liar in the middle of the night."

"You'll be fine." Her eyes shadowed. "Are you going to take Anisa?"

"Why would I do that?"

"I don't know – it just occurred to me to ask…" She scowled. "Stars! I thought she said she was going to stop meddling."

"Do you think I should take her?"

She shook her head again. "I don't know, maybe. I think she knows more about this than she's letting on."

I sighed. "I'll take her. She probably just wants to listen. And then maybe I can ask her advice. She is ancient, after all."

"Yeah, though maybe living one hundred lives turns you mad as a hatter."

I laughed. Cyan had managed to put me at ease, somewhat. She left me alone to watch the sun fade over Imachara. And then I crept down to the loft to meet Drystan.

"Are you alright?" Drystan asked me as we changed into our black clothing to go to Pozzi's. I was shivering like a leaf.

He came over and wrapped me in a hug, offering wordless comfort. I sank into it gratefully. He rested his forehead against mine.

"I'm alright," I said. "Just… it's frightening."

"Hopefully he just wants to check on you and then he'll leave you alone."

I snorted. I doubted things would be that simple. "Come on," I said, pulling the hood of my coat over my head.

We shimmied down the frozen drainpipe again. The night was clear, the just-waning moon bathing the streets in a silver glow. I would have preferred snow flurries for cover.

We made our way to Ruby Street, keeping to the darkest shadows or scaling the roofs. It felt good to have Drystan at my side. I wished I could take him with me to meet Doctor Pozzi, but the less the doctor knew about my new life, the better.

Taking a circuitous route, we entered the side of Ruby Street where we wouldn't have to cross the front of the constabulary headquarters. As we passed the back of the building, I wondered what information they had gathered about me, and how hard they had looked. So far I had more fear of Shadows than searchers or policiers.

Statues of griffins stood guard before Doctor Pozzi's tenement. The large, sweeping staircase in front was welcoming, but the iron bars across the door were not.

We circled around the building until I saw the ivy trellis. I eyed the lit window to the top left, propped open. A silhouette passed the window, waiting. I took a deep breath.

"I'll be right here," Drystan said. "If anything happens, go to the window and signal at me, and I'll be up there faster than you can say "vivisection"."

I managed a weak laugh. Chewing my lip, I looked up at the window again. Then I climbed.

Some of the ivy grew so thick that it was difficult to find a good handhold. I had already lost some of my aerialist calluses. But long years of climbing meant I made short work of it. At the window, I glanced down.

I could make out the glint of Drystan's eyes from the shadows, and only because I knew he was there and my eyesight was keen.

Here goes, I thought, and opened the window to slip inside.

At least I entered the right window. Doctor Pozzi stood in front of me in a pressed suit and white gloves. I swallowed as I closed the window behind me, leaving it propped open in case I needed to make an escape.

Doctor Pozzi smiled pleasantly. "Welcome, Micah. Thank you for coming. Please, sit." He gestured to a chair.

I crossed the room and perched gingerly on the spindly chair. Pozzi's apartments were not unlike Shadow Kameron Elwood's. His possessions were lavish displays of wealth. A large anatomical chart, expertly rendered, hung on one wall, and a cabinet that looked a little like our spirit cabinet dominated another. On the top of it was a glass case with a gilded human skull – or almost human. The canines were pointed, reminding me uncomfortably of Juliet the Leopard Lady from the circus.

Doctor Pozzi noticed my stare. "It is my cabinet of curiosities, housing some of my most prized artifacts from my Vestige collection." He paused, as though he expected me to ask what was in it. I wanted to know, but at the same time, I did not. It could be morbid, like the gilded skull, or, even worse, an artifact could speak to me, like Anisa. I felt her in the corner of my mind. Crouched, listening to our every word.

"I am here, as you asked."

"Still not one for pleasantries, are you?"

"I'm not here for pleasantries. I'm here for answers."

Pozzi smiled again, as if he found my insolence amusing. "Would you like some tea?"

"No. Thank you."

His smile grew. He made his way to the kitchen and brought out a full tea set, setting it on the low table between us. I gaped at the rare Vestige set, made of a dark material that would not burn a hand but keep the liquid warm almost indefinitely. He could have boiled the water last week and it'd still be ready for tea.

Pozzi poured tea for both of us, even though I'd declined, the steam rising between us. My chest tightened, anxiety thrumming through my veins.

"Milk or sugar?" he asked.

"Milk and two sugars," I managed.

He passed the tea to me. I held it in my hands. When did you know if it was cool enough to drink?

"You're not my child," he said. I started. I'd never actually considered that possibility. "I found you on a warm spring evening. I heard the crying from my laboratory. I opened the door and there you were. A perfect little pink thing, squalling at the top of your lungs." He sipped his tea.

My heartbeat pulsed in my throat. He shook his head ruefully, stirring his tea with a spoon. "I have to admit I just looked at you at first. I had no experience with children, you see. But eventually I picked you up and you quieted. I glanced around the street, but naturally nobody was there. So I took you in. I unwrapped you, examined you to make sure you were healthy, and what I found gave me a shock."

I looked away from him, crossing my legs.

"I'd never seen a case quite like yours, but you seemed healthy enough. But I wasn't sure if I could look after you. I couldn't afford the distraction."

At those words I looked at him. His gaze was rueful. "I regret that, but I thought I was doing the right thing."

I wished that Cyan was with me and could read Pozzi. He dripped sincerity, so much so that I was immediately mistrustful.

Slyly, I switched on the Augur in my pocket, reclaimed again from Maske without his knowledge. "I asked a fellow doctor," Pozzi continued, "who specialized in fertility and asked if he knew of any couples of... comfortable means that would be open to a quiet adoption. He found the Laurus family for me and I made my enquiries and found you a home."

"And what did you tell them, exactly?" I found my voice. Why didn't he give me to an adoption agency? Because they might have given me to a hospital to be studied? The Augur was silent. Perhaps he danced around the lie.

"I told them... to cherish you and keep you safe."

I said nothing.

"I never thought they would operate."

"Did you speak to my parents? After I left?"

"I did. They did not mention the surgery."

"Do many know about your anatomy?" he asked.

Such a medical way to describe it. But at least he hadn't called it a disorder. "A few. A few I trust."

He nodded. "Good. That's good. You shouldn't be ashamed."

"But I have been, for most of my life. Unable to trust almost everyone. Growing up my... my mother told me no one could know. My maid was bribed to keep silent. Only she and my brother knew. You have no idea what that was like for me." I kept my voice low but it shook in anger. I rose, ready to leave.

"You're right. I don't."

His words deflated me. I sank back into my chair.

"I'm glad you were not changed, and that you were able to decide for yourself in the end, though it cost you."

I said nothing.

"I meant to make sure you developed as expected and had the support you needed. But... business kept me detained."

"How long were you abroad?"

"One year's sabbatical."

"I'd been around fifteen years longer than that, and you never came calling."

"Business kept me detained in Imachara."

"I ended up seeing plenty of doctors anyway, believe me."

"Quacks, I'm sure, who had no notion what they were dealing with." He made a dismissive gesture.

"And you do." I made it a statement rather than a question, gripping the sides of the armchair so hard I feared ripping the leather. My heart pattered in my chest.

He paused. "I do. Though it's unrelated to your anatomy, I believe."

"What?"

"You have heard, I assume, that there has been a rise in birth defects over the past few decades especially? All around the Archipelago, not only Ellada."

I nodded.

"Many are not malformed, but they are born with certain... anomalies. Children who are special, with unique abilities. Things that have not been recorded in history since the time of the Alder and the Chimaera."

My mouth felt dry. I did not trust myself to speak. I dared a sip of my tea. It nearly scalded my tongue.

"I have a feeling this is not exactly news to you, in some ways."

I said nothing, staring at the patterns of the carpet beneath my feet.

"Telekinesis. Regeneration. Telepathy."

"Are any born physically different?"

"Yes, a few have been born with strange physical anomalies. Scales, a lion's tail, webbed feet. Almost all of them do not survive infanthood."

"I don't have any scales."

"This I know. As I said, your sex may not even be related to these abilities. But I noticed things about you even during the few days I had you as a babe. I gave you an immunity shot and within hours the mark was gone. And you started crying precisely half a minute before someone knocked at the door or the telephone rang."

The tea quivered in the cup I held. What I was might have nothing to do with my abilities. I didn't know how to feel.

"The things these people can do are things that Chimaera could do. Whatever you are, it's extraordinary."

I already knew that Cyan and I were different. Anisa had told us more, and Chimaera was as good a name as any, just as calling myself a Kedi had been. But to hear it from an outside source – from a medical professional – frightened me to the core. Did he know about the different kinds of Chimaera – the Theri and the Anthi? "So you've never come across anyone like me?"

His eyes softened. "I have seen many people on a spectrum of sexual development, but no one with your exact condition. I am sure you're not the only one. The world is a large and wonderful place. What's more, I have come across a few of these other children with abilities. You yourself probably have as well, without ever realizing it." His eyes flashed, and with a twist of my stomach, I wondered if he knew about Cyan after all.

Pozzi cleared his throat. "One of the reasons I brought you here tonight was to make sure you are healthy. On the sexual development side, there can be complications which I am familiar with, but that is not my main concern. I didn't mean to alarm you, but there is a high risk of side effects with some of the children I have studied, and some have been dying without ever knowing they were ill."

"And where are these other children that haven't perished?" I asked.

"They're with their families, but they come to one of the doctors of a group I work with for occasional study. Some of them can be dangerous. Some of them are helping their various countries and the Archipelago at large."

"I don't want to join any such group. I want to be left alone."

"I'm not asking you to. It's entirely voluntary. Now, Micah, will you allow me to examine you?"

"I'd prefer if you didn't," I said, as evenly as I could. "I've seen many doctors in my life, and none of them mentioned any health problems. I hardly feel as though I'm dying."

"That's what a few others have said. The illness came on very suddenly, and within days or weeks, they were gone."

I bit my lip. "I still think I'm fine." I set my teacup down and stood. "Thank you for telling me more about my past. It's appreciated. But I think I'll be going now."

"Any dizzy spells? Or fainting?"

"Only when I met you at the séance. The shock must have gotten to me." I moved toward the window. But I lied, even if the Augur stayed silent for me. I had almost fainted at Shadow Elwood's house and just after the shared vision with Cyan.

"Any strange voices in your head? Or visions? Feeling bizarre around Vestige?"

I stopped.

"I thought so. I already feel like I've abandoned you and not done right by you. Let me make sure you're alright, at least. Please."

"Alright," I breathed.

Doctor Pozzi went into the next room and returned with a medic bag. He took out a stethoscope and asked me to unbutton my overshirt. I did, my hands shaking. It reminded me of all the other doctors I had seen, how I was nothing more to them than a freak on display.

But Pozzi was different to the others. He looked at me like a person rather than an object to be studied. He took off his gloves, and every time the cold clockwork hand touched me, I tried not to shudder. His hands – both the human and the Vestige – were gentle and diffident, but I still flinched when he moved the Lindean corset to take my pulse. It both reminded me of the cold, antiseptic smell of the doctor's offices and of the night Bil "checked" I was female.

I expected him to ask me to undress, but he did not. Perhaps he knew I would bolt at that. Instead, he asked me to describe the intricacies of my anatomy, which was embarrassing enough. He asked for clarifications, and I blushed to the roots of my hair, but I far preferred answering questions to taking off my clothes.

He pressed my abdomen, asking if there was any pain or tenderness, to which I answered no. He asked about menstruation and I answered truthfully – that I did but so far only twice, three months apart. Doctor Pozzi took no notes but I knew he memorized every word I said.

He examined the color of my nails and the veins underneath the skin of my wrist. His false skin of his clockwork hand even had the tiny wrinkles and folds around the knuckles of a true hand. Hidden deep within the brass-like mechanisms, I thought I saw tiny flashes of blue crystal.

"How did you lose your hand?" The question was out of my mouth before I could stop myself.

He released my arm, holding the clockwork hand aloft, the dull brass glinting beneath the translucent muscle and skin.

"A creature ate it," he said.

I blinked. I don't know what I'd been expecting, but it wasn't that. "What?"

He tidied away his medical supplies. "It was night in the Temnian jungle, and very dark. Something attacked me. It might have been furred or scaled. Or both. It attacked me." He pushed up the hem of his shirt, and I gaped at the four deep, red scars that scored his stomach. Claw marks. He tugged his shirt down. "It took my hand. I managed to stab it with the knife in my belt and it fled. It only had a snack as opposed to a meal, I suppose. It still almost killed me, between blood loss and the infection that followed."

"But where did you get your... new hand?" I asked, almost mesmerized by the slow flexing of his false fingers.

"I already had it in my collection."

"Yes," I whispered. "I saw some of it. At the Mechanical Museum last summer. I saw the clockwork woman's head. I recognized your name on the plaque. The night I ran away, I heard my parents talking about the surgery. And you."

The clockwork woman had been beautiful. She had rested in a glass display case, levers attached to pressure points at the base of her neck, which, when pulled, caused her to show different emotions. Aenea and I had gone on an afternoon when we were courting and watched a little boy pull the levers. My eyes clouded with the memory of Aenea's face beneath the glass globes as I leaned in to kiss her.

The clockwork woman had spoken to me: "Two Hands. Penmoon. Penglass. Copper." It did not made any sense until that horrible night when the ringmaster came looking to sell me out to save his circus.

"Ah, yes, I remember her well," Pozzi said, startling me from my memories. "A lovely specimen. I put her in the museum so that others could see and admire her as well." He rubbed his beard with his false hand. "Well, young Micah, I have good news. Physically, you appear to be in perfect health, and I don't see any of the markers of the illness some of the other children have shown, aside from you fainting when you met me."

I sank back into my chair in quasi-relief.

"But if you have any physical problems – a fever, a cough, flu, anything of that nature – you must come see me as quickly as possible. You are without a doubt one of the children with abilities I have come across. I can tell by your color and musculature, and how slowly your heart beats."

His confirmation frightened me. "I was in a circus for months. Maybe I'm just especially healthy."

"No days off from lessons from being ill growing up?"

"I stayed home sometimes and pretended I was ill."

A corner of his mouth twitched. "How often did your brother feel under the weather?"

"I don't know. Twice, three times a year."

"Your parents?"

"Maybe the same." My stomach hurt. Even this winter Drystan, Cyan, and Maske had all suffered small cases of the sniffles. Not enough to lay them down and stop them working, but enough to make them a little crankier. But not me.

"Would you like me to prove it?" he asked.

"How?"

Doctor Pozzi calmly reached over and clamped his false hand over my nose and mouth.

For a second I did nothing. And then I realized I could not breathe. Making a muffled squeak of dismay, I grasped the clockwork hand and tried to pry it from my face. I could not move it an inch. Gradually, my attempts to free myself weakened. My lungs burned, and my vision swam. My head felt fuzzy and my ears rang. Splotches danced across my eyes.

"It takes five minutes before a person loses consciousness from lack of oxygen," Doctor Pozzi said, calmly. "After that it could be brain damage or death. You haven't breathed in seven minutes, nearly eight. You feel terrible, but you're still conscious."

I was, but not for long. My hands drifted to my sides and my eyelids fluttered. The doctor took his hands away.

It was like breaking the surface after being underwater. I sucked in deep, frantic breaths, and air had never felt so sweet and cool. I put my head between my knees, as Drystan bid me to do when I felt faint in Elwood's apartments. Within a few minutes, I felt fine again. As though I had not nearly been suffocated into unconsciousness. I remembered when Bil had drugged me, and I awoke sooner than he anticipated. I put a hand to my chest. My lungs did not even hurt anymore.

"Do not ever touch me without my permission," I hissed.

He held his hands up. "My apologies," he said, unperturbed. "Any prolonged ill effects?"

"No. But what if I had fainted?"

"I would have revived you and you would have come to no lasting harm. I am a doctor, after all." He ignored my glare, pressing his hands together. "So physically we have deduced you are in top shape at the moment, which is encouraging. Now, what about mentally?"

I glowered at him. "Are you asking me if I'm crazy now?"

"I'm not suggesting you are. What I suspect is that you have already experienced several oddities that you cannot explain. Things that shouldn't be possible. Vestige passing along messages, hearing the odd phrase that could be someone's thoughts. A dream that turned out to be prescient. Moving an object with your mind, if only a fraction of an inch."

I stared at him. I felt the damselfly disc, heavy in my pocket. I heard the barest whisper in my mind: *Say nothing…*

"No. Nothing like that."

Doctor Pozzi stared at me, eyes unreadable.

Can you hear me, Micah? he asked.

It took everything in me to not respond. To hear someone else's voice other than Cyan's or Anisa's in my head was so jarring. But I hesitated too long, and I did not think I convinced him.

"Are you quite sure?" he asked aloud. "If you have, it's important that I know. It could prove dangerous."

You're shielded, but I still think you can hear me, Micah Grey.

I had learned how to "think" more privately to guard myself around Cyan, and perhaps Anisa helped shield me from him as well. I kept my face blankly attentive, though my palms dampened with sweat. Was he a Chimaera as well? Did his Vestige limb give him powers he should not possess?

"Dangerous how?" I managed.

A small quirk at the corner of his mouth. "Vestige is something we do not fully understand, and we never will, unless the Alder come back to explain it to us. I have one of the largest collections of Vestige in the Archipelago and most of it is still a mystery to me, despite the experts that have studied it. My hand, for instance," he said, holding it up again. "It was attached to an arm, but I do not know where the rest of the body is, or how many of these... clockwork people were created. I assume the Alder created them, like they did the Chimaera, but for what purpose? Were they guards, or experiments? I'd give a lot, maybe even my other hand, to learn the answers to those questions." He smiled.

I resisted the urge to reach into my pocket and grasp the Vestige disc.

"Some Vestige, however, is dangerous. Several store... echoes. I have heard stories of a gun that would turn on its owner, or a toy that strangled the child who played with it. It's rare, but more prone to happen to people who have an existing sensitivity to Vestige. Which is why, if you have heard these echoes, I need to know. It could be the first stage of the illness manifesting itself."

He waited.

"There's nothing," I whispered. "I haven't experienced any of that."

He let the silence drip between us.

"Well," he said finally, "that is most promising."

"I think I shall be going now." My head swam with all that I learned and all the doctor insinuated.

"Another thing before you go that I've been meaning to ask."

"Yes?" I asked, not without a little trepidation.

"Do you want to go home? Back to your old life?"

I stared at him.

"I could speak to your family. Have them guarantee not to operate. Shadow Elwood no longer follows you." A tightening of the lips, as if he knew I had a hand in Elwood's fate.

I continued to stare at him, helpless. Did I want to go home? Did he want me to go back? And did I want this man meddling in my affairs any further? If I went back, my parents would never dare operate anyway.

"No. That is not my life anymore."

"Very well. I understand." He smiled blandly, as if it didn't matter to him. "And so your new life as a magician is treating you well?"

I was taken aback, but oddly pleased that he bothered to ask. "Very well."

"Good. I am glad. I've heard about the duel between Taliesin and Maske."

Of course you have. As has the entire city. I made sure to strengthen the mental walls I used against Cyan, not wanting him to somehow hear me. "Ah yes. Specter's shadows against Maske's marionettes," I said with a wry smile. "We are practicing night and day, and I am hopeful that we will win."

"I've had an invitation from the Princess Royal and the Steward. I was thinking of attending," he said, almost hesitant. It felt like a peace offering, reaching out past the doctor-patient relationship. After this short visit, I still didn't know what to make of this man who had found me on his doorstep almost seventeen years ago.

"Please do come." I smiled, though the words were forced.

He walked me to the window. Down below, I knew Drystan would be waiting.

"Remember, if anything strange happens to you, come to me immediately. I have medicines that will help, both physically and mentally. And..." He hesitated. "I would feel terrible if something happened to you, after I abandoned you."

I pressed my lips together. "Please, don't worry about that. For all I'm angry with my parents, I had a comfortable life and the best brother I could ask for."

He nodded. "I hope you reconcile with your parents. I remember how much they wanted you."

"Perhaps we will." The memory of my mother's hopeful face at the séance came back to me. "Good evening, Royal Physician Pozzi."

"Good evening, Micah."

Until we meet again.

His words twined through my mind. A promise.

Or a threat.

I ran into Drystan's arms when I reached his hiding place beneath the trees. So many conflicting emotions swirled through me, I didn't know whether to sob, or scream, or laugh. I couldn't shake the feeling that Pozzi was toying with me much the same as Anisa was – dangling answers just out of reach.

Drystan did not ask me about the appointment with the doctor as we walked home, for which I was grateful.

The stairs leading to the loft felt so steep. Exhaustion overwhelmed me.

How did it go? Cyan asked me from her room as I passed.

To be honest, I'm still deciding. But don't worry – I don't think he knows about you. Not definitely. I know why you can't read him though. He can speak mind-to-mind as well. Guard yourself around him.

I'm not the only one? Hope surged through her.

Stay away from him, I warned. *At least until we know more.*

I know. I will. Good night, Micah. She left me alone with my own thoughts.

"Do you want to talk about it?" Drystan asked when we dressed for bed.

"Not really. It was… complicated."

"I can imagine. It's like your past has caught up and careened into the present and smacked you in the face."

He shocked me into a laugh. "Something very much like that." I hesitated. "Can I ask you a question?"

"You can, but it'll cost you," he said, smiling, quoting one of our first conversations together when we had been in the circus, when he had seemed so strange and mysterious.

"Alright, a question for a question." I tried to figure out how to form the words. "Has Vestige ever acted strangely around you?"

"What do you mean?"

"Visions?"

He shook his head. "I don't think so, though sometimes certain pieces make me uneasy. My parents had an automaton of a Naga that used to scare me. Can't remember why, now. Maybe it was just childish fancy." He shrugged. "My question, now." He paused, considering. "Why do you ask? Did Pozzi mention something about Vestige, or did you tell him about the visions?"

"You cheater. That's technically two questions."

"The questions are linked by a comma, so it counts as one."

"Oh, really? I'll remember that for next time and ask you fifteen, all strung together with commas."

"I'm waiting for your answer."

I sighed. "He kept asking me if I'd had anything strange happen around Vestige."

"And you have."

"Well, yes, but I didn't tell him that."

"Why not?"

"I don't know. I felt like... if I told him, he'd have some sort of hold over me. And if I see him again, I want it to be on my terms."

"You want to be in control."

"Yeah, but I'm not in control of anything involving him."

Drystan rubbed his hand over his face. "I wish he'd never found you."

"Me, too. But he's known about me for a while. He knew I was in the circus, I'm sure, when he hired Shadow Elwood. But I think he'll always keep tabs on me." *Me and the others*, I thought. I sighed. "Let's go to bed. We have yet another long day of practice tomorrow."

He groaned. "Like every other day."

We slid into bed. Within moments, the cold quilts warmed with our body heat and within minutes, Drystan was asleep. Drystan had not had any nightmares since we pushed our beds together. Sometimes he still went quiet and haunted, and I took care never to mention Bil or Aenea. Sometimes, they were almost ghosts in the room with us, swallowing our words. But other times I felt a closeness to him that I had never felt with anyone else.

I envied him his easy slumber.

26
THE NIGHT THE WORLD NEARLY ENDED

"Why have the Alder left? Did Chimaera ever exist? Will they ever return? These are questions that have haunted historians for centuries, and will likely haunt them for several more."
A HISTORY OF ELLADA AND ITS COLONIES, Professor Caed Cedar, Royal Snakewood University

In the middle of the night, I crept back to the roof and pressed the damselfly disc. Snowflakes drifted from the sky, and the Penglass of Imachara glowed under the light of the full moon. Anisa swirled into view.

"What did you think?" I asked her.

"I do not trust this Doctor Samuel Pozzi, and I do not think you should, either."

Annoyance flared. "I can make up my own mind about him, thank you. Could you read anything about him? Is he the one who wants to kill the Chimaera?"

"I cannot be sure. It is possible. Like the one who was Matla, he was closed to me."

"Do you know anything about this sickness?" Always dancing around the truth. My patience stretched to a breaking point.

Her lips tightened. "No. Chimaera in my time never succumbed to disease – only injury or advanced age. It has been a long time since Chimaera have been in the world, and we do not know why people like you or the one who was Matla have returned. The abilities seem dampened, and more mental than physical. The one who was Matla is strong, but only when around what you call Vestige. If you and she went somewhere where there was no Vestige, she would not be able to hear a single stray thought. We amplify the latent abilities. I hope that in a few generations, the gene will again grow stronger and flourish. If you have the chance."

I did not follow all that she said, but her words frightened me just as much as Pozzi's had. "Vestige is changing us?"

She shook her head. "I do not know. Some aspects of what is happening are a mystery to me as well. Alder tools have been around humans for millennia. Something else is at work."

"Is Vestige dangerous, as Pozzi said?"

"Anything sufficiently powerful that you do not understand can be dangerous."

I wanted to ask: *are you dangerous?* But I feared I already knew the answer to that.

"Do you think Pozzi is a threat?"

"Perhaps. We shall tread carefully with him. He smiles, but it may be the smile of a snake, hiding fangs."

I sighed, so weary with plans and secrets and danger. "I'm never going to be safe, am I?" Someone would always be searching for me or want something from me. Pozzi thought I could drop dead at any moment. Anisa wanted me for some mysterious plan, the Shadow wanted to turn me in, my family most likely wished I could go back to being their precious little girl… "I want to know something. Clouds above, I want some actual answers."

Anisa inclined her head. "Your path is not easy, but most are not." She reached out her transparent hand and rested it on my cheek. I could feel nothing, but I found the gesture oddly comforting.

"You have been patient. I can show you a few more answers. If you truly want them."

I took a shaky breath. Could I really take any more impossibility this evening? "Yes," I whispered.

She leaned forward and kissed me on the forehead. For a moment, I almost thought I felt it. And then the vision overtook me.

I was Anisa. I could feel the wings flickering softly behind me. I was in Penglass – or Venglass, as Anisa called it – but half of it was dark, as though partly submerged in a cave. It was cold, and the furniture looked wrong to me, as if they were an older fashion than what I was used to. Even though I had cleaned the place for hours, it still smelled musty and disused. Late sunlight filtered through a wall of glass. My two wards, Dev and Ahti, played together in the corner. Ahti laughed as he raised his toys with his mind to balance on the tops of his horns. Dev, the Kedi, levitated glass globes that circled them both, like planets around a star. Both of their brows furrowed with concentration.

"Food!" Relean called from the next room. The toys and globes fell to the floor.

"Turn off the lights, please," I told them, and after a quick sketch of a glyph in the air, the lights in the globes winked out.

We ate. Soft music played and I relaxed. I had been tense since we came into hiding from the Kashura. The world had fallen apart out there, in the cities. Here, we could pretend all was safe for the children, but I knew that it wasn't.

They were turning the world upside-down looking for Ahti.

In less than a week, we would be gone. A few of us were making plans to leave, head for another world where we could hide, at least for a time. The vast expanse between worlds scared me. I had lived most of my lives here. I was scared of the dark, deep sleep as we travelled. But it was a new beginning.

The low thrum of an engine rose outside. I paused mid-chew. It could be allies, coming to drop supplies, but they had come only two days ago. There was no scheduled visit.

We heard a knock on the door. All of us froze in fear. We were as silent as could be, but the music still played, echoing about the kitchen and down the hallway. We heard the sound of the glyph being drawn. I hung my head in defeat.

I could not hear the music over the thundering of footsteps and shouting. They wore armor, faces obscured by visors. They slapped cuffs over my wrists – and over those of the children – and dragged us out of our brief sanctuary. My hands went numb. As they marched us *down the hallway toward the craft, I heard a last snippet of music.*

The children were crying. How quickly the world changes. A generation ago, the Alder would never do something like this, even the ones loyal to the old ways. They would never hunt the world for one Chimaera, no matter how powerful.

But politics can change with the wind. One leader to spark the zeitgeist, and the world changes.

If the Kashura have their way, this would be my last life. My last time with Relean. They would forbid anyone to store my memories in an Aleph, to create a new corporal form. All the history and knowledge I learned as a curator of this world – turned into dust. I had raised countless wards for the Alder, and they had grown up to be good and made the world a better place. All save the ward that I failed.

Our footsteps shuffled as we were escorted into the craft. We flew away, and I stopped the tears, but only for Dev and Ahti. I didn't want them to be any more frightened than they already were.

That would come soon enough.

The vision shifted. I was in a cold Venglass cell. Outside, the world burned. The sky roiled orange, red, purple and gray. Smoke broiled toward the bruised sky. Distant screams were cut silent. The ground was ablaze with angry flames, licking and devouring all in their path. Relean stood next to me, our arms touching. Dev slept in the cot in the corner. They had taken Ahti.

Relean reached into his mouth, wriggling something loose. He popped out one of his teeth and held it in his hand. I stared at him, aghast.

"What are you doing?"

"Shh," he said, and unscrewed the back of the tooth, opening it. Inside were little transmitters. He took one and attached it to my temple, did the same for himself, and another for Dev. He looked down in his hand at the last remaining transmitter. The one for Ahti.

"If anything happens to us, we'll be transmitted to the Alephs I've hidden in a safe place. At least then there is a chance that we'll be together again. I don't want this to be the end."

"Oh, Relean." He'd planned this for a long time.

Dev slept. Outside, comets fell to earth, blooming into roses of fire. So much fire. There wasn't long left.

I drew Relean close for a kiss, clinging to him. We drew our wings around us as a pitiful, translucent shield.

Something large hit the prison. The walls and floor shook. The smell of smoke filled the air. Alarms sounded. Dev woke up, crying. I held out my arm, and Dev came to me as we waited for the end.

Pain.

Pain as we started coughing smoke. The searing heat. We fell to our knees. There was no escape. Not while wearing this body. I spasmed on the floor, suffocating, my vision darkening.

Another blast. I felt the transmitter start to work, and my last thought was that the worst part was knowing that it was my ward, my child, my little Ahti, who had ended the world.

I came out of the vision and back into myself. I shuddered, rubbing my hands against my arms. For a second, I had felt myself die in Anisa's body, felt my heart stop, my limbs burn away. My throat felt raw from smoke and screams.

"What happened after that?" I asked.

"My memories end there."

"How was Ahti involved?"

Her face creased in remembered pain at the mention of his name. She touched my forehead again, drawing me into a vision, but this one was like the first she had shared with me – more of a waking dream than a memory.

This time I was myself and stood next to Anisa. The sea boiled and more fire rained from the sky. All was eerily quiet. An Alder ship flew through the air, racing for the stars. But a piece of debris collided, and the ship floundered before exploding; burning wreckage raining down on the scorched earth.

Anisa spoke aloud. "Ahti had two powers. He could control the elements and telekinetic energy. When I found him in the jungle, the Kashura and their human allies were trying to isolate his power, somehow take it out of him. They succeeded in dampening his abilities, but only temporarily."

Anisa turned to me, her eyes wide and dark. I could almost smell the smoke from the dying flames. "He had it in him to save the world or destroy the world and he fought back against the Kashura the only way he knew how. Only his powers were too great for him to control, and most of the world paid the price.

"Many of the Alder left in their aircraft, and some of

the humans with them. But every Chimaera vanished, disintegrated into nothing. They must have told him it needed to be done, but I do not know how it was possible. The seas continued to rise, everything burned, and so many died..." she trailed off. "So much destruction for nothing. And it could have been avoided."

"How?"

"Dev." She looked back out at the patches of fire, the tendrils of cruel, dark smoke. "My little Kedi. Dev could calm Ahti down, and could almost absorb the effects of the power. If Dev and Ahti had been in the same room, history might have taken another fork in the path."

I reeled from this.

"I have been dormant for millennia. It was only when I sensed you that I managed to fully awaken, to stretch out my senses and see how much I could do in this form." She looked down at her body. In the vision, she seemed real. "It does more than even I knew. It did not feel like an accident that I found you, so close to me. And you remind me so much of Dev."

"What is a Kedi?"

"It is simply a word that ancient humans gave to those who did not identify as solely male or solely female, whether it was in a physical or mental way. It could relate to Chimaera, or human, or Alder."

"And they were worshipped?"

"Some were, just as some men and women were."

"Pozzi told me that what I was... wasn't related to my abilities."

"You and Cyan have abilities that few others in this time

have. You're like the Anthi, but you're something different."

"But me being… both genders doesn't relate to it?"

She contemplated me. "There have been male Anthi, female Anthi, eunuch Anthi, and Anthi like Dev. And the Theri were as varied as could be. I myself have lived as a man, and also as a woman, and as a being made of clockwork. The power exists, and what body it inhabits is irrelevant."

I looked away from her, unsure what to say. The sea roiled beneath us, and a fierce wind whipped our hair.

"Do you miss them? Your family?"

"Every second of every day. But I live in hope. It's often all that has sustained me through the centuries. There's a chance that Relean and Dev's Alephs survived. I want you to help me find them, if you can. I want my family back. And then we also have to make sure that this" – she swept her hands out over the wreckage –*"does not happen again. For it might. And this time, it could end the world for good."*

The fires darkened to dim glowing jewels scattered across the land. The sea still frothed, white and angry.

Cyan shook me awake. I was lying on the rooftop of the Kymri Theatre. I felt so cold. I could tell I had been up on the roof for long enough that a normal person would have suffered from frostbite.

She ushered me back into my room. Drystan did not move. Cyan's gaze lingered on our beds pushed together.

Thanks for finding me, I thought. *You should go back to bed.*

Why won't you tell me what happened? I felt her quest

in my mind, asking me to share the memories so I did not have to explain. Gently, I pushed her back.

We all have our secrets. Let me keep this one for a time, alright?

Alright, she said. She strode to the door, the hem of her robe whispering along the floorboards. She paused, turning back to me. Wisps of her dark hair escaped the long braid down her back.

Sometimes she speaks to me alone, too. You're not the only one with secrets.

The door closed behind her, leaving me in the dark, next to Drystan, wondering what Anisa had spoken to Cyan about, and how I was going to help save the world.

27
SCIENCE, MAGIC, AND STORY

"A good magician's performance tells a story. Each act should build on the next, becoming ever more engaging to fill the audience with wonder. It's a bud that unfurls into a flower, meant to woo the audience."

The unpublished memoirs of Jasper Maske:
THE MASKE OF MAGIC

Time slipped past, drawing us ever closer to the night of the duel.

We shut ourselves off from the world, practicing from dawn to long past dusk. As the snow melted outside the windows, snippets of news found their way to us, through newspapers or visits from Lily when she dropped off supplies from Twisting the Aces. She usually stayed for a cup of tea, telling us of the latest antics of the Foresters.

Lily brought flowers and berated us for staying indoors so much, lamenting the dust that again collected in the corners of the theatre. I did not know how often Lily spent the night.

Finally and yet all too soon, it was the week before the Grand Specter-Maske Duel of Magic. The city was plastered with lithographic posters and tickets at the Royal Hippodrome had already sold out. The monarchy had even offered to lend several Vestige projectors so that people gathered in parks and public places would be able to see the duel as well, even if they could not afford the tickets. The gesture would have been sweeter if it had not so obviously been a token one to try to placate the rising ire of the Foresters.

Two days before the duel, we invited Lily to be our test audience. Cyan's beau Oli was there as well, returned from abroad. We had trained him to be our extra stagehand so he was backstage with me. My nerves fluttered. This would be the first time anyone would see our full repertoire. Lily was so excited she could hardly sit still. She wore a dress of watered green silk and cream lace.

Next to me, Oli took a deep breath. He wore a clean but homespun shirt and braces. His face was tanned from months abroad the ship that sailed to Kymri, where winter never held power.

The lights dimmed and the show began.

I watched Lily's rapt face through the peephole beneath the stage, pushing levers and pulleys when needed.

At the finale, I shifted my attention back to the stage. Drystan sat on the stage in a chair, his head in his hands. Behind him rose a tall gauze curtain that looked a little like an artist's canvas. Drystan stood and twirled, waving his arms and muttering incantations. The gauze fluttered and then pulled away. An automaton in a flowing dress with wide sleeves stood on a podium. Her face was of smooth brass, her false glass eyes fixed on a far-off destination. This was only the second time I had seen Maske's creation, and the first time in action. A shiver passed through me as her head moved mechanically to survey the audience. She looked like a crude and primitive echo of the clockwork woman's head.

The automaton took a shaking step downstage. Drystan reached his arms out to her.

"My creation is more beautiful than I could ever have imagined. But if only she could be transformed from metal to flesh and bone." He paused, his eyes lingering on the props of magic books stacked to one side of the stage. "I wonder…"

He circled the automaton. Her head moved jerkily, following him. Again, I fought down a shudder. This automaton was nothing but metal and cogs and oil. The clockwork woman at the Mechanical Museum had been terrible to behold, like a live woman trapped in a crystal cage, but the blank, dead face of the automaton unnerved me more.

I tried to focus on the illusion, which would be perfect for the audience, for they would love the fusion of science, magic, and story.

Drystan arranged more props around the stage – beakers and a magic wand. He shrugged out of his lab coat and into a magician's tails, waving the wand. The beakers of liquid bubbled, sending swathes of purple and blue fog onto the stage. The automaton raised her hands above her head to cover her face, but midway through we heard a screech and she stopped. Her head slumped forward.

Drystan paused in his motions, mystified. Cyan, who was beneath the stage, waiting to go through the star trap once the automaton dropped through, looked at me and Oli anxiously.

I closed the peephole and opened the trap door to clamber onto the stage and held my arm down to help Cyan up.

Maske fiddled with the gears on the automaton's back.

"I don't understand..." he muttered. "She still has full power. She worked this morning."

Maske could not even unbend the automaton's arms. We all stood on stage frozen as if in a tableau vivant. Then Maske lowered his head, resting it on the shoulder of his creation. And he sobbed.

It was disconcerting to see him cry so brokenly. But I understood. The duel was the day after tomorrow. If his final act was broken, then our chances of winning were infinitesimal. This finale could be incredible. But only if the automaton worked.

Cyan moved toward Maske to comfort him, but he turned away from her. Gently, he gathered his stiff automaton in his hands and carried her away to his workshop.

The rest of us stood in silence. Lily rustled her skirts, rising and clearing her throat self-consciously.

"Oh my, will he be alright?" she asked. "Maybe I should go speak to him. Oh, and it was so wonderful as well before it went wrong. Poor Jasper..." She trailed off.

"You're probably the only one who could comfort him," Drystan said. Lily lifted her skirts and bustled away.

Oli came over and wrapped an arm around Cyan. She leaned her head against him. I wanted to do the same with Drystan, but I did not know how Oli would react, and so my arms stayed heavy at my sides.

I could only hope that Maske was alright, and that the finale could be saved.

I heard low, regretful laughter in my head. I frowned at Cyan. Her wide eyes met mine and she shook her head minutely. It wasn't her.

It was Anisa.

"Excuse me, I don't feel so well," I muttered, leaving the room. I could feel their stares on my back. I took the stairs two or three at a time, trotting across the loft and grabbing the Aleph, as Anisa had called it. I pressed the button and waited for her to appear.

"What?" I asked, too impatient and annoyed to be polite.

She only stared at me, with her infuriating, mysterious smile.

"Why were you laughing? Were you laughing at Maske?"

"More at his crude contraption. Maske doesn't know all he created, and so he does not know how to repair it."

I slumped on the bed. "I hope he has another illusion."

"None will be as good. That illusion is the one he needs to win."

"Why do you care about our little duel?"

Her smile widened, as if she found me amusing. "You know how precious I find you and the one who was Matla. And I find Maske intriguing. He is a man who has lived many lives in such a short amount of time. He pursued a life of magic and it consumed him until he was nothing but a shriveled husk. He then used his magic to steal money rather than entertain. Your lover found him and they brought each other back to life. Your Drystan continued to flourish, but Maske stagnated. It is only now, when Drystan returned, with you and then the one who was Matla, that he grows again."

I sunk my head into my hands. "He wants this more than anything, Anisa. And now it might all slip away from him. Again."

"Not necessarily."

I looked up at her. "What do you mean?"

"Maske did something very unusual when he invented his mechanical woman. He used several of the small Vestige automata – ones that did not work properly anymore or were not whole. He broke them open, learned more or less how they worked, and used some of the parts to power his invention. Little bits of Vestige are scattered within her, and no mechanic will know how to fix it. What Maske did was ingenious. Not many humans could have done what he did. But even for all his cleverness, he hasn't quite managed it."

I deflated. "So all hope is lost."

"I can fix it."

My breath caught in my throat. I gazed at her, this strange incorporeal echo from a time long gone, haunted by her past and the possibilities of the future. "Will you?" I asked carefully.

"That depends," she responded. "On you."

I tried to read her expression, but in the dim light of the loft she was more transparent than she was by moonlight.

"What do I have to do?"

"Nothing at the moment. But at some point in the

future, I will need to use you for something that you would never otherwise agree to. But because of this, you will." She blinked once, owlishly serene.

Everything within me screamed that this was a terrible idea. But over the months I had grown to care for Maske, and I knew he needed this. And I wanted this too. If Maske won, he could perform again. Drystan, Cyan, and I could stay in the haven of the Kymri Theatre. A place where I could dress as a girl or a boy and nobody cared. A home. I'd lost my home with my family. I'd lost the circus. I didn't want to lose this place, too.

Though Anisa frightened me half to death and her ways were strange to me, I never felt actual malice from her. She played her hand close to her chest, but was that evil? She cared for Chimaera, and evidently she thought I was one even if I wasn't sure what to believe, so our goals should align.

In theory.

And with so many people after me, as a fugitive there was always the chance I would be in prison by the time she needed to collect on her favor, whatever it may be.

I closed my eyes. "Alright. I'll do it."

"I thought you would, little Kedi," she said. I opened my eyes. She held her hands out, beckoning me, and I stepped into her embrace. Her image flickered and settled along my skin before disappearing. My body reached down and picked up the Aleph from the floor, sliding it into my pocket.

But I did not do it.

I was a passenger, as I had been with Anisa's visions, as though I was cordoned off in a corner of my own mind.

The part of me that was still *me* fought a rising tide of panic. What if this were a trick and she had stolen my body for good?

I've no wish for your body, never fear, little Kedi. I am only borrowing it for a time.

I could only hope this was true. She walked my body down the stairs toward Maske's workshop. She trailed my fingertips along the walls.

We turned a corner, and Drystan walked toward us. He stopped short when he saw me. "Maske is really broken up," he said, pitching his voice low. "Lily's finally convinced him to lie down and get some rest, try to fix his illusion in the morning. She's even making him tea and soup. Mothering him, but that's what he needs."

My mouth said nothing.

He peered at me. "Are you alright, Micah?"

My lips curled into a smile. "I'm fine, Drystan. Better than ever." And my body reached for Drystan and drew him into a kiss.

I could feel everything. His lips. The stubble of his chin. His arms around my neck. He responded enthusiastically. I railed in my mind, trying to regain control of my body. Drystan pulled away, a small line between his eyes. Had he sensed this kiss was different?

What the Styx are you doing? I screamed in my mind.

I could almost feel it, was all she said in response, sadly.

If you ever do anything like this again, the deal is off and I will never, ever help you with anything. I'll throw your Aleph into the ocean and good riddance!

She did not respond to my empty threat. She told Drystan that she was fine and carried on down the corridor.

My body turned back. Drystan looked at me, confused. With Anisa wearing my body, my posture was different, the cadence of my voice altered with the remnants of an accent from long ago. I made a fervent promise to myself that if – when – I had my body back, I would tell him everything so that if he saw this again, he would know. I hoped I somehow kept that thought from Anisa.

She turned away and made her way to the workshop. She opened the door and the mirror maze met us. Anisa walked through it, unerringly following the path through the mirrors. In the reflections, my face was serene and empty.

My body pushed open a mirror and entered the workshop proper. I smelled grease, sawdust, and the acrid tang of metal. The scents almost reminded me of the circus.

The automaton rested in the middle of the room on the slab of table. The large dress for the illusion hung nearby on a wooden mannequin, an even cruder echo of a real person.

Anisa moved my body to the automaton. The panel over her abdomen had been removed. Inside was a mass of cogs and wires. Anisa leaned forward. Interspersed between the brass and nickel of her interior were flexible strings of Vestige metal dotted with small, blue-tinged crystals, like faceted Penglass.

What are these?

"The hearts of mini automata. The spark that animates them. Gives them life."

Life? An odd choice of word.

"What is life?" she countered. "Am I alive, even though the various husks that housed my mind have long since vanished to dust?"

I had no answer for her. I saw my hands reach into the depths of the automaton, moving, detaching, and reattaching. I felt her hold the tip of my tongue between my teeth. After a few minutes, she took my hands away. I had no idea what she did, but the interior of the automaton looked… tidier. Complete. She fitted the plate back on the abdomen, and screwed it back into place.

The door of the workshop opened. Maske stood, blinking, with Drystan and Cyan behind him. Lily and Oli must have left for home.

"Micah?" Drystan asked, tentative. "What are you doing?"

My face folded into a smile. "I fixed your trinket for you, Jasper Maske."

Cyan blanched at my tone. "That's not Micah."

Drystan opened his mouth in confusion, which deepened when I showed no reaction to Cyan's words.

Before Drystan could say anything, Maske drifted closer to the automaton.

"Turn it on, magician," my mouth said.

He reached shaking hands to place the automaton into a standing position. He pressed a button in her back.

The automaton "awoke". Swinging her head back and forth, she continued to lift her arm into position, her crude fingers making the motion that would fasten the sleeves of the dress together, had she been wearing it. Her movements were smoother than before. She drew her arms down to her sides and froze. At this point of the illusion, she would have been lowered through the star trap.

Maske pressed the button again, and she went through all the movements of the illusion – twisting her head to follow where Drystan would circle her, raising her arms, and lowering them again.

Maske's face twitched, as if he had so many emotions swirling through him that his face could not decide which to register.

"I don't understand. The Vestige didn't work."

"You used Vestige?" Drystan asked. He looked to me again, but Anisa did not deign to meet his gaze.

"Not particularly well," my voice said with a small smile. I felt my hand reach into my pocket and draw out the Aleph.

Cyan stepped forward. "Get out," she said, glaring at me. "You've overstayed your welcome, damselfly."

"Cyan!" Maske said. "What are you going on about? He saved my illusion."

"I'm not speaking to Micah." She crossed her arms over her chest.

A low laugh escaped my throat. Deep, sultry, and completely unlike my own. Drystan flinched.

Anisa set the Aleph on the floor and pressed the button. My arms were held out in front of me. Swirls of blue light danced over my skin and then Anisa's projection emerged from my body until we stood side by side. I felt a sickening lurch within my mind and then I fell to the floor, a marionette with strings cut.

Drystan recognized her – how could he not, after all those nights in the circus pantomime? To Maske, she must have looked especially strange, with the tattoos that snaked along her hairline and down her neck and the large dragonfly wings. And the fact she had just stepped from my body and was completely transparent. The magician was slack jawed as a child.

"All my life, I've wanted to see true magic," he whispered. "And here it is under my roof."

"Magic." Anisa laughed the same laugh she had made with my throat. I put my hand to my neck, so grateful that my body and my mind were my own again.

Drystan took a step backward. "Micah? What is going on?"

I realized: Maske and Drystan could hear her. Why could they hear her, when no one but Cyan and I could before?

"Her name is Anisa," I managed to say. "She first spoke to me in the Pavilion of Phantoms, and I took her with me the night we left the circus. I didn't know why at the time. At the séance the first night we came here, she spoke to me again, and she's responsible for the visions Cyan and I have." My mouth was dry.

Drystan narrowed his eyes. "And you never told me about her?"

I shrugged a shoulder, my tongue sticking to the roof of my mouth.

"It is my fault, White Clown. I stressed the importance of discretion," Anisa said. "They are helping me. They are important to me. And you have many secrets you have not shared with anyone, Drystan Hornbeam."

Cyan's mouth made a little "o" as she recognized the surname.

"Can you see the future, damselfly?" Maske asked.

"Sometimes. What do you wish to ask of me, magician?"

"Will… Will we be victorious in our duel?"

A soft smile played about her lips. She walked over to Maske, a trail of light leading from the hem of her dress and back to the Aleph. She rested a phantom hand against the older man's face. Tears shone in his eyes.

"Won't it be sweeter to find out on your own, dear magician? I will say this, though." She gave Cyan a look over her shoulder, who stood as stiffly as if she expected a blow. "You have gained more family than you know."

"What do you mean?"

"You shall see, magician." She gave him a kiss on the cheek, which I knew he would not feel, and disappeared, until only the Aleph lay on the floor.

I hesitated, and then picked up the Aleph and put it back in my pocket.

They all stared at me. I bit my lip.

"She took control of your *body*?" Drystan asked, horrified. I knew he thought of the kiss.

"Only to fix the automaton for Maske," I said, not meeting his eyes.

"And she offered out of the goodness of her heart?" Cyan asked.

I could not meet her gaze, either. "She wanted to help."

Cyan snorted.

"Whatever her motivations, I am most grateful to her," Maske said, running a fingertip down the automaton's face. "Thanks to her, we have a chance to win."

"To win," I whispered.

Maske looked at the clock. "You all should go to bed. We've all had quite a shock today. And tomorrow's the last day to practice."

The last day to practice.

All that happened recently finally hit me. A doctor had

told me I could start dying at any moment. I had been bombarded with visions from Anisa, telling me I had to help her save the world. She'd taken my *body* without asking permission, which was worse than seeing any sort of doctor as a child – the ones who poked and prodded me, trying to quantify me, put me into a box of their own making. Drystan was confused and angry at me, and a duel that decided our professional future loomed over us.

I felt my eyes roll back into my head. Strong arms encircled me, and Drystan carried me to the loft.

I didn't lose consciousness. It was as though my mind just needed time to process all that had happened and could not be bothered with my body. Drystan tucked me into bed and sat next to me. Gradually, I calmed and felt almost normal. I knew I should be worried about the fainting, perhaps even enough to go to Pozzi. But I couldn't find the energy to care. I pushed away all of the unanswered questions and threats I could do nothing about.

Drystan and I stared at each other, mute, drowning in words unspoken. His mouth twisted. He undressed for bed. My eyes lingered on the muscles of his back in the low light as he reached to pluck his sleeping shirt from the washing line. He slid into bed next to me, but our bodies did not touch. I ached to reach over and take him in my arms, but I was scared of being rebuffed. I realized that often I was not the one to initiate affection, and without a doubt I was always the one to push questing hands away.

I licked my lips and moved closer to him, sliding my arms around his waist and resting my cheek on his shoulder. He sighed, some of the tension leaving his muscles.

"I'm sorry," I said.

"For what?" His tone was not harsh, but clearly implied that there were various things I could be apologizing for.

"About what Anisa did earlier. That I didn't tell you about her..."

He turned his head away. I couldn't see his face or tell what he was thinking.

He sighed and turned to me. "Will you ever trust me, Micah? Will you ever trust anyone completely?"

My breath caught in my throat. "I do trust you."

"There's so much you haven't told me over the past few months."

"Oh, and you're the pinnacle of being forthcoming about yourself, are you?" I said, pulling my chin away, though my hands stayed about his waist. I could feel the ridges of his stomach muscles tighten.

A corner of his mouth quirked wryly. "True, there are things about my past I have not told you in the greatest detail. But I have told you more than anyone. Anyone. I thought it was the same with you. And then I discover... this. Just because I can't read minds doesn't mean I can't be useful. Or help you."

He was jealous. He felt like I hadn't told him because he wasn't Chimaera. I blushed, ashamed. I should have told him much more. When would I ever learn?

"You're right," I whispered close to his ear. "I should have told you, but I couldn't. Every time I tried my mouth wouldn't form the words. Like she blocked them. And we know so much less about Vestige than we thought, Drystan. Anisa was alive once. More than once. She was a

Chimaera, assigned to guard and raise other Chimaera the that Alder gave her and her husband, Relean. One of the last ones she raised was a Kedi. She called the Kedi "Dev". And she loved him. Or her?" I found myself finally able to tell him every detail of Anisa's plan, as if the lock on my tongue had opened: how much she frightened Cyan and me. The horned Chimaera, Ahti. The way the world had nearly ended all that time ago. I whispered the words into his ear, and his arms were around me, his hands gently stroking my back.

When I finally reached the events of that afternoon when Anisa had taken my body, his muscles tensed again, but he waited for me to finish.

"Why are you going along with this plan? How do you fit in?"

"I don't know. Some of the time, I don't believe it. But what if she's right? I can't take that risk. And she's so... so not quite human... but I don't think she's lying. I think she wants to try and find her family, and help make sure the Chimaera come back into the world, and make sure they stay here."

He shook his head. "I'd never have imagined something like this could be possible. Tread carefully, Micah. And tell me about anything else that happens. I want to help. We're in this together."

Drystan tilted my head up and our lips met. I clung to him, tears of relief slipping from the corners of my eyes. He didn't hate me. He smelled of soap and skin. I took off his shirt and threw it to the floor. I ran my fingertips over the lines of his muscles. He had a small scar by his collarbone, and a little constellation of moles along his ribcage. I pressed my fingertips against them. I wanted to memorize every line of his body, until it became as familiar as my own. He tangled his fingers in my hair, dipping his head to nuzzle my neck. I gasped, sensations rushing through me in an avalanche.

He took off my shirt, and it joined his on the floor. His fingers paused on the laces of my Lindean corset. I bit my lip and nodded.

I trusted him.

He undid the laces, one by one.

28
THE SPECTER'S SHADOWS AND MASKE'S MARIONETTES

"Tonight is the night Imachara and Ellada have been waiting for: the duel between Pen Taliesin and the Specter's Shadows and Jasper Maske and his Marionettes. The future of these magicians' lives hangs in the balance. Who will win and who will fail? Place your bets here today!"
                    Sign outside Sunbeam Betting Company

We arrived at the Royal Hippodrome in the late morning, our nerves strung to breaking point. Out in front of the Hippodrome was a large lithographic poster of the upcoming duel, sheltered against the drizzle by an overhang. I craned my head.

The poster was taller than I was and echoed the old posters of when Maske and Taliesin worked together. Back then, they had stood shoulder to shoulder, wielding magic against little devils and smiling beatifically at passersby.

The upper half of the new poster showed Maske and
Taliesin glaring at each other in a battle of wills. Maske
looked younger and more handsome than he was in
reality. They'd put Taliesin in a Kymri turban bedecked
with jewels, and shown him as he would look if the drugs
had not ravaged him. Below Maske were Drystan and
Cyan, drawn as if Maske were the puppeteer controlling
his marionettes. Drystan looked like Cyan's fraternal twin.
In their outstretched hands they held blue fire. Taliesin's
boys had legs that turned into smoke, as though they were
specters, and they held red fire. Small imps with forked
tails perched on everyone's shoulders, whispering into
their ears. Tonight was the night.

We opted not to practice on the Hippodrome stage itself
for fear that someone would spy on us. Instead, months,
ago we had measured the stage to the closest inch and
figured out where everything would go. But an unfamiliar
stage was always a liability.

Professor David Delvin, the head of the Collective of
Magic, decided who would perform first by a coin toss.
We made sure it wasn't double-sided, just in case. Taliesin
and his kin would perform first. Part of me liked this – we
would know what we were up against, so it would be no
surprise. Yet if they were far better than us, it would not be
particularly good for our morale and the audience would
be too jaded against wonder and magic.

We set up as much as we could, but mainly we took our
black-wrapped props into one of the storerooms backstage,
ensuring it remained well-locked at all times. Oli arrived not
long after. He murmured a hello and stood awkwardly near

us as we discussed plans. My nerves jangled even more, like a badly strung guitar. I had been edgy before circus shows, but nothing like this; even if a small mistake during the trapeze act could mean injury or death.

An hour before the show, Taliesin and his boys wandered over to us. Maske stood straight, his eyes flinty as he gazed at his rival.

"Jasper, old sport," Taliesin wheezed, grinning to show the ruin of his mouth. His eyes were so bright I knew he was on Lerium. Sind and Jac were impeccably dressed in their magician's kit, their faces showing only smug derision.

"Taliesin," Maske replied. "It's the night the scales are evened and fair."

Taliesin gave a phlegmy laugh. "The scales were already balanced fifteen years ago, Jasper."

Maske smirked, buffing his nails on his shirt. "Pen, we both know you unfairly weighted the scale in your favor. Let's not have a repeat performance of that, shall we?"

Taliesin leered. "You're one to be tetchy about cheating, old card sharp."

The two boys echoed the sentiment, but it felt forced. The accusations of cheating unnerved them. My stomach sank. We could not afford any sort of sabotage.

"I never cheated except at cards. Not even close. Has your magic faded, now that you're so dependent on magic of a chemical nature?"

Taliesin pulled his lips back from his teeth, as if he'd hiss at Maske like an angry cat. "You arrogant..." The twins made a move as if to strike Maske.

I stepped between them.

"Please." I cut Taliesin off. "It's almost time for you to begin. We'll soon find out who wins, and there will be no cheating. On either side." I met the Taliesins' glares squarely.

They left, and we watched them go.

"Are they planning to cheat, Cyan?" Maske asked.

"The twins aren't," Cyan said. "But Taliesin is so delirious on Lerium I can't tell. I'm surprised he could even focus his eyes, much less speak."

"Let's hope that means he's too addled to cheat properly," Drystan said, his mouth twisted.

"Time to beat the bastard once and for all," Maske said, his calm fractured. His eyes blazed, and I saw the man who had been capable of counting cards in front of hardened criminals.

"We'll beat him." I said.

We had to.

The time had come.

The head of the Collective of Magic, Professor David Delvin, and the solicitor, Christopher Aspall, met us and showed us to our private box in the theatre. Our feet sank into the lush carpet, and the chairs were upholstered in expensive red velvet.

I tried not to gape as I saw who else was in the other private boxes. Directly across from us were none other than the Princess Royal and the Steward of Ellada. The young princess wore a little tiara perched in her dark curls, and a red and gold dress with small cards embroidered on a sash around her waist. Her cheeks were pink with excitement as she craned her head to see the empty stage.

I found myself smiling, but it was tinged with sadness. She was just a little girl, and the poor thing was torn between the Forester protest that could result in civil war, a dour old uncle who wanted to keep the crown for himself, and all the many nobles who only wanted to curry favor with her by virtue of her blood. I sent a brief prayer to the Lord and Lady that we would put on a good show, both to win and to give this little girl some magic in her life.

In other boxes were prominent nobility and some of the biggest merchants and property owners. People occupied every seat below, waving fans and perusing the programs. My palms grew damp. There were so many people, and many more would be out in the parks, bundled against the cold, watching us on the blank sides of buildings. So many to see us if we failed.

The lights dimmed in the body of the theatre and brightened on the stage. The show began.

The twins strode onto the stage from opposite ends, and bowed low. In unison, they turned to the audience and waved. They then proceeded to try to kill each other in a number of ways. Sind took out a pistol and Jac held up his hands in surrender before twisting and grabbing a pistol from his own pocket. They circled each other, yelling insults.

Sind fired and Jac flew back, but when he stood, only colored confetti fell from the "bullet wound" and he bowed. Jac threw a dagger that apparently went through Sind without causing injury. It stuck fast to a wooden post behind him, quivering.

The performance was like the Specter Shows, yet on a larger scale. Gone was the demonstration of small-scale magic. All was stage illusion, meant to impress and be seen from the farthest seat in the theatre.

They caused each other to explode, disappear in a cloud of smoke, and then reappear, looking composed and without a hair out of place. The audience gasped with shock and amazement. Several clutched the hollow of their throats in fear. In the Collective of Magic's theatre box, their faces were impassive as they surveyed the illusions before them.

They next brought out the magic lantern for the phantasmagoria from the Specter Shows. Death again appeared on a shifting curtain of smoke. The magicians bowed before it, apologizing for having just cheated Styx himself of their deaths. Styx began to weave his hands and little figures appeared in the smoke. Chimaera with the wings of bats and angels flew overhead, and below people with forked fish tails and fins on their backs swam through the currents of the River Styx. Beings with the legs of fauns or horses or the large horns of antelope, deer, or bulls staggered toward their fate in death.

"You have escaped me, for your magic is mighty," Death intoned, a disembodied voice I recognized as Taliesin's booming through the theatre. A projection of his face undulated on the shifting smoke. "You are the only ones I will ever bow to. In return, I will give you more power." Death himself bowed to the first twin, and then the other, before disappearing.

The next few illusions showcased the twins reveling in their new power. Coins fell from their pockets to scatter on the floor, rolling and spinning.

They levitated themselves, and I narrowed my eyes in

triumph. Their levitation was shoddy and even from this distance I could see a few of the wires, though perhaps that was only because of my good eyesight. Hopefully the Collective would notice as well. But would that be enough? All of their other illusions were so expertly performed.

My stomach twisted and I bit my lip so hard I feared drawing blood. Every illusion was calculated to show that they held the power – they wielded it over death itself. The message they sent was clear: nobody could defeat them. Especially us.

Micah, Cyan said to me, as though she sensed the trend of my thoughts. *If I wanted to, I could make them stumble. I could distract them so easily.*

Oh, it was tempting. So tempting. If the Taliesins had a mindreader in their midst, they would not hesitate at all to use that power to win, and the Specter's Shadows might have planned something already. I shook my head minutely. *If we did that, we'd be no better than Taliesin all those years ago. Our act is good. We can beat them.*

I knew you'd say that. Was worth a try. With a resigned little shrug, she turned her attention back to the stage.

They stepped backwards into two spirit cabinets, locking themselves inside. There was a large sound and a blast of light. The doors of the cabinet swung open to reveal no one inside.

Another flash of light and a crash of cymbals, and the twins appeared on stage again. But another set of twins were there as well, flanked to either side. I squinted at the stage. It must have been something to do with mirrors, but I could not see the angles. The four twins coalesced into a single person, who bowed low before turning on his heel and disappearing into a wisp of smoke that faded into nothingness.

I sunk lower into my seat, fighting the urge to swear or cry. How could we hope to defeat this?

The applause was deafening.

The show paused for intermission. The audience would be mingling in the gigantic foyer of marble and gilt, sipping drinks and discussing the Specter twins as a dance troupe undulated on the stage to music played by minstrels.

We were not there.

Taliesin's stagehands cleared the props away, and the three of us and Oli labored to move our gimmicks into their proper places. In actuality we should have had another stagehand or two, but Maske did not want to hire anyone he did not trust.

We stepped back once everything was in place, panting with effort. It was almost time.

Maske cleared his throat. "No matter the outcome, I want to thank you. Without you, I'd still be moldering in that little theatre. If I lose this time, I'll know I gave it my all, and had the best help possible." He sniffed. "But Lord and Lady Above, I really want to win."

He drew us into a hug in a rare gesture of physical affection. I returned the hug fiercely. Anisa was in my pocket. Just in case.

Christopher Aspall came through, folding his hands in front of him. "The show will begin in five minutes. I wanted to tell you personally." He clasped hands with Maske. "It will be a privilege to see your illusions on stage once again." His face twitched in the semblance of a smile.

"Thank you, Mr Aspall," Maske said in his stage voice,

deep and mysterious. "We will endeavor to entertain you as best we can."

And then it was our turn.

We took our places and the curtains fell away.

I flitted behind the scenes as the puppeteer pulling the strings of the hidden wires and contraptions. Oli helped me when needed, and he proved to be an apt assistant. I gave him a smile and he nodded back, straight-faced and anxious.

"Maybe I can change callings, be a full-time stagehand, eh?" Oli said, tying a knot tight around a belaying pin.

"If we win, maybe."

He shook my hand. I smiled and nodded my thanks as the show began.

Like the Specter twins, we created a story to twine the acts together. And, through the lens of theatre, it was Maske's tale. Drystan, who went by the stage name of Amon Ayu, played the young magician studying to be a scientist who stumbled upon a book of magic. After performing a brief, furious flurry of legerdemain, with scarves pulled from sleeves and a dove flying from beneath his coattails as it had in my vision at Twisting the Aces, the audience laughed at his unabashed surprise and delight at this new magic.

He learned more, and the tricks grew more elaborate. He set out to impress a lady magician, Cyan, who went by the stage name of Madame Damselfly. At first, they flirted through magic. I smiled to myself as I watched them from behind stage. The illusions were Maske's, but we had all helped with the storyline. He gave her a bouquet of flowers from thin air, which she turned into a shower of glitter and confetti. He levitated her above his head, with me above stage in the gridiron manipulating wires, and she tilted her head down for a kiss.

That bit I didn't like so much.

Reaching toward Cyan smoothed my doubts. Cyan was not even concentrating on the kiss. She was thinking about the next trick and the way she'd have to move *just* so to get it perfectly. In that brief brush of her mind, I felt the heat from the lamps and the stares of countless pairs of eyes. I lingered within her mind, as it was the closest as I would get to the stage that night. Cyan knew I was there, and it was as though she wrapped an arm around me, drawing me close to watch the show.

When Drystan lowered her, he gave her another kiss on the cheek, and when he moved away a small jewel remained where his lips had rested. Cyan planted the jewel into a pot and a tree grew from it before the audience's very eyes, which bore tiny apples. She cut one in half and gave him back his jewel from the core to more applause. The Jeweled Arbor was one of my favorite tricks – another perfect blend of science, magic, and story to enchant the audience.

Drystan became more powerful. His illusions grew darker. He disappeared into the spirit cabinet and bats flew out of the empty interior when Cyan went to look for him. He appeared in the audience instead, striding back onto the stage.

He needed more power. Cyan produced a little mechanical butterfly and it fluttered over to catch his attention. Drystan set it aside and turned back to his books.

"Am I not enough?" she asked.

He ignored her. The answer was clear.

Cyan deflated, moping in a corner, causing lights of candles to extinguish and rekindle.

After a short time, Madame Damselfly packed her bags and left. It was only after that the magician realized how much he loved her. He tried to call her back, with and without magic. She resisted him at every turn, and then with sleight of hand showed him a new, very large engagement ring. She turned to leave and he grabbed her. Cyan struck him. Drystan yelled and took out a gun and fired at her, point blank. The same trick as the Taliesin twins, but in a different context. Cyan paused, almost as if she'd been struck, and then she spat the bullet from her mouth, which skittered to the floor. She claimed she would never see him again. After she left, a flurry of black crow feathers floated through the air, settling silently on the stage.

The light dimmed and darkened. The magician regretted his actions. He held his head in his hands. The orchestra beneath the stage whined. But the loss of his love could not deter him. To prove he was the master of magic, he raised the ghost of a Chimaera.

It had not been easy. Behind a drawn curtain, Oli and I raised the clear plate glass, angling it toward the audience. Down below the stage was a smaller level, like an extra orchestra pit. Down there, all was dark, with Oli swathed head to toe in black velvet. The only objects in the second stage were a moving platform, angled so that a figure standing on it would tilt at the same angle as the mirror, and an oxyhydrogen spotlight that would illuminate the ghostly apparition.

I jumped down and threw the costume of a patched and ragged coat over my black clothes and stuck a pair of antlers on my head. I stood on a platform brandishing a curved prop sword. Oli made some last minute adjustments before lighting the oxyhydrogen spotlight so my reflection showed on the stage. I went through the rehearsed feints and stints so that it looked like Drystan fought a Chimaera ghost. He vanquished me and I fell to the floor and Oli dimmed the light so I faded from view.

Once it was safe, I sat up and took the antlers and costume off and let out a tentative sigh of relief. We were almost done, and so far all had gone according to plan.

I couldn't help but smile ruefully as well. In the circus, I had dressed as a girl for the pantomime, and nobody knew, save Drystan, that I had actually spent the first sixteen years of my life as a girl. Now, I played a Chimaera ghost, and none of the audience knew that I was sort-of Chimaera and hid a Phantom Damselfly in my pocket.

Drystan began the finale, saying he did not need Madame Damselfly and that he could create the love of his life.

"But can I do it?" he asked himself. "Is my magic strong enough?"

Just as in practice the other day, the gauze curtain behind him fluttered. Drystan pulled it away to reveal the automaton on the podium. The audience gasped and whispered. Through Cyan's eyes, I looked up at the box where Doctor Pozzi sat with the Princess Royal. He leaned forward in his seat.

Drystan muttered and gestured as he began the "incantations" to bring the automaton to life. I looked around for Oli, as I didn't see him under the stage and

I wanted him around in case I needed help with the star trap. Cyan was changing hurriedly in a dressing room.

Micah, I heard her say, frantic. *I think something's happened to Oli. I can't sense him. I can't feel him!*

What?

Go check on him. I sensed pain. Can't get much more – too many people around. And something weird. My ability is fluctuating. I can only reach you because I'm "shouting" as loud as I can.

I heard footsteps behind stage. *I'll check*, I said, but I didn't know if she heard me. Biting my lip, I guessed I had about ten minutes before I needed to be by the star trap. I sprinted behind the stage and then stopped. Oli lay sprawled across the floor, half-dragged behind a box of props. I heard a rustle of movement and crouched into a fighting stance.

A large man, bald and muscle-bound, crept toward the stage. I took a step and a floorboard creaked. The man stared at me. Distantly, I heard Cyan yelling in my mind. I rushed him.

The man grabbed me and threw me across the backstage as though I weighed no more than a doll. The back of my head exploded with pain. With a grunt, I rushed him again, dancing out of his reach and landing a punch into his kidneys. His breath left in a *whoosh* of pain but he stayed standing. "Was only meant to be one runt back here, not two," he growled.

I darted out of his grasping arms and grabbed a nearby skein of rope. But I was too slow – he grabbed me and threw me again, harder. I hit the wall and slid down it, all my breath gone from my lungs. With a sickening lurch, I remembered Bil had thrown Aenea much the same way in the circus. I stayed still until he turned away. With painful slowness, I sat up. Knowing I had but moments, I scrabbled about desperately. My hands found a spare belaying pin, a long, rounded metal spike used to tie ropes to. I threw it at him with all my strength, hitting him on the back of the head. He fell with a thump. I panted, my ribs screaming with pain, but I felt a brief glow of triumph.

That glow faded when someone grabbed me from behind and then put their hands around my neck and *squeezed*. All the terror of Bil's attack returned in a rush, and for a moment, I couldn't move. I pretended to fight against the man, making my movements weaker, and then I went limp. The hands loosened. Slowly, I drew more air into my lungs and saw who had attacked me.

It was Pen Taliesin, and in his hand – a hand that had just strangled me – was an Eclipse, the Vestige artifact that would cause all other Vestige in the immediate vicinity to stop functioning. It would turn the automaton from the finale to a frozen statue.

I tried to rise, but my battered body wasn't quick enough. At the movement, Taliesin craned his head toward mine, his lips pulled back from his mouth. I felt the snarl mirrored on my own features.

Gritting my teeth against the pain, I knocked Taliesin to the floor. If I hadn't just been thrown across the room and half-throttled, it wouldn't have been a fair fight. I was young and lithe, far stronger than I had a right to be, and he was so fragile he might as well have been made of old bone and dry leaves. But I hurt, and I was slower. He managed to give me a glancing blow across my cheek, his fingernails scratching my skin. But I pushed him from me as hard as I could. He unbalanced and the Eclipse tumbled from his gnarled hands. I scrabbled for it.

Though he was a weak ruin of a man, he was on Lerium. With a last burst of strength he punched me in the face. For a moment, the world around me wobbled, and he tried to grab the Eclipse. I recovered and wrestled him to the ground, using my entire bodyweight to keep him down.

"I won't let him win," Taliesin wheezed. "Even if he wins today, I'll do everything in my power to make him suffer. He ruined my life. He ruined me!"

"And you ruined his life, too. You were both stupid and hurt each other, but now let it go."

His hand fumbled and he grasped the Eclipse again. "I'll make him sorry."

"Not today, Taliesin," I said, rapping his head smartly against the floor. Power flooded through me, heady and strong, as I held him down. He could not fight back. From far away I could tell that Cyan had "heard" what was happening. Her presence batted at the edges of my consciousness, but I pushed her away.

Taliesin glared at me with his yellowed eyes, his breath smelling of decay and the cloying spice of Lerium. And then the leer subsided and he was only a pathetic man gasping for breath, his face purpling. I realized how easy it would be to kill him. To make sure he never tried to harm Maske. Immediately, I skittered away from that thought, horror growing within me. Was that my own thought, my own bloodlust, or was it Anisa's emotions feeding into mine?

With a shaking breath, I forced my fingers to loosen. Taliesin took great, shuddering gasps, his eyes rolling in his skull. With his henchman subdued and without the Eclipse, Taliesin was no threat. Not truly. We possessed the skill and the magic. Our chances of winning were as good as they could be. If we won and he still attempted to tamper with us, we had the Collective of Magic to petition to, and proof he had attempted to cheat. Taliesin had failed.

"Come on," Taliesin rasped, a last plea. "Let me just press the button. I'll pay you for it. Enough to set you up for life."

"If you go now, I won't tell everyone out there" – I jerked my head toward the audience – "what you tried to do. And your grandsons won't need to know you didn't think them talented enough to win on their own."

His eyes widened.

I let him go and stepped back, bending down to clutch the Eclipse, never taking my eyes off of him.

"Get away," I said, my voice hard and sharp. He stumbled off the stage, barely able to walk without his cane.

I watched him go. The henchman had awoken, skulking off from backstage. He paused and turned, meeting my angry eyes, taking in the Eclipse in my hand. He must have thought it was a weapon, for he held up his hands.

"You go too, or I'll call the policiers after the show," I bluffed. Cyan whispered his name in my mind. "I know your name, Jarek Lutier. And where you live. Trouble me again and you'll regret it."

"How do you know my name?" he asked, blood draining from his face.

"I know more than you could ever guess. Go."

Whatever he saw in my face frightened him. He ran from the stage, and I would be certain he wouldn't tell a soul he was soundly beaten by a boy he thought might have magical powers.

Micah! Hurry! Cyan called from below the stage.

I heard Drystan say, "You shall become the love I never had…" and I raced toward the stage. There was less than a minute.

Don't go up the star trap without me, Cyan, it's too dangerous! I yelled at her.

If I don't go, the act is ruined, and we're ruined. Faster, Micah!

I wrenched open the trap door and jumped down below the stage, even though it was a deep drop, for there was no time for the ladder. Cyan stood near the star trap machine, wringing her hands.

"Thanks," I panted. "You saved the performance."

"Yes, I know. No time. Hurry!"

I fiddled with the machinery. Just in time, the trapdoor opened and the automaton slid down the star trap. I caught her and set her down.

"Come on, Cyan."

She stepped onto the platform. She had painted her face with silver swirls, though at my request, she had made them look less like Anisa's markings. She bent down and gave me a quick kiss on the cheek. An apology. A comfort.

I pulled the lever, and she rose to the stage. She unhooked the sleeves and the audience gasped as she revealed herself to them.

"My love!" Drystan spoke of her beauty and perfection, and she covered her face again, as if in shyness. I pulled the lever, and Cyan came back down the star trap. Up above, Drystan reached for her, and the dress collapsed. To the audience, it was if she had disappeared completely. In reality, the dress was sucked into a tube, which Drystan covered with his leg. The tube and the dress dropped back down the star trap and I caught them.

Drystan cried out in surprise and dismay. He admitted the errors of his ways – and he repented to the Lord and Lady, throwing his magic books into a chest.

Cyan wiped the silver from her face and hurried to the trapdoor beneath the spirit cabinet and climbed the ladder. She emerged from the cabinet up above.

"Is the real girl not better than the magic one?" she asked, teasingly.

Drystan fell to his knees.

"Do you love me?" she asked.

"More than anything, my sweet! More than the moon loves the sun."

"Would you give up your magic for me?"

"In a heartbeat, though it would be like tearing my heart in twain."

She reached down and tilted his head up at her. "Then I will not ask such a thing of you. But you must not let it overwhelm the goodness at your core."

They embraced, and I fought down a scowl again as I climbed behind the stage to the gridiron above.

Stop fretting, Micah. Cyan said. *Though he's a good kisser. Lord's left nut, everyone in the Kymri Theatre has kissed*

Drystan now except for Maske.

There's still time! Cyan teased before breaking the kiss. As they did, I ran across the gridiron, releasing confetti and glitter. Cyan and Drystan bowed to thunderous applause before the curtains fell.

"I can't believe what Taliesin did," Cyan said backstage, clutching Oli close. "He nearly cost us everything."

"Taliesin?" Drystan echoed.

"He tried to ruin us." I said. "He knocked out Oli."

Oli pointed to his head to illustrate, swaying slightly on his feet.

"Oli, you should go get some ice from the dressing room for your head," I said. "You don't want that bump to swell any more."

He nodded and grimaced before weaving his way to the dressing room.

When Oli left, I took the Eclipse from my back pocket. "He had this."

"Hurry up and hide it," Drystan urged. "Anyone sees you with that and they'll either steal it or report you to the policiers."

"Styx." I put it in my suit pocket.

Maske found us, beaming. "Marvelous. You were all marvelous. I couldn't be prouder." He gave all of us rough hugs and a kiss on the top of our heads. It was still so strange to see him so affectionate.

The Collective of Magic went to deliberate, and the guests again congregated in the main foyer, drinking and discussing the duel. I hoped they were not disappointed.

We huddled in the dressing room. Maske downed a large whisky – the smell of which still made me gag – and the rest of us stared at the bottle of champagne morosely. Drystan and I sat close together, holding hands so tightly it almost hurt. Oli held ice against his head and Cyan wrung her hands together next to him, staring off into the distance.

Are you listening to what they're saying?

No. They're too far away for me to hear, unfortunately. I'm listening to Taliesin and his grandsons. The boys don't know what Taliesin tried to do. Her voice warmed with triumph. *They're worried. Couldn't believe how well we performed.*

To be honest, neither could I.

After half an hour of deliberation, the Collective called everyone back into the auditorium. The audience took a long time to settle back into their seats. I fought the irrational urge to yell at them to hurry up so we could learn our fate. Finally, everyone fell silent.

Professor David Delvin stood in the center of the stage, flanked by some of the best magicians of the age – the leaders of the Collective of Magic.

Professor Delvin waved to the left side of the stage. Taliesin came out, limping along with his cane, the feathers of his turban bobbing. He tried to come across as triumphant, but I saw how he favored his arm, and how he would not look at me or Maske.

His grandsons followed, straight-backed, smiling disarmingly at the crowd. My stomach felt as though it dropped to my knees. These twins had been born on the stage and lived and breathed magic their entire lives. Their show had far more money behind it, and was flashier. I could not help but think we had no chance, even if I had foiled Taliesin's plot.

I gripped Drystan's hand even harder.

Professor Delvin gestured to his right, and I released Drystan's hand so Maske, Cyan, and he could walk onstage. They blinked under the bright glass globes of the theatre.

"This was not an easy decision to make. The Taliesin Twins of the well-known and beloved Specter Shows performed wonderfully, illustrating their supposed power over death.

"And the newcomers, whom many proclaimed the underdogs, Maske's Marionettes, also gave a stunning performance, focusing their magic into showing the inherent dangers of letting it overwhelm you. Both acts stunned, delighted, and amazed, just as good magic should.

"And so, how to choose?"

He paused, turning toward the other members of the Collective of Magic. I did not know their names, but they were all men with graying hair, wearing immaculate suits, their blank magicians' smiles giving away no secrets. Had they found us worthy or wanting?

"After a long deliberation by the Collective of Magic, with input from the Royal Princess Nicolette Snakewood of Ellada herself, we have come to our decision."

He paused again, and I couldn't breathe. Maske, Cyan, and Drystan all gripped each other's hands. I tried to read Cyan's face, but if she intuited anything, none of it showed. Taliesin glared past the Collective of Magic and Maske and his marionettes, his gaze resting on me. Now that his fear was gone, it was only rage, but impotent. I glared right back at him, my throat tight with fear and anticipation.

"The winners of the duel between the scions of the great magicians of Pen Taliesin and Jasper Maske are…"

Another pause. The tension in the audience rose. Everyone in the theatre, and all the folk out in the parks on the cold night, I was sure, held their breaths. My entire body tingled, and I could not take my eyes from his face.

"Jasper Maske, and his Marionettes: Amon Ayu and Madame Damselfly!"

My knees shook in relief. I sagged against one of the columns to the side of the stage, my face hurting from smiling so hard.

We did it. We actually did it.

"As I said, it was very difficult – almost impossible – to choose between two teams of magicians of such obvious talent and skill," Professor Delvin continued. "In the end, Maske's Marionettes won due to a slightly superior execution of tricks, a more cohesive storyline, and a truly spectacular finale. Well done to you all." He bowed to them, and they bowed in turn. I couldn't believe it. On the stage, Cyan wiped tears from her eyes, beaming from ear to ear, the grin echoed on Drystan's and Maske's faces. Maske stood straight and tall, a man come back to life.

Taliesin's face darkened with rage. I half-expected him to punch Professor Delvin in the face. Sind and Jac Taliesin, by contrast, were flabbergasted, their eyes wide and mouths open.

Taliesin and his grandsons shuffled to the left of the stage, still visible but no longer smirking. One of the twins looked like he might be crying.

The curtains of the stage pulled back again, and all of our props had been cleared away and the scenery changed to a painted canvas of the sunset over the ocean of Imachara Beach. My gaze rested on the section of the beach where R.H. Ragona's Circus of Magic had camped last summer.

But then someone came onto the stage. The Princess Royal walked toward Maske, straight-backed. She wore a royal smile – pleasant and distant – but her eyes sparkled. She held a small box in her outstretched hands. When she reached Maske, she craned her neck up at him.

Guards flanked the stage, and when I turned my head, a man stood next to me, flanked by more guards. I started as I recognized the Royal Steward of Ellada. I'd never seen him up close. He had a full head of gray hair and deep pouches beneath his eyes that made him look sleepy, though his eyes were bright and keen as black buttons.

"Who's this?" he asked his guards.

"One of Maske's stagehands, Sam," the other said without a pause, and my eyes widened, a shiver running over me. The Steward gave me a cool stare and looked back to the stage.

"Mister Maske, Madame Damselfly, and Amon Ayu," she said, and her small, childish voice carried throughout the theatre. "I congratulate you on your victory tonight, and offer you a small token of my gratitude for an evening of delightful entertainment." The words were rehearsed but I could tell she had indeed enjoyed the performance.

Maske took the box, bowing as low as he could.

"I thank you most sincerely, Your Highness," he intoned gravely. He opened the box, and within were three large pins set with diamonds and the emeralds of Ellada. The young, future queen asked them all to kneel, and she fastened the pins herself. She then bade them to rise, and they did, the pins sparkling on their breasts. My eyes shone with tears as I watched.

She inclined their head at them again. "Thank you again, Mister Maske. I look forward to perhaps seeing you and your colleagues perform at the palace someday."

"It would be a singular pleasure, Your Highness."

She smiled politely at him again and made her way off the stage, toward her uncle and therefore me. Her eyes met mine as she passed. "I recognize you," she said. My mind spun in a panic. Had I ever met the Princess Royal as Iphigenia Laurus? Only once, and she would have been far too young, only a toddler, to remember me among the crowds at her birthday party at the palace.

"You were the Chimaera ghost!"

Sweet relief flooded through me. "I am... I was, Your Highness," I stammered.

She smiled, and unlike the one on stage, this appeared genuine. "And you did everything backstage?"

"I did, though our friend Oli helped."

"Was it difficult?" she asked, and her voice lost that forced, royal cadence. She was like any other curious child.

I smiled back. "It was, Your Highness. I had to run around an awful lot. But it was a lot of fun as well, and very rewarding. I am so proud of my friends."

"I hope you will come and perform at the palace for me."

Mindful of the Steward and his cool gaze, I lowered myself to one knee. "We would love nothing more, Your Highness."

She grinned outright, and I saw she was missing a front tooth. She was so adorable I wanted to gather her into my arms for a hug, future monarch or no.

"Come, Nicolette, it is time to be going," the Steward said.

"Yes, uncle," she said obediently, her smile fading.

"Good night, Your Highness," I said.

"Good night... what is your name?"

I hesitated for a heartbeat, my mind scrabbling for a full name. "Sam... Harper, Your Highness."

"Good night then, Mister Harper."

I watched her go before turning my attention back to the stage. Professor Delvin and the other magicians gave short speeches about the merits of magic as entertainment and praising Maske for his performance. Taliesin had limped off the stage in disgust, but the two grandsons remained; it seemed almost cruel for them to still be there. Professor Delvin now listed the prizes: a sizeable cash sum – enough that we could renovate the theatre in full and still have plenty left over; full support of the Collective for new shows and performances; and, as mentioned, the wager of old was settled. Jasper Maske could perform magic and illusion with no hindrance, and Pen Taliesin and his grandsons would have to shut their doors. The Specter Shows would be no more.

I chewed my lip at that. One morning several weeks ago, I had broached the subject with Maske of what would happen if we won – if he would truly keep up his end of the bargain and ruin the boys' career.

"Why do you care?" he asked. "There's no love between the twins and you. Especially Drystan." The corners of his eyes crinkled in amusement as he remembered the tale of the fistfight after the Specter Shows.

"No, but it's not their fault their grandfather is a tosser, is it?" I asked.

"No, I suppose it's not," was all he'd said.

I stared at Maske, hoping he would remember the conversation.

I willed a thought at him, wishing he could hear it: *Be the better man.*

I could not send it, but Cyan could. I felt her push the thought so that it whispered in Maske's mind. His eyes darted first to Cyan and then to me. I met his gaze.

When it was his turn to speak, Maske cleared his throat. "Thank you to everyone who has watched our performance tonight. I am overwhelmed with the support you have shown for us and for magic. I am ecstatic to be declared the victor." He licked his lips. "However, I wish to amend the wager slightly, if it is alright with the Collective of Magic, of course."

Professor Delvin frowned but motioned for him to continue.

"In the fifteen years I have not performed magic, it has been difficult for me, like missing a limb."

My eyes found Doctor Pozzi in the crowd. His mouth twisted at that turn of phrase.

"I thought that, were I victorious, I would delight in giving that same sentence upon others. That it would make me feel the stronger man. But, I have learned that it would not, and so I do not wish to ban Sind and Jac Taliesin from the Specter Shows, nor take their premises from them. The loss of such a wonderful spectacle would hurt Imachara and Ellada. What the world always needs more of is magic and wonder." He bowed to the audience, and then toward the Taliesin twins.

They looked at him in utter amazement, and bowed back in turn. They were so surprised that I wondered how much kindness they'd had in their lives.

Not much from their grandfather, that's for sure. He speaks to them like they're his servants. Or vermin, Cyan said.

Be that as it may, I still didn't like them.

The audience approved of Maske's speech and everyone applauded, and most gave a standing ovation. Maske, Cyan, and Drystan held hands and bowed again. People threw flowers and coins onto the stage. And then the curtains closed, obscuring them from sight.

I grinned in fierce triumph.

We won.

29
THE KYMRI THEATRE

"I did it. We did it. Somehow, these three came into my life, and now I have a life of performance and magic again. It still doesn't seem possible. I still don't feel as if I deserve it, for all my repentance. But tonight, after much wine and dancing, all feels well."

Jasper Maske's personal diary

Maske threw open the doors to the Kymri Theatre. Many of the people he held séances for, the Lord and Lady Elmbark among them, came to celebrate. Some of the friends he still played cards with every now and again – for buttons instead of coins – arrived, bringing spirits and hearty smiles. Oli was up in Cyan's room, as the lump on his head had grown to the size of a clementine.

I told Maske what had happened in the carriage ride back to the theatre. The Eclipse was tucked into the pocket of my coat.

Maske sighed. "Can't say I'm surprised he tried something like that. Are you sure the boys had nothing to do with it? If they have, I'll rescind my moment of sentimentality."

"They're innocent," Cyan said, with a certainty only she could possess.

He nodded. "Seems I owe you even more of a debt, now."

I waved the gesture away. "It was selfish. We like living here."

He smiled.

In the Kymri Theatre, Maske was the cat with the cream. He could not stop smiling magnanimously at everyone. We held the party in the main theatre. The brass automaton stood on the stage, an angel watching over us. I had changed out of my stagehand gear into my stiff suit. I kept tugging at my cravat.

Cyan came over to me.

"We did it," she said.

"So we did. We made a good team there, with Taliesin."

"Aye, that we did." She tilted her chin toward the other end of the room, amused. "Look at Maske."

He was dancing with Lily Verre, the white of his smile visible from here. He looked twenty years younger. It all felt worth it.

"We saved him."

She nodded, and then she hesitated. "Anisa showed me what she showed you. Those visions with Ahti and Dev."

"Ah."

"Guess it's time to try and save more people, soon enough."

"That's us, heroes of the world in the making." I tried to keep my voice light, but it fell flat. "Drystan knows. He wants to help."

Cyan looked over at him. Drystan was chatting comfortably with Lord Elmbark, no doubt amused that the man didn't recognize the boy who once played with his son at his own apartments. "That's good. You care for him a lot, don't you?"

I paused. Life seemed better, brighter, with Drystan around. One touch and my fears quieted. One off-hand comment and he'd have me in stitches of laughter. Even when I'd first seen him in the circus when his gaze met mine, I had felt a spark. Now, I felt a flame. "Pretty sure I've fallen in love with him."

"Have you told him that?"

"No. Not yet."

"You should. He loves you too."

I blinked. "Have you…?" I tapped my temple.

She smiled. "No. I don't need to."

A rush of warmth flowed through me. I wouldn't believe her until I'd heard the words from his lips, but the possibility was sweet as sugar all the same.

Across the room, Drystan threw back his head to laugh at something Lord Elmbark said. I felt happy, and safer than in a long time. Much was to come, but tonight, at least, was celebration.

"Have you told Maske yet?"

She shook her head. "The right time hasn't appeared. He was always in his workshop, or with Lily, or…"

"Or excuses."

A corner of her mouth quirked. "Aye, excuses. What if he doesn't want me as a daughter?"

"Cyan, he's already shown how much he cares for you. He never considered anyone else for an assistant. He'll be delighted. You should speak to him."

She chewed her lip and nodded, leaving me. She tapped Maske on the shoulder, and he nodded at her question and they made their way to the parlor. I smiled.

Doctor Pozzi came up to me, holding two glasses of wine. He passed me one with his clockwork hand. I nodded at him and smiled, taking a small sip.

"Did you enjoy the performance, Doctor Pozzi?"

"Very much so. It was a piece of art. I thought you would be on the stage, though."

"No, I'm afraid not. I decided it's safer for me to be behind the scenes instead of in the limelight." I swirled my wine around in my glass. I didn't like the taste much.

"Perhaps it is, at that. Are you feeling quite well?" he asked, his brows furrowed in worry.

"I'm in perfect health, as ever, Doctor."

"That's good to hear, Micah." He looked around the theatre. "This is an extraordinary building. Some parts of it mirror the Kymri temples I've been to."

"I'd like to see those one day."

"You should. Everyone should travel the world if they can. Open their eyes to different cultures and ways of life. I feel like a changed man after my time abroad."

"Maybe someday," I said, "we'll do a touring show."

He nodded. "So you plan to stay in show business?"

"I never plan anything for forever. Too much has shifted beneath my feet in the past for that. But for now, this is where I belong."

Doctor Pozzi nodded. "I am glad for you."

"And will you be staying in Imachara long?" I asked, wondering how long I'd have to worry about him looking over my shoulder.

"It depends on a myriad of factors. There's been an interesting birth in Kymri I'd like to investigate – the child can cause his bottle to float to him when he's hungry, which has scared his parents half to death – but I do believe my brief travels are over. I am the Royal Physician, and the young Royal is my charge."

Something in the phrasing reminded me of how Anisa spoke of her charges. Someone who knew Pozzi hailed him from across the room, and he made his excuses to me and ambled over. I watched him go, wishing I could have the measure of the man.

When Cyan and Maske returned, they both beamed brighter than glass globes, Maske with his arm tight around her.

Have things gone well? I ventured, looking over to Pozzi. He did not seem to notice how we spoke, or if he did, he gave no sign.

He had no idea, but he doesn't deny he was with my mother around that time. It's still a little bizarre and awkward, but he's happy. And I'm happy.

She laughed in my mind.

I smiled.

30
THE WOMAN IN THE RED DRESS

"But the spirits show me visions. I see a girl, no, a woman, in a wine-red dress. Her child is ill, eaten from the inside. I see figures on a stage, playing their parts, the audience applauding as magic surrounds them. I see great feathered wings flapping against the night sky. A demon with green skin drips blood onto a white floor. A man checks his pocket watch, and I hear a clock ticking, counting the time."

The words spoken to Micah Grey at the séance

The peace did not last.

A week later, Anisa woke me up.

It's time, she whispered in my mind.

"Hmm?" I asked aloud, still half asleep.

I had a vision. You must go to that place where you saw the woman with the ill child. I think something has happened. Something impossible.

I sighed, rolling out of bed. "Alright, alright," I muttered, tugging on my shoes I rubbed my gritty eyes. My muscles hurt. I yawned.

What about Cyan and Drystan? I asked.

No need to trouble them with this.

My mouth twisted. *I'm at least asking Drystan if he wants to come. We promised each other – no secrets.*

Hurry, then.

I shook Drystan awake, and whispered what had happened. He clambered out of bed and dressed, stumbling to the washroom to splash water on his face. We left. The air was warmer today. I barely needed my coat and left it unbuttoned. All of my clothes were nice and new. Séance requests were flowing in thick and fast, the Collective of Magic had assigned us a manager, and we had plenty of bookings in Imachara and other cities along the coasts and in the Emerald Bowl. We had enough money to flee Ellada five times over, but neither of us had brought up the possibility of leaving Maske, Cyan, and the Kymri Theatre.

We trudged through the city, still yawning. It was so early we doubted we'd see the woman pushing her child about for a stroll. I wanted to ask Anisa for more information, but I figured I would learn soon enough.

"So who's this woman again?" Drystan asked me as I walked.

"In my first vision at the séance, Maske mentioned her. For a time I thought she was the second client of the Shadow, but that was Pozzi. Something about her or that child is important. I can feel it, but I can't explain it more than that."

"Time to find out, it seems."

I nodded.

The café across from the building where the woman lived had just opened. We ordered a strong pot of coffee.

Now what, Anisa?

We wait. She will come here.

She fell silent in my mind. I stirred sugar and milk into the coffee, my hands shaking. I was scared. Anisa's master plan was meant to be a vague event in the future. This was the first step, and I did not know where it would lead. I wished Cyan could tell the future, but she only had that dream about the lion. The one that Anisa sent.

The door of the building across the way opened. A woman came out pushing the wicker wheelchair. I sat up straight, and Drystan followed my gaze. She pushed the chair across the cobbled street, her bonneted head ducked low. When she came closer, I peered into the chair, but a cover hid the child from view.

Before entering the café, the woman came around and told the boy off for removing his scarf and she wrapped him up again. It was only when she turned around that I saw her face.

It was Lily Verre.

"Styx," I swore. She hadn't seen us. Quickly, I grabbed a newspaper on the empty table next to it and unfolded it, feeling ridiculously conspicuous.

"It can't be," Drystan whispered to me. "That's Lily. What's going on?"

I rubbed my forehead, and my fingers came away damp with sweat. "I don't know. She said she didn't have any children." I peeked around the newspaper. Lily was at the till. She kept glancing back at the boy in the wicker chair.

"Two coffees and two chocolate pastries to take away," she said to the woman behind the till, and I reeled again. Gone were her flighty voice and her rough mannerisms. She spoke with the smooth, educated voice of the nobility of Imachara.

"Oh, Lord and Lady," I breathed. "We've been had."

She'd been waiting for us at Twisting the Aces. She'd just joined the week before. But how had she known to lie in wait? I searched my memory... and the first night we went to Maske's, there had been a woman walking down the street. I remember the sound of her heels echoing on the cobblestones. Had it been her?

The woman you saw matches her height and weight. I believe she shadowed Shadow Elwood, Anisa said. *I can see it now. She followed him the last night you were in the circus and knew where you went.* I didn't know if I believed her. What if Anisa had known this all along?

I didn't. Oftentimes what I see does not make sense until many other pieces fall into place.

Lily waited impatiently for the coffees and the pastries.

I went back through every memory with Lily, trying to see her ploy. When I went to Twisting the Aces and I'd had a vision: was she to blame? On the second visit, she dropped something, a glass in a frame. My breath hitched. I had been blind and foolish. That purple glass with the motley frame. Take away the gaudy flame, and wipe off a sheen of thin red paint, and it could have been a Mirror of Moirai. It was the same size, and when she'd wiped off my fingerprints with a cloth, she'd taken care not to touch it herself. She could have known where we were the entire time.

She wasn't the second client of the Shadow. She *was* a second Shadow.

When the coffees arrived, Lily put them on the small shelf below the chair and pushed it back onto the street. We waited for her to leave and then dashed up to the till and paid for our unfinished coffee. I put extra coins into the tip jar to make up for the tea I had stolen months ago.

Lily disappeared around the corner. She wore her wine-colored dress. I nodded to a drainpipe and we made our way up to the roof. As we climbed, I felt a little dizzy. Why hadn't she turned us in after our actions resulted in the death of Shadow Elwood? What did she want from us?

Poor Maske.

She made her way through the streets. She gave one of the pastries to the boy and we finally had a clear view of the boy in the wicker basket.

Despite the mild weather, the child, who must have been around eight, wore a coat, a hat, and a thick scarf that covered most of his face. But the child used his weak arms to tug at the scarf and managed to disengage himself from it so he could eat his pastry. I stared, my mouth falling open slightly. The boy's face was peeling badly, and patches had fallen away. Beneath, the skin was dark green, like the back of a beetle. Beneath the hat, I saw two small protrusions.

Horns.

Like Ahti.

Of course, Anisa breathed in my mind. *I should have seen it. This is why the world is in danger. If someone hurts or frightens this little Chimaera, then all is lost.* She sounded so sad. *Once he finishes his change, he will look identical to Ahti.*

Drystan was staring at the boy as well. "Did I just see what I think I saw?"

"Yeah. That's a true Chimaera. A Theri."

Lily drew the covering back again, surveying the street. But she didn't look up. We followed her as she made her way to the nicest part of town, passing the palace. She paused at the gates, and for a moment I thought she would enter.

Instead, she gazed through the bars and continued onto Ruby Street, to press the buzzer for Doctor Samuel Pozzi's apartments.

She was let in immediately.

Drystan and I froze in shock. The woman who joked and comforted us, helped tidy the theatre and had supposedly fallen in love with Maske was all smoke and mirrors, like any of our illusions. I shivered again, but it was not from cold. I felt very warm. I loosened my coat, sweating. Drystan peered at me.

"Micah, are you alright? You're pale." He put his palm on my forehead. "Styx, you have a fever."

"A fever?" I asked him thickly. "Is this what a fever feels like? It's terrible. I don't like it."

"Come on, let's get you home. There's nothing more we can do here."

It was so difficult to climb back down the drainpipe and trudge home. I kept having to pause to catch my breath. My eyes felt like they were cooking in my skull, and I'd never been so weak.

Drystan didn't seem unduly concerned. "It's just a fever, Micah. You'll take a cool bath, get some soup and liquids, and you'll be fine in a day or two."

In response, I stumbled to an alleyway and retched up my coffee. The bile burned my throat.

In all that happened, it turned out I still kept one secret from him. That if I became ill, it could be the sign of something being very wrong.

Are you going to go see Doctor Pozzi? Anisa asked me as we made our way home again.

Looks like I don't have much of a choice.

"Come on, Micah," Drystan urged. "We're almost there. I'll take care of you. You'll be fine."

I opened my mouth to answer, but my eyes rolled up into my head and I fell into his arms. I had just enough time to be annoyed before I fainted yet again.

31
THE DREAM, THE NIGHTMARE

"A fever may burn a man alive. Some of the old wise men who called themselves seers would bring on a fever. They said the fever dreams showed them their fate, and the fate of those who followed them."

"MYSTICS AND SEERS" from A HISTORY OF ELLADA AND ITS COLONIES, Professor Caed Cedar, Royal Snakewood University

Part of me knew it was a fever dream. That didn't make it any less frightening.

I was not me. Anisa was flying, or falling, through skies on fire. All was red, orange, black and gold. I reached out my hands and they burned to nothing. There was no pain. I closed my eyes.

I woke up and I was no longer myself. My body was human, my skin the peach and cream of a newborn. No swirling silver markings of my family. No dragonfly wings rose from my back. I was clipped. Earthbound. I skulked through the

streets of this strange new city of Imachara, keeping to the shadows. I came to the market square before the palace, with a large stage set up in the middle, but no audience. Storm clouds rumbled overhead.

The phantoms, the parts in this play to come, walked across the stage. The woman in the red dress whose son was eaten from the inside. My new charge knew who she was now, and what she had done. Things might still fall into place the way I thought – hoped – they would. The way the world whispers to me that it might.

The doctor with the clockwork hand appeared onstage, smiling that self-satisfied grin, though he was as ignorant as all the rest. He did not even know what he wore against the stump of his arm. The ones who side with him float around him, waiting in the wings. The young girl with the lie around her neck. The one who was Matla, young Cyan, her powers just beginning to unfurl. The boy Drystan, who despite his lack of power could destroy everything. And my little Kedi, my newest charge, the one called Micah, or Gene, or Sam – my last and greatest hope.

The stage lights extinguished, leaving me in the night. My lungs burned with the memory of smoke and soot. I was alone in the darkness. No one called me forth.

A door in the darkness opened, and the boy Ahti came toward me. But as I reached my arms to him, he fell, his shriveled legs unable to support him, his skin gray and green. He wailed, covering his eyes with his hands. He wasn't my Ahti. A flash of bright blue light. A dull roar. A young girl, screaming. Micah Grey, the one meant to help, to save everything, crying out. A flash of blinding blue.

They were all dead and gone, and the world dead and gone with them.

Darkness fell.

I knew what I needed to do to stop it, but how could I commit that evil, too?

I knew where they were, those two little discs that held the loves of my life. My Relean. My little Kedi, Dev. They had survived the years, just as I have, even if Ahti was gone.

I would do anything to be with them again.

Anything. Even what was to come.

"Micah."

I turned my head away from the noise.

"Micah." A cool cloth rested on my forehead.

I opened my eyes, but the brightness hurt. I closed them again.

A brush of lips against my cheek. "Wake up, Micah." A whisper in my ear.

Drystan. I opened my eyes, meeting his blue ones.

"Are you feeling any better?" he asked, his brow furrowed in worry.

I tried to sit up, but a swirl of nausea drove me back. "No, I don't think I am."

"What's happening?"

"I didn't tell you, but Pozzi warned me... that if I grow sick..." I trailed off, my body racked with coughs. I hurt. Everything hurt.

"Then what?" Panic entered his voice.

"Then I could be dying."

"No." He shook his head. "No. You can't be. It's just a fever. It'll pass."

"If I die…" I started.

"Shut up. Don't speak like that. We'll get you sorted."

"Listen, you numbskull." I managed a weak smile. "I'm trying to tell you something important. If I do die, I'd regret not telling you…"

"Telling me what?"

I closed my eyes again, not brave enough to tell him with my eyes open. "That I love you."

A sharp intake of breath. Silence. Horrible silence. A tear slid down my cheek. *Say something, Drystan,* I wanted to say. *Say something while I'm still conscious.* The dreams, the nightmares, hovered in the corner of my mind. Crouching. Waiting. My mouth was dry with fever and fear. I had never felt so vulnerable.

Drystan leaned close, pressed his palms against my warm cheeks. "I love you, Micah Grey. More than the sun loves the moon," he whispered, quoting the magic show.

I gave a half-laugh, half-sob. Drystan pressed his lips to mine.

I began to shiver, my body jerking beneath the sweat-soaked sheets. The visions of the world ending came closer, pressing close, their whispers filling my ears. I felt even warmer, as though I were a bit of tinder about to explode into flame.

"And now," he said. "I'm going to save you."

Acknowledgments

It's scary, writing these. I'm always afraid I'm going to miss listing someone, because there are so many people who help make a book far better than it would be if I'd been laboring on my own vacuum. So thank you to my earliest readers and some of my closest friends: Shawn DeMille & Erica Bretall, for giving me feedback on what was a decidedly shaky draft. Thank you to my literary BFF Wesley Chu being there every step of the way, including dealing with my anxious rambles with the patience of a champ.

To my many other betas who have each provided such valuable critique: Mike Kalar, Rob Haines, Molly Rabbitt, Vonny McKay, Megan Walker, Mike Stewart, Stephen Aryan, Anne Lyle, Amy McCulloch, Colin Sinclair, Joseph Morton, and my Tuesday writing buddies Lorna McKay and Hannah Beresford. Thank you to my writing groups the Inkbots and The Cabal. To Emma Maree Urquhart for the name "Alvis Tyndall." An especially huge thank you to Corinne Duyvis and Erica for not only reading an earlier draft but also being invaluable at the 11th hour.

Many thanks to the publishing people who helped me with my second book baby: my leopard-print-clad, lindy-hopping, honey badger of an agent, Juliet Mushens, and of course to my editor, Amanda Rutter, and to all the people who have given *Pantomime* and *Shadowplay* a lovely home in Strange Chemistry/Angry Robot.

Lastly but definitely not least: to Sally Baxter, to whom the book is dedicated, for being my number one fan and the best mother. Thanks to my family and friends. And my everlasting gratitude and love to my husband Craig, for listening to my endless plot ideas, for the many cups of tea and cooked dinners, and for forcing me to turn off the laptop occasionally.

And thank you to the readers who followed Micah Grey from the circus to the magician's stage.

EXPERIMENTING WITH YOUR IMAGINATION

"A riveting union of science fiction thriller, romance, family drama, and conspiracy theory."
Page Morgan, author of The Beautiful and the Cursed

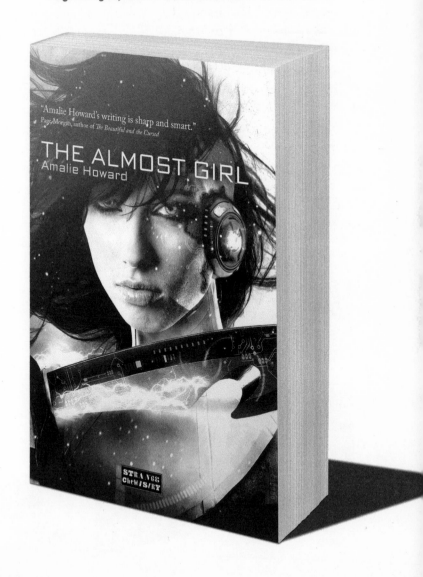

"Amalie Howard's writing is sharp and smart."
Page Morgan, author of The Beautiful and the Cursed

THE ALMOST GIRL
Amalie Howard

STRANGE CheMIS/RY

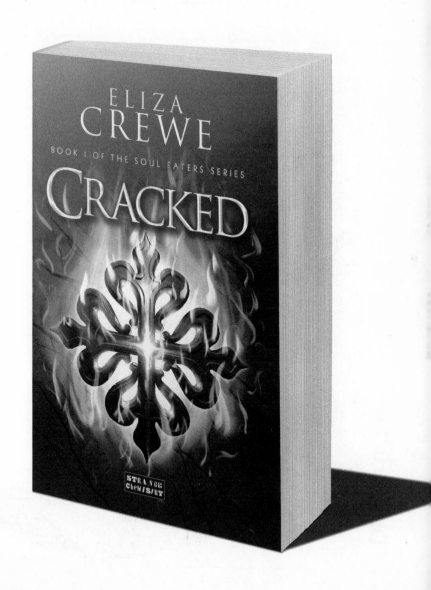

EXPERIMENTING WITH YOUR IMAGINATION

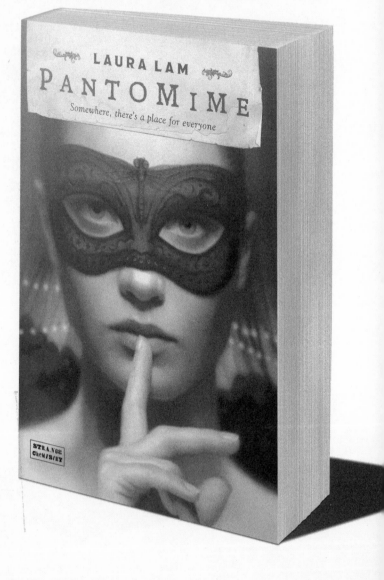

DISCARDED